A Perfect Darkness

"How do you know about this betrayal that's going to happen?" she asked.

"I'll tell you tomorrow, that and everything we know." She saw the regret on his face when he said, "I hate that you're involved in this. We don't even know what *this* is yet." He released a long breath. "Be prepared. Everything you think you know is going to change." His body went rigid as he turned down the radio and cocked his head to listen.

"What is it?" Then she heard a soft *crack*.

He looked at her, fear in his eyes. "Trouble. Protect yourself. Tell them I just broke in and I haven't told you anything. You're scared to death of me." Footsteps pounded across her living room floor. He pulled a piece of paper from his jeans pocket and curled her fingers around it. "Hide this."

Three men dressed in black burst into her bedroom. The man in front aimed a gun at them. "Freeze!"

By Jaime Rush

A PERFECT DARKNESS

Coming Fall 2009
OUT OF THE DARKNESS

JAIME RUSH

A PERFECT
DARKNESS

AVON

An Imprint of HarperCollinsPublishers

AVON BOOKS
An Imprint of HarperCollins*Publishers*
10 East 53rd Street
New York, New York 10022-5299

Copyright © 2009 by Tina Wainscott
Excerpts from *Out of the Darkness* copyright © 2009 by Tina Wainscott
ISBN 978-0-06-169035-8
www.avonromance.com

First Avon Books paperback printing: February 2009

Avon Trademark Reg. U.S. Pat. Off. and in Other Countries, Marca Registrada, Hecho en U.S.A.
HarperCollins® is a registered trademark of HarperCollins Publishers.

Printed in the U.S.A.

10 9 8 7 6 5 4 3 2 1

Dedicated to:
A.D. Copestakes, beloved granddad,
and Jan Copestakes;
Lucy Copestake, wise mentor of things spiritual;
my young friends, who make life just that much better:
Nancy and Al Zokan,
Karen Himes and Cheryl Burgess,
Karen O'Hearn, Betzi Abram,
and gym buddies, Joe, Bob, and Gloria.

CHAPTER 1

"Mr. Bromley, there's no need to fling yourself out of the window." Amy Shane covered her cockatoo's cage with his obnoxious bright orange blanket before he started squawking, like he did whenever she was on the phone. "I have a ninety-five percent retrieval rate." Her love life might be nonexistent, and her plan to eat healthier was feeble at best, but she was damned good at saving people's data.

"My presentation is on that drive," her client said. "My only copy, I know, I'm an idiot for not backing it up, and then to drop it—" He let out an agonized groan.

She returned to the second bedroom of her apartment, cracked open the laptop case and studied the damp interior. "And how did it end up in a pool— You know what, I don't want to know. Is there anything else on the drive that you need?"

"There's one folder titled 'Upcoming Issues' that's rather important. Just business documents, but of a, ah, sensitive nature."

She knew he was lying about the folder's contents.

Whatever it contained held significant emotional relevance . . . and the potential to embarrass him. She didn't want to know that. She didn't want to see the green glow that told her he was hiding something.

She plugged the hard drive into her computer. "I'd better get working on it."

"You'll call—"

"The moment I know what we've got," she assured.

"I hope so," he said, his voice and glow emanating anxiety; if she didn't retrieve his data, she might have to do some suicide counseling. Wouldn't be the first time.

It was bad enough seeing people's glows—what she later learned were called auras—when she was physically with them. That had started when she was a kid, seeing her teacher's yellow glow and knowing the woman was sad, and then doing the really dumb thing and trying to comfort her. Which freaked the woman out and taught Amy a more important lesson than math or reading: seeing colors that indicated people's moods or intentions was weird.

In the last few years they'd gotten pervasive. Everywhere she went she saw that smoky mist. Oh, how people lied and hid their pain, and how that deceit made her distrustful. That was why she worked out of her home and hardly saw anyone. Except now she was seeing glows through the frickin phone!

She uncovered Orn'ry's cage. He made happy clicking sounds, and his crown of white feathers sprang to attention when she opened his door. "Okay, you can come into my office now." She held out her arm, and Orn'ry climbed aboard. She sat down at her worktable, and he climbed up to her shoulder. She liked working to alternative rock cranked loud. For Orn'ry's sake she slipped on her headphones.

Orn'ry pecked at the earpiece. "Stop it," she growled. Then he pecked her nose. *"Ow!"* She shooed him off, and he fluttered to his stand. He wasn't called ornery for nothing. That's how he'd ended up at the animal shelter where she volunteered. No one could stand him, and he languished, destined to become a breeder parrot. She couldn't bear that thought, and besides, she'd come to like the little bugger. More interestingly, he'd come to like her, too. She would have adopted half of the animals at the shelter if her apartment complex allowed more than caged pets.

A quick Internet search revealed that Mr. Bromley was a U.S. congressman. She returned to the drive. "Please don't let me find anything really scuzzy on here," she said to herself. "I don't want to be known as 'the whistleblower' all over CNN and the Internet." Her policy was never to read clients' files unless something screamed, *Sick and illegal.* Fortunately that hadn't happened yet.

She reached for her mug of coffee amidst the clutter of computer parts. The few who saw her work space were always amazed that she could function in it. She told them she had a system, which was sort of a lie. It was more like, if everything was out in the open, she'd eventually find it.

An hour later she popped chocolate-covered cranberries into her mouth as she unearthed bits of data. "Come on, baby, oh, yes, that's it. There's the sensitive folder, but where's the presentation?"

Orn'ry always murmured when she talked to herself, which made her feel not so alone. She opened

Upcoming Issues and found pictures and text documents with innocuous names. She double clicked on one, hands over her eyes, peeking through the cracks of her fingers. If it was something disturbing, she didn't want it seared into her subconscious.

"Yuck." Well, she now had an idea of how the laptop might have ended up in a pool. At least the woman draped over a diving board wearing nothing but high heels was way older than legal age. She would bet that the woman was not the senator's wife, and had no interest in confirming her suspicion.

"Immoral maybe, but not creepy or illegal."

Her body usually started craving sleep at about three in the morning, and at four her scratchy eyes said, *Enough!* Mr. Bromley was in California, and since she was in Annapolis, Maryland, she had a couple of hours in the morning to jump back on it before his meeting.

She was going to transfer Orn'ry to his cage, but he was asleep, his shoulders hunched, the feathers at the side of his face fanning his beak. She left him there and dragged herself off to bed.

She was never too tired to hope for one of her dreams, the ones that woke her in panting breaths and damp with perspiration. A man whose face was always in shadow, touching, kissing, loving her. The same man in every dream. She grinned. Even in her dreams she wasn't a slut.

She *had* seen his body, all of it, lean but muscular, olive skin, with a head full of dark, soft waves. In these dreams, she loved and was loved, there as never in her life. She was safe to let herself go. The only way he would break her heart was if she stopped dreaming about him. Four months ago she had never felt an orgasm. Now she experienced the shattering of her body and soul every night. What an amazing realization, that she could physically experience what she dreamed about.

She slipped through the hypnagogic state of sleep, where she sometimes heard voices, and dove into REM. Deep in an ordinary dream, her eyes snapped open, her heart thrashing against her ribs. She hadn't heard a thing, couldn't see a thing, but she knew someone was there.

Her second thought—after, *Oh, shit, someone's in my room!*—was: *What can I use as a weapon?* Clock. Brass table lamp with sharp corners. Bingo. Her hand darted out to grab it and collided with hard flesh. Before she could scream, he was on top of her, his hand over her mouth.

"I'm not going to hurt you," he said.

Oh, God, he was going to rape her and kill her and cut her up in pieces. *This can't be happening. Fight! Kick!* But he was on top of her, his weight pinning her down. Panic squeezed her chest.

He shifted to the side, reaching for something. She heard a *click*. Knife? Gun?

Light flooded the room. She blinked in the sudden onslaught. Her eyes focused on the man in front of her. Gorgeous, with gray-blue eyes and brown hair, he didn't look like a crazed rapist killer. But that didn't ease her fear any more than his words of assurance did.

It hit her then. He made no attempt to hide his face. *That's because he doesn't intend to leave a witness.* Whimpering sounds emanated from her, as though a small animal was trapped in her chest. She quieted them, because, dammit, she wasn't going to go down like a mouse beneath an eagle's talons.

He leaned close. A gold cross on a chain dangled before her eyes. The sight of it was surreal. A cross on a killer. If he tried to kiss her, she'd spit in his face or, better yet, tear off his lip with her teeth.

His mouth hovered just above her cheek. He spoke in a low, soft voice that would have been soothing if he wasn't a terrifying intruder. "Amy, my name is Lucas, and there are things I need to tell you. I'm sorry, really sorry, I had to do it this way. I didn't have time to gain your trust. Am I hurting you?"

She'd swear by the concern in his eyes that he cared about her comfort. He pressed his hand over her mouth only as much as necessary. She shook her head. Her heart pounded so hard she thought it might explode.

"Good. I'm here to talk to you about your father's supposed suicide."

Her brain scrambled to process his words. Her father's suicide.

Gunshot coming from her house!

Spray of blood.

Shallow breaths.

His eyes wide and fearful, pleading, Save me. Save me.

"Daddy, no!"

Twenty years ago, but it felt like yesterday. She'd found him in the garage that horrible day after hearing the gunshot on her way home from school. The man who claimed he loved her killed himself where he knew she'd find him. Her sole provider made no arrangements for his five-year-old's care.

The bigger question was, why was this possible rapist and murderer talking about her father's suicide? Unless he wasn't a rapist and murderer. She must be crazy, because he didn't feel like either. That's when it hit her: his glow wasn't like any she'd seen before. Not one color but all of them, like static on a television.

Wait a minute. Had he said her father's *supposed* suicide?

He obviously saw her curiosity. "If I release you, you won't scream? I'd rather not continue the conversation like this."

She shook her head, and he freed her. She scrambled away from him, feeling the grooves of the headboard bite into her back when she slammed into it.

He sat back on her bed, his hands on his jean-clad thighs. The hair at his neck curled from dampness. "You don't have to be afraid of me."

She almost laughed. "A stranger breaks in, and I'm supposed to be *cool* with that?"

"Amy, we're not strangers."

The way he looked at her, with a soft smile and his gaze reaching right into her soul, corkscrewed her stomach. She pushed beyond that puzzling statement. "What do you know about my father?"

He reached over and turned on the stereo in her alarm clock. Evanescence's powerful song, "Bring Me to Life," filled the room, the tune she'd cued to wake her this week.

"Why'd you do that?" she asked, her words crammed together. What was he going to do that he didn't want anyone to hear?

"Just in case someone is listening."

"The walls aren't that thin."

"Listening equipment can pick up conversations from over a hundred yards away, through walls thick or thin."

"Listening equipment?"

He leaned forward, and for a bizarre moment she thought he was going to kiss her. His mouth grazed the shell of her ear and whispered, "My two friends, Eric, Petra, and I discovered that someone is watching us. They call us Offspring. You're one, too."

"Me?" she choked out.

"It's how I finally found you. The Offspring we know about have two common links: we lived near Fort Meade, Maryland, during the same time period, and we each had a parent who died either by suicide or accident within a year's time." He gave her a moment to absorb what he'd said, looking toward the window and the darkness beyond.

She pressed her hands to her temples, trying to make sense of it. "Someone is watching you? Me?" When he nodded, she asked, "Who?"

"We don't know. Probably some facet of government, which is why we can't go to the police."

"Do you have any . . . proof?"

He looked toward the window again. "Not yet. We need to find other Offspring so we can put the facts together and figure out what's going on. You're the first one we contacted." He leaned close once more. "I know you have a lot of questions, or you will once you get your mind around all this. We need to meet tomorrow, somewhere we can talk more. I can't stay here much longer, in case they're watching you now. They may suspect I'd come here, which makes it dangerous for me, but I had to warn you. You can't tell anyone what I've told you."

"Warn me about what?"

"Someone you trust is going to betray you, and someone is going to die because of that betrayal. It might be you." She shivered at his warm breath caressing her ear as well as his words.

The depth of his concern baffled her. He looked at her in the way someone who had loved her for a long time might look at her. All she had to go on was the way her father looked at her, and that was such a distant memory. And he hadn't loved her enough after all. Except Lucas had said *supposed* suicide.

"How do you know?" she asked. "About this betrayal that's going to happen?"

"I'll tell you tomorrow, that and everything we know." She saw the regret on his face when he said, "I hate that you're involved in this. We don't even know what 'this' is yet." He released a long breath. "Be prepared. Everything you think you know is going to change." His body went rigid as he turned down the radio and cocked his head to listen.

"What is it?" Then she heard a soft *crack*.

He looked at her, fear in his eyes. "Trouble. Protect yourself. Tell them I just broke in and I haven't told you anything. You're scared to death of me." Footsteps pounded across her living room floor. He pulled a piece of paper from his jeans pocket and curled her fingers around it. "Hide this."

Three men dressed in black burst into her bedroom. The man in front aimed a gun at them. "Freeze!"

Lucas's hands flew up as he stepped in front of her. Despite his surrender, the man squeezed the trigger. Not a loud report but a *whoosh*. A stream of blood squirted on Lucas's collar as his hand flew up to the wound in the neck. A second man stepped into the room and walked toward Lucas, who barreled toward him with his head lowered and shoulders hunched like a bull. He knocked the guy against the door frame, the man's skull hitting the wood with a thud.

Turning, Lucas aimed for the third man, who was running toward him. The two of them clashed and wrestled, ending up in the living room and sending her gooseneck lamp crashing to the floor. Lucas was more wiry muscle than bulk, but he had rage on his side. He jammed the palm of his hand into the man's face, sending blood spurting out of his nose, then turned back toward the second man, who was approaching fast despite the blood trickling down the side of his head.

Lucas didn't even glance at the open door. He didn't want to escape, but to take out the men one by one. With a bullet in his neck. She sat paralyzed, watching as he dug his elbow into the man's stomach. The one with the gun, who appeared to be the leader, made no move to help his comrades. He was waiting for something, which she saw when Lucas's motions slowed and he blinked several times. He wobbled, his eyes rolled back, his body slackened, then he crumpled to the floor with a painful *thump*.

One man limped over as another checked Lucas's pulse and peeled back an eyelid. After a nod to the man with the gun, the two hoisted Lucas up and carried him out the door.

The leader turned toward her, about to say something, but she shouted, "You shot him!"

"He was endangering you."

It was only just sinking in, that Lucas had been shot, that he was probably dead because people didn't survive bullets to the neck, did they? Or if they did, they were paralyzed, but mostly they died. "Who are you people?"

"FBI," he said, flashing his badge so fast she could only see that it *was* a badge. The man, whose features were as stark as a mask, told her, "This guy's been on our radar for months now. We had to wait for him to break in before we could arrest him."

"Arrest him? *You shot him!*" she said again, her scream edging into hysterical.

"He's a serial killer who's eviscerated fourteen women with a carving knife."

"He didn't have a knife."

"That you saw." He looked into her eyes. "Did he say anything to you?"

She was supposed to pretend to be afraid of Lucas. That he'd said nothing. She shook her head.

He studied her. "Nothing at all?"

"He didn't have time. You—"

"You're lucky to be alive, ma'am," he interrupted before turning and walking out of the room.

"—shot him," she finished with a whimper, then fell limp onto the bed, a cold fog starting from her fingers and stealing over the rest of her. Orn'ry was screeching in her office but she couldn't move. Trembling followed the cold, tiny seizures sparking through her muscles.

Offspring. Her father. Betrayal. Lucas's urgent words careened around in her head. Then what the man had said: *serial killer . . . eviscerated women . . . lucky to be alive.*

Lucas was right. Someone had been outside listening, watching.

Watching her.

A violent tremble shook her body. On wobbly legs, she walked to the window and pulled open the drapes, hoping for a glimpse of the vehicle the men had arrived in. The lights that usually illuminated the parking area were off, leaving the night in darkness. She heard the sound of a car start and pull away but never saw headlights.

"Who are you people?"

She became aware of the paper in her hand, now damp from sweat, and tucked it into her pajama waistband with shaky fingers. The most bizarre thing was how worried she was for Lucas, a stranger who'd broken into her apartment and scared the hell out of her. She managed to reach for the phone and dial Uncle Cyrus.

He answered on the first ring. "Amy, what's wrong?"

"A man broke in . . . then these men . . . serial killer . . . they shot him!" Her teeth started chattering and she couldn't utter anything else.

"I'll be right there."

CHAPTER 2

Amy cleaned up slowly, still stunned at the wreck of her living room and the reason behind it. Orn'ry was back in his cage clucking like a chicken, trying to get her attention.

"Not now, buddy."

Her red bean bag chair lay in a clump, kicked into the corner; the gooseneck lamp under which she'd read—and cried over—*Wuthering Heights* twenty times was bent on the floor, bits of bulb glittering in the light. Neither the heat nor the rich cinnamon color on the walls could warm her. She kept pausing, mesmerized by the mess, feeling violated by the sight of it. The constellation globe her father had given her was dented. She should throw it away. Why did she keep it, anyway? He'd abandoned her. Guilt lanced her as it did whenever she let anger lick at her soul. With a sigh she set it back on the side table.

"Amy?" Cyrus took a sharp breath as he pushed open the door. "What the hell happened? The door lock's broken."

The lock wasn't just broken; the metal and wood were shattered.

She made her way to the door and saw the towering man with the shaved head picking his way through the disarray. She was even too traumatized to hide the *True Confessions* magazines scattered on the floor. Red blotches of blood dripped across the wood. Her stomach clenched.

As soon as his arms went around her, she sank into his big, hard body and felt the trembling start again. Cyrus wasn't a true uncle. He'd been her father's best friend from their Army days and had kept in touch since her dad's death.

"You all right?" he asked, kissing the top of her head as he always did.

She nodded even as tears squeezed out. She fought them because she was strong, because she couldn't let herself shatter like that bulb. "I'm sorry to bother you like this."

"That's what I'm here for."

He led her to the couch, and didn't complain about sinking into its plum depths, as he usually did. "Tell me what happened, sweetheart. You said a man broke in? A *serial killer*?"

She grabbed up the patchwork bunny her mom had made before she was even born and shook her head. "No, he wasn't . . . that's what one of the men said. Lucas—that's his name, the man who broke in—he said he wouldn't hurt me, that he had to tell me things." She pulled her fingers through brown hair that couldn't make up its mind whether it was straight or wavy and ended up somewhere in between. "He knew my name. He said I'm an Offspring and that people are watching me. He said the words, 'your father's supposed suicide.' "

It was only then that she remembered Lucas's order not to say anything. He'd meant to those men, though. How could she not tell the only person she trusted?

"Could it be that this guy has been watching you, studying you?" Cyrus replied. "Predators do that, you know. Maybe he found out about your father and figured drawing you into some paranoid conspiracy was a way to get to you. Who knows, maybe he even believes it."

"No, he *knew* me. I can't explain it, but the way he looked at me . . . I know it sounds crazy, but it was like he's . . . cared about me for a long time."

"Sociopaths have incredible people skills, even though they have no emotions. He was just playing you."

What Cyrus was saying made sense, but it didn't feel right. Was she looped to put any stock into an intruder's urgent ramblings?

She hugged one of the pillows. "Then three men broke in and shot him. They just took him out, without reading him his rights or anything. He didn't have a weapon, at least that I saw. The lead guy said they were FBI but flashed his badge so fast there was no way I could see it. Nothing on their uniforms said FBI."

Cyrus shrugged. "Maybe you just didn't see it in the confusion."

"Sure. That makes sense. Except . . . wouldn't they have asked me questions? I'm a witness. Supposedly an almost victim. They didn't even ask my name or get my phone number for a follow-up interview. They were just . . . gone. Poof. No, wait. He did ask if Lucas had *said* anything. Not what he'd done but what he'd said. Don't you find that odd?"

Cyrus thought it over, squirming as the Killer Grape—his name for her purple couch—sucked him down like quicksand. "Law enforcement agencies have their way of doing things." He would know, she thought, having worked for the CIA for over twenty years. "I learned not to question things."

Amy drew her legs up to her chest and wrapped her arms around them. "Not even when they bust into your home, shoot someone, and haul him away without saying more than, 'You're lucky to be alive'?" Her emotions bubbled again at the memory of Lucas crashing to the floor. "That not-questioning thing might work for you, but it doesn't work for me."

"I admit, it sounds a bit strange. I'll look into it."

She nodded. "Ask if he's . . . dead."

"I'll find out everything I can."

"These guys were good. I mean, not good like *good* guys, but professional. Completely controlled. Their glows were so tight to their bodies I could hardly see them."

Cyrus was the only person who knew about her glows. For a few uncomfortable weeks he'd asked her to accompany him on interviews for new recruits and assess their glows.

He grazed her cheek with his fingers. "How about you come over to my house? Your door's busted."

"And leave my place open to anyone who happens by? No way." At his look of concern, she mustered up some humor and flexed her biceps. "Me strong, fight off predators." When he wasn't convinced, she said, "How about we push the Grape in front of the door?"

"I don't like it."

"I'll be fine. Remember, they have the guy."

Cyrus was wrestling his way out of the couch. "I don't like you being here alone. Emotionally more than physically. You might feel brave now, but any minute the adrenaline is going to drain, and you'll fall apart."

The tremors had already returned, but she hid them by using the arm of the couch to push herself up. "I'll call the locksmith, clean up, get some work done. I've got an urgent job to work on. It'll keep my mind focused on normal, sane things."

Cyrus looked as though he were going to argue further, then relented. "I guess."

She kissed his cheek, but he studied her for cracks. "You don't have to be brave all the time, you know."

"I can't help myself." She gave him a feeble smile. Having lost her mom when she was three and her dad at five, she'd learned not to rely on anyone being around for the long haul. Her aunt had taken her in, but Amy had felt that if she became too much of an intrusion she'd be sent away.

"It's not being brave," he said. "You've always kept this wall around you. Do you ever think about reaching out, Amy? Do you ever need anyone?"

She thought of her dream lover, but knew she couldn't mention him. Or the fact that Cyrus, too, seemed to keep a buffer zone between them, which suited her just fine. He was the only other person, besides Lucas, whose glow she couldn't read. Cyrus had explained that he learned to shield himself from assessing eyes.

She forced a smile. "You taught me to be tough. Be proud."

"I am proud of you. But being tough doesn't mean you have to handle everything by yourself."

"Love you for caring," she said, leaning in to give him a hug, feeling a crack open inside her.

He looked chagrined but hugged her back.

"Let me know as soon as you find out something," she said.

"And you let me know when you're ready to talk. You just went through a terrifying ordeal. Talking will help you sort it out."

She nodded, but Lucas hadn't been terrifying, except for those first few moments. It was what he'd said and what happened to him that scared her. Cyrus stepped outside and helped her push the Grape to the door. The sun was beginning to rise, coloring the sky shades of pink and gray.

Standing with the couch between them, he said, "I'll arrange for the door to be fixed. And Amy, I wouldn't mention this to anyone. We don't know what's going on here."

After he left and the door was sealed shut, she spotted something on the floor where the couch had been. Lucas's necklace, the chain broken. The edges of the cross bit into her palm as she curled her fingers around it.

The paper. She pulled it out of her waistband and collapsed onto the couch. At the top was her name and address. Below that:

Bill Hammond, 1416 Cannon Ave.

Maybe this Bill Hammond had something to do with what Lucas was trying to tell her.

Why hadn't she told Cyrus about the paper? Because some guy who broke into her apartment told her not to trust anyone? She felt as though she was betraying him somehow. The confounding part was, she didn't know which *him* it was: Cyrus, for not disclosing all; or Lucas, for telling Cyrus some.

Her energy drained out of her, just as Cyrus had warned. She closed her eyes, loving how the couch seemed to hold her as she sank into the velvety cushion. She needed sleep. Lots of it. But images of the night flashed through her mind, shooting her up from the couch. Surely there would be something on the news about it. She tuned the television to one of those twenty-four-hour-so-much-news-you-could-throw-up channels and listened while she worked on Bromley's hard drive.

After an hour, nothing. She needed answers to the bizarre questions Lucas had posed. She couldn't wait to find out what Cyrus dug up.

CHAPTER 3

Amy was staring at a computer screen filled with jumbled file names when a knock on the door startled her. She jerked around, knocking her empty mug of coffee over. Were they back?

"Calm down, it's probably the locksmith," she said under her breath, and hollered, "Coming!" She turned down the Staind CD she'd been listening to, nudged the couch out of the way, and pulled the door open. Orn'ry took his usual defensive stance on his perch, head down and body flattened. He hated visitors.

Not the locksmith, but Ozzie Stavros, neighbor, friend, and fellow computer geek. Even this early his thick, dark hair was combed back in glossy waves and he smelled like a fresh dose of cologne. He took in the couch barricade with a lift of a thick eyebrow. "Mrs. Cameron said she heard some commotion early this morning. She thought you were having a party." He was looking at the shattered doorknob. "I heard that rock stuff you listen to so I knew you were awake, even though you're hardly ever up this early."

Thank goodness Mrs. Cameron hadn't heard the

gunshot. It probably had a silencer on it. "I'm expecting a locksmith. To fix the door," she added as he stared questioningly at the knob.

Hm, how to explain this to someone she didn't want involved? He eyed the room behind her now. She'd cleaned up most of the mess, but her gooseneck lamp was obviously disabled, and she noticed that her "Last Act of Defiance" framed poster was tilted.

"Coffee?" she asked, buying time. "Fair trade French roast."

Ozzie was the one who'd gotten her into the organic, fair trade kick. He'd told her about those underpaid farmers in places like Uganda and Paraguay and all the chemicals used in traditional farming. She pulled the couch away enough for him to slip his small frame between it and the wall.

He looked around for more evidence of whatever had happened the night before. Ozzie was a true nose bag. Whenever he came over, he snooped through her fridge and cabinets and told her how unhealthy her food was. He grossed her out with tales of what the sinister ingredients did to her body or about the animals sacrificed in their creation. He'd ruined her for veal.

"Harry's broken," he said, picking up one of her Geex creations. During moments of frustration or boredom, she made creatures out of obsolete computer parts. Recycling, as Ozzie had pointed out. Harry was a CD drive with circuits for eyes and a nine-pin plug for a mouth. Well, he used to be. "He was my favorite," he said on a sigh.

"Mine, too." She thought about going for the party lie, but he knew her better than that. "It wasn't a party."

"I never figured you for a party girl, anyway." With a nervous rub to his Roman nose, he added, "And I'd hope you'd invite me. So what happened?"

"FBI raid," she said, sticking as much to the truth as possible. "Wrong address."

"No way! They busted in your door and everything? That is so cool. How come nothing exciting ever happens to me?"

"Boring is good," she said. "Boring is safe and sane." She handed him a cup of coffee with a dash of hormone-free milk.

"So I should take it as a compliment the next time a girl says I'm boring?"

Someone knocked on the door and a man called out, "Locksmith."

The man on the stoop didn't look like a locksmith. He looked like the men who had busted into her apartment. He wore a uniform lacking any logo and carried a black box. "I'm here to take care of the door," he said, and began to step forward.

Like the three who had busted in, he had the kind of face that got lost in a crowd. She suspected that was by design.

She remained in the doorway. "You're one of them, aren't you? The FBI or whoever."

His expression was as deadpan as the leader's had been. "I'm just here to fix the door."

She glanced back at Ozzie, who was hovering behind her. "Oz, can you go in the kitchen and, uh, fix your coffee or something?"

"It's already . . . oh. Uh, I guess." He backed away.

Amy lowered her voice and said to the man, "Look, I just want to know what's going on."

He looked her right in the eye. "I'm just here to fix the door."

She remained there another few moments, hoping he would relent. He was definitely one of them, and he definitely wasn't going to relent. She couldn't see his glow and wondered if the FBI also trained their people to suppress their intentions. "I want to see some ID."

He whipped out his wallet and showed her both a driver's license and a locksmith's license under the name Michael Callahan. With a sigh she let him in.

Orn'ry was having fits over the stranger, so Amy took him into her office.

Ozzie followed. "Just to make sure everything's all right," he said, eyeing the locksmith. Orn'ry tried to bite Ozzie every time he got close to the perch. "That bird hates me."

"It's nothing personal. He hates everyone who isn't me." She also peered out to check on the locksmith.

"I've heard birds live a long time."

"Yeah, something like thirty or forty years. I don't know how old Orn'ry is. Parrots also bond to their owners, and for some reason he never bonded to anyone but me. It's weird because I'm not a bird person, but he's grown on me."

She sat down to work on Bromley's hard drive, digging into her bag of chocolate-covered cranberries, keeping the front door in view. Callahan seemed to know what he was doing. At any rate, he was doing locksmith-type stuff.

Ozzie perched on a PC case. "You should have called me . . . you know, when the FBI crashed in."

"I was fine, but thanks."

She could see the red-orange glow of Ozzie's suppressed passion, his longing. Oh, boy. She liked him, but not in that way.

He looked around at the deep yellow walls, cat clock, and maroon drapes. "Do you have a life outside this cocoon?"

She popped a cranberry up in the air and caught it in her mouth. "I go to the store sometimes." She heard defensiveness creeping in.

"When you don't have it delivered," Ozzie added, raising his thick eyebrow. "I've seen the grocery delivery boy."

"I chat online."

"Personal forums, like, kinky sex or anything?"

"No. Computer stuff." She'd found an affinity with computers, and in particular with fixing them. Out of high school she had apprenticed with a guy who taught her a lot. One day she discovered he was rigging his clients' computers with viruses to get more business. When she confronted him, he got the eeriest glow, and she'd quit and started Disc Angel.

"But that's not you, it's just what you do."

"No, it's me." It was the only thing she was good at. "I used to talk to my neighbors, but they got too nosy so I stopped."

He actually asked, "Who—oh, I get it. Sure, fine. Be a hermit."

"I'm a computer geek. It's what I do best."

"I'm a geek, too, but at least I'm joining clubs, getting out there."

She patted his shoulder. "Good for you, Oz." When he gave her a narrow-eyed look at her patronizing tone, she added, "I visit the shelter animals."

"But they're animals, not people."

She didn't want to get into how she felt when she looked into the eyes of those abandoned and neglected animals and how their glows, so simple and pure, tugged at her. She didn't like feeling apologetic about her lifestyle.

"Ma'am," the locksmith said, appearing in the doorway. "You're all set." He walked out and closed the door behind him. She went to the window to see what kind of vehicle he drove. He was nowhere in sight.

From behind her, Ozzie said, "Amy, you need a man—"

"No, I don't." Uh-oh, he was finally going *there*. "I'm fine and happy and perfectly content being celibate." That line scared off potential suitors, especially since she was damned sincere.

"So you don't like, ah, sex?"

"It's fine. I just don't like dealing with guys in general. You know, that morning after, relationship stuff."

"Are you a . . . lesbian?"

"No, a vibratorian." She had to keep herself from laughing and giving away that she was just poking fun at him. "Thanks for caring, though. You're a good friend, Oz."

"Friend," he repeated.

"I'd love to chat more, but I've got a file to save and an hour to do it in. You know how I hate to hear a grown man cry."

"Sure." As he was about to leave, he turned and gave her a hug that about crushed her ribs. "Next time call me." He let go of her just as quickly, as though she were a hot potato.

"The next time the FBI raids my apartment, you'll

be at the top of my call list." His words touched her despite her sarcastic response.

As she sank back into her chair after locking her front door, she still felt the imprint of his arms around her. She had vague memories of being held and kissed by her parents. Her aunt, happily unmarried and independent, had never hidden the fact that she had no room in her life for a kid. Cyrus was careful about expressing affection, or perhaps he didn't have much to offer either.

She looked at her framed print of a porcupine with the words, *Aw, come on, gimme a hug!* beneath. She didn't need affection. Yes, she could have Ozzie's affection, but that wouldn't be fair to him, considering her lack of romantic feelings for him. Fair trade, after all, she thought with a smirk. No, she didn't need to be held and stroked and kissed. Except in her dreams.

After e-mailing Mr. Bromley his files—she'd still had to hear him cry, but at least it was tears of joy— Amy headed out to get her Days of the New CD from the car. When she opened her door, the sight of someone standing there startled a scream out of her, which made Orn'ry screech.

Cyrus blinked. "It's just me."

She forced a smile. "Come in."

"They fixed your door already."

"Yes, thanks. Chatty guy with lots of personality— not. He was one of them, wasn't he?"

"It's not the kind of thing you can call a regular locksmith over for." He gave her the usual kiss on top of her head, as affectionate as he ever dared to be. "How are you, besides jumpy?"

Her voice cracked when she said, "I'm okay. What'd you find out?"

"I talked to a friend at the FBI." He took a seat and she perched on the coffee table in front of him.

She tried to stay calm and not look too concerned about the stalker who'd been about to eviscerate her. The stalker who'd looked at her like he would die for her. She caught herself leaning toward Cyrus as though she could hear the words faster if she were a few inches closer.

"His name is Lucas Brown. He's been on their radar for some time now in connection to fourteen brutal murders. All cute brunettes in their late teens and early twenties." He gave her a look that added, *Like you.*

"*Cute?*" she said. "I'm definitely not his type."

He crossed his arms in front of him as though accusing her of using sarcasm as a barrier. "The murders he was suspected of were scattered all over, so there wasn't any solid connection. The FBI tracked him here. He started acting erratically, and they figured he was on the hunt. They had to wait until he made a move, which he did by breaking into your apartment. If they hadn't been here . . . well, I don't even want to imagine."

Why did that seem so . . . not right? "How come there's been nothing in the news? Lots of scandals and all manner of scumbagism, but nothing about this major serial killer the FBI apprehended."

"Scumbagism?" His eyebrows quirked. "Do you know the kind of public outcry there would be if it was discovered a suspected killer had been in their midst and no one was warned? Of course, if they'd been warned, Lucas Brown would have fled, and they would have had to start all over again. The FBI is keeping this low key. The important thing is that it's over."

"What about Lucas?" She swallowed hard and pushed out the words, "Is he dead?"

"Sig 229 in the neck will do it every time." He studied her. "It's what he said that's got you a little freaked out, isn't it? About you being a . . . what? Outsider?"

"It wasn't that so much as what he said about my dad's death."

Cyrus pressed his fingers together. "All that stuff he told you was a load of bull manufactured by a sick mind. Brown has a history of psychiatric problems, including psychotic schizophrenic. Paranoia. Nonsensical ramblings about spies and phone taps."

He gave her a sympathetic look. "I know you always had trouble believing what your father did. Me, too, for a while. But he had psychiatric problems of his own. Not like this Lucas guy, but deep depression. Remember the nightmares that sent him screaming out the door?"

She shivered. All too well. "He dreamed people were in his head trying to kill him."

They both grew silent for a moment.

Finally Cyrus said, "Sweetheart, he loved you very much. At the end, he just wasn't thinking straight."

That's what hurt so much. She'd grown up believing he hadn't loved her enough to push on, to get help. She believed she wasn't good enough to live for. "No matter how depressed he was, he had a five-year-old daughter who loved and needed him. It never made sense that depression would take away his sense of responsibility. If I wasn't enough to live for . . . okay, take your life. But at least make arrangements for your kid. And leave a suicide note." She looked into his eyes. "You would have told me—you'd tell me now—if there was more to my father's death, wouldn't you? My dad who showed me the stars and then shot himself where he knew I'd find him. *The dad who said he loved me and then left me!*" Anger washed into her voice.

Cyrus leaned forward, bracing his arms on his thighs. "Did Lucas imply he was murdered?"

"Not exactly. That would explain Dad's behavior, though."

And his glow. She hadn't known what the colors meant then, and thought the glimmer of violet blue meant despair. Years later she'd come across a man climbing over the railing at a bridge. With the conviction of someone who had lost a loved one to suicide, she'd talked him into seeking help instead. His glow had been a deep yellow. Her father's had been the color of anger. Angry people didn't take their lives. Unless, as Cyrus had suggested, she hadn't remembered it right.

"Think about it: who would have wanted to murder your dad? He did administrative work for the Army. And he was a nice guy. Nothing was taken from the house, and it was his gun."

She hadn't realized she was waiting for some revelation until her body slumped in disappointment. "But how did Lucas find out?"

"Maybe he met someone who knew your dad or found some old papers. His mind creates a conspiracy theory. Killing women might be part of his delusion."

"Maybe," she echoed, getting to her feet.

"If you need to talk . . . "

She shrugged. "There's nothing more to say. Lucas is dead and there doesn't seem to be any way to find out more."

"Let it go. Try to forget it ever happened."

After he left, she sat on the floor and spun the constellation globe. When she was seven she'd taped a picture of her dad over his favorite constellation, Ursa Major. He was smiling in the picture, young and handsome.

She tried to convince herself that what Cyrus said must be true. It made sense, right? Well, sort of. So why couldn't she quite make herself believe it? Because Lucas said she hadn't felt right about her father's suicide, she realized, and there was no logical way for him to know that.

The thought that her dad hadn't consciously decided to abandon her tightened her chest. If he hadn't just selfishly killed himself, that changed everything.

Everything you think you know is going to change.

She rubbed the stars on the charm bracelet he'd given her as a child, real silver stars and bright plastic beads that she'd had redone on a silver chain. She remembered how they'd lie in the grass together and he'd show her the constellations. He told her stories about her mom. Sometimes she'd hear him talking to her mom when he thought she was asleep. It broke her heart to hear him cry.

She needed to know more about Lucas Brown. She pushed off the sofa and went to her computer to do a search on his name. Tons of stuff came up but nothing relevant. There seemed to be only one other place to go, and that was the man whose name was on the slip of paper Lucas had given her.

She looked around at her cocoon, as Ozzie had called it. He was right. This was her safe haven. Going out in the dark was not something she liked to do.

Forget about all this. Go back to your nice, quasi-normal life. Dig up lost data. That's what you're good at.

She went back to work, beginning diagnostics on another drive. She cranked Linkin Park and belted out the lyrics to "Crawling." The words died on her lips, though, and her fingers stilled. Her mind drifted to Lucas, to his breath on her ear and his urgent warning. The third time it happened, she gave up. She wasn't going to be able to push this into the back of her closet.

Amy closed her door and steeled herself to step into the darkness, even if it was a bright spring day. What she would tell Bill Hammond, she had no idea; something would come to her. She got to the bottom of her stairs when a woman with long blond hair and the smile of someone who knew a secret handed her a flyer.

"Come alone and tell no one," she said, her smile intact. "Make sure you're not followed." She floated down the walkway and stuck another flyer in a doorjamb, giving her a glance before heading on to another door.

Amy would have laughed—hell, conspiracy theories, *Make sure you're not followed*—except it didn't seem so awfully funny anymore. She watched the woman for a minute before pulling her gaze to the flyer in her hand. The four-color brochure depicted ethereal stained-glass works and announced the artist's appearance the next day at the Blue Rain Gallery, in West Annapolis, near the historic area. Even though she'd lived here for the last nineteen years, she'd been to that part of town only a few times.

When she walked to another door and plucked the flyer the woman had stuck there, however, she discovered that it wasn't for the gallery at all. She looked around. That one and all the other flyers announced the opening of a car wash. The deluge of flyers, then, was a cover. Her finger slid across the edge of the one she'd been given—a message meant just for her.

CHAPTER 4

The next day, Amy opened her refrigerator door, stared at the rows of organic yogurt, and pulled out one along with the container of fresh strawberries. When the toaster dinged, she lifted out the Pop-Tart and set it on a plate, then heaped yogurt and fruit on top. She glanced at the clock: noon, the usual breakfast time for one who worked into the night and slept all morning. She hadn't slept, though. She felt as though she'd ingested four cups of Fair trade French roast coffee on an empty stomach.

Orn'ry flapped his wings and squawked. "Popcorn!"

He didn't talk very clearly, but she recognized the request for food. She poured in fresh birdseed and changed the water. "I've got to go out for a while. Be good." She pointed at him. "Don't make me cover you." Luckily she had only one apartment butting up against hers.

She'd decided to wait on talking to Bill Hammond. She grabbed the flyer from where she'd stuck it on the fridge. "Let's see what this is about first."

As soon as she reached for the door, Orn'ry started

making his plaintive sound. Once the door opened, he went into screech mode, and she quickly left. She headed for the Blue Rain Gallery, not with trepidation but a desperation that thrummed through her veins. That's where she would find the truth—or at least the beginning of it.

They call us Offspring.

They. Who were they? Who was Lucas? More importantly, why did the thought of him being dead leave a hollow feeling in her chest?

She was actually wearing civilized clothing instead of the cotton pants and tank tops she usually wore. As she pulled out of her allotted space, she caught the movement of a car in the rearview mirror. The man behind the wheel had dark sunglasses and bushy hair. When she turned left, so did the car. It fell back, though, and other cars filled in until she couldn't see it anymore. Still, her gaze flitted to the mirror as often as it watched what was ahead of her during the drive.

When she reached the designated address, she saw the white car drive past. Just as her heart started thumping, she saw that the man behind the wheel didn't resemble the one she'd seen leaving her lot. He had wispy blond hair and, more important, wasn't looking at her.

"You're getting good and paranoid now, Amy girl."

The building had once been a Victorian two-story home that, like others in the area, was now converted to commercial space. Blue neon limned the windows and set off the white exterior.

As she walked toward the entrance, her tongue felt like a towel in her mouth. A man stood inside the front window, and he was so still that she wondered if he was a statue. Bells tinkled when she pushed the door open. She expected harp music to match the cool blue lighting instead of U2's soulful song "One." Light poured through stained-glass panels depicting nature scenes that were painfully exquisite. A deer nuzzled her fawn in one, and a rabbit and wolf played together in another, both set against an outer-space-like background.

People milled about, talking softly as though they were in church, and indeed that was the way this place felt. A bearded man was describing his near-death experience that inspired a piece that featured dolphins swimming in a pink vortex. He acknowledged her with a smile. She stared back, watching for some signal. After several uncomfortable moments he turned away. Hell, he probably thought she was a stalker.

The man standing inside the window was real. At least she was pretty sure he was. His bright blond hair, spiked like flames, caught the sheen from the blue neon. His body was perfection, at least six-foot-three, thick muscles and hard lines encased in black pants and a tight bronze shirt. He continued to watch the parking lot, though his eyes flicked toward her once.

No one approached. She'd wait, be patient . . . as impatience screamed through her veins. She turned her attention to the large room filled with artwork of various mediums: statues of lovers melting in a goodbye embrace; a painting of a woman crying over lost love perhaps, her tears turning into a bloody pool. A painting of a couple looking lovingly into each other's eyes, making her think: *Someday one of you will die and the other will be left alone.*

Most of the art was of a sensual nature, though all very tasteful. She glanced back to the man in the window. He was gone. Letting out a long sigh, she continued to look around. Maybe she'd misunderstood what the girl handing her the flyer had said. Maybe it was her own desperate need for information—or worse, her own delusions of conspiracy—that made the girl's words sound the way they had. She couldn't think of a damned thing that sounded anything like "come alone and make sure you're not followed," though.

The soft buzz of conversation calmed her nerves—until she saw a collection of paintings on the far wall.

No.

No frickin' way.

But there they were, as real as the wall they were hanging on: images from her erotic dreams. Heat seared her cheeks. The man's face was in shadow here, too, but her face was clearly defined, even down to her dark green eyes and the freckles sprinkled across her nose and cheeks. These were sexy and romantic and everything her dreams were, painted against surreal backgrounds of blues, greens, and glittering gold. The beauty took her breath away. So did the bizarreness of seeing them here.

She put her hand to her chest to hold back the pressure building inside her. *Me. My dreams. But how?* Her gaze went to the plaque identifying the artist: Jason Stark. No picture or biographical information.

"We wondered if she really existed," someone said beside her.

Amy spun around with a gasp. It was the woman who'd handed her the flyer. She smiled, the silky hair flowing over her shoulders and pearlescent skin reminiscent of a fairy's.

Questions stampeded over one another in Amy's mind. "Who is Jason Stark?" Her abrupt tone grabbed the attention of people nearby. She lowered her voice. "Who is he?"

"You don't know? I mean, you had to be the model for these."

"I've never seen them before."

The woman looked surprised. "He never intended to sell them, you know. He kept them in his office. One of our regular clients was looking for just such a painting, and I showed him one of these. He was blown away and insisted on buying it. Then we got more requests from people who saw his painting, and finally we convinced the artist known as Jason Stark to display and share them. So he did, but he wouldn't talk about them and he didn't want his name associated with them. He's intensely private." She looked at the paintings again, placing her hand against her heart. "They move you when you look at them. The passion. The romance."

Keep calm and don't take off the nice lady's head, Amy told herself with gritted teeth. "Who is Jason Stark?"

In a low voice she said, "It's a pseudonym for Lucas Vanderwyck. He owns the gallery."

"Lucas Vanderwyck," Amy repeated. "Do you have a picture of him?"

"No, afraid not. Wait, the gallery was featured in a magazine last month."

Amy followed the woman to the glass case that held jewelry, but her gaze kept going back to those paintings. All her feelings, her desire, her private moments right there on the wall for everyone to see. *Gawd.*

When she turned around, she bumped into the frame the woman was holding out. Amy tried not to snatch it too fast. The article featured four full-color pictures, but the only one she cared about was the man with the Mona Lisa smile looking uncomfortable about being photographed.

She put her hand over her mouth as her head swam. Lucas Vanderwyck, not Brown. The man who'd broken into her apartment. And even more bizarre, her dream lover. His voice whispered in her mind: *Amy, we're not strangers.*

The dreams . . . they were real.

She looked up to find the woman watching her with open curiosity. Amy asked, "Is he—?"

"Not here," she said quickly, as though she couldn't bear to speak the words. "We don't know . . . where he is." She maintained her pleasant facade even as she spoke words that caused her glow to turn a mix of yellow for sadness and brown for fear. "I have some other pieces you might be interested in, if you like these."

With her fingers at Amy's elbow, the woman led her to an open doorway filled with a curtain of crystals that resembled the blue rain of the gallery's name. Beyond that there was a long hallway, then a small office, and then she followed the woman into a storage room. She was beginning to feel like Alice in Wonderland. If the woman offered her a drink or a square of cake, she would swallow without question.

Down the rabbit hole I go . . .

Her heart thrummed inside her, but not out of fear. It occurred to her that no one knew where she was and no one in the gallery would likely remember her because she wasn't the kind of woman people noticed.

"Wait here, please." The fairy woman closed the door, leaving Amy alone to look at stacks of artwork waiting to be displayed and a box that reminded her of the art supplies container she kept her computer tools in, only it wasn't purple with colored polka dots.

The door opened and the man she'd thought was a statue walked in. She expected him to explain the summons, but he appeared to be there for other reasons. "Excuse me," he said, reaching behind her. As she moved out of his way, something white flashed in front of her eyes. The man had pushed a cloth over her face! A minty odor rushed into her nostrils as he held her in a grip so tight she couldn't move.

She wrenched her head from side to side to get a breath, but his hand stayed with her. Panic escalated her breathing. She felt as though someone had poured soup into her brain and begun stirring her thoughts around. Shapes floated in front of her just before blackness closed in. Her body fell as limply as Lucas's had, and her last taste of consciousness was feeling strong arms go around her.

Amy swam to consciousness, the smell of mint saturating her nostrils and coating her tongue. Gasping, choking, she opened her eyes to find two figures standing in front of her. Or, more precisely, hovering over her, since she was lying on a couch. She lurched to a sitting position, blinking to clear her vision. Nausea rose in her throat at the sudden movement. It felt like fists were pummeling her muzzy brain.

The fairy woman was nowhere in sight. Wait a minute! The *storage room* was nowhere in sight. Amy scrambled to her feet but sank back to the burgundy couch when the whole room rocked.

The man in bronze and a striking woman with long, golden blond hair watched her orient herself. The two shared the same statuesque build, glacial blue eyes, and strong facial structure, though his angles were sharper than hers. The woman stared at her with the same curiosity the woman in the gallery had, though without the smile. What particularly baffled Amy was that these two had the same mysterious glow as Lucas. Which meant she had no clue as to their intentions. As much as she detested her curse, she needed it now.

"Who are you?" she said, her voice still slurred. "Why did you knock me out?"

The woman, wearing a stylish black lace top and black jeans, came closer. "We don't know if you can be trusted."

A laugh bubbled out of Amy's mouth. She looked down at her five-foot-five frame. "Because I'm, what, *dangerous*?"

The man stood with his arms crossed over his chest, a stance that made his biceps bulge. He was built like a damned Hummer. "Because of what you know and who you could tell it to."

The woman said, "We don't want you to know where this place is."

Amy took in the long, large room, part living and dining area and part artist's studio. Not one window or even a door. There was a kitchen behind her, and a hallway that led out of sight. It had the cool feel of a basement. A barrage of artwork styles covering walls that were each a different color looked like something out of a schizophrenic nightmare: a sepia-toned canvas of a woman with a man behind her, whispering in her ear; an Andy Warhol style one of Betty Boop; and at the far end, one of the dream paintings of her lying in a meadow. Stacks of charcoal sketches done in jagged lines crowded a corner. The one on the easel depicted a scary scene of someone falling to the ground.

Before she could study it further, the man said, "What happened two nights ago?"

She turned to them, her chin jutted out and anger prickling her skin. "You summon me here, *drug* me, drag me off to some . . . basement, and you want me to *talk*? Let me out of here."

"Not until you tell us what happened to Lucas," the woman said, worry creasing her forehead. Her glow, Amy saw, was jagged, indicating she was agitated.

"And what he told you," the man added.

Anger surged at their audacity. She got to her feet. "Pardon my lack of manners, but who the hell are you people?"

"I'm Petra. This is my brother, Eric."

"Lucas's friends," Amy said, leaning back against the sofa and crossing her arms in front of her.

"He told you our names?" A vein throbbed in Eric's temple. He turned to Petra. "This is why we can't let emotions get in the way." To Amy, he said, "What else did he tell you?"

Was Eric implying that Lucas trusted her because he was emotionally involved with her?

Petra stepped closer. "What happened to him? Please tell us."

Amy's anger dimmed in light of the fear in Petra's eyes. All right, what would it hurt to tell them? Then they'd tell her stuff, too. She sat on the arm of the sofa. "Lucas broke into my apartment . . . " Reliving the experience as she recounted the events renewed her fear and confusion. She wrapped her arms around herself as she finished. "Then these men busted in and . . . and they shot him in the neck." That's when it hit her. He was gone. No more dreams. "And still he fought those men . . . for a few minutes . . . until he dropped. Then they took his body."

Petra choked back a sob. "Oh my God, he's dead— body, she said *body*."

Eric's jaw tightened, but if the death of his friend affected him, he hid it well. "What did you tell the men?" He stood so close she could feel his breath on her hair. "They asked what he'd told you, didn't they?"

Amy nodded. "Lucas told me not to say anything, so I didn't."

"They didn't interrogate you?"

She shook her head. "I told them Lucas wasn't there long enough to tell me anything before they charged in."

"Did you tell anyone what Lucas said?"

"Only my uncle Cyrus."

His voice sounded strained. "Your uncle?"

"He's not really a blood uncle. He—"

"You told someone what Lucas said?" he repeated. "After he told you not to say anything to anyone?"

Petra added, "Didn't he warn you that someone you trusted would betray you?" Her eyes glistened with tears. "That's why he risked his life."

"Yes, but I didn't think—"

"You didn't think." Eric banged the heel of his hand against his temple. "Stupid."

Amy shrank back but just as quickly felt her own anger rise. "A man breaks into my apartment in the middle of the night, mentions my father's suicide, then gets shot, and I'm supposed to *think*?"

Petra stepped forward. "It's just that we're scared and now Lucas is—"

Eric put his arms around Petra and pulled her close. He closed his eyes for a second, as though gathering his emotions as Petra tried to rein in hers. After a moment he looked at Amy. "How long have you known Cyrus?"

"My whole life," she was happy to assure him. "He was my dad's best friend since their Army days."

Instead of looking relieved, he said, "Is he still in the Army?"

"No, he's worked for the CIA for twenty-some years."

"You may have just signed your death warrant."

"Why?"

"Because Cyrus probably works for them, and now he knows that Lucas told you about our suspicions, so you'll need to go, too."

She got to her feet. "Go? What do you mean by 'go'?"

"Be eliminated. Taken out. Killed. I'm sure we're already on the hit list. They probably suspected that we knew too much, but now, thanks to what you told your uncle, they know for sure."

"Cyrus wouldn't tell anyone. He wouldn't be the person Lucas said would betray me."

Eric looked skeptical. "I told him it was a bad idea to make contact with you, and we all agreed. We figured they'd be watching you." His expression hardened. "But he went to you anyway."

Guilt twisted inside her. She had caused him to get killed. "Why did he come to me if he knew it was dangerous?"

"He wasn't thinking either," Eric said.

Petra wrapped her arms around her waist and paced, her tears flowing. "If only he would have told us. If we'd all gone, we could have saved him."

"Or gotten killed, too. No, he wouldn't tell us because he knew we'd object. No way was he going to let us stop him from going to her."

But why? Amy wondered. Why her? With her hand in her pocket, she wrapped Lucas's chain around her fingers. She followed Petra's gaze to a corkboard above the desk that held several photographs. Most looked old, from maybe twenty years ago. They reminded her of the pictures of her mom and dad she kept in places she looked at frequently. She was ashamed to admit that if she didn't have the pictures, she would forget their faces.

Two photos were of Lucas and his mom, an exotic woman with a head full of dark curls. The one in the center showed five children playing in a kiddie pool on a bright day, grinning at whoever held the camera. Something stirred as she stared at the picture. The little girl, green eyes, freckles, and thick, frizzy brown hair. *Her*. The boy holding her protectively, the skinny boy with dark hair and blue-gray eyes, was Lucas.

Amy, we're not strangers.

They had known each other as children years ago, and, inexplicably, they knew each other in dreams, too.

As she was about to turn and ask questions of her own, something white flashed over her face. Mint assailed her senses. *No, not again!* Before she could think of fighting, everything went black.

CHAPTER 5

She woke in the storage room to U2's "The Sweetest Thing." The fairy woman knelt next to her with a bottle of water. Amy's first thought was to knock it out of her hand and demand answers, but her head was too foggy to put action and intention together. Might as well let the woman help her sit up.

Amy saw none of the suspicion that had been so apparent on Eric's face. She accepted the water and drank half of it in one gulp. Her throat felt parched and her mouth tasted of that minty smell.

"I'm so sorry," the woman said, meaning it. "I'm Kira, by the way."

Breathless, Amy said, "Please tell me what's going on."

"I don't know. It has something to do with Lucas, though, and I'll do whatever I'm told if it'll help bring him back." She gave Amy two aspirin. "For the headache."

"I don't have a—" As though the mention triggered it, she became aware of a distant throbbing in her brain, and it grew larger by the second. She downed the aspirin. "What did they use?"

"Chloroform." Kira gave her a pained look. "I'm so sorry."

"Do you know why Lucas is gone?"

She shook her head. "Eric only told me that something happened to him and to get in contact with you. Bring you back here. Then wait for you to wake up. He promised they wouldn't hurt you."

Kira tried to help Amy to her feet, but she needed to do it on her own. As before, she had to hold onto something as the room spun. "Where was I?"

Kira shrugged. As secretive as Eric and Petra were, it was likely that Kira didn't know, confirming the honesty Amy could see.

"I'll be all right. I just want out of here."

"I'm supposed to give you a message," Kira said. "Don't tell anyone where you were or who you spoke with. If anyone asks, you came here for the showing. Your life could depend on it."

Anger and confusion surged through Amy's body as she shakily made her way through the gallery. She felt like a ghost wandering among living beings. Melting faces leered at her, colors throbbed. She paused to look at the dream paintings. Lucas had looked at her in the way someone who cared about her would, and now she knew why. There was so much more she didn't know, and it wasn't likely that Eric and Petra would enlighten her. Damn them. Double damn them. Cyrus would never betray her. Someone was lying to him, that's all.

She walked outside, blinking in the afternoon sunlight, feeling as though she'd crawled out of a bizarre dream. She collapsed into the driver's seat of her car, letting the cool air and heavy bass of Saliva's "Ladies and Gentleman" surround her. That they welcomed her to a show that would make her eyes and ears bleed seemed appropriate. As they suggested, she even checked to see if she was still breathing.

Now what? Part of her wanted to run home and never come out. The other part needed to know more. Something was going on here, and it was connected to her father—and to Lucas's death.

You're as tenacious as a bulldog, Mr. Bromley had told her when she reported how she'd finally managed to pull his report out of the scrambled data. She *was* tenacious about retrieving other people's data from a puzzle of bits and pieces. She'd go to the moon for her clients. She could at least go one more step for herself.

Energized by anger and determination, she pulled out that slip of paper Lucas had given her. He said she'd been the first so-called Offspring that he and his friends had contacted, which meant they hadn't approached Bill Hammond. He was her only lead to figure out what the hell was going on here.

Bill Hammond lived in a small, neat apartment complex twenty minutes from her place. Just in case someone was watching, she'd taken several detours with an eye on her rearview mirror. She hadn't seen any suspicious vehicles, including that white one. Still, she had the eerie feeling she was being watched. No way could someone have followed her, she'd told herself. She was just being paranoid.

Now she sat in her Rav 4 and stared at Bill's door, wondering how to approach him. *Hey, this guy broke into my apartment and gave me your name.*

Nah.

Ten minutes of mulling produced no brilliant ideas. She got out of the car and hoped something would occur to her before she reached the door. As it turned out, she didn't have quite that much time. Just as she reached his landing, the door opened and a wiry man with cream-and-coffee-colored skin stepped out with a basket of laundry in his arms. He was about her age and clearly puzzled to find a strange gal at his door.

Amy knew her smile was clumsy. She could talk someone down from the ledge by assuring him that his life wouldn't end if his data was lost, but this situation was way out of her expertise.

"You're Bill? Bill Hammond?"

"Yeah?" he said, drawing out the word.

"I'm Amy." She shoved her hand at him, and he limply shook it around the basket. "Sorry to bother you. Lucas said I should talk to you." She waited a beat to see if the name registered. When it didn't, she plunged on. "I'm looking for a place to live, and he suggested I ask you how you like it here. I'm a girl on my own, and I want to find a secure place. My apartment just got broken into and—" She took a breath. "Is this complex safe for a woman? Not that you're a woman, of course, but maybe you could tell me anyway."

Gawd, she wanted to slap her forehead.

"Who's Lucas?" he asked, instead of answering her. He balanced the basket on a slim hip.

She appeared to look confused. "Lucas . . . well, you know, he never told me his last name. I figured he was someone you knew since he gave me your address."

Bill had that same blend of glow colors as Lucas, Petra, and Eric. It meant he was definitely connected to whatever this Offspring business was. And to her. She let her gaze drift behind him and saw an old framed picture of a serviceman on the wall. Below it were three faded roses tied with a black bow.

"Your father?" she asked, walking into his apartment as though riveted by the picture. She recognized Bill's features in the handsome black man. "Army?"

He followed her but couldn't seem to voice his obvious objection to her boldness, which was just as well. His glow, which had started out close to his body, now flared out. He set down the basket with a thud.

"My father died, too," she went on, because babble was good; babble was working for now. "He was in the Army. But he didn't die in a war." She looked at him and the words "He killed himself" tumbled out of her mouth.

Bill's face changed from disbelief to a mix of pain and surprise. He looked at the picture. "My father did, too."

Now she knew why she'd been compelled to say it. *Always trust your instincts.* "Gun?"

"Hanged himself."

"I'm sorry," she said, wincing in sympathy. "When did . . . it happen?"

"January seventeenth, 1989, 5:32 P.M."

Her eyes watered at the date recited from memory, down to the minute. "September second, 1990," she said. "Two-thirty."

Gunshot coming from her house!

Spray of blood.

Shallow breaths.

His eyes wide and fearful, pleading, Save me. Save me.

"Daddy, no!"

She could hear his words even though his mouth hadn't moved. A shocked girl's imagination.

She and Bill faced each other. He was probably remembering as she was. His gaze shifted to the floor. "We'd just moved out of Fort Meade."

"That's where we lived . . . where it happened. Bill, did you ever have a weird feeling about your father killing himself?"

"A million times. But then . . . "

"That would mean it was something more than just despair. Did your father have a history of mental illness?"

"No."

"Did it run in your family?"

"Not that I know of." He was getting impatient with the questions, but she forged ahead.

"What was your father doing at Fort Meade?"

"I dunno, research, I think."

"Mine was in administration. Don't you think it's a strange coincidence, both our dads in the same place, same time, and both killed themselves within a year of each other? I have two friends who also lived near Fort Meade and they each lost a parent, too." Maybe the Army was yet another commonality between the Offspring.

He snatched up the basket and walked toward the door, a signal for her to follow. "Look, I don't want to talk about this anymore. I've got to get my laundry in, so . . . " As soon as she was out the door he locked it, and went down the stairs without looking at her again.

Amy wandered to her car and didn't even remember turning the key and driving home. She should have felt relieved that she couldn't go any farther. She could go back to her life and forget all this madness. Fatigue melted her and she could barely keep her eyes open as she dragged herself up the stairs. Locking herself inside, she curled up on the Killer Grape. She couldn't even make it to the bedroom.

She drifted through the hypnagogic state of sleep, slipping past the frightening voices. Then sleep drew her deeper yet, and she sank into dreams. In the middle of one about the FBI men breaking in and shooting *her* this time, the dream morphed into the one she knew so well. She saw her dream lover approaching, only this time she saw his face. *Lucas.* His expression wasn't tender, though, but tense. As she always did, she ran to him.

"Lucas!"

His image flickered, like a television station that wasn't coming in properly. She felt his touch on her shoulders. His mouth moved a second out of beat with his words. "Amy, forget what I told you. Stay out—of it. Tell no one what—I said."

"Lucas. How are you here? Is this just a regular dream?"

"No, it's real."

"But that means . . . you're alive." She ran her hands over his face, needing to feel him. "Please tell me you're alive."

"I'm alive—shot with a tranquilizer gun."

He was alive! Cyrus had lied about Lucas's name and that he was a killer. It made sense that he'd lied about Lucas being dead. Joy rushed through her.

"Where are you? I talked to Eric and Petra. They wanted to know what happened to you. We thought you were dead. But you're not." She couldn't believe it. "We can save you."

Even with the flickering, she could see his distress. "No. Don't. Forget—me. Keep yourself safe."

Like hell. The words jarred her in their vehemence. Her dream lover was real, and he was in danger. She had a choice: stay in her safe world or save Lucas. She already knew her life would never be the same. Her cocoon had split open, and though she was no butterfly, she had to fly out into the dangerous world. "Lucas, why do you keep flickering in and out?"

"Giving me—drugs, something." He held her face, looking at her. "Amy, stay away. Promise me."

She nodded.

He kissed her, his body pressed to hers, and God, he was real . . . this was real. Her fingers trailed through his soft thick hair. He was hard, pushing into her stomach, and she rocked against him. He held her face, tilting her to just the right angle to plunder her mouth. He paused, looking at her in wonder, his thumbs rubbing the corners of her lips. With a small groan, he kissed her again. His tongue laved hers like a man starved. She ran the tip of her tongue along his teeth, darting it against the roof of his mouth. As she sank into the magnificence of the moment, he flickered.

Then he was back, holding her as though if he held on tight enough he wouldn't leave. She wanted to ask him more about where he was and what they were doing to him, but knew he wouldn't answer. So she took what he would give her. She loved that he would protect her, even though she wasn't going to let him get away with it.

He began to unbutton the dress she wore in her

dream—for some reason, she wore dresses, though rarely in her waking life. She sighed, tilting her head back and letting him kiss down the length of her neck and then lower to the soft indent between her breasts, just as he had so many times.

"Lucas . . . " she whispered, meaning *Take me* and *Help me find you* all at once.

When he didn't respond, she opened her eyes. He flickered out, leaving her in a deep, sudden darkness. She sat up, breathless as always, attempting to button up a dress she wasn't even wearing. That's how real it was. As much as she wanted to cherish those sensual moments, she had to push them to the back burner to savor later. Lucas was in trouble. With fear and adrenaline shooting through her, she lurched up from the couch, grabbed her keys and left.

For a few minutes she wasn't sure where she was going. When she found herself back at Bill's complex, she didn't question it. Instinct again. Bill was a link to Lucas, or at least to whatever Lucas had been about to tell her. She needed to find out more without freaking him out.

This was why Lucas broke in and forced it on me.

As she opened her car door, her gaze caught on something that stopped her. No. Couldn't be. She blinked just to make sure. Yes, Cyrus. Cyrus was there, walking toward the apartment building. Lucas's warning sounded in her mind: *Someone you trust is going to betray you.*

Not Cyrus. So it was surely a coincidence that he was here, of all places, of all times. Surely an even bigger coincidence that he was heading to the stairs that lead to Bill's apartment. He wasn't actually going to Bill's apartment, of course. That would be too much of a coincidence. Yet, he did walk right up to the door and knock. Bill opened the door, and she was shocked to see the two men shaking hands and do the shoulder-patting thing men who know each other well did.

"Huh?"

Amy drooped back into her seat, stunned. The two went inside for thirty minutes, giving her time to look for Cyrus's car. It was nowhere in sight. When he emerged, she could see the frown on his face.

If Bill had something to do with this Offspring business, and Cyrus had gone to Bill's apartment, that meant Cyrus was involved. The thought settled like trans fat in the pit of her stomach. It lurched when she saw him walk to the white car she'd seen when she had gone to the gallery. Not his car.

"Cyrus, you were following me like I was some criminal," she said, raw emotion in her voice.

Amy's brain churned as much as her stomach as she glued together her fifth Geex character in a row. Orn'ry obviously picked up on her nervous energy. He kept walking from one end of his perch to the other, muttering, "What the fluck?" Fortunately, he'd mis-heard some of the words his first owner had obviously used a lot.

A knock on the door sent Orn'ry into his usual screeching spasms. She sprinted to the peephole: Cyrus wearing a somber expression. Maybe he was here to tell her what was going on and why he'd lied to her. She yanked open the door and tried not to look anxious.

His smile looked phony. "Hey, hon. Just stopping by to check on you."

She didn't say a word as she stepped aside and let him in.

The light shining off his bald head looked like a halo. "I've been worried about you. How are you holding up?"

She gave him the so-so sign with her hand.

Orn'ry put up a fuss, and Amy yelled, "Hush!"

"Hush!" he echoed back.

She sank into the Killer Grape, pulling her knees up to her chest.

Cyrus sat in the chair. "I hope you didn't stay around the house all day," he said.

She had an aching feeling she knew where this was going. He was fishing, hoping she'd mention her visit to Bill Hammond or the gallery. That he couldn't come out and ask told her everything.

Someone you trust is going to betray you . . .

Not Cyrus. Please not Cyrus.

"I ran some errands."

He waited for more. She pressed her lips together, holding in words she couldn't let out.

. . . and someone is going to die because of that betrayal.

"Just . . . errands?"

"Trying to get back to normal."

Like normal would ever happen now. They remained suspended in an air of false trust, real suspicion, and hope that the other would come clean. If the party line was that Lucas was dead, they had other plans for him. That sent a jolt of panic through her. Where was he? What were they doing to him? She knew she wouldn't get the answers from Cyrus.

She could see his turmoil even as he tried to bank it.

"Amy, you know you can trust me. Whatever's going on, let me help." He tried to pin her gaze with his.

I can't trust you. I can't trust anyone. She pushed to her feet and walked to the door. "I'm so tired right now. I haven't been sleeping well. Can we talk later?"

He followed but stopped beside her, tilting her chin up. "Sure. Then I want you to tell me what's going on inside that confused head of yours."

She could only nod, the dam barely holding back the tears. The pressure was building. As soon as she heard his footsteps going down the stairs, she slid to the floor and let the Dutch boy pull his finger out of the hole in the dam. It was her father's death all over again. Except this time she had no one to hold her, to comfort her. This time she was truly alone.

As the tears swamped her, though, the comforting presence she'd always felt during dark moments wrapped around her. *Dad.* It wasn't as strong this time, but it took the edge off the ache and brought her out of her sobbing. That abandoned little girl had survived. Yeah, with a few dents and scars, but she'd survived. She would survive this, too. First she had to find out what *this* was.

She hobbled to the sink, splashed cold water on her face, and took a deep breath. "Okay, pity party is over. I need answers. I can't go to Cyrus or Bill Hammond. So I go back to Eric and Petra. They know what's going on. And they're going to damn well tell me everything."

CHAPTER 6

Amy was shaking by the time she reached the gallery. Fear, anger, and a mix of other emotions gripped her. She had taken a circuitous route and was sure she hadn't been followed. It was almost closing time, and Kira was in the process of locking the door. She opened it when she saw Amy.

"I need to talk to Eric and Petra," Amy said, then belatedly realized she'd forgotten a polite greeting. "I'm sorry. Hello. I need to talk to Eric and Petra. Now."

Kira looked unsure.

"Do you want to save Lucas?"

"Of course."

"Then get Eric and Petra."

Kira glanced around, though no one was there. "Wait a minute." She made a call in the office while Amy waited. Naturally, she had to wait by the paintings. Her body stirred at the memory of those particular dreams: Lucas running his hands down her bare back; she artfully lying across his body.

Kira returned with a piece of paper. "Eric said to meet him at this address at nine tonight and—"

"Make sure I'm not followed. Got it."

Amy punched the address into her GPS, which showed it would take forty minutes to get there. She had plenty of time to stop by a jewelry repair shop. She pulled out Lucas's necklace and held it to her mouth. "When I promised I would stay out of this, I was crossing my fingers."

From his car, Cyrus watched Amy walk into the gallery for the second time that day. Lucas Vanderwyck's gallery. Which meant Lucas told her something that intrigued her enough to pursue. It also meant Amy knew that Lucas Brown was a lie.

His cell phone rang. He recognized the number and was tempted to let it roll to voice mail. The man would only call again and again, so Cyrus answered, "Diamond."

"Have you talked to Shane again?"

"Twice now. She's upset, of course, and wondering why the 'FBI agents' didn't follow normal procedure by questioning her, but she bought the serial killer story."

For a moment there was silence. "That's what I needed to know." The line disconnected.

It wasn't the first time he'd lied. Wouldn't be the last.

Amy emerged within a few minutes and headed to her car. Cyrus pulled out a few cars behind her. He knew she'd noticed the white car, so he'd switched to a different one, a different disguise. She was on guard, searching the parking lot, taking convoluted routes to her destinations. She was up to something and she didn't trust him.

That was dangerous for both of them.

* * *

Gerard Darkwell hung up the phone and looked at his associate, Sam Robbins, across a pristinely organized desk. "Diamond says Shane bought the cover story."

"You don't believe him?"

Gerard knew that Robbins, with his round face and brown rabbit eyes, wasn't tough enough for this job. That he was up to his balls in this made him an asset.

Gerard's phone rang again. The man on the other end said, "It's Costa. Amy Shane went to Vanderwyck's gallery. Now she's on the move. Diamond is tailing her, and I'm tailing both of them."

"Good work." Gerard disconnected. "Shane's at the gallery. We need to find out what she knows. Just as I suspected, Diamond is holding back on us. They're both becoming a problem."

Robbins ran his hand over his balding head. "With all due respect, we need to stop now. Resurrecting this is going to destroy us and destroy innocents."

Gerard narrowed his eyes. "Nobody's innocent."

"Is that how you justify your actions?"

He could see that Robbins had grown a bit of a backbone since their last association; unfortunately, it was directed against him. He would have to crush that before it grew troublesome. "I don't have to justify my actions, Robbins. I'm thinking of a higher cause. The noble and brave risk all for the betterment of our society. I'm risking my career, just as I did twenty years ago. Yes, we made mistakes then."

"*Mistakes?* People died."

"Sometimes people must suffer and die for higher causes. Soldiers have died for our freedom since the beginning of time."

"But they sign on for that. They know the risks."

"Keep your focus on the big picture. Look what we accomplished! And we would have accomplished so much more if . . . well, no point in lingering in the past. There's nothing we can do but make use of it. And make good of it. We're going to change the world as we know it. We're talking about victory, justice, everything we dreamed of last time. Everything we almost had." He stared at his clenched fist, remembering how it had all slipped through his fingers. "You and I, we have another chance to attain our goals. This time we're doing it differently."

The recrimination in Robbins's expression softened. "Are we?"

"With our participants, yes. The ones who are causing us trouble are another story altogether. I'm not going to let a few rogue twenty-year-olds threaten everything we can achieve. That's why it's imperative that we crush them."

Amy slid the repaired necklace over her head and pressed her fingers to it. It was like having Lucas with her. God's protection wouldn't hurt either. She made the hour's drive into Baltimore to the park where she imagined walking alone through the dark—and having Eric jump out of the shadows.

As she drove closer, though, she saw lots of cars and people and more rainbow flag stickers than she'd ever seen. Cars were parked all along the roadways and in spots that weren't quite parking spaces. It was almost nine o'clock now. She chewed her lower lip and searched for a spot. "Yes, mine!" she said when she saw reverse lights flash on.

She pulled into the space and got out. Music floated from a distance, as did the sounds of hundreds of people talking and laughing. Many wore costumes as outrageous as those in any Mardi Gras she'd seen on television. Man and man held hands as they headed toward her, women walked with their arms around one another. The banner across the park's entrance read BALTIMORE GAY FESTIVAL.

A bark of laughter erupted. "Oh, Eric, you do have a sense of humor." Likely, he had looked for an event where there would be lots of people in which to get lost.

She glanced behind her as she made her way into the heart of the festival, seeing no one suspicious. Once again she'd weaved and wound through the city, feeling quite clever. For someone who liked her safe little world, she had to admit she was revved up by the excitement of intrigue. She looked around for Eric and Petra, knowing they must be watching her. And again she was in the frustrating position of waiting for them to approach.

The music grew louder and the crowd thicker. A band jammed and a hundred costume-clad people gyrated in front of the stage. The scent of sausage and peppers and fried dough permeated the air. Amy made her way closer, getting bumped and jostled and even pulled into a quick dance with two other women. She begged out and continued on. Someone else swung her around, and before she could protest, a tall person dressed as Wonder Woman draped an American flag cape over her shoulders. The woman's icy blue eyes sent her the message to cooperate. She knew those eyes—Petra. As they twirled, Amy felt a wig settle on her head. Petra swung her away toward a silver-clad man who took her hand and pulled her against his hard body.

Eric. Eric with dark red hair.

He smiled, friendly as could be, except in his eyes. He did his best to look like a guy trying to dance and failing miserably. Or maybe that was real. Petra stalked over and grabbed her arm, looking for all the world like a jealous girlfriend. She gave Eric a *She's mine* look and dragged Amy off, gesturing in angry ways while she muttered, "Play along."

"What is—"

"Look, if you want to go back to being with a *man*, just say so! You don't need to play games."

People glanced over at Petra's tirade, and Amy might have been embarrassed if she hadn't been so confused. With the chaos, no one paid all that much attention.

"I, uh, don't want to be with a man," she said, and then, after a quick breath, "Stop being such a jealous bitch."

Petra's eyes sparked with approval. She swiveled around to face Amy. "Then prove it."

They were standing in front of the restroom door, where, as usual, the women's line snaked for miles.

"Fine," Amy muttered, taking Petra's hand and by-passing all of those women twisting uncomfortably and now protesting their audacity as they entered the restroom.

Petra made no apologies as they snagged the next available stall and crammed inside. "Yes, that's what

I'm talking about," she moaned as she opened her big purse and pulled out two more costumes. "God, Delilah, I'm so sorry I doubted you."

Women grumbled, but no one intruded. Amy slipped into a shapeless but shimmering dress and changed wigs. Petra peeled off the Wonder Woman one-piece bathing suit and the red, thigh-high boots, revealing another skintight costume on a body worthy of it. She splashed glitter over her face, tied on a blue cape covered with shells, and pulled on blue, sparkly high heels.

By now all the women who witnessed their assignation had already peed and left the restroom. First Amy stepped out and then Petra, looking calm and detached. They left the restroom separately, and Amy followed her to the back of the bandstand, where the loud music would cover their conversation. Sheets of colored fabric served as a backdrop for the band, blocking them from the view of the crowd in front of the stage.

Amy would have asked if all of this was necessary, but she knew it probably was.

Eric waited, all of his phony good humor gone. "How the hell did you know about Bill Hammond?"

Ready to scream out that Lucas was alive, Eric's question halted her. "How did you know—*did you follow me*?" She'd had the feeling she was being watched but had seen no one.

"You could say that. And baby, I'm not the only one. I was watching from the parking lot here. Two guys who weren't gay—either sexually or moodwise—got out of separate cars right after you did."

That thought made her sick. "But I was so careful . . . "

"You weren't careful enough. You can't just run a red light and take a few extra turns and think you've lost them. That's what you did, isn't it?"

"Something like that," she had to admit.

Eric took up an arrogant pose with his arms crossed on his chest. "How did you know about Bill?"

"Lucas had a piece of paper with Bill's address on it. He told me to hide it when the men busted in. And no, I didn't show it to Cyrus. When I couldn't get answers from you, I decided to talk to Bill."

"What did he say?"

"He wasn't exactly open to chatting. His father was in the Army, lived in Fort Meade around the same time my father did, and killed himself. Those are the common links between us, right?"

Petra said, "Our parents weren't in the Army and there was no suicide."

"Oh. He's got the same glow you both have, and Lucas, too." As soon as the words came out she wanted to take them back.

"Glow?" Eric asked with a cocked eyebrow.

Damn. He wasn't going to let her get away with not answering. Besides, that would only pique his interest more. "Ever since I was a kid, I see a color around people that indicates their mood or intention. Different colors mean different moods. You three and Bill have the strangest glows I've ever seen, a muddle of all the colors." Would they think she was crazy?

They exchanged a look but it didn't seem to say, *This chick's nuts*. They were giving each other a knowing little smile.

"What?" she asked. "Go ahead, say it."

He shook his head. "What else did Hammond say?"

"Nothing more than that, but . . . you were right. About Cyrus. He went to see Bill right after I did."

Amy wanted to smack the smug expression off Eric's face. Petra looked worried, and her glow was jagged in a different way than Eric's.

"How do we know you're not working with him?" Eric said, checking the area. His gaze snagged on a sexy woman with boobs spilling out of her bustier. He turned back to Amy. "Setting us up?"

"Because I can't trust Cyrus anymore." It hurt to say it. "And the reason I wanted to meet you is that Lucas is alive."

That got their attention. Hope sparked on Petra's face while Eric looked skeptical.

Petra grabbed Eric's hand. "He's not dead!"

"And you know this how?" he asked Amy. "You said they shot him in the neck."

She squeezed her eyes shut for a moment, trying to assemble her thoughts. Now they'd really think she was crazy, and she didn't want them to think that because she needed them. It didn't help that she had to scream over the music. "Lucas comes to me in my dreams. The paintings that he does . . . they're my dreams."

Eric said, "Comes to you?"

"Yeah. We . . . talk. And stuff."

Now they both looked skeptical.

"Lucas and I don't know each other as adults. So how did I end up in his paintings? You can't deny that's my face."

They reluctantly nodded. Eric said, "But how?"

"I don't know. Until I saw the paintings, I thought they were just normal dreams." Well, sort of normal.

"So how does that prove he's alive?"

"He came to me earlier today. He said they shot him with a tranquilizer gun. I asked where he was, but he didn't want me involved."

Eric narrowed his eyes. "Lucas never mentioned any of this dream stuff to us."

"Good," she blurted out. "I mean, they're rather personal. Look, what matters is that he's alive." A group of people walked by, and she waited until they passed before saying, "We have to save him."

Eric said, "No."

"*What?*" both Petra and Amy said.

Petra's hopeful expression sagged. "But—"

He pointed at Amy. "This is why we can't get emotionally involved. It makes people do crazy things. Stupid things. We agreed not to approach Amy or Bill, and Lucas broke the rules. He's on his own."

"But he broke the rules to *warn* me," Amy said.

"So? He took the risk; why should I put my ass on the line to save him?"

Petra said, "Eric, you can't—"

"I can. We don't even know what we're up against yet."

"He's our family," Petra said. At Amy's questioning look, she explained, "We grew up together, after Lucas's mother died. Our dad sort of adopted him." She turned to Eric. "He's like a brother to you. We can't—"

"Drop it. He's the one who had to go to his precious girlfriend here. He didn't think of us when he did that."

Amy saw that Petra was about to say something before she drooped in defeat. Her pain over Lucas was apparent. Eric was obviously a formidable force to go up against. If Petra, who knew and was trusted by him, couldn't sway him, how could she?

To hell with that, she thought, and got up into his face, or as close as she could get on tiptoes. "Lucas is alive, dammit, and if we don't do something, he won't be for much longer. They're injecting him with some-thing—drugs, he wasn't sure. He kept flickering in and out." Emotion rose into her voice. "We're the only ones who can save him. I don't care if you don't trust me or if you don't like me. There's no way in hell we can abandon him while they do God-knows-what to him until he dies!" The music had stopped before she screamed the last line.

Through the applause Petra said, "She's right. We're family, Eric. We don't abandon family."

His expression grew dark. "He abandoned us, re-member?"

"He didn't leave us to die. He left because of you. I know at least that much. If we find Lucas, we can find the truth about what we are. If you want nothing else, you want that."

He faced them, his body stiff with stubborn anger. Amy didn't back down. She flicked her gaze to Petra and saw that she didn't either. However, Petra did give away her anxiety by cracking her knuckles.

Seconds passed. Music pounded the air. Eric's gaze was as hard as his body as he shifted it to Amy and then Petra. The wind kicked up, flapping the fabric and shaking the metal frames holding it. Their eyes never left each other's.

Then Eric ducked his head and ran his fingers through his hair. "Yeah, yeah. We'll get him." He looked at Petra. "I'll start working on it." To Amy, he said, "Thanks for the info. Act like you belong here so the spooks or whoever they are think you came for fun." He seemed to appraise her. "You could pass for a lesbian."

She wanted to deck him, but he started to turn away. She grabbed his arm. "Wait a minute. You're not leaving me out of this."

He looked at her hand on his arm and then at her. After she pulled her hand away, he said, "This is our business."

"It's mine, too. According to Lucas, I'm one of you. An Offspring."

Eric said, "Involving you is problematic."

"Because of Cyrus? I told you—"

"*If* what you're telling us is true, you're still too closely tied to him. He knows your habits, your weaknesses. That makes you a liability. We'll take care of this on our own, but thank you for your interest."

You've been excused, a voice whispered. *You can go back to your cocoon of a life. Leave saving Lucas to them.*

No! Instinctively she knew that together they could save him. That was more important than her safe little world. "You need me. I can communicate with Lucas. And . . . I need you." How she hated the plaintive sound of those last words.

Eric seemed to consider while the band on the other side of the stage butchered Janis Joplin's "Me and Bobby McGee." Then he said, "You have to prove yourself. Trusting the wrong person can be dangerous for us. Look what happened to Lucas."

Yeah, that stung, deepening her sense of guilt over causing his capture. "It wasn't as though I turned him in. Fine, what do I do? Swallow a goldfish? Walk over coals?"

He crinkled his eyes at her sarcasm. "Something useful. Get on Cyrus's computer and get more Offspring names. At least if he catches you, he won't kill you. Probably."

God, the thought of that, that Cyrus would kill anyone . . . She didn't know that side of him, because he never talked about his work. "You think the CIA is behind this?" She didn't want to think that.

"Since Cyrus is involved and he's CIA, yes."

"All right. So how do I know when he's logged on?"

"I'll let you know. The tricky part will be getting you out of there without your spy coming along."

"I could take laundry down to the little building that's at the rear of the complex."

"That should work. I'll call you and say, 'Paul, blah blah whatever,' and you'll play it off like it's a wrong number. Pay close attention because what I tell you is going to indicate what kind of car I managed to get for you. I'll park it behind the laundry building and put the key under the visor, but you'll have to be sneaky about getting to it."

She wasn't going to ask how he would be getting the car. "I'll be sneaky."

"And fast. You've got to get to Cyrus's place pronto. System security will probably log him off if he's inactive for long. Or he may log off when he's done. I'll come up with a way to distract him."

Petra said, "If he's at the main page, it'll look like a Web site. Click on the link for 'DARK MATTER.' At the left of that page there's a list of names with hyperlinks. Have you ever been to MySpace?"

Amy nodded. She'd checked it out and had even flirted with the idea of putting up a profile.

Petra said, "When you click on the links, the pages will look sort of like that. A picture, basic information like addresses, and then more links."

Eric said, "Write down as many names and addresses as you can."

"Is this how you found me? And Bill?"

Instead of answering, Eric said, "I'll be in touch afterward."

"You know, I've answered every question you've asked, but you've answered exactly none of mine."

"Give me your cell number," he said, not even bothering to respond. He glanced around, something he'd done every few seconds.

With an aggravated sigh, she wrote it down on the paper Petra gave her. As distrustful as she considered herself, it was oddly refreshing—as well as annoying—to meet someone even more so.

Eric leaned down into her face, wearing a pleasant expression. "Don't screw with us."

She knew it was more than just a warning.

The song the band had been playing ended, and the crowd exploded in applause. "Time to go," he said, then he and Petra split up and merged into the flow of people.

Amy slipped out of the wig and robe and stuffed them behind the fabric sheets. She walked around the bandstand and mingled with the crowd. A man on stage talked about the joy of living in the freedom of being who they wanted to be, and everyone cheered. She clapped as she scanned the crowd for anyone who looked out of place. For Cyrus. She thought she'd recognize him anywhere, but remembered the guy who'd been driving that white car. Maybe not.

With a false smile on her face, she wound her way around the edge of the crowd. Her heart tripped when she saw the man wearing dress pants and a white work shirt. He'd unbuttoned the top few buttons and rolled up the sleeves, but he was way out of his element. For one thing, he screamed heterosexual, his distaste at being there etched on his face. For another, he was looking at her when she'd swung her gaze in his direction, then quickly looked away.

Though she wanted to march up and question him, she knew the response she'd get—much like the locksmith. So she meandered to the car, trying to ignore the uncomfortable feeling of being followed. From the corner of her eye she saw him trailing off to the side.

A shot rang out then, and she slapped her hand to her chest. The crowd behind her gasped. He'd shot her! Her knees wobbled. More shots cracked. She was going to die!

But wait. Shouldn't a bullet hurt? She felt no pain. She jerked around to see the sky lit up with fireworks.

"I'm not cut out for this," she muttered to herself, regaining her breath. The man surreptitiously watching had paused, too, as though enjoying the display in the sky.

Jerk! Anger at him dogging her engulfed Amy. Without letting herself think about it, she stalked over. He didn't see her until she was a few feet away. To his credit, he gave her an innocuous smile.

She returned the smile. "How about I follow you for a while?"

"Excuse me?"

He was good, just good enough to make her doubt herself. Still, she said, "It's only fair."

"I don't know what you're talking about."

She kept up her smile. Waited. With a get-me-away-from-this-weirdo look on his face, he walked away. She followed him to his bland car, catching his eye whenever he glanced back at her. He maintained a convincing worried-curious expression.

She waited until he pulled away, and for the first time felt as though she'd gained some of her power back.

Enjoy it, she told herself. *It might be the last time you feel this way for a while.*

CHAPTER 7

Just as Amy reached the base of the stairs leading to her apartment, she stopped cold. Cyrus sat at the top.

"It's not a good time," she said, dragging herself up the steps.

"I can't wait for a good time." He looked just as weary as she felt—and resolute.

She nodded, too tired to argue. She didn't even begin to hope he would tell her the truth about any of this.

He followed her inside, and she closed the door and leaned against it.

"Sit, please," he said, nodding toward the Grape.

This was going to be bad.

She walked in and draped the orange blanket Orn'ry had become attached to over the cage. "Uh-oh," he said in his small voice, which would have been comical in other circumstances.

Cyrus gave her those moments when he was clearly agitated. He'd always been patient. Or maybe controlled. Though he masked his glow colors, she could see a jagged shadow all around his head.

Robotically, she walked over to where he stood. "I'm not sitting."

"Amy, you don't know what you're into here."

"You're right. Tell me."

Oddly, he got a wistful look on his face. "When you were a girl, you were scared of things you didn't understand. Remember when I took you to Disney World, how you wouldn't go into the Haunted Mansion?"

"I'm not a little girl anymore."

"I know." He said that on a sigh. "This is something you should be afraid of."

"Are there spooks?" she said, taunting him with a reference to the CIA.

"More than that," he replied, not taking the bait. "You need to trust me. Tell me what you know."

"Tell me what you know." She remembered the listening devices and went to the stereo. "Wait a minute." A few seconds later Green Day's lead singer belted out "American Idiot." She returned to stand in front of Cyrus. "Okay, we can talk now."

"Amy . . . " He closed his eyes and rubbed them hard with his thumb and forefinger. "You don't have to live this way, sneaking around, going to gay festivals, for God's sake."

"You've been following me."

"For your own good. I don't know what you think is going on, what Eric and Petra Aruda told you, but this has nothing to do with you."

"Then tell me what it does have to do with, Cyrus. Let me decide. You want honesty, well, you go first." She'd learned that much from dealing with Eric and Petra.

She saw his frustration, even without seeing his glow. "All I can say is that you're in dangerous territory and you have to back off." He gestured toward her office. "Go back to being your little hermit self saving hard drives and sanity. Forget this."

The second person to tell her that. Of course, that would be the sane and undoubtedly safe thing to do. There was one hitch in that escape hatch: Lucas.

"Not until I see Lucas . . . Lucas *Vanderwyck*." She aimed an accusatory look at him.

"I didn't want you digging." A puzzled expression crossed his face. "Why do I get the impression that you care about him? The guy broke into your apartment. I'm having a hard time understanding why he matters so much to you."

"I would have an even harder time explaining it—" She felt a catch in her throat. "But I need to see him."

"I told you, he died here."

"No, he didn't. He's alive, and they're doing something to him, they're *hurting him*! I want him released, and I can't let this go until that happens."

"Eric and Petra told you that, didn't they? They're lying."

"They didn't tell me." Emotion strained her voice. "Don't ask me how I know, I just do!"

He blew out a breath. "Amy, you can't save him. I don't know what they're doing to him, but neither one of us can save him. If he is still alive, he's going to die, and you're going to have to let him go."

"No!" she screamed, feeling the pain and anger at those words rip through her.

He clamped his big hands on her shoulders. "You can't save him, but you can save yourself. *Let this go.*"

Her voice was a hoarse whisper: "Did my dad kill himself?"

"Yes."

"Cyrus, do you know why he died?"

For just a glimmer, she saw something she'd never seen before—Cyrus's glow. Yellow, sadness, regret. Then it disappeared.

"No," he said, as convincingly as he'd told her about Lucas Brown, serial killer. He squeezed her shoulders so tight they hurt. "I'm sorry you got involved in this, Amy. I'm sorry you can't trust me enough to tell me what's going on. I'm trying to protect you, but I can't if you keep digging. This is way beyond anything you can handle, emotionally or physically. You may not trust me, but you can't trust the Arudas either. That leaves you alone and more vulnerable than you were the day you were orphaned. If you drop this now, things can go back to the way they were. Maybe not between us," he added at her hard look. "But you'll still have your life."

She was seeing him as a man she'd never known. This was his CIA persona, and maybe this was how he really was. He'd thrown that barb about her days after her dad's death to break her down. It hit its mark but didn't weaken her. No matter what, she didn't have Cyrus anymore. But she wasn't alone, not as long as Lucas was alive.

"Am I an Offspring?" she asked.

"If I said no, would you believe me?"

She shook her head.

"Then why bother to ask?" He sounded weary.

"I was hoping you'd tell me what it meant."

"I know you, Amy. You're dedicated. And even

though you try not to, you care too much. Maybe that's what's driving you. But Lucas isn't some cute, abandoned animal. No matter what he told you, he's dangerous. And your dad, he just lost his mind, nothing more."

He walked to the door, but before he opened it he turned to her. "I can't answer your questions. All I can do is beg you to go back to your life before Lucas Vanderwyck broke in. This is your last chance."

Her pulse throbbed at her temple as she met his gaze. Maybe he was trying to protect her in some way. Maybe she should take his advice. She said nothing. With a dip of his head he opened the door and left.

She locked the door behind him. She could never go back to her life before Lucas. Maybe her father hadn't abandoned her out of a lack of love. She might be something called an Offspring. They were up against a big bad government agency that would do everything within its power to squash them. And a gorgeous, mysterious man cared enough about her to put his life on the line to protect her. She could only do the same.

Cyrus's words, though, came back to haunt her: *He's going to die, and you're going to have to let him go.* Grief and helpless frustration swamped her. She might have Lucas in her dreams, for now, but what if she couldn't save him? Worse, he didn't want to be saved, not at the risk of her life or that of his friends' lives.

For a few minutes she didn't have to be strong. She stumbled to the couch, curled up around her bunny, and let the pain engulf her. In the throes of it, though, she felt something stealing through her. Comfort. She knew this feeling; every time she'd felt despair, it filled her with peace.

"Dad?" she whispered. She had always believed it was him, comforting her from beyond. She'd heard stories, and hell, she just wanted to believe he hadn't abandoned her after all. She sank into the comfort and then, a few minutes later, into sleep.

In the dream, she walked down a pathway in a deep green forest. The sound of a waterfall roared in the distance. She knew the feel of this dream, and she anxiously searched for him. Lucas always brought some beautiful place with him, and here he had chosen a spot that spoke to her soul. But where was he?

She saw him up ahead, his hands draped above him on a branch, his body relaxed but eyes sparking with desire. All these months she couldn't see his face, and now she saw all of him: his strong jawline, captivating eyes, and waves of dark hair. He wore a button-down blue shirt that was open to reveal a sculpted chest, and old and comfortable blue jeans tight enough to show muscular thighs. Her heart raced as she came to a momentary stop, taking him in. His mouth quirked in a subtle smile as he released the branch.

As though something broke loose inside her, she ran to him. Her body slammed into his and her hands went to his face, and then up into his hair, and their mouths collided. His hands moved over her, as though he couldn't get enough of her. They moved in circles, getting dizzy and devouring each other.

"Lucas," she said on a breath, just wanting to lose

herself in the fact that he was real and here with her, loving her.

Framing her face with his hands, he looked at her as though etching every feature into his memory. "God, it's good to see you. Are you all right?"

She kissed him again, not wanting to get into everything, not *able* to get into so much of it. None of that mattered right then. She wanted him, to touch her, inside of her.

When they took a breath, she said, "Why did you hide your face from me all these months?"

"Just in case we ever happened to run into each other. Wouldn't that have freaked you out?"

"Yes," she admitted. "But I would have gotten over it. And then—"

"No, it had to stay just like it was."

"Why?"

His fingers massaged her scalp, sending pleasurable sensations through her body. "It's just better this way."

Words begging him to tell her where he was threatened to pour out, but he kissed her and stole them away. Still, she had to know . . .

"Lucas, are you all right? Are they still—"

"I don't want to talk about what's going on here. I want to get lost in you while I can."

He began to kiss her again, but she pulled back. "While you can? What does that mean?"

He closed his eyes, obviously regretting those words. "We won't ever be together, love," he said, warming her heart with his endearment and crushing it with the words preceding it. "Except for here, for now. Maybe I'm selfish for wanting you when I can't give myself to you—"

"No, Lucas, don't even say that. I'm the selfish one, because I want to save you so you'll be mine, so we—"

He kissed those words away, too, and she tasted sorrow and regret. He pulled away to look at her. "I want you, but when I'm gone, when I don't come anymore, I want you to forget me."

She couldn't pretend to agree with that. "What about Eric and Petra? Can't you give me some clue to give to them?"

"I don't want them hurt either. This is my problem."

She wasn't going to mention that Eric had said the same thing.

He held her chin, making her look into his eyes. "You promised you wouldn't get involved with all this. You're not, right?"

How well could she lie in her dreams? "I promise. But—"

He put his finger over her mouth. "No buts." He pulled her close and she heard his soft sigh. "I'm sorry about Cyrus. I'm sorry you have to feel this pain."

She pulled back. "Why did you say that?"

He gave her that provocative Mona Lisa smile. "Remember when I told you we weren't strangers?"

"How could I forget? But that's because we've . . . well, the dreams. Right?"

"It started long before the dreams; I only recently figured out how to come to you." He searched her eyes. "I've been connected to you since we were kids. Our souls bonded when we were all together. After you moved away, I started getting glimpses of this little girl. For a while they were just quick flashes, and I always felt some emotion. Like when you found your father. I was there, in a way."

"You were there?"

"I could feel what you were feeling and I saw what you saw." He brushed her hair back from her face. "I realized your emotions pulled me to you. Whenever you were really upset or really happy. Just a while ago I felt your sadness and frustration. I'm sorry if I had anything to do with that."

"It's been you all these years?" Not her father, but Lucas. Always there, her protector. She felt tears forming in her eyes. "And I'm supposed to just forget you?"

He wiped away a tear that escaped down her cheek. "I won't come if it's going to cause you pain."

"No, don't stop coming. I'll be sad, of course, but"—she forced a smile—"I'll survive. I always do."

A dirty lie, but she'd already gotten away with one.

"You're sure?"

She nodded, unable to say the word. Then she pulled him down for another kiss. She loved the way his mouth felt against hers, the way his tongue wandered through her mouth and his body moved against hers. She pushed back his shirt, and he shrugged out of it. Her hands explored him, feeling his smooth skin and the muscles beneath, the ridges of his taut stomach, every inch of him.

He pulled up her top, and the forest spun around her, leaving them next to the stream and standing on a blanket. Just as suddenly, she was naked. He was the master of the dream, and she the willing slave. It wasn't hard to be willing with his mouth trailing down her skin, his tongue tracing a wet line around the swell of her breast and then her nipple, and when she couldn't contain the pressure growing between her legs, he gave her other breast the same loving attention. She was about to melt when he slid down to his knees and tickled her belly button with a flick of his tongue.

Thank goodness in dreams she didn't have to worry about belly button lint, she thought before he went lower. His mouth nuzzled that pleasurable place over her pubic bone, and then as her fingers kneaded his hair while her head was thrown back and eyes closed, she was suddenly lying down and he was exploring her folds with his tongue and making her toes flex so hard her joints cracked.

He spread her legs, and she completely trusted him, opening for him as she had never done for anyone in real life. She heard her breathing quicken, her heart race, and her body convulse as orgasmic waves washed over her. He kept kissing her sensitive flesh until another wave of pleasure cascaded over her, and then, over the sounds of her gasps, she heard him chuckle as he did it again.

Still, he wouldn't let her up as he kissed along her inner thighs and down to her toes and the soles of her feet. He sucked each toe into his mouth while he watched her arch in pleasure.

"Your turn," she said, trying to get up, but he gently pressed her back down to the blanket.

"I'm not done with you yet."

He took his time kissing and gently sucking every inch of her body, even her ankles, and, God help her, the back of her knees, which she had no idea could feel so erotic. Then he crouched over her, his hair tickling her skin, and kissed her so tenderly she wanted to cry out. Though he had never said the words, he kissed her and looked at her like someone who loved her. She had never been loved like this, loved and cherished, and she never wanted to let him go.

She grabbed onto the waistband of his jeans and pushed the button through the hole. Then she stopped. "How do you do that instantly naked thing?"

His grin was so devilish she couldn't help but smile the same way.

"Just think it. This is like lucid dreaming, where you're aware of your dream and can change it. You can even make me blond if that's your preference."

"I'll take you just the way you are . . . except naked."

It worked! She pushed him down and took the same pleasure he had taken. She'd never realized that giving could feel so good. His naked body beneath her hands and the taste of him as she took him into her mouth filled her with a sensual charge. What had amazed her, those first times she and Lucas made love, was how easy it was. Nothing like that awkward scenario she experienced the first time she had sex with a guy who, like her, was only curious. She'd decided that sex was overrated and not at all worth the effort. Then, as Lucas had seduced her, she discovered how wonderful all aspects of making love were, even the parts she hadn't been too sure about, like this one. She gently scraped her teeth over the velvety tip of his head.

Over the sound of the rushing creek, she heard a bird calling out in a trilling sound. There was something about the bird, something annoying. Not Orn'ry. She tried to make it go away, just as she'd made his jeans go away.

It didn't. In fact, it grew louder and more ominous. The phone!

"No, no, no," she said, willing her mind to shut it out. It had happened one other time, the phone pulling her out of one of their dreams, leaving her grouchy all day. Now it meant so much more.

The ringing stopped. She giggled. She was still in the forest with Lucas. He rolled her over and kissed her again as he playfully prodded her opening. He was never in a hurry to consummate, something she loved. He slid inside her, but only up to his tip, and then slid out again.

"Aaaah!" he shouted, grimacing, falling away from her and then . . . he was gone.

"Lucas!" she shouted, searching frantically even though she knew he wasn't there anymore. Fear clawed at her as she sank back to her knees, hugging herself. What was happening to him?

The bird started trilling again. No, the phone. She was pulled from the dream as quickly as Lucas had been.

Early-morning light washed through the front window. She lurched for her cell phone but didn't recognize the number. "Hello?" she answered in a rough voice.

"Hey, pinto bean," Eric said in a Spanish accent. "You got my green. I know you got company, but I need my cash, man."

Disoriented, she stumbled from the couch and fell on the floor. "I, uh, you have the wrong number."

She tried to make sense of the message. Pinto. Green. You got company?

Oh, she had *company.* Someone to ditch.

That was as daunting as sneaking into Cyrus's house while he was there and getting onto his computer. Still feeling the imprint of Lucas on her skin and in her soul, she grabbed her backpack. Nothing was going to keep her from trying to find him, especially not a little thing called fear.

Okay, a big thing.

CHAPTER 8

Lucas snapped out of the dream when the lights came on like a blast of cold air. For hours he'd been in the dark, without sound or any kind of stimulation whatsoever. Except for his dream connection with Amy. Only that had kept him sane these past two and a half days. He wasn't sure if the deprivation was some kind of torture, but they'd done it for a reason, one he feared he would find out soon. Another less torturous device was the rubber cap they'd put on his head with electrodes hooked to a machine.

Two men entered his room, which, with light green walls that had yellowed with age, resembled a hospital room. One man looked like the Devil, with bushy black hair, feathered eyebrows, and deep grooves that arced up from his thick moustache. The other was pudgy, maybe ten years younger than the Devil, and he very definitely did not want to be there. He pushed a cart ahead of him.

From his angle on the table, where the bonds held him in place, Lucas couldn't see what was on the cart, and his fear spiked. *Surgical tools?*

"Time for your first assignment," the Devil said. He dropped several folders on the cart.

"What the hell are you going to have me do, strapped down like this?"

The man's smile sent a chill across Lucas's skin. "I think you know. What were you doing while you slept just now? We could see your brain waves jumping all over the place. Not ordinary REM waves."

Lucas's mouth tightened in a hard line.

The Devil leaned against the cart. "Don't try getting into our heads," he said, nodding to the man with him. "We know how to block you."

"I don't know what you're talking about," Lucas said, but his mind was spinning. What, exactly, did the Devil know?

The Devil smiled. "Let's get in sync, shall we?" He picked up a folder and extracted a newspaper clipping. "Paul Canyon, who was stalking his ex-wife and had a plan in place to stab her to death." He handed the page to the other man, who tacked it to a bulletin board. "Andy Schmeckfeld, pedophile living next door to a nice family, found dead in his sleep. The girl told police Schmeckfeld promised to get a puppy that she could come over and play with." He handed that one to the other man. "And finally, Stubin Gresto, domestic abuser, found dead in his sleep." He gave a triumphant smile. "Each man asphyxiated without a mark on their neck or anything lodged in their throat. And, hey, I don't give a rat's ass about these scumbags. Good job, in fact. Now I have something bigger and better for you to put your skills to work."

He knew.

Lucas couldn't get his head around it.

Nobody knew, not even Eric and Petra. It was his dark, dirty secret, nothing he'd meant to do. At least the first time. Nothing he was proud of. Still, he wasn't going to fess up just yet. "How do you figure I had anything to do with them?"

"We know what you are, Lucas. You're a dream-weaver, like your mother."

His heart jumped at that. "My mother? How do you know my mother?"

"We were business associates a long time ago. She could do amazing things, and you inherited her skills. You can enter other people's dreams. You can manipulate them. And you can snuff them out while they sleep with no one the wiser for it. That's a valuable skill."

"My mother killed people in their dreams?" The thought stunned him.

The Devil continued as though he hadn't spoken. "Unfortunately, Eric interfered before we could approach you about joining our team. And now it's too late for voluntary service."

"If you think I'm going to help you—"

"Robbins," the Devil said, nodding toward the bulletin board. The other man pinned a picture of Amy on the wall.

Lucas's chest tightened and he struggled against the bonds. "Leave her the hell out of this."

"Only if you cooperate. We've seen those beautiful paintings of yours. If you want her kept out of this, you'll help us achieve our goals." With another nod to Robbins, a different picture went up. "See this man? He's somewhere in the Washington, D.C., area, and he's very dangerous. He's coordinating a terrorist attack on the Pentagon. We want him to die in his sleep."

Rage poured through Lucas. They were using Amy. He was as angry at himself as he was at this son of a bitch giving him orders. He had involved her by going to her that night.

Robbins spoke for the first time since he'd entered the room. "We've been preparing you for the sensory deprivation state that we found relieves the mind from having to filter out the 'noise' of sound and sight. It was probably a bit unnerving—"

"It removes the need for you to be asleep to go into others' dreams," the Devil cut in, shooting Robbins a dismissive look. He turned back to Lucas. "Your nervous system is so starved for stimuli you're more receptive to using your skills. As I think you've already discovered."

He hadn't been asleep when he connected to Amy. His mind was so fried he hadn't even realized it. "So I kill this guy. Then what?"

"You'll be given another assignment. And another."

"Until? Are you going to keep me here indefinitely?"

Without a speck of emotion, the Devil said, "You won't last that long."

The words jabbed him like swords, but he bit back his fear. "What are you injecting me with?"

"We call it the Booster. It amplifies your skills."

"How? What's in it?" When the Devil didn't answer, Lucas said, "If you're putting it into my body, I have a right to know what it is."

No one answered. Robbins walked over to the cart and lifted a syringe. Reluctance colored his features as he stepped toward the table.

Lucas writhed, but he could hardly move. Frustration swamped him; he was helpless. Movement at the interior window caught his eye, and he saw a woman with long, straight, brown hair watching. Both men followed his gaze, and the Devil told Robbins, "Get her out of here."

Robbins went out and spoke to her. With one more glance in the room, she slowly moved away. He pulled heavy drapes over the window, blocking out all light from the hallway.

"What did you do to Trevor Gladstone?" the Devil asked. "We haven't heard from him in days."

"We left your spy at a warehouse. He was tied to a chair. Alive."

"What did he tell you?"

"You'd be proud. He said nothing, except how to log in to your system with a code we figured had let you know something was going on, since his laptop shut down."

The Devil's eyes hardened even more. "Give it to him."

The substance in the syringe was milky blue. Robbins stepped up next to him. "It won't hurt as much if you relax."

Lucas stared right at him as the needle slid into his vein. Robbins shifted his gaze to his task.

The Devil watched, too. "That's the second injection. Have you felt any heightening in your abilities?"

"Tell me about my mother. What did she have to do with you?"

The Devil smiled at the standoff. "You don't know much about your mother, do you?"

He knew very little. She'd been killed in a car accident when he was four, bereft over the fiery death of her friend, Eric and Petra's mother . . . a death she'd witnessed. All he knew was that the two women were working in a lab for a company whose name he didn't know. As his adoptive father said, all that was important was that the Company had paid on two big life insurance policies, put in trusts for them.

The Devil said, "She was a talented woman, the most talented woman I have ever known."

"What was she doing?"

"That's all I can tell you. So? Any enhancement or change?"

"No."

The Devil gave him a skeptical look. He glanced at Amy's picture on the board, and then the man's. "You have your assignment. You'll hear a chime that will signal it's time to go. When you're done, you will be free to roam around this room."

Lucas narrowed his eyes. "And Amy will be safe?"

"As long as she keeps her nose out of our business, and you cooperate . . . yes."

"She'll stay out of it."

The Devil betrayed nothing as he looked at Lucas. "Then you have nothing to worry about."

The two men left and the lights went out. A soft static sound filled the air—white noise. He stared into the darkness, his eyes wide. His body became twitchy.

The shapes began sometime later, triangles and blotches of color floating in the black. He imagined a red glow in the vicinity of the injection site, which still stung.

What the hell were they putting into his body?

The thought of it made him feel cold and clammy. Something he wouldn't survive. He suspected he wouldn't survive this, especially now that he knew why he was there. No way would they have him kill a few people and then let him go. At least he'd die before Amy. That had always been his biggest fear—that he'd experience her death.

Now he had to keep her safe.

He'd never been able to go into the dreams of someone who wasn't somehow connected to him: a woman who'd come into the gallery, whose ex was out to kill her; the pedophile who ate at a restaurant he frequented. That man on the wall had no relevance to him. Panic licked at him. What if he couldn't do it? He imagined the old Pac Man game and saw the yellow guy nibbling away at him.

He had no concept of time. He might have been in the dark for minutes or hours. His mind began to spin, slowly, round and round. He tensed his body even though he knew he wasn't physically moving. Images flashed before his eyes like a photographer's flashbulb, one after the other: Amy, Eric, Petra, and then the faces of the men he'd killed. Now the target's face. A man sleeping in his rumpled bed. Lucas floating above him. An ashtray on the nightstand, a glass with whiskey residue. Papers strewn everywhere, notes, floor plans. In the room, two other men and a woman, all asleep on the floor. The man in the bed, his face . . . the target.

His skills *had* changed. No prior connection. No sketches that foretold the crime. Just an order to kill.

The first time he killed someone, Paul Canyon, he

brought the man's fantasy into his dream, the plan to stab his ex-wife, the vivid details etched in his mind. He told Canyon, "You don't want to kill her."

Canyon had shoved him out. Which pissed Lucas off. He dove back in, and the two fought. Lucas got his hands around the man's throat and choked him. Canyon's death in the dream thrust him awake in a cold sweat. He hoped he'd stopped Canyon's fantasies. The next day a story in the paper about a man's mysterious death stunned Lucas. The police found evidence of the man's murderous intentions.

He had killed Paul Canyon.

He was as much a murderer as Canyon intended to be. Lucas beat himself up over that, even if he'd saved an innocent woman's life.

What he had to figure out was *how* he'd done it. He soon had his answer. The body experiences what dreamers dream. Their hearts race when they're being chased. They cry when someone dies. They jerk when they fall. But their bodies are protected by the paralyzing that happens during REM. His own presence interfered with that protection, and the man experienced what happened in his dream.

When Lucas got another vision of murder, he knew what he had to do. He would do it as many times as he had to. Kill to protect the innocent. Still, he wasn't anyone's hero.

Now, he floated closer to the man, hovering over his face, and then sinking into his mind. The dream was murky, violent, reflecting what was saturating his mind: bombs, death.

Lucas faced the dream image of the man who wished to kill many people in the name of his religion.

He reached out with one hand, wrapped his fingers around the man's throat, and squeezed.

Gerard Darkwell watched the brain monitor from his office. "Lucas is spiking, like he was before we brought him out. I'd like to know what he was doing then." He smiled. "But I know what he's doing now."

Robbins was watching the video monitor that showed Lucas on the table. "Do you think he's lying about his abilities being enhanced?"

"Probably, but that's not as important as the result." Gerard let out a groan of pleasure. "What we could do with him. Too bad he'd never cooperate willingly. What I don't know, and never will, is how much is him and how much the Booster."

"How many injections can he take?"

"At the strength we're giving, not more than four before he loses his mind. As powerful as he is, he's also dangerous, especially since we don't know exactly what he can do. So it's better that he goes soon." His smile returned. "But what he can do for us in the meantime . . . what they all could do for us. We've got to stop the Rogue Offspring before they contaminate any more of the Offspring we haven't found yet. The Rogues are looking for them, trying to figure out the truth. They already know too much. They must be either captured or eliminated immediately. Eric and Petra Aruda are the most troublesome right now."

"What about Amy?" Robbins asked.

"Right now she's dangerously curious. Once Eric and Petra are out of the picture, she may be usable. Or she may have to be taken out, too, but only after Lucas is gone. I have a feeling he'd know." Robbins had always perspired heavily when things got tense. Now the patch of bald scalp between his thinning hair shined with a layer of sweat. Gerard was glad he still had a head full of thick hair, thanks to his mother's Romanian background. He leaned back in his chair and crossed his arms in front of him. "What's the matter? Don't have the stomach for this anymore?"

"I never did, not when we started lying to them. And giving them that *stuff*. You said it was all gone, destroyed by Wallace."

"It was." He looked at Robbins. "You knew what you were getting into when you signed on this time."

Robbins's eyes narrowed. "Like I had a choice. You yanked me out of the Directorate of Support."

Gerard glanced at the monitor again. "You've always been too soft. It's time to toughen up."

The phone rang. It was headquarters—his boss. Gerard had no patience for the other aspects of his job now that DARK MATTER was coming together, but he answered anyway.

"Darkwell, it's Greely. I was expecting the report on the SALON project this morning. You're not in your office, and from what your secretary says, haven't been lately."

SALON was another research project on tactics, one that wasn't nearly as interesting as DARK MATTER. His other line rang in. He noted the number; an important call. Reining in his impatience, he said, "I apologize for the delay, but we've had some personnel issues. I'll get you the report by day's end, sir." He closed the call and took the other one.

"It's Samuels, sir. We found a body."

"Gladstone's?"

"Well . . . we think so. He's been burned to a crisp. You can hardly tell it's a body, much less whose body. But given the information and location, I'm guessing it's him. We'll have to take him back to the lab and run some identification tests."

"Let me know." He hung up. "They found Gladstone."

"Dead?" Robbins asked, a squeak in his voice.

"Very. We're going to bring in the police. I want Eric Aruda now. He's just become a wanted criminal . . . for arson."

"What about murder?"

"We don't need to muddy the waters. The police, and the press, will want to know who was killed. Gets complicated. Just arson. That'll be enough to bring him in, and then we'll take care of him from there. A lot of things can happen when you're bringing in a criminal."

"He'll be killed?"

"He's too dangerous to keep alive. The other Rogues will prove useful, though. They'll be our guinea pigs. Test subjects without limits."

CHAPTER 9

Amy had felt fear before. Usually it drove her inward, to her cocoon. The fear of losing Lucas drove her out. She couldn't help herself; she peered from the side of the front window to spot her "company": a black, generic car parked within sight of her apartment, a man sitting inside. No way could she get out of her apartment without Spy Guy seeing her. How Eric knew that, she didn't want to contemplate.

Pasting a bored expression on her face, she trotted downstairs with her laundry basket, forcing herself not to look at the black car. Her backpack was buried in the bottom of the basket. Too bad she couldn't enjoy the summerlike day. Others were out by the pool or wandering the path that wound through the courtyard. She took that path directly to the laundry building. She dumped her clothing into the washer, dropped in coins, and tucked the basket behind a chair.

A man wearing dark shades and talking on his cell phone walked down the path. She assumed he was reporting her movement. How exciting was she, in her apartment for long periods of time, broken up with a trip out with her dirty clothes?

This wasn't the guy she'd confronted at the festival. This one blended in better, wearing khaki pants and a cotton button-down shirt, but she was sure he was one of them. He had a controlled glow, so tight to his body she couldn't ascertain the color. He wasn't an Offspring, though. What if he came into the Laundromat and hung out? He'd look mighty conspicuous without any laundry.

She settled in a chair off to the side and grabbed a women's magazine someone had left behind. *What to do when you suspected your man was cheating. How to punch up your bra size in three easy steps.* The magazine might as well have been in Swahili. She yawned as she flipped the pages. It was doubtful they'd actually buy that she was returning to her normal life—not after yesterday. Still, even someone sneaking around had to do laundry once in a while, right?

Spy Guy continued down the path toward the recreation center, his head cocked at an angle to catch any movement should she leave through the front door. He was not much taller than she was, looking as far from some government agent as she could imagine. Which was the point, of course.

She eyed the window way up high with an iron grill on it. Great. It should have a release button. Hopefully, the bathroom had a window, too, a much better place from which to escape. She walked into the small room. Damn, no window. She had an idea, though. She closed the door and turned on the water, annoyed at hearing Ozzie's voice in her head chastising her about wasting water. She cracked the door and saw Spy

Guy glance up when someone asked him a question. She exited, quietly closed the door, and ducked out of sight, hoping he'd think she was still tinkling.

He walked past the open door and then around the corner, out of sight. She jumped on top of the washing machine below the window, saw the green Pinto through the grimy window—and Spy Guy! She ducked back. While making sure the bathroom had no window, he looked up at the window she was next to. Could he see her? She held her breath while he studied it for a moment. If he saw her, he'd know she was up to something.

He walked around to the other side of the building and, seeing it blocked by a fence, quickly walked back toward the front again. As he did, she jumped down and ran back to the bathroom. Shut off the water, waited a second, then came out. Now, he was standing in the open doorway. He replaced the worried look with a casual nod and continued on.

Playing along, she tossed her paper towel into the garbage can as though attempting to make a basket, and dropped down into the chair. A second later she launched herself up and on tiptoe and looked out the high, short windows. Spy Guy was pretending to watch the people in the garden area, though his head was turned slightly toward the laundry building. He started to wander back. He wasn't going to give her a lot of time. She jumped back onto the washing machine, opened the window, and pushed the button that released the grill. It was stuck. She pounded it while watching him through the side window.

Fluck, as Orn'ry would say. "Damn it, come on!"

Spy Guy was getting closer.

She pounded on the button. It finally gave. With a rusty screech, she pushed it open. Spy Guy glanced at his watch and then at the building she was in. He was almost there. Five more steps and he'd see her, ass sticking out the window. She only realized how far the drop was when she looked down, half in, half out. She landed on the concrete with an *Oof!* No dignity, and, unfortunately, not unobserved. A woman who stood nearby, next to her car, was staring at her.

"Sorry," Amy whispered. "Trying to get away from my ex."

The inside of the Pinto smelled old, looked old, and frankly, was old. Eric had probably looked for the crappiest car he could find. Didn't these things blow up if you sneezed in them? She found the key and started it. A cap and sunglasses were on the passenger seat, and she slipped them on as she put the car in gear. And not a second too soon. Spy Guy came through the corridor as she passed it.

Stay calm, don't gun it. If this thing can be gunned.

Through the rear view mirror, she saw him watching the car. Her fingers tightened on the wheel. He ran toward her. Stopped, looked at the stairs going up to the apartments near him. Then he glanced in the other direction, looking for her in places other than the Pinto.

Adrenaline shot through her veins. "Ohmygod, ohmygod, I'm crawling out windows and hiding from CIA dudes." She took several deep breaths and then a laugh bubbled out of her. "I ditched a CIA dude. Me! Little ol' computer nerd me!" She started howling in laughter, knowing she was only one step away from hysterical. More deep breaths. She sobered herself by wondering what Spy Guy would have done if he'd caught her climbing out the window.

She'd only felt such an adrenaline rush one other time, six months ago. She had been summoned to look at a guy's drive on his yacht at a marina. Admittedly, she'd been busy looking at the stars in the night sky, thinking of her dad, and only glancing ahead enough to make sure she didn't walk off the dock. She'd entered a dark section where the lights were out and became aware of a guy working on his boat. He said, " 'Evening." He had the same dark glow the creep she'd worked for had.

She had continued walking, trying to appear cool and unconcerned. Animals could sense fear, after all. In a flash, hands grabbed her from behind, a knife was pressed to her throat, and a gravelly voice said, "Walk with me toward the boat. Don't mess with me or I'll cut your throat." He edged her toward his boat, and she frantically tried to figure out what to do.

Then she saw another guy running toward them and thought, Oh, God, there are two of them, except the second guy did a Rambo on the first. He told her to get out of there, and she raced to the office to get help.

By the time she'd returned with the manager, the creep was cuffed to the railing on a boat, her rescuer gone. She'd never even seen his face. The police had asked him to come forward as a witness, thankfully keeping her name out of the press, but he never did. She hadn't gotten to thank him.

One of the things that still haunted her about that night was what the police had found on the creep's boat: ropes and nonspecified instruments of torture (it was better that she not know). The other thing was the blood on the dock, which was nowhere near the creep. She hoped it was the creep's blood, but . . . what if it wasn't?

Now, once she was on the highway, she let out a long sigh. "I'm already exhausted and I haven't even gotten to the tough part yet."

The car coughed, then paused before continuing. She called Eric's number. "Nice ride," she said, her voice dripping with sweetness.

"It runs, doesn't it? You're on your way, I presume."

"After ditching my parasite." She wasn't going to tell him how close it got. "Is Cyrus still online?"

"Yes."

"How do you know? Do you have a camera or something?"

"That's not for you to worry about."

Implying that she had plenty of other things to worry about. Another call beeped in.

"Who's that?" Eric asked.

She glanced at the screen. "A client. I'll catch him later."

"Client? What do you do?"

"I save data from damaged hard drives. Ever heard of Disc Angel?" Even now she could hear pride in her voice. Until she wondered how all this was going to affect her business.

"No way," he said. "*No* frickin' *way*."

"Yes, way." She made a turn onto the highway and toward Cyrus's neighborhood. "And that seems strange to you because?"

"Never mind. All right, remember what I told you to look for?"

"DARK MATTER. Names and addresses."

"Right. Petra is going to show up at his door and use her feminine wiles to convert him to the Order of Brotherly Love. You won't have long, but you should have enough time to at least get a few names. She'll be on the sidewalk by his house. Make eye contact and then she'll wander to the door. Okay, good luck."

He hung up. She passed Cyrus's house and saw Petra in a simple dress and plain top with one button too many left undone. Her hair was plaited in braids and she wore glasses. She held what Amy surmised was a Bible and some pamphlets. They nodded to each other, and Petra walked toward Cyrus's door. Amy turned into the common area and parked, feeling a sick turning in her stomach. She walked along a path that meandered through the green space behind Cyrus's house. Doing this in the daytime was going to be tricky, but she didn't have much choice. Hopefully most of the close neighbors would be at work, as all reasonable people were. Not that she'd ever been reasonable.

Like, for instance, she still held onto some brainless hope that this was all a big fat misunderstanding, and all she'd find on Cyrus's computer would be boring government secrets about the Clintons or Al Qaeda sex orgies.

She slinked to the back porch. Fortunately she'd never convinced him to take one of the shelter dogs that she worked with, so no animal would give her away. As she'd hoped, the back door was unlocked, and she slipped inside just as Cyrus opened the front door.

His office was in a second bedroom off the main hallway. She knew that he conducted CIA business on his Company-issued laptop. She kept one ear tuned to the door, where she heard Petra introducing herself. She knew she probably wouldn't have time to get out of the office when Cyrus shut the door in Petra's face, which would be as soon as his patience wore out. If that happened, she would duck into the closet he used for storage. Maybe she would learn more by listening for a while.

Now, however, she slid into his chair, which was still warm. He was logged into exactly what Petra had described as a MySpace page. She was startled to see her god-awful driver's license picture staring back at her: green eyes, hair she'd tried to tame until she stepped out into the humid day. On the left were several links: *Background, History. Skills,* and *Notes.* He was typing in a Notes section of the page. Resisting the urge to read more on herself, she clicked on the *Home* link and saw links for *BLUE EYES* and *DARK MATTER*. The CIA logo wasn't at the top, but rather, DEPARTMENT OF TACTICS AND DEFENSE. She clicked on *DARK MATTER* and saw a list of about a dozen names, hers included.

"But I can tell that you're lonely," Petra was saying in her effort to keep Cyrus talking. "We're all lonely until we accept God into our hearts. Don't you want a family to embrace you, to keep you warm during the cold nights?"

Good grief, she was mixing seduction with religion, and she wasn't very good at it.

She saw Lucas's tab, too, and her finger twitched to click on it. But she needed new names. Unease shivered down her spine, as though someone was standing right behind her. She jerked around. No one. Eric's camera?

She clicked on the name Randall Brandenburg. His driver's license picture showed a good-looking guy who could be in a rock band, with his goatee, eyebrow piercing, and two-toned hair. She jotted down his address, using the pen and the pad she'd brought, then went back to the main page and clicked on the next link.

"But sir, I really need to talk to you more," Petra said in an urgent voice. "I've got to save someone's soul or they'll punish me." Time was running out.

"If you belong to some cult that punishes you for not getting converts, you need some intervention. Unfortunately, I've got too much on my plate to do it."

Next she chose Nicholas Braden, going right to his address. Then Jerryl Evrard, only memorizing his address when she heard Cyrus say "Get help" and close the door. Just as she was about to scram, a thought hit her: she had to go back to where he'd left the cursor. No time! If she didn't, she'd be busted anyway. She clicked on her link again and positioned the mouse at the end of the last sentence: *Still no indication of . . .*

If only she had time to read it. She pushed away from the desk. His footsteps sounded across the wood floor. Coming down the hallway. She opened the closet door. Oh, jeez, it was more jammed than she remembered. Boxes stacked up to her waist, and Cyrus had been tossing stuff in.

Footsteps came closer.

She climbed up on the boxes, feeling one collapse a bit beneath her. She folded her legs up and pulled the door closed just as she heard Cyrus walk into the office, muttering about religious crazies.

She realized she was holding her breath and released

it in degrees. The box beneath her crumpled more. She squeezed her eyes shut. *God, if You get me out of here I'll never . . . I don't know, cuss or something, again.*

The phone rang.

"Diamond . . . Yeah? All right, I'll be there in thirty minutes."

Could she dare hope that he'd leave his laptop sitting there logged in? Not reasonably. She heard him snap his laptop closed, and a minute later he walked down the hallway and out the front door. She gave him plenty of time to leave before emerging. Feeling fully paranoid, she half expected Cyrus to be standing at the doorway.

He wasn't. She did note that he'd taken his laptop, and she knew he didn't keep anything work-related on his regular computer. She searched his desk and the file cabinets but found nothing about DARK MATTER, whatever that was, or any familiar names.

"Names."

She picked up his telephone and scrolled down his speed dial entries, writing each one down. Bill Hammond, the Offspring she'd tried to talk to, was there. The phone rang, startling her into dropping it. It was, in fact, Bill's name on the caller ID screen. She was tempted to answer it, but knew that would be a bad idea. She wrote down the last entry and set the phone in the cradle, then waited until Cyrus's outgoing message finished and the machine beeped.

"Hey, it's Bill. I've been picking up some weird energy. And there's some guy hanging around who's definitely putting out a vibe. This all started after that weird chick came over talking about her dad. I've got a bad feeling about this. Call me."

Weird chick. Didn't sound like he would be open to another visit. But what did he mean? Did he have a CIA spook watching him, too?"

"Damn, maybe because I went over there. Were they watching me that day?"

She shivered and quickly left.

Amy ditched the car near the City Docks in the historic section of Annapolis. The boats and salt air reminded her of her terrifying encounter the last time she went near the water, but she tried to pretend to enjoy the breezy day, like many of the others who were eating their lunches in the sunshine. The smell of food made her stomach rumble, though she didn't feel hungry.

She walked around the edge of the square brick area where people sat on benches. She'd been there only a couple of times in recent years. Too many people, too many glows. As she glanced around at the yachts tied along the seawall and the shops and restaurants, she scanned for anyone who looked suspicious.

She spotted Eric and Petra standing in the shadow of a tree on the opposite side, where the boardwalk edged the common area. It gave them an escape, she realized. It scared her that they had to think in those terms.

Petra looked like a fashion plate, as always, with slim black hip-huggers and a tight shirt with a butterfly painted on the front. Eric's now red hair looked even more like flames as it spiked up.

She meandered over to them. "I'm sorry, I only got three names."

Eric shrugged. "Three's a start."

She realized she should be pleased she got three names, under the circumstances, instead of apologizing. It was a bad habit, always feeling sorry. "Randall Brandenburg—"

"Rand," Eric said to Petra. "He's the fifth kid in our group."

"In the picture you saw," Petra clarified.

"Who else?" Eric asked.

She glanced at the paper on which she'd written down the names and addresses. "Jerryl Evrard."

"Never heard of him." Eric leaned close to look at the paper. "Or Nicholas Braden."

At the strange sound near her ear, she turned, furrowing her eyebrows. "Are you sniffing me?"

"You smell good."

"I smell sweaty."

"You smell like a woman."

She stepped away from him. "So are you going to tell me how you knew Cyrus was online?"

"Nope," he said without apology.

Amy let out a frustrated sigh. "Have I proven myself?"

"I suppose," Eric said. "Be a hell of a lot easier, and smarter, if you just walk now and let us handle this."

She met his gaze. "I know that."

A breeze blew Petra's silky blond hair across her mouth. She pulled it back and wrapped her fingers around it like a ponytail. "He's ours. Our concern, not yours."

He's mine, Amy caught herself about to say. *Whoa.* Did she feel that way?

She didn't know for sure, but it was everything and more that she'd read in all those tragic romances—a tidal wave lifting her skyward, ready to plunge her down to drown in the depths. She'd kept herself safe by not connecting emotionally. Now, she had to admit, she'd torn her cocoon as much as those three men had back at her apartment. She had fallen in love with a man who might die before she ever saw him again. That thought tore through her, leaving a gaping hole inside.

Eric interpreted the grief on her face as fear. "You have every reason to be afraid. Get the hell out of this while you can. Petra and I live off the grid now. No credit cards, no freedom—"

"Living in fear," Petra added. "Never getting to just go out to the mall and shop."

Eric said, "Walk away now, go back to your life, and forget all of us."

The breeze blew her thick hair around, too, but it wasn't long enough to twist into a ponytail. "I thought you wanted to round up all the Offspring, band together. Why give me an out?"

"You're too emotionally involved. That's dangerous."

She, Amy Shane, too emotional? She would have laughed if . . . if it wasn't true where Lucas was concerned.

He said, "So get the hell out of here and save yourself. It's okay to admit you're scared. Tell your uncle you've decided we're crazy, all of us."

Or was she crazy to think he was trying to protect her as well as get rid of her? Maybe she looked scared. She felt scared, oh yes, she did. Just as much of finding out the truth about who she was, or of getting killed, as she was of losing Lucas. She could walk with her pride intact. But could she walk?

Amy Shane would run *whee-whee-whee,* all the way home. Something hit her: she wasn't that Amy anymore. She'd always considered herself a bit on the cowardly side, but look at what she'd done since Lucas broke into her apartment. She'd escaped spy guys, sneaked onto Cyrus's computer, and met with two people who, frankly, she didn't trust or like. She'd done things she'd never thought she could or would do. For love.

"I'm in."

She was both terrified and excited to find out who this Amy was.

Neither Petra nor Eric looked especially happy.

Petra leaned against a large piling with her arms draped in front of her. "Why are you so passionate about finding Lucas? You don't even know him."

"You saw the paintings. They weren't just any dreams." Her cheeks reddened, and she saw Petra's do the same. "I can't explain what Lucas and I share, and I won't. But I'm here, so that should tell you what you need to know." She met their gazes. "I want the same things you do. To rescue Lucas. To find out how my father was involved in all this . . . whatever 'this' is. Why am I an Offspring? Who are these people watching me? I can't walk away from those questions . . . or from Lucas."

Eric nodded, a grim expression on his face. "You realize that once the bad guys figure out that you're working with us, you're going to have to go into hiding. There's no turning back."

Amy finally used her hand as a hair band. "That's why we've got to keep our alliance hidden for as long as we can."

"Our alliance?" Eric said.

"We want the same thing. That makes us allies."

He scrubbed his hand through his stiff hair. "Right now we have no idea where Lucas is. That's the first problem."

Petra asked, "Can't you find out anything from him? During your dreams," she added in a harder voice.

It hit Amy then that Petra was jealous of her connection with Lucas. Was she an overprotective stepsister or did she have other feelings for him? No matter, she knew she couldn't deal with that right now. "He won't tell me anything. He doesn't want me or you to rescue him."

Eric shook his head. "Noble son of a bitch. Typical Lucas. Look, you're the only one who has a connection to him. You've got to find out something." Frustration made his glow flare out from his body. "Can you connect to him?"

She shook her head. "I tried."

"He told you they were injecting him with something."

"Yes, but he doesn't know what it is."

"They're keeping him alive," he said, his mouth a grim line. "They could torture him to find out what we know, but Lucas would downplay that. Besides, they already know we're on to them."

"How do they know?"

The two exchanged a look that clearly said: *should we tell her?*

When the answer was their silence, Amy let out a huff of breath. A sea gull, squawking as it swooped by, mirrored her frustration. "Look, whether we like it or not, we're involved in this together. I need to know everything."

He raised an eyebrow at her. Made her wait a few seconds. "I'll tell you what you need to know," he said at last, propping his arm on the same piling Petra was leaning against. "It started when I was arrested for suspicion of arson two months ago—bogus charges. The questioning just stopped all of a sudden, and this guy in plainclothes comes in, says he's Trevor Gladstone. He doesn't ask me more questions about the fire. He wants to recruit me for the Department of Tactics and Defense.

"I said 'Hell no' and that was the end of it. Or so I thought. Except I keep seeing him around. I even followed him once, but he lost me. Then Lucas mentions someone's been breaking into the gallery, looking around but not taking anything. He installs a video security system and shows us the video of this guy creeping around his office. And holy shit, it's Gladstone."

Petra said, "Then I wigged because he was a guy who'd been friendly to me at Hooters, where I worked."

"So we realize this guy has been casing us. There's no such thing as the Department of Tactics and Defense, but he's probably government, has to be, with the clout to interrupt an interrogation."

"That was the organization Cyrus was logged into," Amy said.

"So we kidnapped him," Eric said in the casual way he'd say they invited him to dinner. That was what unnerved her about him; one of many things. "He didn't give up much information, though. Lucas got onto his computer, and with a little bit of cooperation we found what you saw at Cyrus's. We saw our profiles, Hammond's, and yours before his computer shut down."

"That's how Lucas found you," Petra said, not hiding her disdain at that. "Until then he only knew your first name."

Eric pushed away from the piling. "We figured Gladstone gave us a code that alerted his people he was in trouble. We ditched the laptop in case it had GPS capability and left him there. Since they knew which profiles we'd looked at, we decided to wait to approach you and Hammond. Gladstone was monitoring us, trying to get to know us. Cyrus is probably your monitor, yours and Hammond's."

Amy felt a jab in her heart. Cyrus had been reporting on her. Was that the only reason he'd been in her life? She pushed past her pain. "I saw two program names on the home page on Cyrus's computer: DARK MATTER and BLUE EYES."

"What the hell is BLUE EYES?" Eric asked.

"That link was on Gladstone's computer, too," Petra said.

"I didn't have time to check it out." Amy flipped over the list. "I did, however, write down everyone in Cyrus's speed dial memory." She got a pen from her backpack and marked lines through several names. "These probably aren't Offspring. I don't know who Zoe Stoker is. Oh, Bill Hammond left a message while I was there, saying he had a bad feeling about me coming over and that someone was watching him."

Eric's expression grew grimmer as he looked at Amy. "Don't go to Hammond again. Right now you're the wild card. They're not sure what you know or what you're up to. Let's keep it that way."

Amy hooked her thumbs through the loops in her jeans. "Um, isn't that what I said?"

"Maybe we can get you onto Cyrus's computer again. Speaking of computers . . . " He looked at Petra and nodded toward Amy. "She retrieves data from damaged hard drives."

Petra's face perked up. "Really?"

"I checked." He lifted a cell phone that could obviously get onto the Internet. "She's got a reputation for her expertise, even got a small write-up in *Wired* magazine."

Though Amy was proud of that, she was annoyed that he hadn't believed her. "And what is the relevance of your interest?"

His smile was smug. "We ditched Gladstone's laptop, but I took out the drive."

All annoyance fled. Her fingers twitched. "Give it to me."

"We'll do it together," he said.

"Look—"

Petra shushed them and cocked her head. She kept a pleasant expression on her face, but her glow grew jagged as she shifted her gaze toward the parking lot. "Eric, see that cop car? He's calling into the station, citing your description. They're talking about the arson suspicion. Even though they didn't have enough to charge you, they were sure you were guilty. You need to get out of here." Despite the words, she turned to Amy and said, "Laugh and pretend that Eric was trying to pick us up. We're so not interested." She waved him off and grabbed Amy's arm as they walked away, laughing like teenagers.

"You're good at this stuff," Amy said on a peal of laughter.

"I'm good at pretending to be something I'm not." Her smile was hollow at that.

They glanced back and giggled again. Shaking his head at the silly girls, Eric casually strolled toward, ironically, the police substation, taking a walkway that went behind the small building.

"How could you hear the officer?" Amy asked as they got into a burgundy vintage Barracuda.

"I have really good hearing." The engine roared to life, smooth as whiskey, and Petra pulled away. Worry permeated her features.

"Eric seems like he can handle just about anything," Amy offered as consolation.

"That's what I'm worried about."

U2's "Numb" played on the not-so-vintage CD player. "You guys must have a thing for this band. I heard it at the gallery, too."

Petra's fingers tightened on the wheel, and her voice tightened around her words, too. "This is Lucas's car. He says that U2 is the only band that is a perfect blend of music and consciousness, whatever that means."

With that, the car took on a whole different meaning for Amy. She looked around, studied the perfectly maintained interior. Mixed with the scent of leather was the faint echo of a citrus men's cologne. It was like being inside Lucas, feeling the warmth of him, hearing the rumble of his blood. Her fingers automatically went to the cross at her neck, caressing the edges and remembering it dangling from his neck that night he'd changed her life.

Petra dropped her off near her apartment building a short time later. She was surprised to find her laundry still in the washer, and she moved it to the dryer. She heard the scrape of shoes on the concrete floor and looked up—to find Spy Guy staring at her. She didn't need to see his violet blue glow to know he was pissed.

CHAPTER 10

Rand Brandenburg sat at the blackjack table in Atlantic City, four hundred dollars on the line. He'd drawn eighteen, a high enough hand that no sane gambler ever took another card. Rand gestured for another card. The dealer raised his brows as though to ask, *Are you sure?* Rand nodded, and the dealer slid the card and turned it over. A three. Twenty-one. The dealer busted.

Rand acted surprised, shocked even, what friggin' luck. The dealer narrowed his eyes as he pushed a pile of chips toward him. Rand had changed tables, played recklessly, and lost enough not to arouse suspicion. He collected his winnings, tossed a chip to the dealer, and departed. He knew to stay under the radar.

He'd gotten a little greedy lately, coming into the city twice in one week. The woman next door whose daughter had leukemia was selling off her possessions one tear at a time to pay the medical bills. Damn insurance company was stringing her along. Then an anonymous benefactor deposited thousands of dollars into the account set up for donations. Her "garage" sales had stopped and that fearful look on her face had lessened just a little. He had another two thousand in his pocket for her.

He wended his way through the crowds to the cashier. Unfortunately, he hadn't thought to check ahead. Real bad luck that. He walked right into a brick of a man wearing a suit.

"Excuse me," Rand said, knowing better than to react to the man's rudeness or lack of manners when the man stepped in front of him again.

A beefy hand clamped onto his shoulder. "You need to come with me."

Shit. He sighed, as though accepting his fate, but at the same time bolted. Or tried to. One second he was turning, and the next he was on the floor with a knee jammed into his back. He was hauled up as though he weighed a hundred pounds and shoved through the gawking bystanders to the back of the casino.

"What's the deal?" he said.

The man said nothing as he propelled him through a door that read EMPLOYEES ONLY and down a hallway. Another man waited inside what looked like an interrogation room in a police drama. He would have actually welcomed the sight of a detective. These dudes were definitely not cops, which meant they didn't have to follow any rules. No phone call. No bystander videotaping the incident. Plus the police needed proof that he was cheating, and there was no proof.

These guys didn't need proof. They'd obviously decided he was guilty. Both men felt him up, and they were none too gentle about it.

"Hey, watch the merchandise. I don't have any weapons."

They threw his wallet on the table, his car keys, his winning chips, and kept looking.

Please don't let them do a cavity search.

"No electronic devices," Tall and Mean said to no one in particular.

He shoved Rand into a chair and started throwing pictures onto the table: pictures of him playing roulette, blackjack, craps.

"We've been watching you," he said.

"Well, that's obvious. I realize I'm a stunner and all, but really, you shouldn't have."

A whack on the back of his head snapped his neck forward.

"You have odds way beyond the normal sucker who comes in here."

"Guess I'm a lucky guy," Rand said, and got another knock on his head.

"That ain't it. You've got a system. Since you don't only play the cards, it ain't card counting. So what is it? Tell us and maybe you'll walk out of here on two bruised but not broken legs."

Rand swallowed hard but kept his body slack and relaxed. "I don't have a system. You said it, buddy. How can I win at different kinds of games? I'm telling you, it's luck."

This time the fist came from the front, smashing his nose. Blood spurted onto the pictures on the table, giving him multiple views of bloody Rands.

Tall and Mean smiled; oh, yeah, the son of a bitch was enjoying this. Someone was cheating his casino, which regularly cheated people and preyed on their dreams, but that part didn't matter. "Try again, dickweed."

The other guy, Big and Beefy, stood against the wall, his body sculpted like concrete, muscles ridiculously big and veiny. He was also enjoying the show. Likely he was backup in case the muscular but-not-even-close-to-beefy Rand Brandenburg caused trouble or Tall and Mean got tired of getting blood all over himself.

"Don't I get a phone call? How about a towel, at least?" Blood continued to gush. When he tried to stanch it he heard a crackling noise. Damn, it was broken.

That got him another slam, this time in the side of his head. His ear rang and pain shot right through his head. Thankfully it wasn't the other side; that could have torn the gold bar that lanced the top of his ear or ripped his spike right out of his eyebrow.

Big and Beefy said, "I can do this longer than you can stay conscious, I bet."

Rand was going to say something about him messing up his pretty hand but thought better of it. He closed his eyes for a second and saw another fist coming—he opened them. "All right. I'll tell you my system." He noticed the camera up in the corner of the room. So he *was* being taped. Would the police ever see it? Coercing a confession by brutality wouldn't fly in court. With a jab of fear he realized this would never see court. He might not, for that matter, see another day. "I can see ten seconds ahead."

Silence.

Then the fist he'd already seen.

For a second worms wiggled in his vision. Did he dare want to see ahead again?

"Try again," Tall and Mean said.

"That's all I have. I've been able to do it all my life. I concentrate and see ten seconds ahead. I can see what cards the dealer has, what number comes up in roulette and craps. That's my system. It's prescience. Psychic. Whatever you want to call it."

Another slam to the head, and this time the room blinked in and out. "What kind of device do you use? What'd you do with it?"

"Device?" His words were slurred. "No device. Just here." He tapped his temple and grimaced in pain.

A phone rang, and Big and Beefy answered it. After listening for a second, he said, *"What?"* He looked at Rand. "Why?" After a second he hung up and looked at Tall and Mean. "We gotta stop. Someone else wants him."

"Who?"

"Boss didn't say, but they must be pretty powerful. We don't get to finish him."

Tall and Mean grunted in annoyance. "This ain't right." He aimed a look at Rand. "You must be messing with some pretty big shit."

The two men walked out. The lock clicked behind them. Rand got up and made his way over to the phone. He glanced at the camera and smiled, though it felt more like a grimace with his face swelling up. He lifted the receiver. No dial tone. He tried 9 and a number but still got nothing. He wandered over to the door and twisted the knob. As he suspected, it was locked. He paced, wondering who these people were who wanted him.

An hour later the door opened and his two buddies reentered and leaned against the wall. They looked at him but said nothing. A few minutes passed with Rand trying to appear unconcerned as he sprawled in one of the chairs. The door opened again, and the guy who stepped in made Tall and Mean look like a teddy bear. He didn't need brawn or mass either. He would have made a perfect villain in an old horror flick, with his winged eyebrows, bushy moustache, and eyes so dark the devil could lurk inside. A gratified devil, by the smile that spread across the man's face when he looked at him.

To the two beefcakes he said, "He say anything?"

"Just some bullshit about seeing ten seconds ahead. You with the FBI or something?"

"Something."

Rand wasn't sure whether he should be relieved or not. He sure as hell didn't *feel* relieved. So who was this guy? And why was he being cagey about what agency he was with?

The man picked up his wallet and tried to compare the driver's license picture to the bloody mess in front of him. "I see you guys have been having fun."

"It's just a job," Tall and Mean said with a shrug.

He tossed the wallet on the table. "Randall Brandenburg. You're a hard man to catch up with."

"I don't like staying in one place too long."

"Any particular reason for that?"

He'd been running loose since he was a kid. His mom was too busy making love with her bottle of vodka to care. "Not really."

Two other men came in, neither in uniform. The cagey guy nodded, and the two lifted Rand by his arms to his wobbly feet. He felt cold handcuffs snap around his wrists.

"Is there a back way out of here?" the cagey man

asked the two beefcakes. "I don't think you want customers seeing your handiwork."

Reluctantly, the two led them down the hallway and out a back entrance. A black car pulled up. Cagey Man opened the door while the other two helped him into the back, and then he got into the passenger seat.

"Am I under arrest?"

Cagey Man turned toward him as the car pulled away. "Not technically."

"Then let me out."

"Since I saved you back there, I think you owe me."

"Owe you what?"

"Your cooperation." He seemed to assess Rand. "You're not a cooperative guy, are you?"

"Not technically." He crossed his arms over his chest and sat back in the seat. "I don't like games. Beef. Drama."

"Do you like money?"

"Money's not important to me."

"Why are you using your—shall we say—talent, to cheat? I have a better use for it."

This had *bad* painted all over it in bright red. "Look, I appreciate the offer and you saving me, but no thanks."

Cagey Man turned forward again. No one talked as they left Atlantic City and headed south. Rand wasn't in a talkative mood, and he knew they wouldn't answer his questions anyway. He was pretty sure they weren't with the FBI, police, or the New Jersey Division of Gaming Enforcement.

The silence was oppressive. The two men in the back with him checked their watches periodically. After four and a half hours, not too long after he saw the sign telling him they were in Maryland, one of the men turned to Rand. "That's where we're headed." He pointed to a cluster of buildings, though there were several in the distance and Rand couldn't figure out which one he pointed at, or why he was even bothering.

Something sharp punctured his neck from the other side. His first thought was a vampire, because he read every vampire book he could get his hands on, and then his body slowed. His thoughts ground to a halt. And he slumped into darkness.

Petra curled up in the 'Cuda's driver's seat as she waited for Eric and tried to imagine that she was on Lucas's lap. Though they grew up together, she had never seen him as a brother. Unfortunately, he'd only seen her as a sister, and she kept hoping that would change someday. She'd never had the courage to tell him she wanted more. The last time he hugged her and told her he loved her like a sister, she'd pushed him away, and every day she kicked herself for that. Especially now, when she might not be able to tell him it wasn't his affection that had angered her but the type of affection.

The driver's door flew open. She screamed before turning. "Eric! How did you find— Never mind. What happened?"

He motioned for her to jump over the console to the passenger seat, always having to be in control. He smelled of sweat and maybe fear, and his shirt was filthy. "I ditched the cops."

"You . . . didn't hurt them, did you? They're not our enemies, even if they're doing our enemies' work."

"I didn't hurt them. I just lost them. We need to talk to Dad."

"What are we going to tell him about Lucas?"

"Only what we need to. But mostly I want answers." He glanced in the backseat. "Where's Amy?"

"I dropped her at her place."

"I don't know whether she's going to be a help or a hindrance. So far she's handled everything all right."

Petra couldn't help but smile at the charades Amy had gone along with. "I hate to admit it, but she's pretty good. The question is, can we trust her?"

"I'm not sure. We'll only tell her what she needs to know."

After dinner they drove to their dad's house, parking a short distance away and walking through the night to the kitchen back door. Eric unlocked it and they slipped inside. Rick Aruda dropped the potato he was peeling. "You startled me." His surprise hardened to anger. "What are you doing here, Eric?"

Eric's body stiffened. "I didn't know I was unwelcome."

There hadn't been any warmth between the two for years, and Petra suspected they kept their civility for her sake. Now it appeared even that was gone.

Rick set his peeler down with a *clack*. "You're wanted for arson. The police were here asking about you just an hour ago."

"It's a bogus charge, Dad."

"Like the solicitation for prostitution last year? Like having sex in a public place six months ago? Like the fires they've linked to you? Like our house?" he said in a low voice.

"They haven't arrested me for any of those fires. There's no proof because I'm innocent."

He seemed to look just past Eric. "I wanted to believe you were innocent. As a dad, it's my duty to believe in my son. Deep down inside, Eric, I don't. Ever since you were a kid, suspicious fires have broken out. Unexplained fires. And then our house. Candy." His mouth trembled. "I know your mother's death shattered your world. When your mother burns alive, it's got to have an effect on a kid's psyche. That's why I got you into counseling. But I can't help you anymore, Eric. Now something else has to be done."

Their father was lean, almost too thin, and looked years older than he was. He'd lived alone since his second wife's death.

Eric walked closer to him. "I didn't kill Candy. Look, this arson thing, it's bogus because someone higher up is after me. After me and Petra. Something's going on here, something we don't understand. Lucas is missing."

Rick rolled his eyes. "And the paranoia continues. I thought we'd gotten past that."

"This is real."

"It is, Dad," Petra said.

He finally looked at her. "Now you've got her convinced."

Eric flattened his hands on the island's counter. "I don't want to tell you too much. I don't want you involved, but I need some answers. Twenty years ago we lived in Fort Meade. Where Mom died. What did you do for a living then?"

"What I've been doing all my life, engineering."

"What about Mom? You never want to talk about her or what happened that day."

He picked up a knife and chopped a potato in half. "And I'm not talking about it now."

Petra stepped closer and implored with her eyes. "Daddy, please." He was actually her stepfather. Her mother married him when she was still a baby, but he had always treated her like his own.

Rick set his knife down again. "Wait a minute. You think that whatever you're hung up in has something to do with your mother?"

"She was our mom," she continued, pinching Eric before he could speak. "We shouldn't need a reason to ask."

"I told you, she worked with a chemical company. There was a fire in the lab."

He shut her out as he always did when the subject of his wife's death came up. He continued cutting the potatoes with deliberate motions.

"What company?"

"Maryland Chemical Corporation or something like that. They're not in business anymore."

"What was she working on?" Eric asked.

"I can't say. I mean, I don't remember."

Eric edged closer. "You *can't* say?"

"I'm not having this discussion with you. It's painful and it's in the past, where it needs to stay."

Eric slapped his hand down, hitting the cutting board and making the potato cubes jump. "You can't say. Because I'm damned sure you would know what she was working on that caused her to die in that horrible way."

Petra said softly, "Whatever it was, it's been a long time. It's okay to tell us."

Her father didn't take his gaze off the potatoes spilled on the counter.

"The money," Eric said after a moment of silence. He turned to Petra. "The big life insurance settlement Dad got after her death. Our trust funds. It was hush money."

Rick's face reddened as he met Eric's glare. "Get out of here or I'll call the cops."

Eric stared him down. "You wouldn't do that. I'm your son."

Rick held firm, not intimidated by his hulking son. His mouth trembled. "No, you're not. Your mother had an affair when she was . . . working at the chemical company. I still raised you as my own, even after your mother died. Even after the fire. But I'm not going to harbor a criminal, no matter whose name he carries."

Petra saw Eric's face harden, but for a second she also saw something in his eyes soften with pain. He spun around. "I'm looking through Mom's things."

He went down to the basement, but Petra remained. She cracked her knuckles. "Is it true?"

Dad nodded, not meeting her eyes. "I never intended to tell him. But I don't know who he is anymore. Whatever schizophrenic scenario he's cooked up, stay out of it. And get him out of here or I will call the police."

Petra flew down the stairs and saw Eric tearing open boxes. "I remember finding a box down here years ago," he said. "Dad—that man up there—told me to leave it alone."

She touched his shoulder. "Eric, I'm sorry—"

He pushed her hand away. "Don't. Don't touch me." He tore open another box and stopped. "This is it. Here's a picture of Mom and . . . him. Look, her death certificate."

Nothing odd there. He kept digging until he came across a yellowed envelope with the return address that read *SPP,* located in Washington, D.C. He pulled out the letter from Calvin Hobson, president of the Society for Psychic Phenomena.

Dear Mr. Aruda,

We have just learned of Camilla's death, and we wish to extend our sincerest condolences. She was very special to us here at SPP and will not be forgotten. We were never comfortable with her involvement in the program and continue to have our suspicions. If you wish to discuss any of this, please contact me at the above number.

While Petra was reading, she picked up sounds in the kitchen. She didn't have many skills, beyond the dumb luck of her beauty, but her heightened sense of hearing was definitely one. She could hear her father on the phone.

"Yes, he's here now. In the basement . . . No, I don't think he's armed, but I don't know for sure."

She squeezed Eric's arm. "Dad just called the police."

CHAPTER 11

Amy tried to act calm. Not easy, considering Spy Guy was probably armed. Even though he wasn't much larger than she was, he'd had all kinds of training to take down armed criminals.

This isn't happening, right? Not happening, and yet, here's this guy, and I've got this bizarre urge to jump up in the air and slow-mo kick him in the nuts. The mental picture actually made her smile.

He sneered. "Are you enjoying this, you sneaky little bitch? You think this is a *game*?"

Her eyes widened. "Are you allowed to talk to me like that? Is that in your etiquette manual?"

The menacing expression wilted for a moment, and that gave her the juice to say, "You're probably a greenie just out of training and pretty pissed that a *girl* made you—isn't that how they say it?—and then ditched you." Her derisive gaze swept him from head to toe. "Then again, maybe you're used to that."

The menace returned, flushing his face red. He surprised her by pushing her against the wall with his forearm pressed against her throat. "You don't know what you're dealing with."

"Do you?" she rasped. "Do you even know what this is about?"

She could tell by the look on his face that he didn't; he was a peon following orders, but he was a pissed-off peon with a wounded male ego. Amy didn't know where this attitude, or her inner strength, was coming from or whether it would help or hurt. She was angry enough not to care at the moment.

"I know better than to mess around with the CIA," he growled, pressing harder against her throat and digging his fingers into her shoulder. "And so will you."

So the CIA *was* involved.

A gasp jerked their attention to a woman who had walked in with her basket of laundry. Amy didn't think. Instinct drove her knee into his balls. He doubled over, and she shoved him backward. He fell against the washer and slid to the floor, hands clutching his groin.

"Should I call the police?" the woman asked as Amy backed toward the entrance.

"No." Definitely not. "Creepy guy's been stalking me for the last two days. I don't think he'll mess with me again."

The woman backstepped, obviously deciding to choose another time to do her laundry, a time when a red-faced man wasn't writhing on the floor muttering vicious expletives.

Amy turned and walked right into Ozzie, impeccably groomed as always, who had obviously seen some or all of that charming little scene. She kept walking, her heartbeat throbbing in her throat.

Ozzie matched her stride. "Are you all right?"

"Fine."

"What was that about?"

"Just like I said, some creep—"

He halted her, putting his hands on her shoulders. Still bristling with adrenaline, she shot an irritated look at his grip on her.

He backed off physically. Not verbally. "That raid on your apartment, it wasn't a mistake, was it? Amy, I'm your friend. You're obviously"—he glanced back to the Laundromat where Spy Guy was hobbling out—"in trouble," he finished with a whisper. "Let me help. I'm up for adventure. I know you're not into drugs or weapons smuggling or anything. You're an innocent citizen being targeted by thugs because . . . because you saw files you shouldn't have. I'm right, aren't I?"

He had a vivid imagination, but that wasn't a bad cover story he'd offered. Amy lowered her voice. "You figured it out, Oz. I appreciate your willingness to help, but you have to stay out of this."

She watched Spy Guy as he angled his body onto a bench and tried to look tough as he stared her down from a distance. She felt his hatred just as she saw it in his spiked glow that verged on purple—violent intent.

"You're up for adventure?" she asked.

"Yes!"

"Good. I may . . . have to go away for a while. Will you take care of Orn'ry?"

He rolled his eyes. "No way. That bird hates me."

"Please, Oz. You said you'd help."

His glow was a vivid turquoise color. Worry. "God, what are you involved in?"

"Gotta go."

She turned toward her apartment, sending one last glance at Ozzie and then at Spy Guy, her feelings going from sad to angry. A thought popped into her mind: *Won't Cyrus be proud of me for handling that situation?* That pride soured when reality reminded her: No, he wouldn't be so happy that she'd just nailed one of his guys in the nuts.

She locked the door behind her and leaned against it. Her body trembled from both fear and anger and . . . pride. Yes, pride. Her own pride, not anyone else's. That would have to do.

She turned on the television for something to distract her. The news was on. It was already dinnertime and she hadn't eaten all day. She went to the fridge and searched for something substantive. She found a container of hummus and some organic pita chips and dug in. Yuck. She was going for the Ben and Jerry's when she got the gooey stuff down. She'd liked the idea of being earth-conscious and healthy . . . at least in theory.

The television droned on about the shift in weather in the Midwest and then on to the next story and the next as she scarfed New York Super Fudge Chunk.

"An Annapolis man is wanted for arson in a January fire. Eric Aruda was brought in for questioning at the time, but authorities didn't have enough evidence."

Amy shot from the kitchen to the living room, where she stood rigid as Eric's driver's license picture flashed on the screen in front of a news video of the burning building. It switched to an interview with someone from the Annapolis police, who was saying, "I'm not at liberty to discuss the evidence at this time, only that we have enough for an arrest."

The reporter came back on. "No one was injured in the fire, which caused $400,000 in damage. The abandoned building was owned by the Porter Canton Company, which was involved in allegations of fraud and other illicit activities. Those charges were later dropped, and it was speculated that the fire was an act of revenge. There is no record, however, of Aruda having any affiliation with the company."

Amy dropped down onto the Grape and turned off the television when they moved on to another story. She knew he'd been questioned for arson, but she didn't know whether he'd done it or not. "This has nothing to do with that fire," she said aloud. "And I bet if they arrest Eric, he'll disappear forever." She thought of Lucas, the "deranged serial killer" whose arrest never made the news.

"Lucas." The thought of him hurt, and filled her with an urgent longing at the same time. "Lucas, come to me. I need you."

It took a while for her mind to stop buzzing over everything that had happened. Finally she drifted into sleep. In her dream, she was running from Spy Guy, down alleys glistening with rain, on a marine dock where creepy guys lurked in the dark, and then she ran right off the end and into the darkness.

"Amy."

As she hit the water, she heard him. Everything changed, then, to a sunburnt desert with dunes and pyramids and miles of sand all around. She fell into the warm, soft sand with her arms and legs spread mid-jump. She had to catch her breath as she rolled to her side and found Lucas sitting on the sand with his wrists propped on his knees.

She ran over to him, her feet sinking in the sand. "Why did you pick a desert, for God's sake?"

His smile filled her with joy as he stood. "I always thought it would be cool to make love in the shadow of a pyramid."

She fell into his arms, and the world felt right again. "Not your typical male fantasy."

He smiled. "I'm not your typical male."

"So true." She kissed him, wanting to feel him inside her mouth and inside her body and everywhere.

But he held her away and studied her. "You're okay with this? Being with me knowing it could end anytime?"

"I have to be."

His expression grew serious. "You, Petra, and Eric, you're all right?"

"Yes, why?"

He held her chin. "You're not trying to rescue me, right? None of you?"

"No, but . . . there's a problem. Eric's wanted for arson. It's a scam to bring him in."

A shadow passed over his face. "Maybe, maybe not. He's always been fascinated by fire. His and Petra's mother burned to death during a lab experiment. He became fascinated by fire. He'd stare into fireplaces for hours, just watching the flames and, when no one was looking, throwing things into the fire. Instead of fearing it, he became drawn to it. He's never been directly linked to a fire, but he's been circumstantially tied to several. Have you talked to them?"

She couldn't lie about that. "A few times. They're worried sick about you. Lucas, what's happening to you? Please, tell me."

He stroked her cheek. "It's better if you don't know."

"No, it's not. I'm imagining the most horrible things. You screamed in pain when you left last time."

"Not pain, surprise. I was in the dark, and they snapped the lights on."

"You said they're injecting you with something. What is it doing? Tell me."

"I don't want you thinking about me, not like that."

"At least tell me where you are, what it's like, if you're comfortable."

He paused but relented when he saw her determination. "I don't know where the building is; I was unconscious when they brought me here. They're doing experiments, giving me this stuff and checking my reaction to it. I saw them wheeling someone down the hall on a gurney. I was worried it was one of you. I think it's an Offspring, though."

"Do you have a window? Can you see what's outside?"

"Just an inside one, where they can watch me. There's a small exterior window way up high, but they blocked it off."

"These people that are doing this, they're with the CIA, I think."

"Definitely government, which is why I don't want you involved. The head guy—I call him the Devil—is on a power trip. His secondary, well, he's not as bad. He's come in a few times, gave me a toothbrush and toothpaste." He cradled her face in his hands. "We don't have much time. I came here to escape, to eat you up so you'll be inside me, keeping me alive."

"Oh, Lucas," she groaned, in both pleasure at his words and pain at what they meant.

After a long kiss, he said, "Now, for the shadow . . ."

Suddenly they were on a blanket in the shadow of the pyramid, her sitting on her knees facing him. He poured champagne into two glasses and handed her one. They toasted and sipped, and she choked on the bubbles. "I've never had champagne."

"Really? There's so much I wish I could do with you." At the agony in her eyes, he said, "Forget that. Kiss me."

After a long, soulful kiss, she looked down and saw that she was naked. "Why am I naked and you're not?" Then she remembered that she could change the dream as well, and a moment later he was naked, too. "There, that's better."

With a growl, he kissed her, his hands roaming over her body, drinking her in as much as his mouth was. She pushed her fear for him from her mind, not letting it steal away her pleasure. He kissed and nibbled down her neck, and as she arched, he kissed down the center of her breasts and then laved each one until she ached with need.

"Make love to me now, before something happens and you leave," she whispered on a hoarse breath. "We can do the foreplay later. I want you inside me."

He was also on his knees, and he sat back and pulled her astride him. Their sexual positions were always inventive; none of that missionary stuff for him. He was hard and ready, and she slid around him as their bodies connected. His hands grabbed her derriere and pulled her closer, and she gasped from the feel of him so deep inside. She moved in his rhythm, her hands on his shoulders and then in his silky hair as she tilted her head back and lost herself in him. He kissed and teased her breasts with his mouth.

She heard sounds of pleasure coming from him and then realized they were coming from her, too. Instead of feeling embarrassed, she let them vibrate through her body. Then it was more than the sounds, it was a feeling that poured through her in waves, eroding her composure and pulling her closer to sea.

He slowed his movements, pulling her down to kiss her. His breathing came raggedly as he strained to control his orgasm. "Not yet," he whispered. He meant *hers,* not his.

"Oh, no you don't." She started moving again, way out and way in, feeling the hard length of him moving against her vaginal wall, the tip of him pushing, stretching deliciously. She clenched her Kegel muscles, and he groaned. His fingers tightened on her behind and he pulled her hard against him. She felt his body spasm, but she was overwhelmed by the waves of pleasure crashing down on her.

He laid her down on the blanket and dove into her again. She saw him above her, and rising up behind him the pyramid, and she lost it all over again. She pulled him down and wrapped her arms and legs around him so tightly he grunted.

When he tried to lift himself up, she held him tighter.

"Amy, I don't want to crush you."

"I want you to crush me," she whispered hoarsely.

He pushed up and must have seen the pain in her expression. "Oh, babe . . . "

She placed her finger over his mouth. "You want to be with me as much as possible before . . . " She shook her head. "I want that, too. So don't you dare think you're going to spare me any pain by not coming to my dreams. Either way I'm going to be devastated, so keep coming, every chance you get—"

He kissed her hard, taking her by surprise. He looked at her, all of his pain and—dare she think?—love in his eyes. "I never wanted to hurt you. I was selfish to start coming into your dreams. I justified it by telling myself you wouldn't remember by morning."

She laughed. "Oh, I remembered them, all right, in every wonderful detail. They're the only sex I get." She laid her palm against his cheek. "But I didn't realize they were so much more than that."

"Then I dragged you into this mess, and now I'm going to leave you—"

"Remember, we're not talking about that. Lucas, before the dreams . . . the only time I ever *felt* something was when I listened to music that moved me. I felt the pain or the love in the song. That was all I ever let myself feel. That was safe. Then with the dreams, I felt, and again, it was safe. Or at least I thought it was. But the thing is, I got a taste of feeling something, and it felt good. So even if I have to feel pain, it was worth feeling love."

He traced lines around her eyebrows and down to her mouth as he listened. "Being with you this way was safe for me, too, though I knew it was real, so I could enjoy it for what it was. I've never felt this way about anyone, Amy."

Those words warmed her. "Did you ever try to find me?"

His expression grew somber. "It was better for me to stay in your dreams."

"But why, after what we've shared?"

"There are things you don't know about me." He flickered then. " . . . dark . . . you safe . . . " He grimaced, squeezing his eyes shut. His voice was warped when he said, " . . . going . . . " He put his fingers to his mouth, held them out to her, and was gone.

She was empty where his warmth had just filled her. The pyramid was gone, too, leaving her sitting in the cold desert.

"Lucas!" she screamed as she came awake.

Bill Hammond had been on the Internet for what felt to him like days now. Ever since that crazy chick's visit, he'd been thinking about his father. No, he'd never believed that his father killed himself, but that was the attitude of a boy who couldn't accept that his father was a weak man. Then the crazy chick—or was she?—got him thinking. He'd been on the computer trying to find out what his father had been doing around the time he died. The same general time the crazy chick said her dad had killed himself.

As he followed yet another link, he heard a sound. Body tense, he got up from the computer and quietly walked into the living room. A shadow shifted in the dark room before he doused it with light.

Nothing.

"Hello?" he said, and then thought, That's dumb. Like if someone were sneaking around in here, they'd answer.

He was being paranoid. He hadn't heard from Cyrus, and he couldn't find his cell number. He'd gotten to know Cyrus, and the man had become a good friend. Then he slipped up, and Cyrus encouraged him to share a secret he'd told no one else. A secret that, much to his surprise, was actually accepted and useful to Cyrus's work.

He walked into his bedroom. Listened for any sound. He reached for the light switch. He felt someone behind him and turned around—but it was too late.

CHAPTER 12

Cyrus walked into the old building where, a long time ago, he had spent years working on something that was supposed to change the world for the better. It had ruined his world . . . and many others' worlds, too. He'd been summoned here by Darkwell, and that could only mean trouble.

He nodded to the guard as he pushed open the glass door. The place smelled the same, of aging linoleum and cleaning fluids. It felt the same, too; the essence of deception, triumph, and failure . . . the screams and blood and chaos. Even long before he'd ever seen this place, he was sure there were screams. This building had always been a place of agony; would it ever change?

The west wing had been set up as residential quarters when the place was miles away from civilization. The center portion consisted of offices, and beyond that were rows of rooms where patients and prisoners were kept. Olivia, waiting by the large reception desk, gave him a grim smile.

He took in her willowy frame, delicate features, and

soft brown eyes. "This isn't a come on, but you're too young and pretty to be stuck in this place."

She wasn't ruthless enough to be CIA either; maybe that was why Darkwell kept her here as office and personnel manager. "As you know, Darkwell has a way of convincing people to buy into his vision. Besides, it's only for six months." Her sweet smile faded. "I'm supposed to take you directly to his office. Do not pass go—"

"Do not collect two hundred dollars," he finished without humor. Last time he'd had the run of the place, everything but the cabinets of research. Not this time.

Darkwell sat at his desk with a look of satisfaction at whatever he was reading. He looked up and his expression hardened. Cyrus wasn't afraid of much. Twenty-seven years in the CIA, working in Clandestine Service in hostile countries, dealing with terrorists, and still he'd never encountered the kind of evil that sat before him.

"Sit down, Diamond."

The power play. Cyrus took his time settling into the chair.

Darkwell got right to the point. "I know you've been covering for Amy Shane."

The words hit Cyrus like barbs. Sweat broke out under his armpits.

Darkwell leaned back in his chair, fingers laced together at his stomach. "Don't bother to deny it. I had a feeling anyway, when you couldn't coax her into displaying anything useful. I let that go because we had other prospects. Now you're endangering everything, and I won't stand for that."

"I don't want her hurt," Cyrus said. "She doesn't know what's going on. She's got a few pieces, thanks to what Lucas Vanderwyck told her."

"What did he tell her?"

"I don't know. She doesn't trust me. Enough to have her asking questions, anyway."

"And sneaking around consorting with the Rogues. She ditched my men twice now, and nearly took out one guy's nuts today. Kill the proud papa grin, Diamond. She's smart enough to be a problem."

He couldn't help the grin, but it faded as he realized the gravity of the situation. "Then take out the Arudas. Without them she'll have nothing." He didn't want anyone taken out, but they were already on the list.

"I will. They killed Gladstone, by the way. Burned him to a crisp."

Cyrus cringed. He'd never liked the guy, but still . . . what a way to go. And that meant the Rogues were dangerous. "Amy had nothing to do with that."

"I know. The Arudas, especially Eric, are the big problem. We only want Amy so she'll lead us to them. Then, as long as she goes back to her little data business, she's fine. But you're not. You've been reassigned. I can't afford to employ people I can't trust, not on this program."

Cyrus didn't argue. Once Darkwell made up his mind, there was no changing it. "Where am I going?" He didn't want to be far from Amy.

"I haven't decided yet. One of the hot spots, most likely."

His jaw tightened. He'd quit first, and to hell with them all. He stood. "Is that all, sir?"

"I'm disappointed in you, Diamond. I didn't realize you were soft. Not when so much is at stake."

"It didn't turn out very well last time."

Darkwell's face reddened. "We were close, damned close, to solving a lot of the world's problems."

"People died. My best friend died."

"He was in the Army to serve his country. Look what he accomplished."

Darkwell didn't care about human life; all he saw were instruments of destruction. He didn't want the glory either. Everything that happened here was hidden, even within the CIA. He wanted secret power and victory, and he would do anything to get it.

"I don't want Amy harmed. She's just a kid."

"They're all just kids. But they're dangerous kids. They're amazing kids. As long as they either work for us or stay out of our way, they'll remain safe."

Cyrus knew that was a lie. Frustration swamped him over Amy's stubbornness. He would swear that she was in love with Vanderwyck, and that made no sense at all. If Darkwell wasn't enough of a danger to her, so were the Rogues she'd chosen to trust.

It was early evening by the time Cyrus returned to his home. He checked the message on the machine and heard Bill's anxious voice. Why hadn't Bill called his cell phone? The man had skills, but organization wasn't one of them.

He called Bill at home. No answer. His own sixth sense kicked in and he slid back into his shoes and headed out again.

He couldn't keep the questions at bay. Had the Rogues done something to Bill? Kidnapped him? How desperate were they? He had access to all the Offspring files, but he was only familiar with the three with whom he was involved. He did remember Eric Aruda's mother, though, and if Eric had inherited her volatility, there was no telling what he would do. He remembered Darkwell's words about Gladstone. Eric had obviously inherited her ability.

He pulled up to Bill Hammond's apartment complex and headed up the stairs. His place was dark, but he'd seen Bill's car in his spot. It was too early for Bill to have gone to bed and he had no social life. That was why it had been so easy for him to insinuate himself into the man's life.

Though he knocked on the door, he didn't expect an answer. He picked the lock and entered.

"Bill? It's Cyrus."

He advanced into the darkened apartment, his senses alert for any sound, walked down the hallway and turned on the light. The bedroom was neat and unoccupied. He doused the light and walked into the bathroom. With his eyes still adjusting to the darkness again, he didn't see whatever was blocking the way on the floor. He fell forward and hit the side of his head. Instantly he was back on his feet, even as the room swayed. He turned on the light.

"Oh, God."

Bill was lying on the floor . . . with a rope around his neck that someone had tied around the light fixture on the ceiling. It hadn't held his weight and broke, but not in time.

Cyrus had been trained to face anything without losing his cool. He backed out of the room, turned off the light, and wiped down the switch. He wiped down everything he'd touched and then locked the door. Outside, by his car, he retched into the bushes.

He'd seen men gutted by explosives and shot down in front of him. Those were men who'd agreed to put their lives on the line. But Bill hadn't known he was involved in anything life threatening. Because of him, Bill was dead. He didn't believe for a second that Bill had taken his life. The guy wasn't jolly, by any means, but he wasn't despondent. Cyrus knew he'd been afraid when he left that message on his machine.

"Bastard."

There wasn't time for anger. If Darkwell had given orders to bring in Bill, or just take him out, then no one was safe. That included Amy.

He had to call her. And someone else, too.

"Amy, you're scaring me."

"Look, Oz, it's nothing. I just may have to leave very suddenly if my sick aunt takes a turn for the worse. I need someone to take care of things here."

He was looking at her with pure distrust; she didn't even have to see his glow to determine that. "And your aunt has something to do with that guy who's been sitting in his car outside your apartment all day? A guy very similar to the one you kneed yesterday."

She sighed, falling back into her chair in her office while he perched on top of a computer case. "Oz, it's complicated."

He'd been trying to casually look for clues since she'd called him over. "I'm actually a pretty intelligent guy. Maybe you could try me."

She closed her eyes. "It's not that." How could she tell him she wasn't insulting his intelligence but keeping him out of trouble?

"It's more than some files you weren't supposed to see."

One eye popped open at that. "What makes you say that?"

"Your apartment is raided, you've got men watching you, and hell, you've been acting plain weird lately."

"I was always weird."

"More weird. Usually you're all prickly, kinda sarcastic, and hey, that's what I like about you."

She gave him a humorless smile. "It's my charm."

"See, that's your normal self. But lately you've been kinda . . . raw. Like if someone said the wrong thing, you'd crumble. And that is definitely not you."

It was annoying to think she'd been that transparent.

He went on. "You pretend to be strong and tough to push people away."

She'd never tell anyone she got teary at the end of *Extreme Home Makeover* and every time she saw a commercial by the organization that rescued dogs and cats. She didn't want to tell anyone she volunteered at the animal shelter, though she'd had to explain to Ozzie why she smelled like wet dog on bath day. "I am strong and tough," she said.

"On the outside, but lately I'm seeing the real you, I think. You're afraid and angry, and it's scaring me. Let me help."

She looked at the geeky guy with the thick dark hair and Roman nose and felt both irritation and softness. "I fell in love with a guy who's in big trouble. Still want to help?" She saw a flash of pain cross his face, saw his yellow-pink glow, indicating sadness and jealousy.

Still, he said, "I don't want you to get hurt."

"But romance is like that. Haven't I been telling you that? If you love someone, you get hurt. Maybe even die or . . . or be wanted for some crime you didn't commit."

"That's just those movies you watch," he said, nodding toward the living room where he'd nosed through her collection of sorry-ass-ending movies.

"That's life." She tossed a chocolate cranberry into her mouth and reached for a box. "Okay, here are my personal belongings. I know you'll be nosy, so I'll save you the trouble." She pulled out the globe. "My dad gave me this. And my mom made me this bunny and blanket when she was expecting me." Her heart always tightened at the thought of her pregnant mom sewing the rabbit. "Some of my Geex guys, pictures, and paperwork." She closed the flaps on the box and picked up one that was on her desk. "And this Geex is for you. My way of saying thanks."

Out in the living room Orn'ry was squawking away.

"What about that thing?"

She gave him a pleading look.

"Oh, no, no, no."

"I know he's a pain—"

"That's an understatement."

"It'll just be for a little while." She handed him two sheets of paper. "Here are some instructions."

"Can I leave"—he nodded toward the parrot—"here?"

"Lord, no. He'll have fits, go crazy, pluck all his feathers out. Put him in your back room. At least he'll know there's someone around. If he gets too noisy, put his blanket over his cage."

Her phone rang and she saw Cyrus's number on the screen. What could he possibly want? Maybe he had some news on Lucas. She answered for that reason only.

"We have to talk," he said. "Now."

Amy shot up out of her chair. "What happened? Is it Lucas?"

"It's you, Amy." The fear in his voice shot equal amounts of fear into her. "Meet me at the place where we went for your birthday two years ago as soon as you can. I pulled out the wooden post on the right. Bring anything you might need. You won't be going back home. I know you're good at ditching the guys following you. Be even better tonight."

"I gotta go," she said to Ozzie, shooting out of the chair. "Here's the key to my place. I'm going to be gone for a while. Keep an eye out for deliveries and route them to the guy listed in my notes. He's expecting referrals. Take Orn'ry home with you. The rent is paid up for the next couple of months." She handed him another piece of paper. "Here's a list of things I'd like you to get out of here if I'm not back before then. Everything else can go. All the stuff I thought was important . . . well, it's just not."

He'd stood, too. "Amy—"

"I was going to take these around to three apartment complexes that allow pets." She handed him flyers she'd made featuring several dogs and cats from the shelter. "Just post 'em in the community center. And let the shelter know I'm going to be gone, too. Maybe you could take my place, visit the little buggers, give 'em some love."

He grimaced. "You know I'm not comfortable around animals."

"That's because you didn't have any pets growing up. You'll love when a litter of pups climbs all over you giving you doggie kisses. You'll purr when a cat rubs against you, and when they start running toward you as soon as they see you . . . " She sighed. "It's something special."

"Amy, please tell me—"

"Thanks, Oz. For being a friend. For everything." She eyed him. "For your shirt."

"What?"

She turned up the music. "I love this song."

He winced. He wasn't into alternative rock or the squawking Orn'ry started again. She leaned close to him. "I need your shirt. And the key to your apartment. I'll leave them on your table. Just give me twenty minutes. Oh, and the keys to your car. I'll be careful, I promise." She ran to her room and grabbed one of her white shirts. "This should fit you, at least to get you home."

"Amy—"

"You wanted to help me."

"Yeah, but I wanted to sneak around *with* you."

"I'm sorry, but I can't involve you."

Ozzie stripped out of his blue-and-white-striped dress shirt. It was warm and smelled of that god-awful cologne he always wore when he came over. Her hair was close enough to his in color. In her bedroom, she pinned it back so it didn't stick out. She changed into blue jeans and stuffed her backpack beneath her shirt to match Ozzie's little pooch. Her heart was already thudding. Cyrus wasn't going to tell her to butt out again. Something had happened.

Lucas. No, please don't tell me he's gone.

A sinister thought popped to mind: was this a setup?

She walked back into the living room. "Thanks, Oz." She handed him the remote control. "Hang out, enjoy. I'll see you soon."

He didn't take it. "Will you?"

"I . . . I don't know." She gave him a quick hug.

She hadn't turned on the light outside her door, so her spy guy wouldn't get a good look at her. He would have taken note of the guy who'd come over, if he was any good at his job. She saw the black, innocuous-looking car and tried not to look at it. She walked like Ozzie in that quick way that hardly used any body motion. Two buildings down she walked into the—thank God—first floor apartment. As soon as she closed the door she looked out the window. She didn't see anyone following her. With a breath of relief, she slipped out of Ozzie's shirt and put on one she'd stuffed into her backpack.

She grabbed a Baltimore Ravens cap sitting on the end table and walked out the back door to the courtyard after checking to see that it was clear. She then got into Ozzie's bright green Prius and headed out of the parking lot.

Cyrus hadn't mentioned Quiet Waters Park, obviously because he'd been concerned about someone listening in. She pulled up to the park entrance twenty minutes later. It was closed, of course, being long after dark. But the moon was nearly full, casting everything in a two-dimensional light. The gate was closed, but she spotted where Cyrus had removed two posts so she could drive around it.

Beyond the gatehouse and where the road curved to the right, she saw a flash of light in the woods. She took the right that led to two pavilions. The light beckoned, and she pulled into the parking area of the first one. Her headlights lit up the pavilion that people used for parties. Cyrus stood by one of the white columns. The night air was in the low fifties, and she hadn't thought about grabbing a jacket. She wrapped her arms around herself as she approached him, feeling as cold inside as she did outside.

He glanced toward the road on the other side of the woods as he stepped out from under the roof. She could hardly see his features, only the flat planes of his face in the silvery light and the halolike shine of his head. For the first time, though, she could see his glow. It was brown and jagged: fear and lots of it. It was contagious.

As soon as she neared him, he said, "Amy, it's too late to go back now. All you can do now is get out of here." He shoved a thick envelope at her. "Take this. It's all the cash I could get my hands on without alerting anyone."

"Cyrus, I can't—"

"Take it, dammit. Now is not the time to be noble or argue." He slid out of his jacket and wrapped it around her. "There's enough money for you to live on for a while, and the name of someone who can help you change your identity. There's also an address and description of a car along with a key. I just bought it from my aunt, but it's still registered to her."

"Cyrus, you're scaring me," she said, echoing Ozzie's words.

"I didn't do a very good job of it earlier. I wish I had. But I don't think it would have made any difference."

"It wouldn't have."

"Amy, your new friends, Eric and Petra Aruda—and Lucas—they killed a man. A CIA officer named Gladstone."

She could hardly breathe the words, "Killed him?"

"You can't trust them. Eric, in particular, is very dangerous."

"What is this all about?" she asked, hearing desperation in her voice and not caring. "Please, tell me. I need to know what I'm up against."

"I don't suppose it matters anymore. I'm done at the CIA."

"Because of me?" It hit her then, that he'd been trying to dissuade her for her own protection. "I'm so sorry."

"I deserve it, so don't go feeling guilty. In fact, I hope you can forgive me. I can't keep doing this, and if I leave the DST, I'll be ruined anyway. I know too much. And now they don't trust me." He took a ragged breath. "Back in the seventies and eighties, several government divisions were running experiments on using psychic abilities, mostly remote viewing. Back then we thought the Soviet Union was way ahead of us in their psychic warfare programs. The president's staff, as well as Secret Service agents and CIA officers, were trained on blocking someone from getting into their minds. We weren't just being paranoid.

"In the eighties, the pressure to find hostages was tremendous. Reagan put the thumbscrews to Casey, the CIA director at the time, and he put them on us. The psychic programs had achieved some success, but not enough to keep the funding. They were shifted from one entity to another and eventually shelved. But one program went further than the others, a program called BLUE EYES that only a few knew about. The subjects were people with high perception. A scientist created a secret blend of nutrients that boosted their abilities even more."

"Psychic abilities? Like mind reading and telling the future and . . . what did you say? Remote viewing?"

"The ability to see a place psychically."

The thought stunned her. "Like . . . psychic spying?"

"Exactly." He looked into the woods again before returning his attention to her. "Though it wasn't publicized, three hostages were located and rescued due to our efforts. The results were astounding, and the possibilities unlimited. But there were side effects, whether from the Booster or the stress of their missions, we don't know."

"Side effects?"

"Their sexual appetites were ramped up. Not only with their significant others but with their fellow participants. That, we could have lived with, but their psychological states began to deteriorate, too. One went on a rampage and killed three people. A few others committed suicide."

"Dad?" she whispered, the pieces coming together in loud crashes inside her mind.

"Your dad was one of those subjects. When I brought him in, I didn't know how it would turn out. I knew he had extrasensory perception, and he was excited about serving his country in such a progressive way."

"Dad was . . . psychic?"

"One of the best in the program."

"Oh, my God." She clamped her hands on either side of her head, trying to compute it all. "That's why he was crazy at the end."

"I'm sorry I couldn't tell you before. The program was shut down and hushed up, and we were all sworn to secrecy. It was something we wanted to forget, everyone except the man who ran the program. He was devastated, couldn't stop talking about what we could have accomplished.

"Nobody thought about the effects being passed to their offspring. Extrasensory abilities do run in families, but what about our enhanced subjects?" His voice grew low, and she heard regret. "Several months ago I brought up your uncanny ability to read people to the man behind BLUE EYES. I was worried that if you'd inherited your father's abilities, you might inherit the psychological problems, too. Unfortunately, he wasn't concerned about you; all he could see was the possibility of reviving his beloved project. You should have seen the look in his eyes. The thing is, the cause is a good one. Rescuing hostages, finding terrorists. But at what cost? I couldn't talk him out of it. He assigned three officers to track down the offspring of the subjects and analyze them."

Her voice was hard when she said, "And I was your Offspring."

He lowered his head. "Yes."

At least that meant he hadn't just been in her life to assess her. "And Bill Hammond."

He nodded. "A lot of you don't know you even have abilities."

"Wait a minute. You're saying that seeing glows is a *psychic* ability?" She shivered. "You tested me on those recruits a few months ago. But you weren't test-ing them. You were testing me, weren't you?"

"Yes, and you passed. But I failed you, at least as far as my reports went. I didn't want you involved. Somehow the Rogues—that's what he calls Eric, Petra, and Lucas—figured some of this out. And now we're here." Sadness permeated those last words.

"Cyrus, I can't get my head around this."

"Amy, what you've got to do is get it out of your head. I told you so you wouldn't make yourself crazy trying to figure it out. Now let it go—let Lucas go—and keep yourself safe."

"Lucas said they were injecting him with something. Are they giving him this Booster stuff?"

"It was supposed to be destroyed, but I don't know if it was. I've been a reluctant participant this time, so they've kept me out of the lab and out of the loop." At the sound of a branch hitting the ground, both of them jerked their heads toward the woods.

Cyrus's voice became more hurried when he said, "There's something else. We believe that the children born of affairs between two subjects may be even more powerfully enhanced. And more dangerous. They're called Ultras, and they're likely to become psychologi-cally unstable. Eric and Lucas are Ultras. But Amy, here's the important thing—the two men behind BLUE EYES are the most dangerous and most powerful of all. Their cause is all they care about. You won't win if you try to fight them or find Lucas. You'll only die, and I couldn't handle that. Take the money and the car and get lost for a while."

She stared at the envelope and then stuffed it into her backpack. Since it contained her identification and her own money, she wasn't leaving it behind. "All right." Even as she uttered the words, though, she knew she couldn't abandon Lucas. Her heart tore at the mere thought of it. "How can the CIA sanction this kind of project?"

"They think it's a program to predict terrorist attacks using computer programs and intuition."

"DARK MATTER," she guessed.

"How did you know?"

"That's not important. Who are the men behind these programs?"

She heard a strange sound. Before she could even turn, Cyrus groaned and fell forward. She tried to catch him, and warm blood spattered her hands. The strange *whoosh-thump* sounded again, and with sudden and startling clarity she knew what it was— bullets.

They were shooting at her!

She couldn't hold Cyrus up. He slumped to the ground in a heap.

Ohmygod, they're shooting at me, they shot Cyrus, and they want me!

She crouched and ran into the dark woods, her heart beating so hard it was slamming against her skin. Her footsteps sounded as loud as sonic booms. She zigzagged to the left. She had no idea what lay beyond, but anything was better than what was behind her.

Another bullet whizzed by, so close she heard it hit the tree next to her. They could see her! They probably had those night goggles on. They'd heard everything Cyrus had just told her, and now she would die and Cyrus was probably dead, and . . . *oh, God, please help me!*

CHAPTER 13

Lucas shot out of his mission. One second he'd been looking at the Arab man's face and the next he'd seen Amy, or rather, felt her: fear, horror, her dry mouth, and pounding heart. He smelled pines and her sweat. But he couldn't see anything.

The darkness around him swallowed him up. He yanked off the cap and jumped from the table, needing to do something, to move, to bang on the door. They didn't restrain him anymore, except when they gave him a shot. What could he do? He'd already ascertained that there was no escape from the room. The threat to Amy kept him painfully compliant.

"What are you doing to her?" he screamed at the camera mounted in the corner.

He wasn't able to hold onto her like he used to. His connection to her came in pulsing images that hit him hard and then were gone.

"What are you doing to Amy?" he screamed again, slamming his fists against the glass.

The curtain opened. A guard stood a few feet away. The brown-haired woman he'd seen earlier looked in, a serene, pretty face that showed a hint of disconcertment at his behavior. She pressed a button outside the door. "What appears to be the problem, sir?"

Sir? Was she kidding? "They said they wouldn't hurt Amy if I cooperated."

She looked puzzled, and then Robbins rushed into view and ushered her out. She kept glancing back while Lucas continued to bang on the glass.

Robbins returned a few minutes later. "Lucas, what's going on?"

"That's what I want to know." Fear strained his voice. "Something's happening to Amy. She's running away from someone in some dark place. It's got to be you guys. You said she wouldn't be hurt if I cooperated, and dammit, I've been cooperating."

Robbins looked as in the dark as Lucas was. "I'll find out what's going on."

Lucas paced in the spill of light coming from the hallway. He squeezed his eyes shut. "Come back, baby, come back."

After a few minutes he hit the glass again. He couldn't bring her back. "Dammit! What are they doing to me?" Since they'd been injecting him with God-knew-what, his skills had grown stronger but more out of control. He used to be able to pull Amy into his consciousness when she experienced a strong emotion.

Another storm of images sent him to his knees.

Oh, God, please help me!

"Amy!" He couldn't talk to her other than in the dreams, but he could always comfort her. Only if he could keep the connection, though, and it was gone as quickly as it had come.

He couldn't help her. He pressed his forehead to the floor and drowned in helpless rage.

Gerard Darkwell was in his office watching Lucas having a meltdown when Robbins returned. They'd been observing Lucas while he undertook his second mission when a call came in. At the same time, Lucas shot up and yanked off the sensors. Gerard sent Robbins to check it out.

The officer on the phone was breathless. "We've got her in our sights."

"If she's going to escape, target her legs. I want her alive, if possible."

"Yes, sir."

His razor instincts had proven themselves again when he'd had Cyrus tailed. Damn traitor. Why did people let their personal loyalties and their misguided sense of righteousness keep them from seeing what was important? Could they not feel the power of justice, the victory of taking out dangerous enemies, and at the small price of a few people's lives?

He hadn't wanted Hammond taken out, though. The asset, known only as Steele, reported that Hammond took him off guard and he had to change the plan. Gerard hated losing even one of the Offspring. Each was useful, either voluntarily or not. Except for Eric Aruda. He had to be removed.

Robbins returned and stood beside one of the chairs in front of Gerard's desk. Half circles of sweat beneath his armpits darkened his white cotton shirt. "He's got a connection to Amy. He felt someone chasing her." He wore a questioning look.

"Cyrus just betrayed all of us by telling her about

DARK MATTER. We can't let her go back to the Arudas with this information." He gave Robbins a hard look. "Diamond has left the program."

"You're firing him?"

"I'm afraid it's worse than that."

Fear robbed the man's face of color. He looked at the monitor, where Lucas was again banging on the glass with the flat of his hand. "What should I tell him about Amy? We promised we wouldn't hurt her."

"*If* she kept her nose out of our business."

Damned connection to Amy Shane. He wanted to get as many missions out of Lucas as he could, for as long as Amy was alive and as long as Lucas's sanity held out.

Frustration at the slow progress of the war ate away at him. Now, after twenty years of watching the war on terrorism flounder, he had a chance to make something happen. He needed this to succeed. Not for the glory his older brother sought. No, he needed success because it filled an emptiness he'd always felt inside him. Patriotism gave him purpose. It didn't matter that his father or brother would never know what he'd achieved. *He* would know.

"Amy Shane, we can see you. Come out and you won't be hurt," a man called.

She crouched behind a tree, trying to hear her pursuers over the hammering of her heartbeat. No matter how clever she had been in escaping her spy guys, she knew she wasn't going to get away from these men. She was going to die or, worse, be captured.

I'll be with Lucas. Not with; they won't put us together. But near.

A sterner voice said, *You can't save Lucas by being captured and shot up with whatever they're giving him. And you damn well can't give up. And don't, for God's sake, think about Cyrus lying there with bullets in him.*

The sharp pain in her chest had nothing to do with exertion.

They might be able to see her, but with all the trees in the way, they wouldn't have a clear shot at her. If she could get to her car . . . but that was only viable if there wasn't an officer left behind to watch it.

"Hey, what's that?" one of the men said to another.

She took the opportunity to run. Branches whipped against her face, stinging her skin. A loud flutter exploded beside her. Birds? Whatever it was made a racket. She saw a light in the distance. The gatehouse? She had no idea where she was in relation to the road. Her shoulder rammed a tree trunk, shooting pain down her arm and throwing her to the side. Branches beat her up. Here in the woods the moonlight barely penetrated. She was running blind in an obstacle course. She needed to get out in the open, or no, maybe not, or—get to the highway. Stop a car and pretend she was being chased by a rapist. Yes!

With a plan and hope, she didn't even feel the bite of the branches. She ran toward the light. Several minutes later she came upon a building that looked like it held maintenance equipment for the park. One large light illuminated the door and part of the parking area. She ran for the corner, planning to be out of sight in seconds.

"Hold it right there!" a voice barked from way too close behind her.

She turned, heaving in oxygen. Her body sagged at the sight of two men emerging from the woods with guns pointed at her. One of them whispered, "If she moves, nail her in the knee."

Guess I'll go with Plan B: get captured and find Lucas from within.

She reluctantly raised her arms. She saw the night vision goggles around one man's neck. How could she, Eric, and Petra hope to win against the CIA?

"We've got her," one of the men said into a phone earpiece that reminded her of *Star Trek*. "Alive."

They wanted her alive.

The other man kept his gun aimed at her. Both men advanced slowly.

Grief and fear crashed through her the same way she had crashed through the trees. Her knees wobbled. She felt light-headed. So she thought she was imagining the odd light that suddenly appeared on the right man's sleeve. Until he jerked his arm with a painful yelp.

The other man backed away. "What the hell?"

The first man's arm was on fire. Just as bizarrely, another fire erupted on his pant leg. Both fires intensified as though someone had thrown gas on them. He dropped his gun, fell to the ground and rolled. The other man just stared in horror, and she stared as well, though part of her brain was screaming, *Run!*

Despite his rolling efforts, the fire grew worse. He was now screaming in pain. The other man stripped off his jacket and threw it over him, but it, too, flared up. The air filled with an acrid scent—

Oh, God, the man's burning flesh.

The presence of someone nearby jarred her, and she

jerked around to find Eric watching the flames with a look of eerie satisfaction on his face. Not just watching, but mesmerized.

"You did that?" she whispered fiercely.

The man on fire stopped moving, his screams dying. The other man looked up, his face ashen. He saw her and Eric, and then he ran—away from them.

"Let's go," Eric said, grabbing her arm and hauling her around the side of the building. They ran down the short road, through a copse of trees, and out the other side, where a car waited. The Barracuda roared to life. He opened the door and shoved her into the back while Petra pulled out of the hiding spot.

Eric said, "Those two won't be following us, but I don't know if they have friends."

Petra jammed the gas pedal and raced down the road.

The horrors of the past twenty minutes bombarded Amy as she trembled in the backseat. As on the night Lucas had been taken, the adrenaline drained from her and left her a boneless lump.

"To the tomb?" she heard Petra ask.

"Yeah."

"What happened?" she asked him.

"She met with Diamond. I wish you'd been there; I couldn't hear what they were saying. Then these two guys appear out of nowhere, shoot Diamond, and go after Amy."

"And then Eric set one of them on fire!" Amy said, unable to hold in her horror any longer. She would never forget the man's writhing and screams and the smell, God, the smell.

"*What?*" Petra said.

"We'll talk when we get home," Eric replied.

Amy's teeth started chattering, and she clamped down on her jaw and curled up into a ball. She had to get herself together before they got back to . . . had Petra called it "the tomb"? She just wanted to go home.

Home. She could never go home, could never again be Amy Shane of Disc Angel, slightly dysfunctional but mostly a normal person. Yes, she had made the decision, but now it was real. Cyrus was dead and she wasn't who she thought she was. Her only allies were two people she couldn't trust . . . and one was a double murderer.

Gerard Darkwell watched Lucas's monitor while he impatiently awaited word from the two officers. He didn't know what Amy's skills were, since Cyrus had probably lied to protect her, but he didn't think she was dangerous. She wasn't an Ultra.

Lucas suddenly stumbled to the chair, tilted his head back and closed his eyes. His features relaxed and Gerard could see relief on his face.

He exchanged a look with Robbins. "He's not worried about the girl anymore. Why?"

He hated this. Everything had gone smoothly until the Rogues got involved.

His phone rang. Finally.

"Sir . . . " The man was trying to catch his breath. "Oh, God."

Gerard stiffened in his chair. "What is it?"

His voice sounded strained. "They set Stephano on fire. First his arm and then his leg and suddenly . . . he was covered in flames and screaming, and I couldn't do anything to help him. It happened so fast. I never saw anything. The flames were just there."

"You said 'they.'"

"We were chasing her, and then Stephano went up in flames and then there was this guy standing next to Shane, just standing there watching. The son of a bitch was smiling!"

Anger suffused Gerard. Eric Aruda. He must have gone with Shane. The idiot had lost her again at the apartment complex, but they'd tracked Diamond through the GPS in his vehicle after he'd given them the slip. When the officers reported that he was meeting with Amy, Gerard knew he had officially crossed the line to traitor. He harbored no hard feelings toward the man, though. Cyrus had given him his project back. In fact, he'd always been concerned about Cyrus's dedication to the cause, even back then. Robbins was another one who needed to be watched.

The most dangerous, though, was Aruda. They had to step up their efforts to find all three Rogues and dispose of them accordingly. Now Amy was one of them. She would be treated accordingly.

"Report to me immediately. Say nothing about what you saw. We'll take care of Stephano."

He would tell the officer that Aruda had some kind of device that shot flames from a distance. The two men he'd tapped had been removed from active duty because they went off half-cocked on a mission in Afghanistan. The Agency was trying to figure out what to do with them. He hadn't told them they were acting unofficially or about the abilities of their quarry.

"Robbins, go check on our friend, see what you can find out."

Obviously annoyed at being left out of the loop, Robbins exited with a huff.

Gerard phoned Steele. "I need you over here as soon as possible."

Steele was a free agent the CIA used on unofficial business, though he was semiretired now. If he were ever caught during a mission, he couldn't be traced to them. In addition, Steele knew what the Offspring were and exactly what they were capable of. He would have no problem eradicating "those freaks," as he'd called them twenty years ago.

Gerard walked down the hall to Lucas's "quarters." Robbins was there, too. Gerard smiled after the guard locked the door.

"I found out what happened," he said to Lucas, who gave him a wary look.

Not knowing what Lucas knew, he had to stick as close to the truth as possible.

"The two officers who went after Amy thought she was someone else."

"Petra? I don't want her hurt either. She's as innocent as Amy."

Tough thing, human emotion. It always got in the way, made one vulnerable. "Eric is the only one I have a problem with."

Lucas started to say something but stopped himself.

"You and I both know he's not innocent, don't we? I'm not going to protect him. He's interfering with my plans. He's already killed two of my men. That makes me very unhappy."

That shocked Lucas, or he pretended it did. "Killed them?"

"Set them on fire."

Robbins's eyes bulged at that. But that shouldn't have surprised him. He knew what Eric's mother was capable of.

Lucas cringed but said nothing in defense of the man he'd grown up with.

"Did you know Eric could set fires psychically?"

"No."

"Come on, all the fires that sprang up in your neighborhood, and the deadly one that destroyed your home, your stepmother . . . that's how he set those fires when he wasn't in the vicinity. We found Gladstone. Fried to a crisp."

"I don't believe you."

"Sure you do."

"We left that man alive."

"Maybe you did, but Eric went back and killed him." He could see that Lucas's disbelief was genuine. "Eric's always been trouble for you, hasn't he? Once he's out of the picture, the girls won't be snooping around anymore."

Even with their history, Lucas still looked pained at Eric's demise. "Look—"

"No more bargains, Lucas. If you want Amy and Petra kept safe, you'll do your part. We'll get back to where we were in an hour."

Robbins followed him, and when they were out of the guard's earshot, said, "Two men? On fire?"

Another of Robbins's weaknesses was his fear. It would eventually destroy him.

"Do you see why we have to find them? They're not only a danger to our program—they're a danger to us."

And now *they* would be dangerous to the Rogues.

CHAPTER 14

Amy used the drive to collect her scrambled thoughts and put her emotions into a box to deal with later. She recognized the neighborhood as the one where Lucas's gallery was located. They passed that and turned down a gravel lane that went between the commercial and residential areas. Eric cut the lights and pulled into the driveway of an old house. Petra jumped out and hoisted the garage door, then Eric drove inside and she closed the door behind them, dousing them in darkness.

They slipped out the side door and through the backyard to a vine-covered shed at the back edge of the property. This is their hiding place? Amy thought as she followed them through the silvery night. Eric reached beneath the vines, unlocked a dead bolt, and opened the door, nodding for the two women to precede him. They ducked beneath the vines to enter. When they were inside, he pulled the chain, and a dim bulb lit the cramped space, which she saw was filled with rusted junk. The three of them could barely fit inside.

Eric turned to her with a hard look on his face. They were mere inches apart. "You're one of us now. Not exactly by our choice, I might add. But you have nowhere to go now."

She caught herself about to apologize. She wasn't sorry, not half the time she felt compelled to say it. "Is that supposed to make me feel warm and fuzzy?"

He laughed despite himself. "You might have noticed I don't do warm and fuzzy."

That brought back the scene at the park. "No, just pyro tricks with a dash of psychopath."

Petra looked confused by the comment.

"We'll talk about that later," he said, his expression serious again. "You can stay in our hideout, but don't do anything stupid to give it away to our enemies. It's all we've got."

"Yes, sir."

If he was expecting blathering gratitude, he would have to wait awhile. He moved a derelict lawn mower aside and pulled up a piece of the rotted wooden floor, revealing a hole about four feet wide. Petra went down first, then Eric nodded for her to go next. She did, thinking again, Down the rabbit hole I go.

She climbed down for several minutes in darkness, feeling her way down, understanding why Petra had said tomb. Eric's footsteps echoed above her, Petra's below. With every foot they descended it grew colder. The first stirrings of claustrophobia tingled inside her, and she took a deep breath. She heard Petra's feet land on a solid surface, then a dim light was snapped on, lighting a vertical tunnel.

Petra waited while she and Eric joined her, then he took the lead down the tunnel. He flicked a switch and several more small lights lit the rest of the way. They walked for a few minutes, their shoes scraping on rough concrete and echoing along the walls. At the end of the tunnel stood an enormous steel door. Eric blocked her view as he punched a code into a keypad. The entire door slid to the right. She followed Petra into a huge room—a room she recognized. Except, on the wall where Betty Boop once hung, she now saw a sailing regatta painting.

"This is where you took me when you kidnapped me."

"Now you understand why we couldn't tell you where you were," Petra said.

The door slid closed, looking now like a wall.

Amy took in her surroundings. "What is this place? Wait a minute. It's a bomb shelter, isn't it?"

Eric came up behind her. "Smart girl. Back in the fifties three families in the neighborhood went in together to build this thing. At least that's what we surmised, given the access from three different houses. Lucas found it a couple of years ago when he was renovating the first floor of his house into the gallery."

Petra added, "The house where we parked the car is vacant. We're renting it from a woman who now lives with her son in Alabama. Under another name, of course."

"What about the third house?" Amy asked.

"Obsolete," Eric said. "Years ago the owners, probably unaware of the shelter, tore down the shed and built a garage over the entrance. The access from Lucas's house enters into his bedroom."

"No one knows about this place?" Amy asked.

"It wasn't exactly publicized. They didn't want the whole neighborhood crowding in during an emergency."

Petra walked into the kitchen, nodding for Amy to follow. "They set it up for three families to stay here as long as necessary for the radiation to clear." She opened a pantry door, revealing a room with stacks of white buckets and several cabinets. "These are filled with nitrogen-sealed food. There's a generator and all of the communication equipment we need, and down one level, more rooms, a water tank, and a gym."

"Wouldn't we be trapped if they discovered us?" Amy asked.

"They wouldn't take us alive," Eric said, his mouth in a firm line. "The doors are one-ton blast capable. We have weapons if we need them, but I doubt they'd be able to get in."

So they'd eventually run out of food, Amy thought.

"It's home away from home," Petra said in a cheery voice that didn't match her expression.

"You called it the tomb."

"Okay, tomb away from home," she replied, letting her real disdain show.

Eric said, "That's why we get beat over the head with color."

"I couldn't stand the bland walls. I need color. Scenery."

"Change," Eric added. "She changes the paintings every other day."

Petra looked at the sepia-toned painting of the woman and man. "These are from Lucas's personal collection. Sometimes I sneak upstairs and change them."

Amy noticed Lucas's taste in artwork was bent toward the sensual. Like in the dreams. Like the man himself. She caught herself sighing and coughed instead. "You'd think it would smell musty."

"It has ventilation units and pumps for sewage," Eric said. "The walls keep the place sixty degrees all year 'round, and one little space heater keeps each level livable."

She remembered how they'd chloroformed her and interrogated her and then disposed of her before she could ask any questions. That made her all the more pissed off now, knowing they hadn't been straight with her.

"Tell us what you were doing meeting Cyrus," Eric said.

She walked up to one of the paintings, an alley in an Italian village painted in odd angles and too-bright colors. She made Eric wait several long seconds before turning to him with her arms crossed on her chest. "He called, said he had something important to tell me. He told me it was too late to turn back, that I had to go on the run. And . . . he told me what it means to be an Offspring."

That got their attention. They waited for her to continue. Eric became impatient when she didn't. "What did he say?"

"Uh-uh. I'm not telling you anything until you tell me what you know. I've answered all your questions honestly, but you've answered very few of mine, and even then, I'm not sure how honest you were."

Eric narrowed his icy blue eyes. "Don't play games with us."

"I won't if you won't. We're a team, like it or not.

You said so yourself. That means I know everything you know and everything about you. Frankly, what you did back there freaked the hell out of me. You're not like any firebug I've ever heard about."

Petra asked him, "What did you do?"

He started to move toward Amy, and she stiffened her shoulders and met his angry gaze with one of her own. Yes, she was afraid of Eric. She couldn't forget Cyrus's warning: *You can't trust them. Eric, in particular, is very dangerous.* What if he set her on fire, too? He'd killed two men that she knew of, and he was potentially unstable. But right now she was valuable to him, so she stood her ground.

Petra said, "Eric."

He tried to stare Amy down for a few more seconds, and she was proud that she didn't wither. Finally he released a breath. His muscles relaxed, and so did hers.

"We don't know all that much," he said. "One of the things we suspect the Offspring have in common is some kind of bioenergetic ability."

"Bioenergetic?"

"Energy transformation. Psychic. Since we were kids, Lucas had these weird episodes where he woke up at night and drew prescient sketches. He has no memory of doing it."

"Like these?" Amy said, walking over to the one on the easel that showed someone lying dead on the ground. His warning. She sucked in a breath.

"What?" Petra asked, coming up beside her.

"He said I would be betrayed and someone would die because of that. He thought it would be me." She turned to them. "Cyrus did betray me, in a way, but he was the one who died. Lucas was right."

"He's usually right," Eric said. "When he gets the same sketch four nights in a row, what he draws always happens on the fifth day."

Amy flipped past the one on top to his previous sketches and stopped at one that depicted a woman getting slashed with a knife. She flipped to the next sketch and was about to turn away when she saw it was of a woman who looked a lot like her, with frizzy, thick hair and a boyish-straight body. A man had grabbed her, a knife to her throat.

Her hand went to her mouth. The man who intercepted, who stepped in to save her . . .

Lucas.

"The guy was pretty pissed that Lucas got in the way," Eric said beside her.

"He got twenty-six stitches," Petra added in a voice that indicated she wasn't pleased that he'd sacrificed himself. With her finger, she drew a long line across her stomach.

Amy felt that knife in her gut now and even bent forward in pain. "The blood on the pier. I never . . . I didn't know . . . "

Eric stared at the sketch. "It was the first time he'd had one of his premonitions about you. I could tell it wigged him out. It was also the first time he got enough information to prevent what he drew. You were a strong incentive."

Petra turned away, and her gaze went to the painting from Amy's dream. "Lucas obviously can get into dreams, or at least yours. I didn't realize the man in his paintings was him." Raw jealousy colored her expression, and she started cracking her knuckles.

"He kept his face in shadow to me, too." Amy turned to Eric. "And you . . . you can set people on fire. Is that some trick or is it . . . what did you call it? Bioenergetic?"

"I got that word from a book about the Soviet psychic programs. Yes, I change the energy and create fire. It's called pyrokinesis."

Petra just stared at him. "Since when?"

"As far back as I can remember."

"All those fires . . . " Her face paled. "Not our house?"

He turned away. "No. Some of the fires I started. Abandoned buildings and, yes, the one I was brought in for. Bastards deserved it. No one was hurt."

Petra said, "Amy said you set a man on fire back at the park."

"Out of necessity. They had us at gunpoint."

Petra's hand went to her mouth. "I can't believe you burned a man to death. You murdered someone."

"He also deserved it." Eric walked over and dropped down on the couch. "Enough about the fires. I can also remote view."

Amy followed him, perching on the coffee table across from him. "Psychic spying. Cyrus mentioned that."

"What else did he say?"

"Uh-uh, not yet. What about you, Petra?"

She looked down. "I don't have any ability."

"Yes, you do," Eric said, surprising Petra. "Your superior hearing."

"I thought that was just good hearing."

He propped his feet up on the table next to Amy. "I think it's more than that."

Petra's shoulders stiffened. "Why didn't you ever say anything?"

"I didn't want you to get too full of yourself."

While she grappled with that, Amy wondered about their dynamic. Very interesting, and Eric's need for control and superiority very telling.

Be careful of him, her instincts warned.

Amy took off Cyrus's coat and hugged it to her chest. "What about the CIA officer you killed? Glad-something-or-other?"

Again Petra's eyes widened in surprise. She hadn't known, which hopefully meant that Lucas hadn't known either and therefore had nothing to do with it. She didn't realize she'd been wondering about that.

"Eric!" Petra said. "You killed Gladstone?"

Again he didn't look the least bit chagrined. "I killed him before he killed me. Lucas drew four sketches of me dying. In the last one we saw the man's face." He looked at Petra. "It was Gladstone, wasn't it?"

"Maybe," she said.

"Probably."

"Did you burn him, too?" Amy asked, not sure she wanted to know.

He couldn't hide the trace of a smile. "Yes."

Amy said, "*You* were angry about Lucas coming to me, yet you killed a man without their knowledge."

"That guy was an enemy. Lucas got himself caught by warning you."

Stubborn son of a bitch.

"We also suspect that whoever these people are, they're trying to recruit us for our bioenergetic abilities. When Gladstone cut into my arson interrogation, he asked if I'd be interested in using my fire-setting skills for the government. He didn't say 'your pyro-kinesis skills,' but I now know that's what he meant. That's why he was casing Lucas and Petra, too, trying to determine their skills."

"Cyrus was, too," Amy said in a quiet voice. "On the profile pages, there was a link called 'Skills.' I wish I'd had time to look at them."

"What are they after?" Eric asked her. "Why are they interested in us?"

Amy wagged her finger at him. *Not yet.* She had to admit, it was damned nice to have the power for a change. "When Lucas broke in, he said my dad's *supposed* suicide. Why?"

Eric put his arms behind his head, looking like he didn't care about the power shift. But by the twitch in his jaw, she knew better. "Our mothers, your dad, and Hammond's dad all died either by accident or suicide. Something's not right there, but we don't know what."

Sensing he was telling her the truth, she proceeded to tell them everything, or nearly everything. She left out the Ultra part. As he'd told Petra, she didn't want him to get full of himself.

They both listened and didn't interrupt until she mentioned the sexual side effects. Petra looked at Eric. "That's why you're so horny."

Amy raised her eyebrows.

"Petra," he warned in a low voice.

Amy was glad she didn't take the warning. "He's been arrested for sex in a public place and solicitation for prostitution."

"I don't consider a canoe in the middle of a lake public." He recited it as though he'd said it many times. "I've never had to pay for sex."

Amy imagined he didn't, not a muscular guy with sculpted cheekbones and riveting eyes. His personality, though, wasn't exactly a plus.

Petra giggled. "When he hit his teens he was more sex-crazed than other boys. I'd heard the girls talk about how the boys would go off in about three seconds, but I heard Eric moaning and groaning for forty minutes."

"You listened?" Eric said.

She shrugged. "I had to learn somehow. Dad couldn't even utter the word 'sex' around me. I didn't have a mom around to explain it."

Amy nodded. "I know that feeling. My aunt, who raised me after my parents died, was too busy to talk about the birds and bees." She glanced at the sepia painting. "What about Lucas?"

Petra's humor vanished. "Though Eric would do it just about anywhere, Lucas was private. And quiet. He chose older girls, not high schoolers, so there wasn't any gossip about him. Neither ever had a long-term relationship. Eric eventually drove them away by being his charming self. Lucas . . . I don't know."

Amy didn't want to think about Lucas being with another woman. "The other side effect of being in the program was . . . well, going crazy."

When Petra looked at Eric, he said, "Don't even go there, little sister."

"I was going to ask if you think that's why Mom set herself on fire."

Amy's mouth dropped open. *"Your mother set herself on fire?"*

Petra said, "Dad told us it was an accident at the lab, but we overheard him saying she'd set the fire.

And she probably did it through pyrokinesis. Not on purpose, like suicide. Maybe she lost control."

Amy continued. "Now they're looking for the offspring. For us."

"Did you find out how many there are?" Eric asked.

"I wish I'd had time." She looked away. "They call you—us—Rogues."

"Rogues." A smile spread across his face. "I like it."

A thought jumped to mind. "Eric, if you can remote view, you can go to Lucas, see where he is."

"Normally I could. I think I'm there, but it's pitch-black, eerie."

"But she can connect with him," Petra said to her brother. "Or rather, he can connect to her."

"Yeah, I know," he muttered. "Maybe the dream connection works differently."

They grew silent. Finally, Petra said, "Lucas asked you about those fires, even the ones that happened when you had an alibi."

"Don't look at me like that. That's why I never told you."

"You killed a man," she whispered.

"Two men," Amy clarified.

Petra looked at Eric, confusion in her eyes. "I can understand that, if it was the only way you could escape. But Eric . . . Gladstone was tied up. He couldn't hurt you."

"Not then, but he would have. Petra, this is a war. They're out to kill us. Get over it."

She winced but said nothing.

Eric walked down the hall and returned a minute later with the hard drive for a laptop. He handed it to Amy. "Gladstone's drive," he said. "Find out what's on it."

CHAPTER 15

An hour later Gerard and Robbins watched Lucas on the monitor as he sank into a receptive state. His brain waves jumped erratically. Gerard typed preliminary notes at his computer.

"Now that he's had three injections," Gerard said, "we're starting to see a difference in his brain wave patterns."

Robbins's expression was dour. "When will his sanity start breaking down?"

"I think we'll get another mission out of him, maybe two if we're lucky."

That stopped Robbins. "How long?"

"For what?"

"How long until we start secretly giving the new recruits the Booster?"

"We're only giving the Booster to the Rogues."

"How long before you grow impatient? Look what happened last time."

A knock at the door interrupted him. Olivia peered in. "Leon's here."

"What the hell does—" Gerard cut himself short as

his older brother pushed past Olivia. He forced a smile but didn't put too much effort behind it. Civil was as much effort as he and his older brother could expend toward each other. "Robbins, we're done."

Robbins left. Olivia paused with a questioning look on her face but closed the door and left, too.

Leon didn't sit, nor did he bother with any kind of greeting. He walked around the room, looking at the monitors. "Who's that?" he asked, nodding toward Lucas, who, thankfully, didn't look like a prisoner.

"What can I do for you, Leon?"

Leon spun around and narrowed his eyes at Gerard's nonanswer. Leon was taller, better looking, and, in some ways, smarter, a fact he had always rubbed in. That and his major general status. "I've heard that you've been preoccupied with a new program, and it smelled like the last one that nearly destroyed our family's name."

Gerard remained in his chair, relaxing his tense muscles before his adversary picked up on it. Leon could smell fear like a snake sensed movement. "Are you spying on me? Or is it Father?"

Leon Darkwell Sr. was a five-star general and as fiercely protective of his status as Gerard was of his program.

"Gerard, you don't think you were able to climb back up to where you are at the CIA just by your abilities alone, do you?"

Gerard's face flushed. "I sure as hell do."

He hated Leon's smug smile. "You always were delusional, little brother."

That propelled Gerard to his feet, something he instantly regretted. Never let your opponent force you into defensive action. "Get to the point. I've got work to do."

"That is my point. I'm here to find out what you're up to. Like a child, you have to be checked on."

"Get out of here. I only have one boss to answer to."

Leon, as always, looked unruffled by his unwillingness to cooperate. "Yes, you do. I'm sure he'll be interested to know how you nearly brought down the CIA twenty years ago."

"He already knows. He trusts my judgment."

"Why the armed guards?"

"To keep out the riffraff. Obviously they aren't doing their job."

Leon gave him a humorless smile and left.

Lucas wanted to get this mission over with so he could connect to Amy. He had studied the picture of the terrorist living in London. The Devil had given him the gory details of what this man had done to hundreds of innocent people . . . if he could trust a man who had abducted him, was injecting him with some unknown substance, and would probably kill him as soon as he outlived his usefulness.

In the sensory deprivation state, his mind quickly sank into the murky depths. First the shapes floating around in the darkness. Then flashes of images. This time every image that flashed into his brain came with a tearing pain like nothing he'd ever felt. He saw Eric and Amy, the dancing light of fire on their faces; Amy at . . . at the shelter. She was there now or would be. He couldn't tell what was past or future. The storm seemed a mix of both. No matter, if she was at the shelter or would be, she was safe.

He saw a man strapped to a table like him, writhing against the restraints, his face bruised. Before Lucas could get a good look, he was gone. Ripping pain. More images coming faster, so fast he couldn't grab hold of them. Gunfire. Eric's scream. Pain. Blackness. Then the target, sleeping, nice room, woman next to him, dreams of destruction, hatred, dreaming of death to the enemy . . . Americans, Brits.

He went in.

A second later he was out again, like a diver who kept floating to the surface just before he could grab the treasure on the bottom of the sea.

He dove in again. This had never happened before. He was losing control. And the pain, God, the pain was so bad. He brought his mind back to the target, but other images slammed in: more gunshots, Amy falling to the ground. Again, gone before he could see any details. The Booster was making him lose control. Not that he'd ever had any real control of his abilities, but at least he knew them. He'd learned how to use them to help people. These images were painful and so fleeting he couldn't do anything with them.

He pressed his fingers to his closed eyes until he saw crazy purple lines. *Focus.* He had to do this. If Amy hadn't gone to the shelter yet, he had to cooperate and be useful long enough for her to get there.

The fact that he saw her there meant things had gotten ugly. Damn, he didn't want to think about that. Not now. He would go to her, find out what was going on.

He focused his thoughts again, imagining the target's face. The storm of images now centered on the man: meeting with other men; hatred; a bomb exploding in a large department store, screams, children, blood . . .

Lucas felt the familiar anger that engulfed him whenever he tried to get into a murderer's dreams. He saw the man again, still asleep. He dove in.

Eric led Amy to a small room that held a rack of car batteries, a desk and computer, and security monitors showing four frames, including the entrance they took to get there. She pointed to a frame of an interior door. "What's that?"

"That's the door from the gallery. We've seen someone snooping around twice already." Eric gestured to the computer on the desk. "Here are some tools, hopefully what you need to get into this drive."

"Eric," Petra said. "Why don't we get her settled in first? Give her a breather?"

"No time for breathers."

Amy smiled at Petra's thoughtfulness. "Thanks, but doing something will help me forget . . . well, at least it will help put tonight on the back burner for a while."

Eric said, "You know you can't return to your apartment, not even to get anything you need."

She patted her backpack. "I have most everything here. Except Orn'ry."

"Orn'ry?" Petra said, her eyebrow raised.

"My cockatoo."

"No pets in here," Eric said. "Not that it matters because you can't get it anyway."

"I've already got a friend set up to take care of my things should . . . I disappear. If he can handle Orn'ry."

Eric slapped his hand to his forehead. "Don't tell me you've told someone else about this!"

"He thinks I stumbled onto a file I shouldn't have seen and now someone's after me."

"Perfect," Eric said with a nod of approval. It annoyed her that his approval felt good.

"I'll need some clothes, though," she said, gesturing to her sweaty, torn shirt and pants.

"I've got a bunch of stuff here," Petra said. "After we found Gladstone"—she looked at Eric—"I packed up and moved down here. Eric's been here for a while. You can use my clothes until we can get out and buy some."

"You're a lot taller than I am," Amy said.

"Only an inch or so."

Amy realized Petra was right. She'd seen Petra as tall and herself as short. She'd always felt not enough, at least on a personal level. Now everything had changed. Who she was had changed. No time to delve into that, though. "Let me clean up, and then I'll get right on the drive."

Later, when the fear and grief had drained from her body, she would sleep. Hopefully Lucas would come, and she would tell him what had happened. Now that she was fully involved, he didn't have to protect her by withholding information about his whereabouts.

Other than having no windows and concrete walls, the shelter resembled a regular home. She took a shower and washed Cyrus's blood from her arms, nearly gagging and crying at the same time. She found a pair of jeans and a red stretch top on the sink cabinet afterward. Feeling a little revived, she pushed herself on the drive for two hours.

"Any luck?" Eric asked for the umpteenth time as she stood.

"It's not physically damaged; its sectors were scrubbed by something resembling a virus. Not impossible but more difficult than the coffee-spill type of job. Files are made up of thousands of bits, and those bits aren't stored contiguously; they're placed wherever there's space, a sector here and a sector there. Without the file name placeholder, I'll have to pick through the sectors and piece things together. I did find what looks like bits of word processing documents that look hopeful."

"Then why are you getting up?" He tried to steer her back to the computer.

"Because my brain feels as though it's being attacked by a computer virus." She held herself stiff, resisting his effort. "I have to sleep." When he looked like he would argue, she said, "Show me where I'm sleeping."

"There are three bedrooms on this level," he said, leading the way. "Mine's to the right, Petra's is at the end of the hallway, and Lucas's room is here. I guess you can sleep there."

Lucas's room. Had he slept here? The bed was loosely made, so she guessed he had. The walls were a gray-blue, like his eyes, with two dream paintings that added vivid color. She felt an ache at the sight of them. A cabinet in the corner held more sketches. An open door revealed a bathroom.

"Good night," she said to Eric.

Without giving him time to respond, she closed the door in his face. She stripped out of her clothes and looked through the drawers in the long dresser. "Oh, yes." She pulled out a shirt that had to be Lucas's and nearly stumbled to the bed. She could smell the faintest scent of a man on one of the pillows. She breathed in deeply, whispering his name. Her last coherent thought as she tumbled directly into sleep was, *Lucas, please come to me.*

During the hypnagogic stage, she heard the voices for a few seconds, whispers, words here and there. Then her name. Not Lucas, not his voice.

Along with the voices came a cold fear that poured through her body.

No, no, no. She pushed the voice away. Was something from her darkest dreams trying to reach out? She imagined a brick wall as wide and high as infinity blocking whatever was trying to get in. She dreamed of death, of Cyrus being shot, of running through the dark woods and the trees reaching out to grab her. Then the forest melted away, though the darkness remained, and Lucas flashed in. He said something but his words were warbled.

In the next instant he was holding her, touching her as though he believed he wouldn't again. "Are you all right? What happened? I felt you . . . scared."

He had a shimmering quality, as though he were there and not. She felt him, but his image was vibrating and his words choppy. "I'm okay. I'm in the tomb with Eric and Petra." She felt her emotions welling up. "They killed Cyrus!"

He was gone. In the next instant they were kissing by the beach, his mouth all over her, and then everything changed again and they were in the shadow of the pyramid making love, and then in a dizzying second they were by the waterfall.

She grabbed onto him, feeling his body against hers, holding on tight. He pulled her just as close and kissed her as though she held the only oxygen he'd had for hours. "Amy, Amy, Amy," he whispered between kisses. "You're all right."

Had he heard what she'd said? She let him sweep her away for a minute, needing his touch as much as he seemed to need hers. His hands ran over her shoulders, her back, and then up to cradle her face again. His eyes were closed as though he was absorbing her. "What hap—"

"I'm with Eric and Petra," she said.

But he was gone again, replaced by images of a previous dream. For those seconds, she could feel him just as she always had. A second later she was alone again, in the dark.

"Lucas!" she called, and heard her voice echo back.

"Amy—" First his voice and then a flash of him a few feet away. " . . . don't know what's happening . . . whatever they're giving me . . . changing . . . can't hold on."

She reached out to him, their fingers grazing, and pulled him toward her. "I know you tried to keep me safe, but I'm involved now. Help us find you."

"No . . . too dangerous."

She stood in the darkness, searching for him. "Lucas!" Somehow she knew he was gone this time, but she waited anyway. Then, awake, she got up, intending to go back to work on the drive.

Her gaze went to the cabinet that she knew contained Lucas's drawings and paintings. Needing to feel close to him, she sat down and pulled them out. It seemed these were his personal collection. She could see his style, even in the earlier ones, and could see how his talent had grown. Most were of her, snapshots of various moments in her life over the years.

One was of her lying on the grass, with a dog as close to her as it could get, its snout on its paws. Tears filled her eyes as she thought of Buzby, a golden retriever at the shelter where she volunteered. She cheered when a family adopted Buzby. They returned him a week later, their veterinarian having found a cancerous lump with which they weren't equipped to deal. She had given Buzby love and comfort until he died. The sketch showed exactly the way they lay in the grass together during those last weeks, and the grief on her face.

Other paintings showed happy moments, sitting up in a tree at the park, joining an impromptu Frisbee game, soaking in the sun. The most amazing part was how beautiful she looked in the paintings, and yet her hair was still that in-between straight and wavy, her body too boyish.

So this was what she looked like through the eyes of someone who loved her. That thought startled her. Did he love her?

She was about to put them back when she saw one of those horrid dream sketches stuffed way in the back. She pulled it out and saw a man lying dead on the ground. Why was this one here? She felt darkness descend on her as she recognized the man's features.

Lucas. He had seen his own death. She searched for more sketches. What was it that Eric had said? He drew it four nights in a row and then it happened the next day? Only one sketch, though. He had hidden it here. Which probably meant he hadn't told Eric or Petra.

Urgency thrummed through her. He had seen his own death, and he'd been acting as though he would die in that terrible place. He wouldn't last much longer. She had to find him.

CHAPTER 16

It was six in the morning, and sitting at the desk in the tiny office, all Amy could hear was the hum of the fridge. She needed her music; working without it was like working without one of her senses. Thank God they had a coffee maker, though no fair trade coffee. Darn Ozzie, making her all socially aware.

Ozzie! She had to call and tell him where to get his car and to find a home for Orn'ry. She started to reach for her cell phone but realized the charge was dead. Actually, better not to call from here. Maybe she was being paranoid, but she couldn't take any chances. She'd watched crime shows where the perp was caught because of cell calls that linked him to a certain tower.

She'd nuked some popcorn and was tossing them up in the air and catching them when a husky voice startled her from behind, making her miss.

"Hey." Eric came in wearing athletic pants and a faded, tight T-shirt bearing the words 2002 BEER FESTIVAL on a stein. He looked like a sleepy little boy with his hair matted down. She remembered how she'd thought his spiky hair reminded her of flames. How accurate she'd been. He picked up her purple phone. "What's this?"

Seeing his hair made her smooth down her own wild hair. "Uh, they call them cell phones. Very handy devices."

He smirked. "I mean, you've got to get rid of it. Some of these have GPS chips in them. In any case, they can get a bead on your location by which tower picked up your calls."

"Yeah, I just thought of that."

"We bought untraceable phones. I'll get one for you."

She sighed. No more purple phone. "I think I've got it, or at least a part of it."

Petra wandered in, wearing velvet pajamas that showed a slice of her flat stomach, her hands wrapped around a mug of coffee. "Got what?"

"I found a document named 'E-Aruda.' Give me about ten more minutes and I think I'll have it."

Unfortunately they waited, looking over her shoulder as she worked and releasing huffs of impatience. They eventually flopped on the floor, scarfing her popcorn. Petra got up and left, returned, and Amy smelled nail polish. When she turned, she was shocked to see Eric painting her toenails.

Petra said, "My legs are so long it was a hassle to paint my toes. One day Eric saw me struggling and did it for me."

It was such a touching gesture it was hard to believe it was Eric doing it. Seeing her expression, he said, "Don't be jealous. I can do yours next."

She tucked her feet beneath the chair and went back

to work. While the computer did its thing, she itched for parts to glue together. What she would have given for an old motherboard and some pliers.

Okay, maybe it was more like twenty-five and a half minutes. These things couldn't be rushed. "It's a log, like a diary," she said, bringing them to their feet behind her.

March 15: EA getting suspicious. Probably that creepy psychic ability. Must be careful. The guy is definitely trouble.

April 24: EA followed me; lost him eventually. Official report is that EA will not be cooperative, and in fact, will only create problems. He's volatile, into trouble, and has displayed tendencies that endanger us and others. He has no value at all to the program. My recommendation is to terminate him. Then again, I think they should all be terminated. They're a bunch of freaks, but the boss won't buy that. Getting rid of this one, and possibly Vanderwyck, would be a good start. Think the boss will agree on EA, at least.

Petra gasped. Eric said, "Now you see why I had to kill the guy. With Lucas's sketches and now this, we know he was gunning for us. For me, especially."

"Maybe so. It's just scary to think my baby brother killed someone."

He touched her arm. "I'm still the same asshole you've always known and loved. But now things are different, and I'm willing to kill to protect myself and my own." He looked at Amy.

Was he including her? The thought made her flush.

Petra leaned over her shoulder. "What's the deal with all the weird symbols and stuff?"

"That's the part I can't recover. I found another document called P-Aruda."

"Open it," she said in a low voice.

"Give me another ten minutes."

They both sighed and walked out this time, leaving her in peace for the fifteen minutes it took to finagle some data out of that file.

"Not much," she announced when they returned after her summons. "All I could get was a few random things."

Beautiful. Too bad she's one of them. No apparent ability. Keeps to herself. Periodic outbursts for no apparent reason.

Amy swiveled around in the chair with a raised eyebrow. "Outbursts?"

Petra narrowed her eyes and jabbed her finger at Eric. "You! Everyone at Hooters thought I was crazy because of you."

Eric actually looked chagrined as he shrugged his shoulders. It was the first time she'd seen any contrition, and not over killing people but annoying his sister. He was an enigma. "That was your fault for getting so uptight about it."

Amy took them both in. "'Splain, Lucy."

Petra said, "He would remote view to me at work. I could always feel him looking at the girls, even in the changing room. Perv. Then I'd get mad at him, and they thought I was yelling at myself."

"I had a funny feeling when I was on Cyrus's computer," Amy said to Eric. "That was you watching me, wasn't it? That's how you knew he was online." She popped another piece of popcorn.

"Yep. And how I knew you were at Hammond's, too." He eyed Petra as he tossed a piece of popcorn into his mouth. "And now you know why I'm a *perv*."

Petra rolled her eyes. "Great, now he has an excuse. Have you seen his room?"

"Hey, it's art."

"Naked women art."

Eric took her hand. "Come here, Amy; you tell me if this is porn."

He escorted her one door down to his room. Oh, brother. When he flicked on the light, she was surprised. She expected boobs and va-jay-jay's, not sepia-toned paintings of passionate embraces, a woman with a towel draped artfully over her body, and an angel leaning over a man on his knees before her.

"Tomasz Rut," he said with a touch of pride. "I've been buying them at art auctions. Lucas has a few, too."

"They're beautiful," she had to concede.

From behind them, Petra said, "And what about the *Playboy*s?"

"I need a diversion. It's not like I'm going to get a chance to do the bump and grind anytime soon."

Amy returned to the office. She didn't want to pursue that line of conversation. As she printed out the documents, the others in the room with her again, she remembered something. "We have access to a car that's not tied to any of us. Cyrus gave it to me."

Petra said, "But I like driving Lucas's car. It's like having him with us."

Eric shook his head. "It's also a good way to get

caught. Even with changing the tags, it's a risk every time we take it out. It's too recognizable." His expression softened, another surprise. "If you want to feel close to him, just go sit in it." He told Amy, "But getting Cyrus's car is too risky. They might be watching it. They were probably keeping tabs on Cyrus; they knew he was meeting you, after all. We don't know if they followed him to the car's drop-off location."

"I *have* to get the car."

He raised his eyebrows at the emotion in her voice. "What do you mean, 'have to'?"

"Cyrus risked—and lost—his life to warn and protect me. As much as Lucas's car means to Petra, this car means as much to me." It would be the last thing he'd ever do for her. "Besides, we need it. Like you said, we can't take Lucas's or our cars."

"No."

"I think you just like being contrary."

"I think *you* like being contrary."

She slapped her hand on her forehead. Orn'ry had nothing on Eric. "I'm going to get the car, with or without you."

"If you want to take the chance, go alone. Now, about the hard drive: is there anything else you can scavenge?"

"There's a file on here for Lucas, too, but that one is beyond reconstruction. We won't know what he reported."

Eric leaned against the rack of car batteries. "Probably not much, since he kept his sketches down here. There were a few times, though, that he was in the middle of doing the four sketches when they were in his bedroom. Gladstone could have seen those."

"Did you know that Lucas saw his own death?"

By their expressions, they didn't. Petra especially looked scared. "How do you know?"

Amy walked into the bedroom and returned with the sketch. They both studied it with horrified expressions.

Eric said, "He didn't tell us a lot of things."

Petra's fingers curled around the edge of the paper, her gaze riveted to the sketch. "How could he not tell us something like this? He saw his own death and didn't say a word about it!"

"He was always private," Eric said. "Even as a kid. But he probably didn't want to worry us. Sometimes I hate that noble son of a bitch," he muttered, pinching the bridge of his nose.

Amy ran her hands down Lucas's shirt, which she was wearing, along with Petra's black leggings. "I think he's in real trouble. I connected with him last night, but he wasn't able to hold on. Whatever they're injecting him with is changing his abilities." Fear welled up inside her. "We have to get him now."

Eric clenched his fists. "I'll try to remote view him again." He stretched out on the floor and closed his eyes. "You need to be quiet. And patient."

"Like you were about the hard drive," she asked with a slight smile.

"I was *Saint* Patience. You were just taking too long."

Petra sat next to him. He took deep breaths, his stomach rising and falling in rhythm. His body stiffened and the veins at his temples filled with blood. His face reddened. His fingers twitched. He looked as though he was having a seizure. Amy looked at Petra, who was watching and seemingly not worried about his behavior. So this was normal. Well, normal for this.

During all this oddness, she felt a surge of joy. It took a moment to figure out why. She belonged for the first time in her life. Not a misfit or oddball; maybe more like part of an oddball group. With Eric and Petra, she was normal.

They waited, watching Eric. He began to mumble, and then little epileptic tremors moved through his muscles. Sweat beaded on his skin, glistening on his upper lip. His breathing quickened. Something was happening.

Please see him.

A minute passed. Two. He opened his eyes, and she could see his frustration. He was drained, and Petra helped him sit up.

"All I see is darkness. I hear nothing. If he's there, he's in a void. Creepy as hell."

Amy felt something stir inside her. "Once, he said something about being in the dark and someone startling him when they turned on the light. Maybe you've been there but couldn't see anything."

"Now you tell me."

"Lucas and I have a connection. What if you and I worked together to reach him? Your ability to go there and mine to connect to him? Maybe I can bring you into his mind with me."

He banged his hand against the wall. "I shouldn't need anyone else to see him."

She pursed her lips. "Well, you do, so get it over it."

He turned to say something, leaning into her face. "You are . . . you . . . "

She met his hard glare. Seconds ticked by. Petra cracked her knuckles, and Amy could see in her peripheral vision that she was watching them.

"Let's do it," he growled, instead of saying what was clearly on his mind.

Petra gave her an admiring look as she brushed her long blond hair back from her face. "Are you strong enough to do this, Eric?" she asked him. "You just—"

"I can do it," he muttered.

Amy and Eric sat on the floor facing each other, and Petra sat cross-legged in the chair next to them.

"We should probably hold hands," Amy said. "To make the connection between us."

They awkwardly clasped hands. His were big and squeezed hers a little too tightly. She didn't say a word about it.

"You go, like you usually do," Amy said. "Take me with you."

He took a deep breath and closed his eyes. For a few minutes she felt nothing. *Please let this work. It has to work. We need more to go on.*

A few more minutes passed.

She felt a tingle go through her body. *Yes, more!* Eric's hands grew hot, creating a dampness between their palms. She put her focus back on the tingling. Something tugged at her consciousness, a strange swirling in her stomach that moved up into her head. Involuntarily she pulled back, but he squeezed tighter and kept her in place. She felt a constriction, something closing in around her, heard a heartbeat and knew it wasn't hers.

One image after another flashed in front of her like a movie trailer, lingering a moment on each scene before moving on. A young boy and girl, Eric and Petra, and then a burned-out house, and then a teenage Lucas screaming, *"What did you do?"* Flames licked away at another structure. She experienced what Eric did when he saw fire, a deep, erotic sensation curling through her just as smoke curled into the air. She was seeing things from his mind, feeling what he felt.

She saw a man tied up in a chair, looking at Eric with disgust, and felt Eric's frustration and rage. She heard the man say, "You're done for, freak of nature!" The man's face changed as a flame ignited on his pant leg. Eric's satisfaction, his deep hunger for revenge, flowed through her, too. Then the scene changed, and she experienced Eric making love with a woman. Then she saw the paintings Lucas had done of her, and an embarrassed flush rushed through her when she saw him looking at her, her body, and then her in bed sleeping, feeling a different kind of hunger.

Before she could even ponder all that, she felt herself lift up, not physically but spiritually. A blur of colors surrounded her, spinning her around as she was propelled forward.

Dizzy. What's going on? No control! Eric? Are you there?

No answer.

Don't panic, I'm still with Eric or I wouldn't be here. It's not like the voices where I'm alone and scared. I'm going to Lucas. Hang in there.

The movement stopped so suddenly it made her stomach spin. She was floating in a pitch-dark sea, or so it felt. She kept turning, spinning slightly, and then with a jerk she straightened.

It was hard to breathe. Her chest was tight, further

convincing her that she was somewhere miles beneath the ocean's surface. She heard nothing. *Wait!* A sound. Breathing, quick, shallow breaths.

We're here, Eric's voice said, though it seemed more like an echo in her mind.

Thank God. *It's . . . it's a perfect darkness.*

This is what I see whenever I come. I don't even know if Lucas is here. That's your part.

I hear breathing. Is that you?

No. I hear it, too. His voice had risen.

He's here! I can feel him.

She followed the sound of the breathing. The closer she got, the more she felt Lucas. He had been tuning into her most of her life. She should be able to connect to him, too.

Lucas! Are you there?

After a pause, he said, *Amy. What are you doing here? How—*

Eric is here. He remote-viewed and brought me with him.

She expected him to be happy to see her, or at least relieved, but he was terse. *You shouldn't be here. Neither of you.*

Eric spoke. *Lucas. Can you hear me?*

Yeah, man. He sounded weak, as though he had to push out every word. *Promise me you'll stay out of this. These people are powerful and ruthless. Keep Amy and Petra safe, you hear me?*

And you get back here. Your girlfriend is a pain in my ass.

What's she doing? Lucas asked. *She's not supposed to be doing anything to rescue me. None of you are.*

No, it's not that. She's getting under my skin,

Lucas. I'm going to have to kiss her smart-assed mouth, and since she's yours, that would be wrong.

Before Amy could even react to that, Lucas said, *You son of a bitch, you're not trying to get me jealous, are you?*

No, I just don't want to live with the guilt of taking your girl. So you need to get the hell out of there. Let me help. What if it's just me, and I leave the girls out of it?

The indignity of that hit Amy, but she held in her objection. If Lucas thought she was helping, he'd never cooperate.

No, man. It was my choice to go to her that night, and I regret that to hell now. She's in more danger than she might have been if I hadn't.

Uh, guys, I'm here. Don't talk about me as though I weren't.

Eric ignored her. *Lucas, stop being so frickin' noble and let me come after you. You know I love this kind of shit. The girls'll stay in the shelter.*

The lights came on, startling Amy just as Lucas had been startled out of their dream. Two men walked in, and she was horrified to see Lucas on what looked like a hospital bed. The room was sparse, with mint-green walls and what looked like a door to a small bathroom. She couldn't take her gaze from him, or the white cap on his head that was covered in electrodes and hooked to machines.

"Lucas," said the taller man, whose back was to her. He tapped Lucas's cheek. "Come out of it. What's going on? Your brain waves are going crazy."

They were monitoring his brain waves. They'd known something was happening. Did they know about his visits to her? Oh God, those horrible men. She wanted to scratch their eyes out, to wrap her hands around their throats.

She could see the other man's face, shorter, rounder, with a balding head. He looked concerned as he stared at Lucas. "It's too much. The dosage and frequency, the sensory deprivation, it's breaking him down. He can't take any more."

Those words gripped her heart. Their last encounter had been so scattered. He said he didn't have control. They were making him crazy! Cyrus had said the side effects of the Booster probably caused her dad to kill himself. That had to be what they were giving Lucas.

The other man said, "I'll decide when he's had too much."

Rage washed over her, but before she could let loose a howl of anger, a third man said, "One of them is here. I can feel him."

The lights went out again.

"Block him," the tall man said.

She spun away into the mash of colors. Her chest constricted again. With a gasp she opened her eyes. Eric's eyes were already open. Their hands were still linked, and she pulled away with a jerk. Her body was soaked with sweat.

Petra couldn't have been any closer if she'd been sitting between them. "What happened?"

He ran his hands over his face and into his damp hair, his shoulders hunched over in exhaustion. "Lucas won't cooperate. He's trying to protect us. I hate that guy sometimes."

Amy had to take a deep breath to muster the energy to talk. "They're monitoring his brain waves. Keeping him in the dark. Sensory deprivation." She heard the fear in her voice. "Whatever they're giving him is breaking down his sanity."

Petra said, "Could it be the same stuff Cyrus said our parents got?"

"That's what I'm worried about. Cyrus didn't know."

In a grim voice, Eric said, "They knew we were there. Someone else, not the two spooks. *Someone knew I was there.*" He slammed his hand down on the carpet. "And he kicked our asses out."

Petra shot to her feet. "It keeps getting worse and worse, and there's nothing I can do. I feel so helpless. There's nothing we can do to save him, is there?"

Amy felt the same vibration of fear as Petra's. "I'm not giving up. We can't give up." She looked at Eric. "What were you doing, telling Lucas that stuff about kissing me?"

"Well, you are a pain in the ass, but no, I don't want to kiss you. I was trying to get him riled up."

But she had seen those images of her through his eyes. He was super-sex-charged. That he was looking at her, watching her sleep, made her all the more nervous around him. Too nervous, even, to call him on it.

He tried to get up but slumped back onto the floor and curled up on his side. He could barely keep his eyes open. "Have to sleep."

Petra said, "He's tired after one trip. Two will wipe him out."

Amy wasn't even sure that he heard. They left the room and closed the door behind them.

"I'm so scared," Petra said, wandering into Lucas's

room. She looked at one of the paintings, the mysterious man she now knew was Lucas.

"You love him, don't you?" Amy asked. "More than like a brother."

Petra paused, deciding whether to tell the truth. "He lived with us since he was a boy. But I never saw him as a brother." She looked at the paintings again. "All my life people told me I was beautiful. I've had men tell me they loved me, dozens of them."

"Must be nice," Amy said, feeling the bite of jealousy. A glance in the mirror told her why: no makeup, baggy clothes, psycho hair.

Petra laughed without humor. "Not really. They loved my looks, not me. Lucas saw beyond my facade. I loved him, innocent love." She looked at Amy for a second and then away. "When I hit puberty, I felt that love shift to something else. I kind of assumed that Lucas was mine, that we'd be together romantically. I never got up the nerve to tell him that my feelings went deeper. But a few times, when I tried to broach the subject, he hugged me back and said something to the effect that I was like a sister and he loved me very much. I didn't react very well to his innocent proclamation of love, and he hasn't said anything since. I just couldn't tell him the truth.

"I guess I kept hoping someday he'd see me in a different light. Sometimes I get testy with him, and poor Lucas, he has no idea what's going on. He probably thought it was PMS, though he was never crass enough to say it. I let him believe that because the truth is so much more sensitive."

She wiped away the moisture in her eyes. "I was always jealous when he talked about you. He didn't talk a lot until he got the sketch of you being attacked. I could see how much you meant to him. I was competing with someone he didn't even know."

It seemed crazy that someone like Petra was jealous of her. "I'm sorry," she said, but she wasn't really. It just seemed like the thing to say.

"And now I'll never get to tell him why I acted the way I did."

"We're not giving up." As tired as she was, she heard the conviction in her words. "Do you hear me? We are not giving up on Lucas. We will save him because we love him."

Petra turned to her. "You love him, too."

"I do." The words just slipped out. She was sure now, or at least her heart was. "I know, it sounds crazy. A man I've only known in my dreams."

Petra's face lit with hope. "Do you believe we'll save him?"

She looked at the paintings. "I have to." The man who painted them was sensitive, sexy, and he loved her. Had always loved her. She took a deep, halting breath. "I'm going to get the car, before someone reports it abandoned. I'll walk a ways and call a cab."

Petra said, "You need a disguise."

"I can wear sunglasses and a hat."

"Then you'll look even more suspicious. Come with me."

Petra led her into her bedroom and to the dresser. The top drawer held hair and skin products. She grabbed a couple of tubes and turned to her. "I've been wanting to do this since I first saw you." She squirted some liquid into her hand, rubbed her palms together, then grabbed locks of Amy's hair and scrunched them.

Amy watched in awe in the mirror as her straight, frizzy hair became defined with waves and darker with the wetness of the gel. Petra backed up and assessed her work. "There. Now . . . " She reached in and grabbed more products, and before long Amy wore makeup, red lipstick and rouge.

"They'll never recognize me now," she said. "I don't even recognize me."

"You're a pretty girl. I don't know why you hide it."

Petra, now she was pretty. While she was just . . . well, Amy. But looking in the mirror, she did look pretty amazing. She caught herself smiling.

Petra went to the small closet and pulled out a hot red dress. "Here, put this on. If they've been watching you at all, they know you wear drab, boring clothes that hide your figure. This will throw them off."

"I'm not trying to impress anyone," Amy said in her defense, slipping into the dress. She looked at her reflection. "Wow." Amy Shane, sex goddess, in three easy steps.

"Yeah, wow. Now you don't look like a woman trying to be invisible, which would attract their attention." She pulled out a pair of red high heels.

"No way. I don't do heels. Besides, your feet are bigger than mine. I'll have to go with the sneakers."

Petra winced. "I suppose they'll have to do. All right, let's go."

"What do you mean, *let's*?"

"I'm going, too. I'll leave a note for Eric."

They headed down the tunnel to the garage. It would be the last time they could take a chance driving Lucas's car. In the garage, they looked out the windows for suspicious cars.

Petra said, "I'm sure they're watching the gallery. One of the times I snuck into Lucas's house to change the artwork I saw a car parked across the way."

Though Amy wanted to drive, to feel what he felt when he was behind the wheel, she got in on the passenger side. "Could they find out about the shelter?"

Petra got into the driver's side. "It wasn't public record, and it's not permitted, but the house was owned by people who worked in the government. It's always possible, I guess, but I try not to think about it."

They backed out and headed away from the gallery. Amy stared at her surroundings. There was a world out there, a normal world where people went about their business and worried about things like bills and the argument they'd had with their lovers. A woman walked her dog, tugging at its leash. A toddler girl picked a flower and stuck it in her mouth. It all looked so normal that it seemed pretend.

She pulled her attention back to the interior of the car. The Edge sang about being numb, and she could relate. Numb was safe. It kept the fear at bay, if only for a while.

"You said you could feel Eric remote viewing you," she said. "What does it feel like?"

"It's kind of a shiver that starts at the back of my neck. Like that feeling you get when you say, 'Someone just stepped on my grave.' Then it tickles down my spine. It's not a bad feeling, just . . . weird. And annoying, like having my big brother checking up on me."

"I hate to bring this up, but . . . if someone else were remote viewing you, could you tell that, too?"

She shot Amy a startled look.

"Well, if Eric can do it, others can, too. Someone in Lucas's room knew we were there."

"I can sense, but I can't remote view, so maybe that person can't either."

Amy watched their surroundings as they drove. Every bland car caught her eye now, and she waited for it to turn around and follow. "Cyrus said that the Offspring have powers they might not even know about. You could, too. I didn't know seeing glows was a psychic ability, and probably the voices, too."

"Voices," she said. "You hear voices?"

"Put that way, it sounds crazy." And damn, she hadn't meant to mention it. "Between wake and sleep I hear bits of conversations and stuff. Maybe it's not an ability at all." She could have convinced herself of that if she didn't feel so damn scared when she heard them.

"Eric thinks my extraordinary hearing is an ability." She smiled at that for a second. "I don't know if I could sense someone other than Eric watching us." Her gaze darted around. "I don't even want to think about that."

"You have to. We know that the men behind this are trying to recruit Offspring. Maybe they already have."

CHAPTER 17

"Why did Cyrus send you out of town to get the car?" Petra asked, looking in her rearview mirror.

"I think he chose someplace that was open twenty-four hours so the car wouldn't be noticed."

"He loved you a lot, didn't he?" she asked softly.

"He made mistakes and he wasn't honest with me, but yes, I think he did."

They drove in silence for a few minutes. Petra pointed to an old building with a cartoonlike picture painted on the side. It depicted a craggy auctioneer lifting his gavel next to a building on the platform with the words MARKET HOUSE on it, and a bubble that said, SOLD OUT TO THE HIGHEST BIDDER!

The Market House, down by the City Docks in the historic section, had been a great place, with local cafés. Its management had been handed over to a firm that filled it with chain eateries and ousted the little guys, much to the ire of the locals, even four years later.

Petra laughed. "That guy just kills me."

"Freedom. I've read about him: a graffiti artist with a message."

Freedom's real identity was a mystery, though the authority figures wanted that to end.

Amy said, "The paper did a write-up on him once. He's almost a hero. They showed this area of Baltimore where the sidewalks were full of cracks and holes right by a retirement home. He'd painted a three-dimensional picture on the sidewalk that showed an old man trying to climb out of a hole. It looked so real, at least in the photo. The city fixed the sidewalks real quick after that."

Just as Amy was thinking how nice it was to talk about something other than spies and danger, Petra's fingers, nails polished a bright red, tightened on the wheel. "Crap. I got *the feeling*."

"Eric?"

She narrowed her eyes in concentration. "I don't think so. It feels . . . different."

"Whoever sensed us when we went to Lucas was able to kick us out. Can you do that?"

"I don't know, I don't know." She waved her hand as though she'd burned it on the steering wheel. "What do I do?"

"Turn in at that gas station. We need to fill up anyway, and it'll give you a chance to calm down."

Petra's hands were shaking as she punched the Cash button. Amy removed the gas cap.

"Do you still feel it?"

"Yes, and it's a creepy feeling. Creepier than when Eric does it. I don't like it."

"Visualize yourself kicking that person out. Create a ball of energy and hold it in your hands. Then throw it out at the person watching us."

"Okay, I'll try."

214

Amy had no idea if it would work, but it would keep Petra focused on something other than her panic. She went into the station to pay. It was an annoying habit to glance at the newspaper machines as she walked by them. Cyrus's face glued her feet to the concrete.

CIA OFFICER KILLED BY MUGGERS AT PARK.

She fumbled for change and bought a copy before going inside to pay.

Petra was pumping the gas when Amy returned. "Do you still feel him?"

"I don't think so."

"Let's get out of here."

"You drive," she said, walking to the passenger side. "I'm too nervous."

Amy slid into the driver's seat and then had to shift the seat. She could hardly enjoy driving the car, though, not with that headline looming in her brain and the fear of being watched thick in the air. She handed the paper to Petra. "Read the article about Cyrus."

She took a side road and wound back to the main highway the long way, in case their spy was able to pinpoint where the gas station was.

"'Cyrus Diamond, Annapolis resident and long-time employee of the CIA, was mugged and shot in the Quiet Waters Park last night. The incident happened after hours. It is not known what Diamond was doing there. He received two bullets, the fatal one piercing his heart. A CIA spokesperson maintains that Diamond was not there on CIA business, and another unnamed coworker told us that Diamond liked to walk in the park at night.

" 'Park officials claim that this is the first incident of violence of this nature at the park and that it remains safe for visitors.' " She looked up. "This is how we're going to end up, isn't it? As victims of some random crime, only it won't be random."

"No, we're not. We're going to rescue Lucas and find out who's behind this. Then we're going to expose them all."

"I hope so." Petra opened the paper and took another breath. "There's more about Eric, too. At least it's only second page news now. They're still looking for him. And . . . oh, crap."

"What?"

"They've identified this car. The police are looking for it."

If the police pulled them over and questioned them, they'd be taken into custody and never heard from again.

"They're calling him a dangerous criminal."

"He is," Amy said. "But he's our dangerous criminal." She shuddered, remembering that man going up in flames.

"He gets on the edge sometimes. He's always been like that."

Was it the Ultra thing?

They drove without speaking for a few minutes, but the silence was uncomfortable. It gave her too much time to think. Like Petra, she kept watching the mirrors for any car that stayed with her as she changed lanes and occasionally took a detour before returning to the main road.

"Uh-oh." Amy flicked her gaze to the rearview mirror.

Petra held up her hand. "No more 'uh-ohs.' I can't take any more 'uh-ohs' or bad news or feelings." When Amy remained silent, she said, "What is it?"

"A police cruiser coming up behind us, don't look," she added quickly as Petra started to turn. "No lights."

It remained a few car lengths behind. Amy moved into the far right lane and slowed her pace so it could pass. She didn't want to give the officer any more time to notice the car. The police car moved closer. Changed lanes to the one next to hers. It finally moved up next to her. She trained her gaze ahead, looking as much as she could like a gal out to enjoy the day.

Someone honked the horn behind her, sending her jolting out of the seat. The driver gestured for her to speed it up. She was going ten miles below the speed limit. She cringed. *Please don't let that bring the officer's attention to me.*

She dared a look. The cruiser had pulled away, now three car lengths ahead. "Whew. We've got to get this car into hiding. Could you get my cell phone out of my backpack and dial a number for me?" She recited Ozzie's number and then took the phone from Petra. "Oz, it's Amy."

"Where are you? I didn't recognize the number. What the heck is going on? Some men questioned me when I left your apartment. They said you were in big trouble. Then another man came around this morning asking how my car ended up at Quiet Waters Park. I told him I'd given you a key a while back and you must have borrowed it. I acted kinda annoyed at you over it, but I don't think he bought it. He tried to bully an answer out of me, and I guess it's good that I don't know anything. Even if I did, I wouldn't tell them. But I'm worried sick about you."

"I'm sorry."

"Don't be. I wanted to be involved, remember?"

"You can't tell anyone I called. I forgot to ask you to change the message on my machine to send clients to my backup. Is that Orn'ry I hear in the background?"

"Amy, I'm going nuts. He's been screeching since I brought him here. Yes, I've fed him and given him water. The neighbors are complaining."

"I'm sorry, Oz." She felt just as bad for abandoning Orn'ry. "See about finding him a home. A good home."

"No one's going to take this bird."

She took a deep breath. "All right, I'll try to get him. Just hold on until I do, okay? And Oz . . . thanks." She disconnected and tossed the phone to Petra. "We've got company."

Lucas tried to swim through the fog in his mind. His body was burning up but he felt water all around him. As he struggled to open his eyes, a storm of images crackled through his brain like an electrical current. Amy driving his car. Her fear. Petra beside her. A man with dark hair, tan complexion, and hard, nearly black eyes. Gun on his lap. Following them. *Capture. Kill if necessary.*

No!

He struggled to open his eyes, but he was too weak. "Amy." He could barely even say her name.

"Shh," a woman said.

Amy? No, not her voice. He would have felt her if

she'd been there. He didn't want her there. Anywhere but there.

He felt a cool wet cloth across his forehead. Water cascaded down his face. He sank back into the ethers. Find Amy again. She was in trouble. Because of him. Where was Eric? If he was with them, he would have been driving the car. Was he hurt? Everything was falling apart, and it was his own fault. If he hadn't gone to Amy . . .

Then something else might have happened to her. His original fear. These people were after her. They were going to get her one way or the other.

He tried to summon her. Nothing. Too weak. Helpless.

"Try to relax, Lucas," the woman said.

No way could he relax, not when Amy and Petra were in danger. Eric. He'd never tried to get into Eric's dreams. Was it nighttime? He had no idea. But Eric had just come here. That hadn't been a dream, right? He'd been here, with Amy. He'd told Eric to keep her safe, but she and Petra were off somewhere without him. If he had remote-viewed here, he'd be tired afterward. Lucas wasn't even sure how long ago that was, but he had to take the chance.

He tried to home in on Eric. If he could get into other people's heads, he could get into Eric's. He pictured the man he considered a brother even though he'd nearly disowned him years ago.

After the fire, Lucas went to France for a few years and lived with a well-known but reclusive sculptor who'd become his mentor. He'd gotten to know other struggling artists and connected them with the galleries he dealt with. He found a love of beautiful things, a counterpoint to the darkness within. For a while he was happy . . . until the sketch that foretold his mentor's fatal fall down a staircase. Until Lucas's warning freaked him out and he returned to Annapolis. He'd grown up enough to know he couldn't sever his few connections to family. He'd kept a wall between him and Eric, though, and would until Eric told him the truth. Now he needed to reach Eric.

It was a struggle, but he pushed hard. A blurry image grew clearer. He saw Eric passed out on the floor. The water sliding down Lucas's face pulled him back to the world again. *Stop.* He opened his mouth but couldn't push out the word. What was happening to him? His body wasn't cooperating, but he still had his mind. For now. He imagined a thread leading to Eric, and he climbed through the ethers by that tenuous thread. He slipped but grabbed hold again. Eric. He got closer. *Got to get in.* Then he dove into his dreams.

There were no dreams, though. His brain was recovering. Lucas pulled in all the strength he had. *Eric! The girls are in danger. Wake up! They're in my car. Find them!*

Lucas, is that really you?

Listen to me. Don't try to rescue me. I won't be around much longer. I don't want you risking your lives for my dead body. Find the girls, Eric.

As hard as Lucas had worked to get there, suddenly he was out of the dream and back to this wet place.

"Just relax," he heard the woman say.

He struggled to lift his eyelids and saw the brunette he'd seen at the window. She was sitting next to him. He was in a tub. Through the slit of his half-opened eyes he saw he was naked but for his briefs. He was way too tired to be embarrassed or even wonder how he'd gotten there. Just beyond the woman was a guard. Lucas's eyes drifted shut again.

A few minutes later a man's harsh voice jarred him out of his slumber. "What are you doing in here, Olivia?" The Devil.

"Peterson had to leave. I told him I'd take over. I have some medical training, you know."

"So does he. And I told you I didn't want you near the criminals. Leave."

"Who's going to stay with him?"

"I will."

So he was considered a criminal. He would have slid beneath the water and let himself drown, if that was possible. He couldn't take being there anymore. But he couldn't leave Amy, not yet. He needed to know she would survive the man with the hard, dark eyes.

Eric woke, hearing Lucas's words echoing from the dream. Or was it a dream? He pulled himself out of bed and wandered out to the main room. No sign of either woman.

"Petra? Amy?" He checked their bedrooms when neither answered. When he returned to the living room, he saw the note on the table. "What the hell? Are they crazy?"

He grabbed his cell phone, intending to call Petra, but stopped. What if they were in a precarious situation and the ringing phone gave her away? She might not have the presence of mind to turn off the ringer.

Lucas's visit wasn't a dream. They were gone and they were in trouble. He tried to remote view to them, but he was still too wasted. He slammed his hand against the wall. He had no way to get to them, no way to know where they were. He let out a string of curses he expected would melt the violet paint on the concrete wall. This was falling apart. The enemy was winning. And there wasn't a damned thing he could do about it.

CHAPTER 18

"Don't turn around," Amy said as Petra began to look. "He doesn't know that we know yet. We need that advantage."

"How'd you get so good at this stuff?"

Amy gritted her teeth. "Same way you're good at it. Necessity. Like that thing at the gay festival."

Petra laughed nervously. "That kind of thing is different. It's acting. This is drive-for-your-life stuff. What kind of car is he in?"

"Blue Buick, one car back. I only see one guy."

"Two against one . . . no problem."

Amy smiled. "That's the way to think."

"I wish we could, like, blow something up or make it go up in flames."

"You never know; we just might be able to." Amy slowly accelerated. She couldn't take a chance of flagging a cop's attention with erratic driving. "Okay, here's what we do. We're only a couple of miles from the car. We need to get out of Mr. Buick's sight long enough to hide the 'Cuda. Once we're on foot he won't be able to find us easily."

"What if we get remote-viewed again?"

"Remember, Eric can't remote view for very long, and it drains him to do it more than once. We have to hope that person gets the same way."

Petra curled her fingers around her seat belt. "How can you be so positive?"

"Because I can't afford to be negative."

Traffic was holding her back. Mr. Buick was getting closer. He was way better at maneuvering than she was. At a light, he pulled up just behind her in the next lane. He had a Latin or Middle Eastern look about him.

"Pretend to laugh," Amy said, pointing at a lingerie store.

He inched closer as the car next to her readied for the green light. He wanted to get a good look at them, apparently. That gave her a good look at him. At, in particular, his glow.

"Purple."

"What?"

"He's not one of us. That's the good news." The light turned green, and she accelerated at a normal rate even though she wanted to stomp the gas pedal.

"Do I want to know what the bad news is?"

"He's got a purple glow. Violent intent. I saw it when that man grabbed me at the marina."

They crossed the Patuxent River toward the US 301 exchange. She'd studied Cyrus's map and knew they'd loop onto that and head south. The blue Buick followed at a respectable distance throughout the maneuver. Almost there. She had to come up with a plan. She searched the area, one with which she wasn't familiar.

"Hand me my backpack." As she drove, she released

her seat belt and slid out of it. The car key was in her pocket, and Petra had the extra key on her. "Be ready to go. You *had* to put me in this dress, didn't you? At least I have sneakers on."

Petra released her belt, too, looking around with wide eyes. "You just passed the Wal-Mart."

"I know. I'm going to take the next road and come from the back side. We need to ditch this car—"

"*Ditch* it? No!"

Amy turned onto the next road and drove through a residential area. "We've got to. It's too risky driving it when it's been in the paper. Maybe we can come back and get it."

Petra let out a whimper but didn't argue further. She worried her plump lower lip. "If we get caught, Eric will just kill me for coming with you. Even if I'm already dead, he'll kill me again. He didn't think you'd really get the car by yourself."

"Let's not worry about that right now." Amy cased the area, the Buick behind her.

"We're going to get caught, aren't we? Then we're going to be in that horrible place where Lucas is, and we're going to die."

Amy glanced over at Petra, whose face wore a mask of despair. She reached into her mind for her counseling skills. "Petra, listen to me. We're going to be fine. We will get out of this. If we think we're done for, then we are. We must believe that we'll get away. Got it?"

Petra nodded.

"If we get separated, we meet in the lingerie department at Wal-Mart at eight o'clock."

Amy saw her break. Both lanes were crawling, a school bus slowing the right lane even more. The bus lights began to blink, indicating it was going to stop. She zipped in front of a car in the left lane. The Buick butted in two cars back. The car in front of her sped up, trying to outrun having to stop. The Stop sign was just swinging out. The car in front of her passed the bus. The kids would be in a line, ready to board the bus and not scattered around.

She swung in front of the bus and turned right. The bus driver honked, but she breathed out in relief that there were no kids in front of the car. Seconds later she turned into a large apartment complex. She saw a strip of woods to the right, just beyond a small park area. Luckily it was too cold for anyone to be using it. Good thing. She tore right through it. She aimed for an opening in the trees she hoped was big enough to accommodate the car. Branches scratched along the sides. She stopped once the car was completely in the woods and cut the engine. They both threw their doors open and ran.

"This way," Amy said, breathless from fear. "Damn!"

The Buick screeched in. He pulled into a close spot and left the car as fast as they had. He made better time, too, running just outside the edge of the trees.

Amy headed back toward the road on the other side. Running in a dress wasn't cutting it. The skirt rubbed against her legs and hindered her movement. She hiked it up to her thighs.

Between gasps, Petra said, "We should go . . . different ways. That way he'll only . . . get one of us. We'll stick to our backup plan." She continued straight.

Even with a plan, Amy could see that the whole thing was falling apart. Damn remote viewing! She broke out of the woods into the backyards of clusters of town houses. Her chest hurt. She was out of shape for running for her life. Over her heartbeat she heard something else: footsteps. He had gone after her.

She ran to the front of the town houses and crouched at the rear corner of one of the cars in the parking lot. Her throat was so dry she could barely swallow.

A man said, "Can I help you find something?"

Another man said, "Girl just stole my wallet. I saw her run this way."

"What is it with kids these days? I saw a girl over there a minute ago."

"Thanks, man."

Amy grimaced.

"Should I call the cops?"

"I am a cop. I'll take care of her. Please go back inside."

Like hell he was. Wearing loose pants and a light jacket, he was dressed to move quickly. She bent down low enough to see the black sneakers of the man she thought of as Buick coming toward her. She crept around the corner and saw him with his hand at his waistband, ready to grab his weapon. He had handcuffs clipped to his belt. She dashed to the low bushes along the side of the building. In the near distance she heard the 'Cuda's throaty engine start. Petra had doubled back and gotten the car. *Good, get out of here!*

"Yeah, it's me," Buick said in a low voice. "Petra is in the Barracuda in the Bowie area. I've got the other one in my sights. I'll bring her in soon."

Amy shivered. She hoped like hell he couldn't actually see her. In a crouch, she ducked around the back corner, toward the next set of buildings, and then into the space between them. She paused, hearing his footsteps close behind her. Dammit, she didn't have enough time to get any distance away. She picked up a rock and lobbed it toward the bushes along the back of the next building. Make him think she'd gone that way.

She ran toward the front and came upon a muddy black truck jacked up on huge tires. With a glance to make sure Mr. Buick hadn't come around yet, she climbed into the bed of the truck and dropped down. The bed floor was covered with beer cans and camping equipment. She pulled a tattered green tarp over her. His footsteps crunched on the grass as he walked back to the parking area. While she was holding back her ragged breaths, she heard no breathing effort from him.

If he caught her, she'd be trapped. He'd cuff her, take her away. The thought of it squeezed her stomach. She said the Lord's Prayer as his footsteps grew closer, and then it morphed into, *I can't do this anymore. I can't. If I get away, I'll forget everything and go into hiding.* Panic welled up inside her, washing over her in waves.

Remember that speech you just gave Petra. I will get away.

Dammit, it was a lot harder to take her advice than to give it.

Petra wanted to take the car and haul ass. She wanted to get herself and the car safely back to the tomb. But she wasn't alone in this. Their pursuer had gone after Amy when they split up, and now she was in trouble, big trouble. How could she just leave Amy? Then again, she might get caught, too.

No, no, think positive like she does. Even if it is annoying.

She opened her cell phone, pressed a button and said, "Eric," to activate the voice command.

He answered on the first ring. "Where the hell are you?"

"Bowie, near the Wal-Mart, getting the car. Before you rant, I need to tell you, they can remote view us. That's how they saw where we were. There's a guy after us, and he means business. Amy and I split up, and he went after her. I'm in the 'Cuda."

"Get back here," he said. "If she's going to risk her ass for a car, let them catch her."

"You don't mean that, Eric. We're a team."

"Obviously not, if you're going to run off without me."

"You wouldn't come anyway." She had to admit that having him with them would have been nice, but she never wanted to see him blowtorch anyone. "I'm going to get Amy. I've got to concentrate on my driving. 'Bye."

Feeling stronger, she tossed the phone onto the seat and turned down the street from which they'd turned. Amy had to be there somewhere. She expected to see her dart across the street any second. When she didn't see her, Petra pulled into a complex of town houses, and saw Mr. Buick stalking toward a black truck. He held a gun close to his thigh. She tuned in her hearing. Amy's breathing. She could hear her someplace close. The truck!

Panic grabbed her throat. He was about to find her, and she had to stop him. How? She punched the gas pedal and drove right at him. When he jerked up his arm to shoot at her, she fell sideways as the car rammed the truck. He fell backward, and Amy shot up out of the truck, shock on her face. Even more shock when she saw Petra waving her on.

Amy jumped out of the truck bed and dove into the open window of the car as Petra backed up. Mr. Buick was scrambling for his gun as residents came pouring out of their homes to see what the commotion was. He'd snatched it up and tucked it under his jacket as Petra tore out and turned onto the street.

The light was green, then turned yellow. Petra floored the accelerator.

Gotta make the light!

One more second.

She flew through just as it turned red.

Only then did she glance at Amy, sprawled in the passenger seat. "Are you all right?" she asked.

Amy looked shell-shocked, with her hair sticking out and her face flushed. "Yeah, I think so. I'm just . . . surprised."

"That I hit the truck you were hiding in. I didn't actually mean to do that."

"No, that you came for me. I thought you'd hightail it."

Petra gave her a sheepish grin. "I considered it. But I knew you'd do the same for me."

"Thanks."

She turned into the Wal-Mart entrance. Amy pointed to the far right corner. "The car is over there. Drop me off near it and then park behind the building. I'll pick you up. We can't bring his car back," she added, anticipating Petra's protest. "I heard Buick calling someone to tell them you were in it. I'm sorry."

Petra knew she'd never see it again. "Me, too."

Amy jumped out, and Petra drove around to the back of the building. She pressed her cheek against the steering wheel and then punched the CD player Eject button. She grabbed the U2 CD and the case and got out. The front corner of the Barracuda was dented, but the car had withstood the ramming well. A minute later Amy drove up in a beige older-model Toyota Camry. Plain, common . . . the perfect car to blend in.

As they pulled away, Amy's cell phone vibrated in her backpack. Petra recited the number on the screen. With a sigh, Amy said, "Ozzie, my neighbor and friend. Put him on speaker phone . . . Yeah, Oz."

"Amy, you're scaring me to death here. I've been trying to call since you hung up on me. Let me help. I need to help. I've watched movies where an innocent person is being chased by the bad cops and stuff. I saw that Will Smith movie like ten times. You need someone on the outside."

"You are helping. You're taking care of Orn'ry until I can get him. That's really important to me."

"No, I'm talking about big help. Like getting you supplies or joining up with you."

Petra couldn't help but grin. This Ozzie guy reminded her of Eric, jonesing for adventure.

"Okay, here's something you can do," Amy said. "I had to leave a really special car behind the Wal-Mart in Bowie. Go get it and tuck it away somewhere. I'll hide the key . . . Petra, take the key off the ring." Amy slowed down. "I'm on North Crain Highway at the light at Governor Bridge Road, heading to Annapolis. I'm throwing the key next to the road."

"How will I know the car?"

"Look in the paper today. There's a description of it. By the way, that's because the police are looking for it. 'Bye, Oz, gotta drive."

Hope spiked. "Will he do it?" Petra asked.

"Probably not."

"I'd better call Eric, let him know we're all right," Petra said, pulling out her phone. "Hey," she said when he answered. "We're on the way back."

She expected him to harangue her, but he was eerily calm. "All right, I'll see you soon. Be careful."

Petra leaned against the door. "There were a few moments there when I didn't think we were going to make it."

"Yeah, I know."

"You, too?"

"You think I'm brave all the time? I'm scared a lot. I just don't let myself get walloped by fear."

Petra smiled at Amy's candor. "I didn't want to like you."

She grinned back. "I know."

Petra laughed. "I'm glad you're on our team."

"Thanks."

They sank into silence, both lost in thought.

She'd been scared, all right, but she'd done it, Petra realized. She wasn't the pretty, helpless girl that she always felt like. She glanced behind them, then turned back to the front. There was no looking back now. They could only look forward. If only she knew what lay ahead.

CHAPTER 19

"You are both idiots! I can't believe you took such a stupid risk," Eric bellowed as soon as they walked into the main room. He grabbed one of their arms in each hand and squeezed so hard Amy yelped in pain.

She tried to pull free. "They didn't know about the car."

Petra was right, Amy realized: he hadn't thought she would go on her own to get it. And Eric certainly didn't think Petra would go with her.

He gritted his teeth. "Do you think this is a game?"

Petra trembled, her eyes wide. "Of course not!"

Amy was willing to bet she'd seen him like this before. Again she tried to pull away from Eric's grip, but he held on tight. "Let me go—you're hurting me."

He leaned down into her face. "Good. You need some sense hurt into you. You could have gotten yourself killed. Or even worse, caught."

Amy shivered, thinking of Lucas. "Every hour that goes by increases the chance that we lose Lucas forever."

He flung both their arms free in disgust. "Don't let your desperation and your emotions make you stupid. I'm in charge of our little operation, understand?"

"Why you?" Amy asked. Not that she was challenging him, but she didn't like that he'd made the assumption.

"Because I'm—"

"Please don't say 'a man,'" Amy said, her hand out to stop him.

"First of all, someone has to be in charge. Are either of you volunteering?" He didn't give them a chance to respond. "I'm the one who figured out that we were being watched in the first place. I've got the strongest ability. And"—he leaned down into her face—"*I'm the man.*"

"*Argh.*" She turned away, shaking her head.

"And you almost got caught," he went on. "Do you see a pattern? Lucas goes against our protocol and gets caught? You run off by yourselves and almost get caught?"

Petra said, "We would have been fine if they didn't have someone remote viewing us."

"Yeah, what'd you mean by that?"

"I felt him, just like I can feel you. Then we had a tail, this creepy guy with dark eyes and a gun."

"And handcuffs," Amy added. "He's trouble. And not one of us."

"How do you—"

"No glow."

Having spent his rage, Eric dropped down onto the couch. His expression, and arms-crossed posture, still radiated anger. Then he saw Amy, really saw her. "Whoa. What happened to you?"

She scanned herself. Had she been cut? Nope, no

blood anywhere. Her dress was torn, and it and she were filthy. "I had to run through the woods."

"I don't mean the dirt, I mean the dress. The hair, makeup."

She didn't like the spark in Eric's eyes as he took her in. She tugged down the short skirt. "Petra's idea. So I didn't look like frumpy ol' me." *Had* she been hiding under her clothing?

"Interesting."

"Not really." She had the urge to change but didn't want him to think he could affect her behavior. She averted her gaze to the Warhol-like sun painting.

"Lucas came to me," Eric said.

Amy spun around. "What?"

"In my dreams. He warned me that you were in danger, said you were driving his car."

She began to pace, agitated and restless. "We have to find him . . . now."

"I'll try remote viewing him again tonight, when I'm rested. Maybe the lights will be on."

Amy rubbed her arms. "But they have someone who knows when you're there. He'll just kick you out again. And now they can view us."

Petra said, "I'll stay on alert. I think I was able to push him out like he pushed you out, Eric."

Amy said, "We have to *do* something."

Petra looked at her. "What about the voices?"

Eric narrowed his eyes. "Voices?"

"She hears voices. Maybe it's another ability."

He got to his feet. "Tell me about the voices."

Amy said, "I don't even know if it's an—"

"What voices? As you said, we don't know what we're capable of. We can't dismiss anything."

The fear she always felt about the voices crept down her spine. "I hear people whispering. It never makes much sense, but then again, I don't really pay attention to what they're saying. It's spooky. Then I fall into sleep and they go away. It only happens when I'm between wakefulness and REM sleep."

"Who could it be?"

"I don't know. I hear both women's and men's voices. For a while I thought it was someone in the apartment next to me. Then they moved and I still heard them. And last night someone called my name."

"Lucas?"

"No, he can only visit me when I'm in REM sleep."

"Talk to the voices, Amy. Let them in." He ran his hand back through his red hair in frustration. "We don't have a lot of options."

She shivered. "I'll do anything I have to do."

Petra was staring at the sailing painting. She climbed on the couch and took it down. "Voices can't hurt you."

"I don't trust anything anymore. Look what Eric can do."

Petra shivered. "Sorry I mentioned it." She removed the sun painting and hung the sailing one in its place.

Eric rolled his eyes. "There she goes again."

"I need change." She regarded the violet wall. "Maybe I'll paint this wall a deep red."

Amy steeled herself for Eric's objection when she said, "I have to get my parrot."

"Say what?"

"I have a cockatoo, and he doesn't like anyone but me. My friend Ozzie is taking care of him, but he screeches and makes a ruckus because I'm not there."

Petra added, "His name is Orn'ry."

He lifted an eyebrow. "And this is supposed to warm me to the idea? Uh, no. No pets in here. We've got enough to deal with."

"I'm getting my bird."

Eric gestured to the room. "Whose place is this, anyway?"

"Lucas's, technically," Amy said. "Look, I can't leave my parrot behind. Ozzie won't be able to keep him and he'll have a hard time finding him a home. Parrots bond to their owners forever. I can't leave him to be euthanized or sold to bird breeders." She wrapped her arms around herself. "I'm too tired to argue about it right now. I'm going to lie down. Maybe I'll hear the voices."

She closed herself in her room and slipped into another of Lucas's shirts. It didn't have his scent, only fabric softener. Still, wearing it made her feel closer to him.

Someone knocked and Petra peered around the door as she opened it. "You want me to stay here while you sleep?"

No, she wanted to be strong and not need anyone. So why had she nodded?

Petra closed the door and sat in the chair. "You're scared of the voices."

It wasn't a question, and she couldn't make the effort lying would take. "Seeing glows never scared me because I was used to them by the time I realized they weren't normal. But the voices . . . they started a year ago, and I know they're not normal. I don't know what I'm letting in."

Petra nodded, understanding and yet not. "If what

Cyrus said is true, none of us knows what we're capable of. That's scary. I don't know what I'd do if I started hearing voices or seeing things that weren't there." Her gaze went to Amy's collarbone, and she got up and walked over. It wasn't until Amy felt her tug gently on the necklace that she understood what Petra had seen. "Lucas's necklace."

"He lost it at my apartment when they . . . when they got him."

Pain crossed Petra's face at that thought, but it lessened when she looked at the cross. "This was his mom's. She was always afraid of things. Of evil. She bought him a necklace when he was just a baby. It was lost when our house burnt down, when we were in high school. His mother's necklace was in a fire-safe box with all of our important papers. Now he wears hers." She bit her lip. "Wore it."

Amy unclasped the necklace and handed it to Petra. Her voice was tight when she said, "Take it. If you hadn't come back for me, you might still have his car."

Petra wrapped her fingers around the cross even as Amy's fingers involuntarily tightened. But she didn't pull it out of Amy's grasp. With a sigh, she released it. "He loves you. It should be yours."

Amy met her eyes, seeing pain but also acceptance, and smiled. "You're all right."

Petra smiled, too. "So are you."

Did Lucas love her? Amy wondered. Look what he had done for her all these years. How he made love to her. She'd always felt unlovable, inadequate. But she was lovable. She was enough for Lucas.

She put the necklace back on, breathing an inward sigh of relief that she didn't have to part with it, then pulled the covers over her. "You can leave when I'm in REM. When my eyeballs start twitching and stuff." When Petra nodded, she said, "Thanks," and rolled onto her back. A minute later she heard soft popping sounds. Opening her eyes, she saw Petra slouched in the chair, cracking her knuckles.

"Oh, sorry. Nervous habit." Petra tucked her hands beneath her thighs.

Amy closed her eyes again and let fatigue sweep her into darkness.

Memories crowded into her mind: images of running from Buick, the fear, hiding in the truck. Then nonsensical thoughts floated through. That was when the voices started, when her mind was open . . . vulnerable. She heard the whispers and felt her instinctual urge to push them back. Her body stiffened, but not her mind.

Several voices spoke:

I don't want . . .

She's not going to . . .

. . . climbing up the sheer wall . . .

Most didn't make any sense. She waited for her name.

Amy. A man.

She fought her urge to shut them out. *Yes.*

Thank God. It's Cyrus.

That almost knocked her right out of her state. *Cyrus! Are you . . .*

Dead. His words came in pieces, the way Lucas came in when he was fighting the drugs. . . . *you're . . . channel . . . how Lucas connects . . .*

Other voices tried to intrude. One carried an ominous feeling: *Kill you . . .*

Cyrus! I've got the car. Thank you. Was she actually talking to the dead? To Cyrus? She had so many questions, about her father, about who she was. But there was only one she had to have the answer to right now: *Please tell me where Lucas is.*

Don't . . .

I know you don't understand, but I have to rescue him.

Silence for a few moments. Had she lost him? Then: *Old insane asylum . . . not far . . .*

She took the tumble from a hypnagogic to a dreamless state. She had no control over that transition. She floated in some kind of void filled with swirling blue smoke. Before she could steep in frustration over losing her connection with Cyrus, she heard her name again. She knew that voice, and her heart rate jumped as she turned to see Lucas. In a flash he was holding her, kissing her, his hands on her face. "Amy, you're scaring the hell out of me."

"Ditto," she said between kisses.

They both parted and said at the same time, "Are you all right?"

He searched her eyes, worry in his. "You're at the bomb shelter."

She heard the emotion in her voice when she said, "They killed Cyrus. He was trying to warn me to go into hiding and his own people shot him."

"I'm sorry, love." He cradled her face, his pain clearly visible on his face.

"Don't blame yourself. I needed to know what was going on. Who I am. They would have come after me sometime."

"What happened this morning?"

"Petra and I went to get the car Cyrus arranged for me. They're looking for your car in relation to Eric. And . . . I'm sorry, but we had to leave it behind."

He shook his head. His image wobbled. "Don't worry about the car. I only care about you." He ran his thumb over her lower lip. "All three of you. Stay away from me." He leaned down into her face. "You promised you weren't trying to rescue me."

She nodded.

"Your job is to keep yourself safe. The Devil—that's what I call him—promised not to hurt you if I cooperate. But only as long as you're not trying anything funny."

"I'm not trying anything funny. What about you? You seem better." Every now and then, though, his image warped or his voice warbled.

"I had a reaction to the Booster—that's what they call it—that they're giving me. I'm better now. But . . . I don't know how much longer I'll be able to connect to you. Stay with Eric and Petra until the heat dies down. You can trust them. Eric's a bit . . . "

"Off the wall," she finished as he tried to think of a nice way to put it. "He worries me sometimes." Her heart hurt as she took him in, looking so beautiful, the waves of his hair brushing the shoulders of his black shirt, his blue-gray eyes soft with longing and regret. She placed her hands on either side of his face. "It's you I'm scared to death for."

"Dying is better than being here. I'm not afraid to die. The worst part is losing our connection."

The thought of hearing his voice, along with Cyrus's, was as frightening as the voices themselves. "Lucas . . . "

They came together at the same time, crushing each other's mouths, trying to swallow the other up. They took the pleasure of undressing each other the old-fashioned way, stripping off clothing one piece at a time. The feeling that this would be the last time permeated every kiss, every touch. He wasn't even strong enough to bring scenery with him. She held back tears and focused only on him, still with her, still loving her.

"Lucas, I love you."

He closed his eyes. "Don't." He kissed her with such fierceness she knew he was only trying to protect her by withholding the words.

He laid her down and then sat facing her with his legs flanking her. He pulled her legs up over his shoulders and slid into her. He teased her by barely filling her. He kissed her feet and her ankles and all the way down her thighs. He trailed his tongue in the indent behind her knees, sending such pleasure through her she couldn't believe it was coming from a nonsexual part of her body. His movements pushed his penis deeper, sliding in and out just enough to remind her of the agony and ecstasy of the tease.

His fingers played in her folds, sliding in her wetness, sending shivers through her. Oh, yes, he was teasing her mercilessly, and dammit all, she loved it. His biceps flexed with each movement. She drank in his beautiful body as she was connected to it in such an intimate way. She felt the orgasm bloom without warning, enveloping her in heat. Her toes curled and her hands clutched his knees and felt the coarse hairs that sparsely covered his legs. He was watching her come with a look of satisfaction, of pleasure, and before she could register that, he took hold of her hips and started slowly moving her against him.

He moved in rhythm and then increased the intensity until she could barely stand it. He never took his eyes from her. She felt the growing pressure beginning at her core and sweeping her body. Then his orgasm hit and he tilted his head back and let it take him with a soft moan of surrender. She watched him, the way his neck muscles stretched and his eyes squeezed shut so his eyelashes brushed his skin. His fingers tightened on her legs. Slowly he came back, in degrees, his eyes fluttering open to find her smiling.

She held out her hands, and somehow he knew she wanted him to pull her up so they were still connected, yet face-to-face. Her eyes drank him in, his cheekbones, the straight line of his nose, his chin . . . every feature that she wanted to touch now and tomorrow and next month and next year. And she couldn't. She might never actually touch him. The agony of that washed away the joy she'd been feeling at watching him experience their joining.

Before he could see that agony on her face, she hugged him hard, crushing her breasts against him. To no avail; the sobs that rose up inside her burst out. He ran his fingers through her hair, holding her tighter yet, whispering, "Please, don't cry."

She didn't want him to see her like this, had tried so hard to stop the tears. He pulled her back, though, and wiped away her tears with his fingers. She hoped she didn't have snot coming out of her nose in dreams. No, she'd be beautiful, just as he always saw her. She tried to speak, but heaving gulps came out instead.

He held her close again, stroking her back. "Oh, baby, don't cry, please don't cry. You're killing me." She heard the kind of pain she was feeling in those last words.

How could she live without him? She had the terrible feeling that this was the last time she'd see him if . . . if they didn't get him out of there. She pulled back and gripped his face with her hands. Her words came out between gulps. "Lucas . . . fight. Fight to stay alive. For me. For us. Don't . . . you . . . dare . . . give . . . up."

He turned, as though he'd heard a sound, then faced her. "Goodbye, Amy."

"No, don't say goodbye!"

He was gone.

She still felt his arms around her even as the emptiness tore through her. The tears were real, the sobbing was real . . . and as she woke, the arms around her were real, too.

Not Lucas.

Petra held her, arms awkwardly around her shoulders as she sat in bed next to her. For a moment Amy felt too wrecked to even be embarrassed. For a moment. Then she grabbed the sheet and wiped her face, snot, tears, and all.

Petra was looking at her strangely, a mix of curiosity and sympathy. "You were with Lucas, weren't you?"

Amy sucked in a deep breath to clear away the emotion. She could only nod at first.

"I drifted off to sleep for a while," Petra said. "When I woke, I could see your eyes moving beneath your eyelids and I was about to go."

What had she looked like? Her body had experienced everything that her dream body had. She was still throbbing, flushed, spent. "And?"

"The look on your face. You were . . . so in love. It's like those paintings, isn't it? He's making love to you."

Amy nodded. "What am I doing in my sleep?"

"Just arching a little, sighing. Then just as I was really going to leave, you started crying."

Movement at the door caught her eye. Eric was just outside, watching them. "Is he better, then?"

"He tells me he's fine, but I don't believe him. He said he had a reaction to the Booster. And they're going to keep giving it to him." Tears threatened again. "They're going to keep giving it to him until he dies." She took a deep breath, getting her act together. "He's in an old insane asylum." She wrapped her arms around herself at the thought.

Eric's eyes widened. "Lucas told you that?"

"No, Cyrus did. The voices, they're . . . people who have died. Cyrus was one of them. He said the asylum was near, but I don't know if he was going to tell me it was near here or near something else before I lost the connection."

Eric said, "We'll research old asylums. Once we find some likely candidates, I'll remote view them. Let's eat. Then I'll check it out."

Amy knew she was going to be holding her breath all through dinner. Time was running out.

Gerard Darkwell woke Lucas from whatever had spiked his brain waves. "What's happening?"

Lucas blinked awake, his eyes hazy, his voice weak.

"Amy. She said someone was tracking her down. She's only trying to get safe . . . not rescuing me."

He looked like hell. They'd almost lost him, and he was still fading.

"She has no powers, so she's not valuable to us," Gerard said. "As long as she stays away from here and any other Offspring, she's perfectly safe."

Lucas struggled to sit up on the bed. "I hope to hell you're a man of honor." He looked doubtful.

Gerard knew that Lucas would be gone by the time Amy was apprehended. At least at this rate, he thought. Damn Steele had failed to catch two women. Two *women*, for God's sake. He hadn't even come up on Mr. Pyro yet.

"One more mission, Lucas, and your work is done. This one is very important. Very sensitive." Gerard tacked a photograph on the corkboard, followed by a map. "And easy. We know exactly where the target is. Right here, where the red arrow is. Study the information; I'll have to take it with me."

After a minute Lucas said, "Got it."

Gerard removed the two papers and walked to the door. "Don't see this as doing it for me. You're doing it for your country."

He walked out, where Peterson was waiting. "I'll need you here tomorrow at five in the morning," he said to him. "We'll put him in deprivation mode, have him complete one last mission, and then we'll give him the fourth injection."

"Are you sure, sir? That will finish him."

"I'm sure. He's not strong enough to put up a big fight, but bring one of the guards with you just in case."

Peterson nodded, showing no emotion at all. Like a good soldier.

Having Lucas around was becoming more of a liability than an asset, particularly with his connection to Amy Shane. What if she were caught or shot? He didn't trust an enraged Lucas, even in a weakened state. Look what Eric Aruda had done.

No, better to finish him off sooner than later.

Gerard walked back to Robbins's office, but he wasn't there. He located him in the doctor's lounge with the orange walls, sitting on one of the gray sofas watching CNN.

"Breaking news," Robbins said. "They just found out that Muhammed Muzaham is dead in a London flat. Died in his sleep. Without him, the cell turned on each other. There have been fourteen arrests."

Gerard smiled. "I heard. Lucas's second mission was a success. You have to admit it's satisfying to have that kind of impact on terrorism."

Robbins reluctantly nodded. "We saved lives."

Maybe there was hope for Robbins yet. "Hundreds of lives, and think of the terror we've prevented people feeling. We're doing a good thing here." Now he would seal Robbins's loyalty with a bit of information he'd just learned. "This was the group that bombed the house where your cousin was hiding out in Afghanistan. These are the people who killed him."

Robbins stood. "You're sure?"

"We're sure."

He lowered his head for a moment.

"Feels good, doesn't it?"

Robbins curled his hands into fists. "Yeah, it does."

"Back to the problem at hand. We're still having trouble locating the Rogues' hideout. They've either got a block on it or maybe it's near an energy or magnetic field. I could torture Lucas for the information, but I know he'd never give them away and I need him for other things. Any luck on your end?"

Robbins stood. "I've looked up their families' properties going back three generations. Now I'm working on friends, but that's a short list."

"We'll find them. They're obviously in the area. Go home, celebrate our victory. It's yours, too, you know."

Robbins tilted his head. "I notice you call Lucas by his first name."

"I address him by his first name to sound . . . friendlier. It just becomes habit to refer to him that way. Don't think I'm getting soft on him." He narrowed his eyes. "He's the enemy. The enemy is just a machine, Robbins. A machine we're going to shut down."

CHAPTER 20

It was 5:30 A.M. Amy, Eric, and Petra had spent most of the night researching insane asylums, unearthing article after article, and consulting maps. Or rather, Eric and Petra did, because Amy sat next to the map feeling left out. Sitting at the computer, Eric read off story after story on military hospitals and sanatoriums, and Petra marked them on the map. Occasionally Amy was able to find the location before Petra did.

Amy said, "I can get around the Internet fast." *Faster*, she didn't say. She wiggled her fingers.

"If I need something typed up, " Eric replied, "I'll let you know."

She grimaced in frustration. "You type with your pointer fingers. Tap. Tap. Tap."

"Shut, shut, shut up." He rolled his neck. "Petra, give me one of your miraculous massages. My shoulders are killing me."

She stood and rubbed his shoulders as he kept trolling the Internet.

Amy held her tongue on Eric's smart-assed remark. "Miraculous massage?"

Petra shrugged. "Everyone says my massages cure them. Headaches, shoulder aches, that kind of thing."

"Her hands get warm, too," he said.

"I even thought about training to become a massage therapist, but the thought of touching strangers"—she shuddered—"I couldn't do it."

"Why not?"

"It's literally uncomfortable, like the time I pushed a wire out of the way and it was still charged. It went through my body. That's how it feels when I touch someone." That bothered her on a deeper level. "Maybe I'm just cold or . . . uncuddly."

Amy thought of her porcupine poster.

Eric made groaning noises as he rolled his neck under Petra's touch. "Much better."

"Good, get back to work," Amy said.

He tilted the chair at a precarious angle. "Here's something. It's dated eight years ago. The Merrill State Mental Hospital was a civilian asylum and then was used for military personnel suffering from things like post-traumatic stress disorder. Funding disappeared and the place was closed. Apparently it needs a lot of work or should be demolished altogether."

"That sounds promising. Print it out," Amy said. "And keep looking."

"Yes, ma'am," he said, giving her a mock salute.

She gave him a mock salute back with one particular finger extended. She nearly ruined the moment by laughing at his shocked expression.

He gave Petra the coordinates to find it on the map, ignoring Amy. Petra rolled her eyes. "Look, we're stuck down here together for God knows how long in this place with no windows, no sunlight, sameness." She shuddered. "We have to get along or at least be civil." To Amy, she said, "If you're engaging Eric in a power struggle, forget it. You won't win and everyone will be miserable." She shot him a look. "Everyone but him. He'll love it."

Amy saw the challenge in his expression. "I'm not interested in a power struggle," she said. "But I do insist on respect."

Eric had already tuned them out, continuing to tap on the keys. Tap. Tap. Tap. Amy twitched with each tap.

"Here's another promising one, and it's near Fort Meade. It was built in the 1800s, went through a few different transitions, but has always been military something or another. I can't tell what it is now." He printed it out. "How many do we have?"

"Three possibilities in this area, three more farther out," Petra said.

He got down on the floor with them and studied the map. His fingers touched one of the marks Petra had made. "I'll start here, the last one I found."

He rolled onto his back and closed his eyes. Like before, he took several minutes to sink into a semiconscious state. His body began to tremble. Sweat broke out on his upper lip. His breathing deepened.

Even though Amy knew what he was experiencing, it was still spooky to watch. She'd endure it a thousand times to see Lucas. She glanced at Petra, whose expression tensed with fear as she stared at Eric.

"What are you afraid of?" Amy whispered. "Is there something dangerous about remote viewing?"

"There wasn't until someone was at the other end. Someone like us."

Amy nodded. They didn't know the boundaries of their powers. Or the dangers.

Eric's mouth, usually in a hard line, softened. She imagined this was what he looked like in sleep, those strong features relaxed, the anger muted. He mumbled for a few seconds and then his words became intelligible. "People. Busy place. Checking out basement." He winced. "Dead people."

Amy's heartbeat jumped. "Who?"

"One's getting cut open. Autopsy. Oh, shit. This is the morgue."

She exchanged a relieved look with Petra.

"Coming back," Eric said.

A few moments later he opened unfocused eyes. They met hers, and she got that uncomfortable feeling that accompanied her memories of what she'd seen in his mind. She always used her plain clothing and unruly hair to create a wall around her, so she rarely had to deal with admiring looks or sexual innuendo. Ozzie was subtle, and certainly not sensual. Seeing blatant desire made her feel clammy inside.

"It was just a regular hospital," he said, his voice softer now that he was tired. He sat up and studied the map. "I'm going to try the next one." He settled on the floor again and closed his eyes. "This is the one that was shut down eight years ago."

It took several more minutes before he sank into the ethers. "I see the building. It's not as big as the last one, only one story, but it's wide. There's a tall fence around it. Weeds growing all over, looks abandoned. Except . . . ah, very interesting. There are two armed guards patrolling the perimeter. I see about five cars in the parking lot. I'm going to get closer."

His eyebrows furrowed. "I can't get through the roof. It's like there's a shield. I'm going to try to punch through—" His face tightened. His body stiffened. "Almost." A moment later his eyes snapped opened. "I got kicked back again, just like when we went to Lucas."

"That's it!" Amy said, hope rushing through her body.

Eric's voice sounded weak. "That's the good news. The bad news is they probably know that we know."

"What do you mean?" Petra blurted out.

"If an enemy Offspring put the shield on, he might know if someone tried to come through."

"We may be looking," Amy said, "but if we can't get in, we don't have verification. They can't be sure we'd try anything based on a hunch."

Petra nodded toward her. "Annoyingly optimistic, isn't she?"

"Just annoying," Eric said, and stretched out on the floor again. "I'm going to go back but stay overhead and not alert anyone to my presence."

This time Amy didn't watch him. She read through the article on the defunct asylum. "This has to be it," she whispered, handing it to Petra, who was watching Eric.

It didn't take him long to open his eyes. He looked more tired than before, but grabbed a notepad and sketched the building's outline and perimeter. "The building's a wreck. I don't get the impression this is a high-level operation."

Amy popped a raisin in the air and caught it in her mouth, a poor substitute for chocolate-covered cranberries. "Remember, this program is off the records.

Whoever's heading this isn't going to be able to requisition a bunch of guards."

Eric said, "They still have the resources of the U.S. government behind them. Do you know how many experiments have been done under the shield of 'Classified'? Dozens, if not more. While I waited to see if you two made it back here alive, I trolled around on the Internet. I didn't find anything about DARK MATTER or BLUE EYES, but I found secret psychic projects that were declassified. In one they even explored remote viewing, though without any concrete results. And no one had pyrokinesis," he added with a touch of pride.

"That the public knew about," Amy added, just to keep him in check.

He gave her a frigid smile but with a shrug conceded, "There was plenty on those reports that was still blacked out. I saw nothing about a cocktail given to the subjects either, but in one program, subjects were secretly given LSD. One guy flipped out and threw himself out a window." He got to his feet and stretched.

While the computer was free, Amy got on and typed in the asylum's address on Google's satellite image maps. "Here it is, about forty minutes from here, give or take, depending on traffic. And if I'm not mistaken, tomorrow—well, today, technically—is Saturday, so traffic should be light."

Eric said, "We're not going today. We've got to make a plan."

"Every hour that passes brings less hope of rescuing Lucas alive."

He looked at both of them and took a breath, as

though gathering strength. "We're not going to bring Lucas back alive."

"What?" Amy balled her hands into fists, ready to fight. "The hell we aren't."

"When he came to warn me you were in trouble, he said he'd be dead soon. There's no hope, Amy."

She felt a rush of cold wash over her. "There's always hope!"

He shook his head. "Lucas's right. We're not risking a rescue. Only a recon."

She got in his face. "No! We are not giving up!"

"He doesn't want us risking our lives for his dead body."

She pounded on his chest. "We can't leave him there! He's just trying to protect us."

He grabbed her wrists, jerking her against him. "That's right! He's trying to protect us from getting killed. Or getting caught. They're putting something in him that's tearing him down. Killing him. We have to accept that we're not going in to bring Lucas back. We're going in to find the truth. We have to be stealthy. That means being unemotional, cool, and calm. You are not unemotional about Lucas. So you'd better get that through that pretty head of yours."

The truth about her dad's suicide and who she was had been important to her in the beginning but now had taken a distant second to finding Lucas. "Maybe you can be unemotional. Maybe you don't have a heart. I can't!" Her breaths were coming quickly. "You can pretend you're cold and detached, but that's a damned lie! We are *not* giving up—"

Eric kissed her, hard and without mercy.

After a moment of shock she shoved him away. "Don't you ever touch me again."

"You're getting hysterical. That seemed better than cuffing you."

"Eric!" Petra said.

Amy wiped her hand over her lips, rubbing away the imprint of his mouth on hers. Okay, maybe she'd gotten a bit overwrought. She took several calming breaths.

His glow was jagged. "We can't go in guns and emotions blazing. Doing that will get you killed."

"You know that Lucas is just telling us not to get him in order to protect us. You said earlier that he was noble. So forget what he said. What we know is that he *will* die if we leave him there. If we rescue him, we at least have a chance of saving him. I don't care what condition he's in; we're getting him out of there."

Eric studied her face, obviously seeing her conviction and hearing it beneath her calmly spoken words because he said, "We need to rest today. Don't go off and do anything stupid. We'll go tonight."

"To bring Lucas back," Amy said.

He met her gaze, then Petra's. "To bring Lucas back."

Lucas woke in the dark, sure that he was in an oven. He'd heard the chime. Time for his third mission. He tried to sit up but had no strength. Sweat covered his body. Not an oven. The heat was inside him, burning through his veins.

Got to get through this. One more time. Amy will be safe.

He had no choice but to believe, to cooperate. He summoned the memory of the man's picture. Dark hair, wavy, something exotic about his looks.

When he tried to sink into the zone, though, his mind faltered. He was already seeing the shapes floating in the darkness. This deprivation was driving him insane. Or was it the Booster? He was slipping away from sanity. That's the only thing he was sure of anymore.

The shapes morphed into images. Memories, of his childhood, of the five children at the inflatable pool, Amy with her freckles and wild hair, each image coming faster. Then the storm began. He saw the man with the beaten face again. He was screaming, arching his body. Another man standing by him. Giving him an injection. The same brawny man who had given Lucas the first injection and claimed to be a nurse. The Devil's voice: *Your mission . . .* The man telling the Devil to go screw himself. The Devil: *If you want your grandmother to live . . .* Then, strangely, he saw the children again. Zeroed in on the boy, the fifth child . . . saw the boy's face. Rand. Then he saw the bruised face. He was here. The person he'd seen being wheeled down the hall.

Hell, they had him, too.

The images ceased. For a moment, quiet, and then he saw the target. The man was sleeping in an elaborate, four-poster bed, the dawn light spilling in through an immense arched window. The woman next to him lifted her head, looked at the clock, and then lay down again. Lucas centered over the man and then floated away. He was losing control, like a Macy's parade balloon with only one rope holding it to the earth. He struggled to maintain his position. He was tired, so damned tired.

Even in sleep the man's face was all hard lines and furrowed brows.

Let him be a bastard.

And he went in . . .

Olivia returned to the facility later that day, feeling anxious and restless. She'd forgotten some papers she wanted to work on, but in truth just needed to escape her family's dynamics. This place was no serene escape, though. It gave her the creeps, especially when there weren't many people here.

She found herself again in the east wing, where the criminally insane had once been housed and the prisoners were kept now. She passed the darkened room where the newest one was being held. Farther down, where a guard was hovering just outside an open doorway, she heard Peterson's tense voice: "Come on, stop moving already. Let's get this over with."

"What's going on?" she asked.

Harry Peterson, a big, muscular guy with a military haircut, jerked his head toward the door where she stood. "What are you doing here on a Saturday?"

"I have no life."

"I told you I could fix that." His cheeks actually reddened. He wasn't the man she wanted to fix her lonely life. Though she liked him, it was one of the subjects who had caught her attention. Any kind of relationship there would be frowned on. His expression sobered. "You shouldn't be in this wing."

"I know. Darkwell's a hard-ass."

Peterson smiled. "Yeah."

She walked in, and saw that the prisoner was burning up again, feverish and delirious. He was on the bed trembling and murmuring, his eyes closed. "Boy by the pool . . . get him out . . . "

"What's going on?"

"I need to give him an injection, but he's shaking so hard I'll never hit the vein."

She nodded to the needle that contained a milky blue substance. "What is it?"

"Something to help him."

"Like what?"

"Not my place to say."

"Why the secret?"

He shrugged. "Look, I'm just following orders. To be honest, I'm not even sure what's in it."

She digested that for a moment. He was probably telling the truth. Darkwell was notoriously secretive about things.

She leaned over and put her hand on the man's forehead. "He's burning up again. We need to cool him down."

"It doesn't matter. He—" Peterson held his words. "He'll sweat it out eventually."

"He won't sweat it out. This man's probably got a temperature of a hundred and five." She unbuttoned his shirt. "Help me get him out of these clothes and in the tub."

Darkwell called Peterson a nurse, but Olivia doubted he had more than sketchy medical training. They maneuvered Lucas out of his clothing. His skin nearly burned her.

"He should be taken to a hospital."

"Can't do that."

"Why not? Prisoners have a right to medical treatment."

"Not this one. Let it go, Olivia."

She took the man's feet, Peterson took his upper body, and they carried him down the hall to a room at the end. The shower area had a musty smell. They carried him through the open room and to the far stall that held a tub. It was probably for patients who couldn't stand. The once white porcelain was now gray and stained. She ran the water as she had the last time, and they lowered Lucas in.

The guard who patrolled the hallway had followed them. Olivia said, "Look, this guy isn't even going to open his eyes, much less attack me." She looked at the gorgeous man in the tub. He must have done something terrible for Darkwell to deny him medical care. He didn't look like a terrorist, but looks were deceiving.

The guard paid her words little attention, still hovering in the hallway.

She turned to Peterson. "You look exhausted."

"I've been in this morbid place for ten hour shifts." He looked at his watch. "I'm on my last hour, and all I've got to do is give him the injection, and then I was going to eat dinner and grab a snooze in the lounge."

"Why don't you go home early? I'll take care of him."

Peterson frowned. "I can't leave. Darkwell wants us around. He's wary of trouble."

"He's always wary of trouble. Well, go, grab your dinner and a nap." She looked at the man in the tub. "His name's Lucas, right?"

"Yeah. All right, maybe I will take a quick snooze. Hey, you haven't grown keen on this guy, have you? You seem to like hanging around, taking care of him."

"Of course not." She looked at the prisoner, with enviable cheekbones and the kind of mouth a woman might want to lose herself in. Not her, but another woman. Like maybe this Amy he kept asking for. "But I am interested in what he's done to end up here and what Darkwell's doing to him."

Peterson shrugged. "You'll have to take that up with—"

"Darkwell, I know. He won't tell me either." She ran a wet washcloth over the man's forehead.

"Thanks, Olivia." As Peterson left, his footsteps echoed through the shower room and down the hall. She continued to drip water over Lucas's face, wondering what his story was.

A few minutes later she heard footsteps coming back. Didn't Peterson trust her?

He walked in, looking agitated. "Someone took my dinner. Again. This place drives me crazy, no pun intended. You don't have any crackers in your desk, do you?"

"Sorry, no. Why don't you go to that bikers' bar down the road? I'm sure they've got some kind of food there."

Again he looked conflicted.

She said, "No one will know. Darkwell won't be back tonight. As soon as Lucas is stable, I'll give him the injection. I'm good at sticking. Go on. Eat and sleep. You look almost as bad as he does. Mr. Personality out there will keep me safe."

Peterson nodded, though he still appeared doubtful. "All right. You've got my number in case you need me." After another moment of indecision, he left.

She stopped the water when it just covered Lucas's body and checked his pulse. It was fleeting.

His body wrenched as if in pain. His muscles contracted, defining them sharply. "Amy. No, Amy!"

"It's all right, Lucas," she said, trying to calm him. It wasn't, but she couldn't tell him that. His body finally relaxed and he sank back into unconsciousness. "Who is Amy? And why are you so worried about her?" She expected no answer. She moistened the washcloth and dabbed it over his face. "You must be one bad dude," she whispered. And unfortunately for him, she thought, he was probably one dead dude, too.

CHAPTER 21

"I'm a *decoy*?" Amy shouted as Eric outlined the plan. "No way. I want to go in. Let Petra be the decoy."

They sat around the table with a rough sketch of the facility in front of them. Eric gave her the kind of look a tired parent would give a child. "I need her hearing ability. And she's fired a gun before. Have you?"

"No, but—"

"Distracting the guards is a damned important job, Amy, so stop bitching. Have Petra sex you up like she did before."

"I'm going in."

"You just want to find Lucas, and what I don't need is you getting hysterical or going off when you find him dead or something."

She crossed her arms over her chest, trying not to think about Lucas being dead. "This coming from the man who sets people on fire."

"Stop, you two," Petra said, rubbing her temples. "You're getting on my nerves, this place is getting on my nerves, and I just want this over with."

He leaned back in his chair. "I'm not trying to be contrary or leave you out, Amy. We need someone to keep the guards distracted in the front while we go in."

He had pulled up old blueprints of the original asylum on the Internet. The outbuildings had been torn down over the years. "And we need you to be ready with the car when we come tearing out. I'm going to try to find Lucas. If he's still alive, he'll probably be in the east wing where the patients were kept. Petra's going to try to find anything of value to us, records, someone's computer, whatever. I don't think there are a lot of people on-site, judging by the few cars parked in the lot." He put his hands on the table and looked at each of them. "Ready?"

Amy's heart thudded in her chest. She nodded.

Eric went to a storage room in the far corner of the kitchen and opened it. He took out two rifles and two handguns and then pulled out boxes of ammo. She hadn't known all that was here, which was probably better. She wasn't comfortable around guns. Neither was Petra, by the look on her face, but she was resigned. So was Amy.

He said, "The people who set up this shelter armed it, too. There are eight twelve-gauge shotguns here. The .357 magnums are mine."

"Do I get one, too?" Amy asked.

"You can't shoot," he said, loading the ammo into a leather satchel.

"I bet I can at close range."

He looked at his watch. "We've got ten minutes. Let's go downstairs and I'll give you a quick lesson. For emergencies only." He met her eyes. "Just don't shoot one of us."

She wrinkled her nose. "Don't tempt me."

* * *

As soon as the sun went down, Amy, Eric, and Petra walked around the old asylum. The woods surrounding it contained the foundations of the old buildings that had once been scattered throughout the property. A tall fence surrounded the asylum itself, enough to discourage the curious but not necessarily keep out the determined. Not that Amy could imagine anyone being simply curious about the creepy, dingy building. The thought of men and women imprisoned there, as well as in their minds, was disturbing. The thought of Lucas imprisoned there was horrifying.

The asylum was a wide building, with a center portion deeper than the two wings on either side. The entrance was simple, and inside they could see a reception desk and an armed guard. The left wing sported large windows with curtains, some of the rooms with lights on. The right side had small windows, and these were high up.

Amy said, "Lucas said his room had a window but it was blocked."

They moved around to the back of the building.

Eric said, "I wish I could take a look."

They had agreed it would be better if he didn't remote view. They didn't want to alert their enemy, and he needed all of his strength.

Amy pointed at a window in the middle of the wing. "It's blocked out with wood. There's another one at the far end."

Eric held the binoculars to his eyes. "He's got to be in one of those. Or at least that's where he was."

Pain lanced her. She had to believe he was alive, though Eric kept reminding her of the unlikelihood of that. But Lucas's words about dying came back to her, the ones she'd chosen to ignore: *Dying is better than being here. I'm not afraid to die.*

She suspected he was suffering far more than he let on. Trying, once again, to protect her. He couldn't protect her heart from shattering, though.

They continued to trek around the perimeter, staying in the shadows of the woods. A light burned in two windows of the far corner of the west wing. Petra tuned in to see if she could hear anything but shook her head.

The scrape of shoe against concrete froze them. One of the two guards walked toward the fence. Amy held her breath. Had he heard them? She could only see his silhouette, the lights in the parking lot casting him in shadow. When he got to the fence, he reached inside his coat. Was he calling for backup? Getting a weapon? His glow was hard to discern from a distance. Normally if someone were agitated or impassioned, their glow would flare out, but these men were trained to remain calm. She could tell, however, that neither guard was an Offspring.

The flame ignited at his chest level. Both Amy and Petra jerked around to look at Eric, who raised his hands and then nodded toward the man. The flare of a lighter sent relief through her in more ways than one. The guard walked slowly along the fence until he reached the far corner, then returned along the same path.

"Carl!" a man called out, and the guard near them walked toward the front.

They tensed again. Now they wondered if the other guard had seen something. The two men converged at the center of the lot, and Petra aimed her ear at them to listen.

Eric said, "You don't have to do that. You hear them in your head."

"Shh."

Another light flared and the second man lit his cigarette. They spoke for a few minutes, laughing about something, then parted to continue their patrols.

"All right," Eric said. "Time to get in gear. Amy, you ready?"

She nodded even as her gaze returned to the two blocked windows. She wanted to go inside and look for Lucas. Instead she was wearing a little black dress and a ruby necklace.

They made their way around to the east side again. They heard noise at the front entrance. Laughter. Distance voices. Petra tilted her head.

Two people in coats walked out and toward the parking lot. Both had a casual glow . . . of muted colors. A few minutes later a car started and pulled around to the front gate, where one of the guards let them out.

Petra said, "It was a man and a woman."

"Offspring," Amy said.

Eric watched the car's taillights disappear down the road. "Two of them." He looked at Petra. "What'd they say?"

"He said he was glad to get out of there for a while but they had to be back soon. When they walked closer to the car . . . " Her expression was rigid, her gaze still on the place where the two had been. "He told her that he'd try to lock onto me when they got back."

"We don't have long," Eric said. "Let's move."

Amy watched them get in position as she walked back to the car they'd appropriated and was now parked off the road where no one would see it. Alone, she pulled out the small note with some cash tucked inside and slid it beneath the front seat. The note read: *Sorry for any damage to your car.*

She took a swig from the bottle of tequila, dumped part of it out in the grass, and got behind the wheel. "Here goes."

A few minutes later she was swerving down the road leading to the asylum. The tires screeched as she slammed on the brakes just before the gate entrance. The car then swung out of control for a few seconds before coming to a stop. The guard ran over but stayed within the fence.

"Ma'am, are you all right?"

She feigned a disoriented look. "Who put the fence in?" she screamed, a hysterical edge in her voice. "When I left a few hours ago, there wasn't a fence!" She got out of the car, her body like rubber. Her feet were bare since sneakers would have looked strange. She blinked at the building as she tugged down her dress.

"I don't know where you think you are—"

"The Hyatt, of course."

The guard was probably in his thirties, and as she got close, he winced at the liquor on her breath. "Ma'am, this is a government facility."

The other guard came over, too. "What's going on?"

"Oh, God." She slapped her hand over her mouth, trying hard not to let her gaze stray to the right where she saw a dash of movement. "Where am I? I'm lost!

First my boyfriend, who I flew down here with, blows me off, and now"—she jerked around, panic in her expression—"I don't know where I am. And I think I'm going to get sick . . . " She wobbled, and they quickly backed away. "I'm so dizzy." With a cry in her voice, she said, "I had too much to drink." She slumped to the ground.

"Hell," the first guard said.

That's when the smoke alarm went off. Thank God they still worked. Eric was worried that with the building being so old they might not.

Both men raced toward the entrance.

She was hoping they'd have opened the gate first so she could run in, too. But, damn it, her job was to be the getaway driver. She got back in the car, adrenaline shooting through her body, and bounced in her seat, wringing her hands. *Please let them find Lucas.*

Petra wanted to stay with Eric. His job was to find Lucas, and she wanted to find him, too. She couldn't bear the thought of Lucas being dead, and every time Eric tried to ready them for that possibility it cut her to her core. She knew that was why he'd given her and Amy other jobs. What would she do if she found dead the boy she'd loved since almost forever?

She pushed away the thought and watched Amy do her number while she waited in the bushes near the front entrance. When the alarm went off, she jumped. *Here I go.*

The outside guards ran to the entrance, and someone inside unlocked the door. "There's a fire in the back hallway! Help me get it out. The sprinkler system hasn't kicked on."

No one bothered to relock the door. She slipped inside and ducked behind the big reception desk. Smoke drifted in, along with an acrid smell. Men shouted, shoes squeaked on old linoleum floors. A fire extinguisher hissed. Not much time. She surveyed the area. The fire had started straight back from the desk. To the left she saw a darkened room with cafeteria tables, and past that another hallway led to the west wing. Directly to her right were offices. Bingo.

She darted down the hallway and ran into the first office. It was neat and feminine, with a vase of flowers on the desk. Knowing that two men ran the program, she moved on. The next office was empty but for a broken desk and credenza. She ran to the next one. Papers and pencils littered the desktop. She opened file drawers looking for anything relevant but found nothing. The last office looked more promising. Through the window in the door she saw two monitors, one showing vital signs and another that showed a room. She turned the knob. It wouldn't budge. *Damn!*

"Find another extinguisher!" a man called.

Footsteps echoed down the main hallway. She pulled out the pin Eric had given her and inserted it into the lock.

"There's one over by the offices!" someone yelled.

She looked up. An extinguisher was mounted on the wall at the end of the hallway. Within her sight.

Within sight of her.

She ran to the opposite door. An empty room, no place to hide. She ran to the next door and opened it. This room was filled with hiding places: cabinets, a desk, shelving.

Footsteps just around the corner.

She dashed in and closed the door just as a man yelled, "Found it!" Wedging herself beneath the desk, she pulled the chair as close as she could. A second later someone opened the door.

Eric worked on the lock by the side entrance. Somewhere inside he heard a man shout, "Get out! There's smoke coming down the hallway!" Then the alarm went off. He just about had the lock picked when the door flew open. He stumbled backward but caught his balance. A woman with long dark hair rushed out. Then she saw him. Before she could scream, he decked her. She fell to the ground in a heap.

He ran in and ducked into the first room on the right, the one with the lights on. It reminded him of his high school locker room, with its little green tiles, cruddy drains, and the smell of sweat and mildew. His footsteps echoed as he followed the light to another room. A large therapy tub sat off to the side with a chair next to it.

Lucas was in the tub. In his briefs. His head was tilted back, his eyes closed, his hair plastered to his cheeks. He knew Lucas wasn't relaxing; his face was too slack for consciousness. He ran over, dropping to his knees as he tapped Lucas's face. "Hey! It's Eric. Come on, man, wake up!"

Lucas murmured.

"You're going to make this hard on me, aren't you?"

Lucas slumped farther into the tub.

"Shit."

He pulled Lucas up by the shoulders to get a good grip on him. Or the best grip he could get on a wet body. A deadweight body. But not dead. He didn't let himself feel relief yet. With a groan, he lifted Lucas out of the tub and over his shoulder. Water sluiced down over him. He lost his balance. Regained it. He walked back through the shower, ready to encounter someone who might stop him. He hoped the woman was still out cold. He peered into the hallway. Smoke drifted like the ghosts this place probably had. He heard voices, but not frantic ones. They had the small blaze under control.

Then he heard a voice, muffled, accompanied by a banging sound. "Hey! Let me out of here!" It came from two rooms down the hall.

No time to investigate. He headed to the exit door. The woman was indeed still out. He stepped over her and then had a most disturbing thought: how was he going to get Lucas over the fence?

Amy kept scanning the front and the side entrances, looking for movement. Every muscle was knot-hard, ready for action and beginning to ache from it. Soon the guards would return. Eric was only supposed to start a small fire, nothing that would catch and burn the place down. That also meant it wouldn't take long to extinguish.

The movement she'd been poised for caught her eye at the east exit where Eric had gone in. She saw him lumbering out, and . . . he was carrying someone!

"Lucas!"

Except he was *carrying* Lucas, which meant he wasn't conscious or—please, God, no—alive. Eric weaved as he made his way toward the fence. The fence! How would he get Lucas out?

With a whispered prayer, she jammed her foot on the gas and headed right at the fence. She got a glimpse of Eric's surprised face in the headlights, then the fence came at her, and then she heard the screech of metal scraping metal. The fence collapsed over the car. Eric climbed under one piece. She jumped out and ran around the front of the car.

"Get the door!" Eric said, obviously thinking that she was running over to see Lucas.

"That's what I'm doing!"

She opened the rear door and helped pull him onto the backseat. Lucas, here, finally here. "He's wet. He's naked." But hot, which meant alive. Tears momentarily blinded her, and she blinked them away. "Where's Petra?"

He scanned the area with jerky movements. "I don't see her."

"What do we do?" She scrambled out of the back-seat and closed the door.

Pain and indecision wracked his face. "We gotta get out of here. She knows the backup plan." In case anyone got left behind. Or caught.

Two guards ran out the front entrance.

"Go," he said. "I'll keep an eye out for her."

They both jumped in. She wished he was driving so she could check on Lucas, but they didn't have time to switch places. She tore out of the parking lot just as the guards reached the gate.

"Go faster," he said, and she envied his calm.

They burned asphalt and rubber down the road before turning onto the highway. Within a few minutes they reached the place where they would ditch the borrowed car, then transferred Lucas to the Camry. Looking at the front of the banged-up car they would leave behind, she realized she hadn't left enough money.

This time Eric ran to the driver's side. She climbed into the backseat of the Camry and wedged herself around Lucas's body. He was on his side, bent into the fetal position to fit him in. She kept her gaze behind them, fighting not to look at Lucas. She knew she'd get completely lost if she did, and she needed to watch for pursuers.

Two minutes passed. Ten. Fifteen.

"I think we lost them," Amy said.

"We lost Petra, too." Anger permeated his words.

"She's all right. We have to believe that."

"She was supposed to scream if she got caught. I never heard her scream. I would have heard it." He was trying to convince himself.

"She's hiding. There are probably lots of places to hide in a building like that."

"But how do we get her out?"

"I don't know." She let her gaze fall to Lucas. Water glistened on his body. "Why is he wet and almost naked?"

"He was in a tub. He's burning up, so maybe they were trying to cool his fever. There was a woman with him, I think. She ran out the side door, and I cold-cocked her. Maybe she was a nurse."

Amy touched Lucas's skin. "Damn, he *is* hot. Open the windows, let in the cool air." She opened the two windows in the back. Wind soon swirled in, ruffling Lucas's hair. She placed the back of her hand against his cheek. "Lucas. Can you hear me?"

"He's out of it." Eric glanced at her in the rearview mirror. "And he might not come out. Just be prepared for that."

"I will not prepare for that."

"Amy, *he* doesn't think he'll make it."

She'd read and watched stories of tragic romance and thought that was how true love always ended. But now that she'd found love, she could not accept it ending that way.

She brushed her mouth against his cheek and whispered, "You will not die and leave me alone, Lucas. Do you hear me?"

CHAPTER 22

Petra held her breath when the door opened. She saw black pants and blue pumps.

A woman said, "I'm okay. I just need to sit down."

Someone pulled out the chair Petra had been using to shield herself from view. *Oh, no, I'm busted!* But it was only turned to face away from the desk. The woman dropped down onto it.

"What happened?" the man asked. He opened a cabinet, but Petra couldn't see what he was doing.

The woman hissed in pain but stilled it with a deep breath. "I ran outside when Hanson told me about the fire. I was going to pull the prisoner outside, if necessary. Someone was standing right there, and he hit me with something. Son of a bitch."

Eric. Despite the circumstances, Petra smiled. This woman was the enemy. She couldn't be bothered to feel bad for her.

"Did you see him?"

"Just a blur. Big guy. It was dark."

"Here, press this on the wound. You're going to have a real goose egg. Any dizziness?"

"A bit. I'm fine, though."

"Too bad Peterson left. He'd know what to do. Maybe you should go to the hospital."

She said, "I can't do that. Too many questions."

"Good point."

Petra let out shallow breaths, praying that she didn't sneeze. *Good job, introduce that thought in your head.* Dust bunnies had made whole colonies under there.

Another man ran in, breathless. "They're gone. Carl's trying to track them down, but they had a head start."

They were gone. She felt both relief and bereft. Well, that was the plan. If one got caught, the others had to scram. No point in all of them getting caught. Her phone. She could call them. *Please, don't let them call me.* Even though the phone was on vibrate mode, she couldn't take a chance on them hearing something.

"The prisoner is gone," the woman said, fear in her voice. "I'm never going to hear the end of this. It was my idea to cool him down by putting him in the tub."

"Did he have anything to do with this? Was he faking it?"

"No. He couldn't fake a fever like that. The man is nearly dead."

Petra winced at that. But Lucas was free.

"Does Darkwell know?" the woman asked.

"We called him as soon as the fire was under control. He doesn't know Vanderwyck's gone. I sure as hell don't want to be the one to tell him."

"He still has the other one. I hope he'll be satisfied with that." The tone in her voice was doubtful.

The other one. Her? No, they didn't know she was there. Petra shivered. What did that mean?

The woman stood. "I'd better clean up before he gets here, face the music without mud on my face."

"The other two Offspring have been called to come back, too. Their little date just got messed up."

The woman remained after the man left. She pressed the pads on her cell phone. "Harry, it's Olivia. You'd better get back here. The Rogues broke in and took Lucas."

"Oh, hell," the man on the other end said. "Tell Darkwell I gave Vanderwyck the shot, okay?"

"Why is that important now?"

"Trust me, it is. Get that plunger and shoot the contents down the sink."

After a pause she said, "All right." She hung up and walked out. In the second that the door was open Petra saw the pin in the hallway that she'd been trying to use to jig the lock. Her heart dropped right down to her toes. If they saw it, they'd suspect someone had made it this far, and possibly hadn't made it back out.

The room went dark and the door closed. She crept out and, in the dim light from beneath the door, tried to get her bearings. She needed a better hiding place before the man that woman was afraid of showed up. Because whoever this Darkwell was, he was going to be pissed.

Lucas was there. Amy could touch him. See him. He was lying on the bed, naked but for a sheet corner that covered his private area. Though they had only briefly met, she knew every contour of his body, knew the feel of the stubble on his chin and the sparse hairs on his chest. He was as gorgeous in person as in her dreams. His olive skin looked sunburned and was covered in a sheen of sweat. The waves of his hair were damp at his neck.

The tub wasn't big enough to comfortably accommodate his body, so she exchanged damp washcloths in the refrigerator and rubbed them over his skin as he lay in the bed. She paused at the red scar on the right side of his abdomen: from when he'd saved her from the attack. And she hadn't even sustained a bruise during his rescue. It didn't seem fair somehow.

His glow was so faint she could barely see it. That scared her more than anything else. His body was fighting whatever they'd put into him. He had murmured a couple of times since they returned to the shelter but nothing intelligible.

Her heart was a lump as she ran the cloth over his chest in slow sweeping motions. She followed it with her fingers, trailing over his breastbone and the ridges of his stomach and down to the pale area above his pubic bone.

An indefinable feeling made her turn toward the door. Eric was standing there watching her. He was statuesque again, staring at Lucas or perhaps her hand on him. She saw something in his eyes that looked like a curious longing.

"He's the same," she said, uncomfortable with his scrutiny.

He walked closer, handing her a fresh cold cloth. "He's not trembling as much."

They'd turned off the heat, and the temperature hovered at sixty. "His pulse is stronger, too." She didn't know much about how fast it should be, but it seemed frighteningly faint when they'd gotten him here three hours ago.

. "Do you need a break? I can sit with him for a while."

"No," she said too quickly. "I'm fine. Thanks." She didn't want to leave him. She ran the back of her fingers against his cheek. "Lucas. Can you hear me?"

Nothing. She turned to Eric. He wore such an odd expression, she asked, "Are you all right?"

He nodded, turning away. "I guess you've got everything under control. He's in good hands." He glanced back at her. "Call if you need me. I'm going to crash for a while." He closed the door behind him.

She nodded but was already focused on Lucas. She leaned close to his face, touching her mouth to his so softly she barely felt it. "Lucas," she whispered. "Come back to me."

He shifted. Response! She was afraid to hope and yet couldn't allow herself to consider the alternative. She stretched out beside him, tucking her face into the crook of his neck and placing her arm over his stomach. It grew so hot, though, that she had to pull it off. "Lucas," she whispered. "It's Amy. I'm here. No more dreams, sweetheart. I'm here."

She drifted off and dreamed. She was on a train, feeling the tremble of the tracks vibrate through her. She reached to the door of her compartment; it was wet. She held out her palm, seeing a sheen on her skin.

She opened her eyes, thrust out of the dream by a realization: her hand really was wet. She was trembling. No, not her. She pushed herself up. Lucas. His body was covered in sweat. His fever had broken! He was still either asleep or unconscious. She ran to the hallway to tell Eric. He was asleep on the couch, the cell phone in his hand in case Petra called. She quietly got dry towels from the bathroom and returned to her room.

Lucas had pulled into a fetal position, shivering from cold. She turned on the heater and then wiped his body down. "Lucas. Can you hear me?"

This time he did murmur, and she thought he'd said her name. It made her heart jump. She pulled the blanket over him and tucked it over his shoulders. She glanced down at the sweatsuit she was wearing. Without a second thought she stripped out of it, climbed into bed, and wrapped her body around his. She willed her body heat into him as she held on tight. He felt so good against her. Alive. His heartbeat thumped beneath her ear. She closed her eyes and savored the sound and feel of him. If they could get through the night, he'd be all right. That's all she hoped for at the moment.

She drifted into sleep again until she heard a distant phone ringing. Not her ring. Her eyes popped open. Someone was calling Eric's phone. She hated the lack of windows in this place. Perpetual night. The clock read 3:32. Lucas was breathing softly, nice and even. She slipped out of bed, threw on her sweats, and walked out to the living room.

"Where are you?" Eric said into the phone, then looked at Amy as she sat next to him and said to her, "Petra."

Amy craned to hear the other end of the conversation. Petra's voice was barely audible. "I'm still in the asylum. I'm in some kind of medical supply room. They don't know I'm here. The man who's probably in charge of the program came in and he was over-the-top pissed about us getting Lucas out. I . . . I heard him say that as long as he got the last shot, he wouldn't be a problem. But he didn't get that shot so he should be okay. He's okay, isn't he?"

"His fever just broke," Amy said. "Now we need to get you out of there."

Eric said to his sister, "For God's sake, don't wig out."

"I'm . . . I'm doing all right. Everything has settled down a bit. I had to wait until it was quiet before I took the chance of calling. I'm going to try to get into the locked office. I dropped the lock pick in the hallway, though. I've got to get that before they see it."

"Shit," Eric muttered.

"I'm getting a sense of the guards' routine. I think I can manage it before daylight. Then I'll get out of here. I'll call and you can pick me up."

"I want you to call me every hour," he said.

"I don't want to use up the battery."

"All right. If you don't get out by tomorrow night, we're coming in."

"I'll get out. I have to go. It's time for the guard to come by. I'll talk to you soon." She disconnected.

Amy moved away from Eric. "Thank God they haven't found her."

"It may be a good thing, her being in there. She can pick up information. As long as she doesn't get caught." He pressed the phone against his mouth in thought. "You said Lucas's fever broke?"

"Yes. I'd better get back to him. I'm keeping him warm."

"I bet," he said under his breath. "At least I can get some real sleep. Petra's okay. Lucas is getting better." His relief was audible. When she stood, his gaze swept over her in the too-big sweats. "Keep me updated."

"I will."

She returned to Lucas and checked him in the dim light. He wasn't sweating or trembling anymore. She stripped again and climbed into bed with him. He was on his back now, his hand on his stomach. She snuggled against him and laid her hand over his. She rubbed her cheek against his shoulder, breathing in the faint scent of him. That was the one thing she'd never experienced in her dreams—his scent. She synchronized her breathing with his even breaths, not as shallow as when they'd brought him here. She had monitored his breathing by counting between his inhalations.

As she drifted back to sleep, his hand moved against hers. She opened her eyes. "Lucas?"

His face was still slack. An involuntary movement, probably, but movement nonetheless. She sighed, leaning her face against his shoulder again. She closed her fingers over his, twining them together. Sleep eluded her now. She wondered who the woman was who'd been with Lucas. An odd jealousy filled her; that woman had been with him while she hadn't. The woman had cared for him when she couldn't.

"Amy . . . "

She lifted her head again. He was struggling to open his eyes. She got up and sat beside him so he could see her. His mouth moved but no sound emerged.

"I'm here, baby." She traced her fingers over the curves of his face. "I'm here."

He opened his eyes. Beautiful blue-gray eyes, sleepy, slightly unfocused. Looking at her. Her joy transcended her smile, coming out as a laugh.

His voice was so soft she could barely hear it. "Am I dreaming?"

She shook her head and took his hand in hers, kissing it. "You're in the tomb. You're safe."

"*You're* safe," he said, a smile slowly forming. He touched her face as though he still couldn't believe she was real. He trailed his fingers down her neck, down between her bare breasts. She'd forgotten that she was naked. His hand rested on her stomach, warming her skin. No trembling. His smile widened.

She knew the relief that he felt. It burst in her heart. "Here, drink." She helped him sit up and then grabbed the bottle of water on the nightstand. He drank small sips until he'd finished the bottle. "I'll get you more."

"Did you put me in the tub?" he asked, his eyebrows furrowed. "Everything seems hazy."

"No, that was a woman at the hospital. You had a raging fever. We think she was trying to cool you down."

"How did I get here?"

Amy smiled in pride. "We busted in and rescued you."

"You shouldn't—"

She pressed a finger to his mouth. "Save your strength. I'll get you some more water."

She pulled on the sweats again and paused at the door, drinking him in just as he had drunk the water. Seeing him awake and lucid *was* like someone who was dying of thirst drinking water. He wasn't going to die, like he'd drawn. She closed her eyes and savored the relief in that. "Be right back."

Eric was sitting on the couch with his back to her. As she rounded the corner, it took a second for her to realize what he was doing. The steady movement of his hand, the flash of his naked leg—she caught her breath in embarrassment, which made him swivel around. He muttered an expletive as he pulled the blanket over him.

She grimaced, pressing the palm of her hand against her forehead. What would Miss Manners say? "Sorry," she murmured, keeping her gaze averted as she headed to the kitchen.

She heard him pulling on his pants behind her. "Lucas is awake," she went on, trying not to listen.

Eric walked into the kitchen as she took out two bottles of water and turned to find him too close. He didn't look exactly embarrassed, but possibly a bit chagrined. "How is he?"

"I think he's going to be all right. Come see."

He was asleep again, his head cocked to an angle on the pillow Amy had set behind him. "Lucas," she whispered.

He didn't answer. She could see a difference in his expression now; he wasn't out, just asleep. He looked content. Secure. She set the bottles on the nightstand and forced herself to turn to Eric. "I'll see you in the morning. Maybe he'll really be up then."

"Look—"

"Don't." She shook her head. "Don't worry about it. Good night."

He left, closing the door behind him. Amy pressed her fingers against her eyelids. Oversexed Offspring males. She took in Lucas. It sounded like he was ramped up sexually, too. Her mouth quirked. She hoped so.

After stripping bare, she lay against him. He rolled to his side and pulled her close, as naturally as though they'd been sharing a bed for years. Something swirled inside her, curling like smoke through her veins. How long had it been since she'd been held? Physically held? Long, long years filled with lonely months and weeks and days and hours of a yearning she'd buried deep inside her.

No more.

She pressed her cheek against his arm and, with a smile, drifted off to sleep.

Petra waited for the guard to walk past the room and turn the corner. She counted to three and opened the door. She was most exposed here, not knowing if anyone was within sight or whether someone would come from either end of the hall. The fluorescent lights washed everything in a harsh glare.

She saw no one. Except for distant footsteps, she heard no one. She crept out and reached for the pin, then ran toward the last office and tried the lock again. She heard someone breathing in the next hallway. Footsteps growing farther away, but another set coming closer. She jammed the pin into the lock as Eric had shown her. This was no flimsy lock. The man had something to hide. She looked through the open blinds in the window. File cabinets. They probably contained information about them. About her mom. About what they'd injected into Lucas.

Footsteps came closer. She spun around and ran back to the room. As she reached the door, a shadow fell at the end of the hall. She flung herself into the room and closed the door. At least she had the pin, this time tucked in her back pocket. She had to figure out how to get out of this place. She walked to the cabinet of medicines, wondering if there were any knockout drugs she could slip into their coffee machine. Except the cabinet was locked.

She heard voices: two men. She guessed there were rooms on the other side of the wall, in the hallway where Eric had set the fire.

"Are you telling me that that son of a bitch can start fires psychically?" It sounded like the man who'd walked out with the woman earlier.

An older man said, "You may be capable of the same thing." Darkwell, the man everyone was intimidated by. She'd heard his thunderous voice demanding answers earlier. "What you can do now is just the tip of the iceberg."

"No, shit . . . ah, sir. When can I learn that kind of thing?"

Darkwell chuckled. "I like your enthusiasm. As soon as we find the Rogues, you can practice on them."

Petra shivered.

Their voices got fainter. She heard a door close and strained to hear them again.

Darkwell said, "I'm going to try something that was effective for the prisoner: sensory deprivation. Depriving your senses actually sharpens them, heightening your ability to both locate and remote view."

"I'm ready. I want to take these guys down."

Darkwell said, "You can still only see Petra, right?"

"Yes, sir. For some reason she's easy to pull in."

"That's a start. Let's work on that now."

He could only see her? Why? Then it hit her: he was going to see her! He'd see the room and figure out where she was. She had to get out of there.

CHAPTER 23

Amy heard a soft tapping noise at the door and lifted her head. She'd been half awake for hours now, keeping her senses tuned to Lucas. She pulled the blanket over her shoulders as the door opened.

Eric peered in. "I'm going to drive out to the asylum so I can stay close in case Petra calls," he said. He nodded toward Lucas. "How is he?"

"He's been asleep since I returned with the water, but his temperature has stabilized and so has his breathing."

He nodded. "I'll be back soon. I hope," he added ominously. "I'm going to pick up some food and supplies, too. Need anything?"

"Can you bring me back some chocolate-covered raisins or cranberries? Preferably cranberries. I'm dying for something to pop in my mouth."

He choked, which brought on coughing spasms.

"Sorry." Her cheeks flushed at her faux pas. When he regained his composure, she added, "And a box of Pop-Tarts. Strawberry. No, chocolate. I deserve chocolate. But I should eat fruit, I suppose. And organic yogurt."

With a salute, he closed the door, leaving her in silence again. She turned on the soft light beside the bed to check Lucas. He was in deep REM sleep. His mouth moved slightly and his jaw clenched. It wasn't a pleasant dream. She had watched dogs and cats dreaming at the animal shelter, their paws and mouths flexing as they chased mice or ran away from abusive owners.

Lucas jerked his head to the right, his body rigid. His eyes blinked beneath his lids as though flashbulbs were going off. Sweat beaded on his upper lip. He grunted as though someone had punched him in the stomach. She touched him, trying to gently bring him out. He pushed at her, caught in the grip of a nightmare. She grabbed his arms and tried to still them as he thrashed.

"Lucas. Wake up."

He gripped her wrist as he came to a sitting position, his eyes wide as he breathed in gasps. The sudden movement sent her backward onto the bed. She scrambled up beside him. "Lucas, it's okay."

He continued to stare ahead, still caught in the dream or somewhere in the confusion between that and reality. He swung his gaze toward her.

"Lucas, it's all right. You're in the tomb, remember?"

He didn't. He looked around the room before coming back to her. He ran his hand down his flushed face, rubbed his eyes, then looked at her again.

She smiled. "Hi." The word came out soft and shy.

His gaze swept down her, and she remembered that she was naked. He then looked down at himself. Oddly, she felt a bit awkward. They'd never been naked in reality before.

"You had a fever when we rescued you. And you were . . . well, nearly naked, soaking in a tub to cool you down. I kept cool cloths on you through the night. Then you broke the fever and were cold." She pulled the sheet over her, feeling really, really naked now. "I gave you my body heat."

He touched her face, and she automatically leaned into his hand.

His voice was raspy. "You're real. You're here."

"It's not a dream." She reached across him for the bottle of water on the nightstand. "Here, drink." She watched his throat convulse as he gulped the water. "Not too fast."

He wiped his hand across his mouth, took a breath, then finished the water.

She set the empty bottle on the stand. "Want more?"

"I'm fine for now." He looked at her in disbelief. "You said you weren't trying to rescue me. You promised you weren't."

She nodded. "I didn't want to worry you."

"Eric? Petra? Are they all right?"

She didn't want him to worry about Petra, not yet. She didn't exactly lie. "They're both out right now."

He was grappling with it all, she could see: her lie, that they had risked their lives for him.

"Lucas, we weren't leaving you there, so don't waste your energy being angry about it."

He pinched the bridge of his nose. "I didn't want you involved like this."

"But I'm an Offspring. How can I not be part of it?" She scooted closer, her sheet falling away. "We're in this together. All of us. And you and I . . . God, Lucas, how could I leave you there to die?" She brushed her fingers through his hair. It was almost curly, probably because it hadn't been washed in a few days. "So don't you dare tell me I shouldn't have rescued you. Don't you tell me I should have just forgotten you, forgotten everything we shared. You brought me to life. In those dreams, you made me breathe again and feel things I'd never felt. You saved me from being raped and God knows what else."

His mouth tightened at the passion in her words. "You know about that."

"I found your sketch. I wanted to know the man who knew me so well." She shrugged. "I snooped."

"Only fair. It's been a bit one-sided all these years."

She touched his scar. "You did that for me. Getting your ass out of that horrible place was the least I could do." She smiled, trying to lighten the mood.

He reached toward her neck and touched the cross pendant.

"You lost it at my apartment that night . . . " It seemed a lifetime ago. "I got it fixed. Here." She raised her arms to unclasp it, but he stilled her.

"Keep it." He pressed his finger against the cross. "It looks right there."

He cupped her face in his hands and rubbed his thumb across her lower lip. "I am furious with you, Amy, because you could have gotten killed or captured trying to save me. And I don't know what they put into me, what it's going to do."

That sent fear through her. "But you're all right. You're here, awake . . . you."

His smile was faint. "Me, but different. It's like I'm . . . bent. Inside." He leaned forward, pressing his forehead against hers. "I don't want to talk about that right now. I just want to feel you here with me."

She took his hand and turned it so she could kiss his palm, all the while looking into the eyes of the man who had captured her heart. She wouldn't believe that he was bent inside, or if he was, that he couldn't be healed with her love.

"I keep thinking I'm dreaming," he said.

"I know. I've pinched myself twelve times already."

He smiled and pulled her close, tracing his fingers along her face as he looked into her eyes. Then he kissed her. Softly at first, as though she might break, and then deeper, deeper, and soon she was spiraling into bliss.

Their hands were touching each other, absorbing. His body heat had returned, but for far different reasons. A different kind of fever. She felt his rigid penis pressed against her stomach as he lay her down on the bed. His gaze took her in, and she knew he didn't see that too-straight body she cursed when she looked in a mirror. He saw someone beautiful, precious, someone he desired. The awe in his eyes filled her heart. People said that something was a dream when it was better than real life. This was better than a dream.

They were both sweaty, and their musky scents blended into one erotic fragrance as their bodies intertwined. Their movements were languid, as though they were under water. There was no hurry now. No impending sound to wake her, no terrible thing to yank him away. They were here, together, always. She wouldn't believe anything else.

He slid into her, and she knew that what she'd felt in the dreams was only a shadow of what real love-making was. He teased her as he did in their dream encounters, filling her body and soul, moving in and out, kissing her all the while. His eyes were closed, savoring her. She wrapped her legs around him and joined his rhythm. She lost herself in being with him at last, her dream lover.

Her emotions pushed her orgasm to the surface, where it burst. She let out a scream and held tight to him. He kept going, moving in and out, bringing her to a second mind-blowing orgasm. He came seconds later, quietly but no less intensely. He ran his fingers into her hair and tilted his head back and lost himself for a few moments. When he came back, he kissed her again.

As soon as she could breathe, she said, "I love you, Lucas."

A shadow passed over his features, and he buried his face by her neck. "Don't."

That word she'd heard before stabbed her. She pulled back to look at him. "I don't care if you're bent inside. Don't try to protect me. I don't want anyone to protect me anymore. Cyrus died trying to protect me. You got captured trying to protect me. I can take care of myself."

"I don't want to hurt you."

She planted her hands at her waist. "What, you going to cheat on me?"

He smiled at that, shaking his head. "Never."

"I saw your sketch. Of you, dead." She shivered, thinking how close he'd come to that. "But you're safe now."

"What I saw . . . it wasn't necessarily me dying in that hospital." He took a deep, halting breath. "Amy, I don't want to hurt you by leaving you."

"Too late," she said, her fear making her words sound like broken glass. "I already love you. Stopping now isn't going to make one bit of difference. And you know what? You do love me. I could feel it in our dreams, even when I couldn't see your face. I can see it now."

He rubbed his thumb over her chin. "Eric's right. You are a pain in the ass." He tempered his words with a soft smile. "You seemed so soft and sweet when I first came to your dreams."

And lonely and inadequate. "I was. That girl is gone now."

"I'm sorry."

"Don't be. I like this Amy much better. I'm alive now. I wouldn't trade that for anything."

She wasn't quite convincing him. A shadow still hovered in his eyes. Was he not telling her something? Then she remembered Cyrus's words about the Ultras: *They're likely to become psychologically unstable.* Was that what Lucas meant when he said he was bent? She didn't want to think about that.

"Let's get a shower," he said, giving her a quick kiss.

He was still shaky as he got out of bed. He looked gorgeous, even after all he'd been through. She suspected that he hadn't eaten much, though; he looked too thin.

"Did they feed you?" she asked.

"I don't want to talk about that place."

She felt that shadow inside her. What had happened to him? Why wouldn't he share it with her?

He reached for the doorknob but paused. Turned back to her. Held out his hand. She took it, and they walked into the bathroom.

* * *

With heartbeat thudding, Petra crept to the door and listened. Footsteps came down the hallway. Closer. She shrank back beneath the desk. Eventually someone would come in and use this desk and she'd be discovered. Was this the person? She held her breath as the footsteps stopped outside the door. A doorknob turned. She expected to see light from the hallway flood in. Nothing.

A door opened. Not the door for her room but the one across the way. Releasing that breath, she listened. The person shuffled papers, and then a few minutes later she heard the keys on a phone beep. "Hello, this is Sam Robbins. I need someone to come out as soon as possible and fix a fence. A car accidentally ran through it . . . Ten feet high . . . Asphalt . . . Monday morning? Is that the earliest you can get out? . . . Uh-huh, I see . . . Your truck will definitely be repaired by then? . . . All right." He gave the man directions and hung up.

A few minutes later more footsteps came down the hallway, and Petra shot back into panic mode again. She had to get out of there. The stress was eating at her, and speaking of eating . . . she was surprised they hadn't heard her stomach growling. Any minute now the enemy Offspring was going to remote view her, and *wham*, they'd find her. She kept trying to imagine a shield all around her, as she'd imagined that ball kicking him out before. So far she hadn't gotten that eerie feeling.

Again footsteps slowed just outside her door. *Please, please, go on.*

Darkwell's voice. "Are we getting the fence fixed today?"

Robbins said, "Monday's the best we can do. The only company that answered was Calistoga Fence. The man promised they'd be out in the morning."

Darkwell made a disapproving grunt. "The guards will make sure no one gets through, but I want it fixed as soon as possible."

"You don't think they'll come back, do you?" Robbins asked, an undercurrent of fear in his voice. He was afraid of them.

"They got what they came for. Lucas could be a problem; fortunately, he won't live long. I've got my star Offspring working on locating them. It'll be over soon."

She was still caught on his words about Lucas not living long. What had they done to him? Even more frightening, that man would do the same to her if he caught her.

Have to get out.

She got the first inkling of the *feeling*. It tingled along her skin. She closed her eyes and concentrated on pushing him out. The tingling subsided for a few moments but came back again. She pushed. How long could she hold him off?

I've got to get out of here. Oh, God, I'm wigging out. I am totally wigging out. The air got thicker, harder to get into her lungs.

The older man said, "Let's get started with the other prisoner. I don't think he's as talented as Lucas, but he's all we have right now. What did you find out about him?"

Robbins said, "He's got a grandmother who raised him, lives in Baltimore. He sends her money every week."

"Good, an attachment."

She felt the tingling again. This time it was more of a struggle to push him out, as though she were pushing against a huge balloon.

Wigging out. No, not wigging out. Can't wig out. If I wig, they'll catch me, so stop using the word wig, Petra.

And stop talking to yourself.

The two men's footsteps and voices faded as they moved away. She had to move herself, and made a quick call to Eric. "I'm getting out of here," she whispered, and disconnected.

The place was quiet, though she knew the guards were still making their rounds. She cracked open the door and peered out. No one in sight. Leaving the sanctuary of the medical room, she edged down to the reception area. That was the trickiest part, as it opened to the right, where their "star Offspring" was trying to find her. To the left was the front entrance, which might be locked.

She craned her neck to see to the right. No one. Another step and she would be able to see the entrance. Her heart leapt. A guard stood at the door looking out. *Breathe, stay calm.* She walked calmly past the desk and toward the hall opposite it. A door opened to a darkened cafeteria on the right.

The tingling was becoming persistent. Pushing harder. *Go away!* She ducked into the cafeteria, overwhelmed. He could see her now. Hopefully he wouldn't see much with the darkness, just as Eric couldn't with Lucas. She imagined the ball and sent it up. The tingling vanished. For now.

She glanced out in the hall again, which led to

what looked like a lounge. Three doors on either side indicated that these offices were large. She walked down the hall, her chest hurting from lack of breath. The windows in the offices had curtains. She heard a woman talking in one of them but didn't focus on her words.

The tingling started again. She picked up her pace and was nearly running as she reached the lounge: two couches, a coffee table, and a table and television in a room painted a dark orange color. She was only interested in the exterior door. She looked out the window and saw the parking lot beyond. Could she make it over the fence before the enemy Offspring finally broke through?

The tingling pressed against her and swept down her spine. He could see her. She heard running footsteps and a man shout, "She's here, in the lounge!"

She slammed against the door, praying it wasn't locked. It opened into the cool morning sunshine. She tore across the asphalt toward the fence. *How did I do this last night?* She wasn't out of breath and scared to death then. Amy's voice filled her head. *I have to be optimistic. I have no choice.*

She could do this. She crashed into the fence and started scrambling up it. Men shouted behind her. One of the outside guards ran toward her. Her foot slipped. She jammed it back into the hole in the fencing and kept climbing. The fence began to shake as someone else climbed up behind her.

Petra reached the top and saw one man just below her and two more running toward the fence. She dropped to the ground on the other side with a thud and then dashed toward the woods. She knew them from their reconnaissance the night before. Once she hit the shaded area she turned to the left, toward the highway. She had to get far enough away to call Eric with her position.

She heard people running through the woods behind her. Their shouted directives clashed in her brain. She changed her course. Changed it again. She could hear the sound of traffic in the distance and aimed for that. The way she figured, it was better to get hit by a car than caught by these animals. The highway noise grew louder. *Almost there.* Her chest hurt, her legs hurt. *I promise if . . . no, when I make it out of here, I'm going to use the gym at the shelter!*

Louder than her heartbeat, louder than the cars on the highway, she heard footsteps to her right. She saw a blur of movement. Turned. One of the guards broke into view, his gun aimed at her.

CHAPTER 24

In the shower, Lucas closed his eyes and let the water wash over him. He still couldn't believe he was here. Safe. With Amy. He was relieved, furious, and elated all at once. A wave of dizziness seized him.

Her arms wrapped around his waist. "Are you all right?"

"Light-headed."

"I told you we should have eaten first."

"I'll be fine." He needed to wash off the sweat and the musty smell of the asylum that seemed to cling to his skin.

When he turned to her, she held a round gauzy thing loaded with bubbles. She was studying him, probably looking for some sign that he was going to drop.

"I'm fine," he said again, touching her chin. "Stop worrying."

"You were nearly dead a day ago, and I'm supposed to just stop worrying about you? Forget it."

He had to admit he liked this sassy and confident side of her. She ran the gauzy thing over him, gently, slowly, focusing on every part of his body. He was hard again. Well, that part of him wasn't screwed up. The rest . . . he didn't know. Watching her cleaning him, something shifted in his chest. Her words about loving him generated more conflicting feelings. Yeah, he loved her. He'd always loved her. It seemed she'd been living inside him nearly all his life. All he'd wanted to do was protect her, from this Offspring business, and now . . . from him. From what he was and what he'd become.

She stood, catching him with who-knows-what expression on his face. "What's wrong?"

"You're beautiful."

He loved the way her face transformed from worry to a mix of disbelief and love. He looked at the freckles on her face, her dark green eyes and thick eyelashes beaded with water. They reminded him of the tears he'd seen her cry in their dreams. He ached that he'd caused her pain, that he would probably cause her more.

She had an intriguing mouth, lush and pink, her lower lip with its square corners. He'd loved this face for so long. He drank her in, her throat, the swell of her breasts and hardened nipples, pale skin with more freckles, nest of dark hair that was also beaded with water.

"Turn around," she said. "You're making me feel funny."

"Why?" he asked, but allowed her to turn him.

She scrubbed his back, long strokes from his neck all the way down over his buttocks. "I've never had anyone look at me like that."

He turned his head. "I don't believe you."

She laughed, a sweet sound that was nonetheless filled with cynicism. "I'm not beautiful. And until our dreams, which I don't know if that actually counted, I was celibate."

He selfishly liked that idea. "I bet that drove the guys crazy."

"There *were* no guys. I didn't date."

He turned back around to look at her. Even before their encounters, she hadn't dated, so it wasn't his fault. "Why?"

She grabbed the shampoo bottle, squirted some into her palm, and reached up to wash his hair. Her fingers felt heavenly massaging his scalp. He leaned forward to accommodate her.

"I didn't want to be hurt," she said. "I lost my dad and my mom. I never wanted to lose someone I loved again. So I didn't want to love anyone."

At the emotion in her voice, he looked up.

"Until you," she added.

Damn. That made his mind up. He had to keep his distance from her to keep her heart safe. How the hell was he going to do that now? He leaned back into the water to rinse out the shampoo.

"Lucas, don't you dare close down. I'm not going to lose you."

"Amy, I—"

She pressed her finger over his mouth. "I made the decision to stop hiding in my cocoon even when I wasn't sure I'd ever see you again. Seeing your sketch of you dead . . . that didn't change my mind. I'm sure not going to back away now that you're here, and neither are you."

He released a breath. In his mind he saw Amy through the years, as a shy, sweet girl, with her frown, her tears, and her happiness. How could he turn away from her? "Come here, your turn." He reached for the shampoo.

"You're going to be all right, Lucas."

There was so much he hadn't told her. She wasn't going to like the one thing he had to say.

Pain ripped through his head. Electricity crackled through the darkness he now saw. He grabbed onto the shower head. It was happening again. In the far distance he heard her call his name, fear in her voice. He thought she was touching him but couldn't be sure.

Images crashed into his mind, each separated by a blinding light that he swore tore into the tissues of his brain. The boy in their childhood group, then the man, fighting the straps on a bed like the one he'd been strapped to . . . now Petra, scared, running, being chased through the woods. Amy falling with a scream. Hitting the floor. Blood.

"Lucas!"

Her voice broke through. He opened his eyes. He was on his knees gripping the shower head that was no longer attached to the wall. The shower was off. She was crouched beside him, holding onto his arms. He dropped the shower head, and it clanged loudly.

"What happened?" she asked.

He pressed the heel of his hands against his temples to push away the residual pain. "The Booster . . . " It was hard to get his tongue around words. "Different."

She turned him toward her, staring into his eyes. "What's different?"

"I used to get the dreams . . . the sketches. I could do something then. But now I get . . . it's like a slide show, one after the other. Too fast to see much. To do anything. And it feels like someone tasering my brain."

He grabbed her shoulders. "Petra's in trouble. You said they were all right."

"I said no one got caught." She chewed her lower lip. "I didn't want to worry you. Petra didn't get out of the building last night. She *is* all right. She called and was hiding. They didn't know she was there."

He stood, willing his legs to stop wobbling. "She's not all right now. Or won't be."

"Lucas, I don't understand."

"The sketches were always the future. I don't know if these visions are future or something that's happening now."

"Eric went back to the asylum—"

"The asylum?"

"That's what the hospital was once. He went back to be nearby. She's supposed to call when she can get out."

He stepped out of the tub. "We've got to get over there."

"Eric has the only car, and that place is an hour away from here. Besides, you're in no condition. You can hardly get your clothes on. We have to trust that Eric will handle it. If she's running, she hasn't been caught."

He dried off. "But they know she's there. They're after her."

Amy dried off, too, fear in her expression. "She'll be all right."

"You don't know Petra. She wigs, panics. She's not good under stress."

"She's gotten stronger. Come on, let's get some food into you. I'll tell you all about it."

He was going to need his strength, and he had to

admit that his stomach actually hurt with hunger. He let her lead him to the kitchen and watched her put ham and cheese sandwiches together. She kept looking at him with a worried expression. He wasn't going to let her pretend he was all right.

"Tell me everything that's happened since they took me from your apartment."

She brought the sandwiches to the table and they ate as she told him. He felt a swell of pride at what she'd done, how she'd escaped, how she'd kneed Spy Guy in the nuts. That he didn't remember anything about the rescue itself bothered him. He barely remembered the woman, of particular interest to Amy, but not the last time he'd been in the tub.

She said in a soft voice, "The funny thing was, I wasn't as scared for myself as I was for you. None of that compared to seeing you unconscious." She smiled. "And nothing compares to seeing you sitting here now."

"Did you fall?"

She looked up in thought. "I don't remember falling. Why?" When he didn't answer right away, she said, "You saw me falling, didn't you?"

He dropped the crust of his second sandwich on the plate. "So that hasn't happened yet."

"And it won't. You changed the future when you saved me from that creep at the marina. What you see doesn't always happen."

"How do you know about that?"

"I found the sketches."

He turned away and rubbed his temples. That time, he knew enough about the event to prevent it. With the images flashing so fast, he couldn't see the events leading up to it. He had a bad feeling it was connected to what he had to tell her when Eric and Petra returned.

Petra stopped, her breathing heavy. The man slowed, too, eyeing her warily. He was one of the outside guards. She couldn't take her gaze from the gun he pointed at her. He hollered, "She's over here!" To her, he said, "Don't move. I don't know what you all are, but you give me the creeps. I don't mind shooting you, even if you are a pretty gal."

She didn't doubt that he would shoot her. This couldn't happen. She couldn't let them capture her. Footsteps sounded from several directions. She still had a minute before they arrived. She dove for the ground and rolled. A shot rang out, hitting the dirt and spewing it up. She zigzagged toward the highway. He wouldn't shoot her in front of witnesses, would he?

Almost there. She could see the road through the last of the trees. Cars whizzed by. As soon as she ran into the open she'd wave her arms. *Thwang.* Another bullet flew past. She glanced back. He was trying to run and shoot at the same time, which skewed his aim. As she turned ahead, something grabbed her and threw her backward. She landed with a thump, dizzy from the sudden change in motion.

Her eyes focused. She'd run into a fence separating the forest from the highway. The guard ran up, his gun trained on her. He was gasping for breath as much as she was. Worse, she heard footsteps coming up on her right.

"Now I'm . . . going to have to . . . hurt you." He lowered the gun to her legs.

She heard a shot. Flinched. A scream of pain. Not her scream. Not her pain. His gun flew out of his hand. Blood spurted from his wrist.

Footsteps near her head. A hand reaching toward her. "Come on."

She jerked around to find Eric standing there. She took his hand and let him pull her to her feet. "How did you—"

"No time. Let's go."

She followed him along the fence line. The man's screams covered the sound of their footsteps but also blocked her from hearing where their enemies were. Several yards away Eric climbed over a place where the fence had been torn away from the post and bent down. She saw the Camry parked along the side of the highway. Both doors were open.

Sometimes she really loved her pain-in-the-ass brother.

They jumped into the car and he pulled onto the highway. She slunk down in the seat and watched the woods to see if anyone had spotted them. She saw two men running toward the fence. Eric drove at a calm pace, glancing at the woods only briefly, his hand still gripping a gun.

"Did they see our car?" he asked.

"I don't think so." She pressed her face against the glass to look back. One man had jumped over the fence and was looking around, but not at their car. "I think we're okay . . . Yes, we're okay." She allowed herself to collapse completely, her head on his thigh. "Thankyou thankyouthankyouthankyou," she said on one breath.

He tucked the gun beneath his seat and stroked her forehead. "I remote-viewed you. I could see the woods around the facility. I saw you running. I was already in the area, ready to pick you up. Or bust you out of there."

She gathered the strength to sit up. "How's Lucas?"

"He woke up last night for a few minutes. Amy said he seemed good."

"The men at the asylum kept talking about him not being around much longer."

Eric handed her his cell phone. "Let Amy know you're all right."

Her fingers were still shaky as she dialed the numbers. Amy answered on the second ring, her voice breathless. "Eric!"

"It's Petra."

"Thank God! You're with Eric?"

"He got there in the nick of time." It warmed her to hear Amy's relief at her safety. "How's Lucas?" She so badly needed to hear that he was all right.

"Here, ask him yourself."

Her heart lifted when she heard his voice. They both said simultaneously, in a rush of relief, "You're all right."

"Petra, were you running in the woods?"

"Yes, how did you know?"

"I saw you."

"In one of your sketches?"

"No, a flash of you running. In danger. Tell Eric to drive carefully. Get back here safe."

"We will." Her voice got soft when she said goodbye. She slumped back in the seat with a sigh.

Eric's fingers tightened on the wheel. "You're going to have to give him up." At her questioning look, he added, "He's got Amy now."

"What are you talking about?"

He kept his gaze straight ahead. "I know you're in love with him. I'm just warning you that you're going to have to let that go. He's loved Amy for a long time. And she loves him just as much. Whatever they've got—and I don't understand it—is stronger than that damn bomb shelter."

"Was I obvious?"

His mouth quirked in a half smile. "I'm intuitive, remember?"

It was strange that he had even noticed, stranger that he'd never mentioned it until now. And strangest yet that he was trying to ease her into the harsh reality that she would never have the only man she'd ever romantically loved. "You don't think he knows? Oh, jeez, I hope he doesn't."

"I don't think so."

"Thanks," she whispered. She rubbed the dirt from her arms, wincing at a red mark. "I knew as soon as Amy joined us that I'd lose him. The truth is, I never had him. All I ever had was hope. Now that's gone."

He scrubbed the top of her head, an affectionate gesture that surprised her. She felt a bond open between them. "Eric, I'm sorry about Dad."

His expression hardened. "He's not my dad. I don't want to talk about him."

Way to go.

They sat in silence. She wondered if his hard glare was from thoughts of her father or of something else. All around them people went about their business, beeping at slow drivers, talking during their drive. Normality right there, yet so far away. Finally she couldn't stand the silence anymore. "What's the plan now?"

"We need to stay low for a while, try to find other Offspring, put the pieces together."

She liked the prospect of laying low. She needed that.

Eric's mouth tightened. "Then we'll take that damned asylum by storm and find out what the hell they're doing. And what they did to our mother."

CHAPTER 25

Amy was watching Lucas sleep on the couch when she heard footsteps coming down the tunnel. He woke, too, and in a flash shot off the couch and ran to the storage room in the kitchen. "Come here," he whispered, waving her over.

She joined him as he pulled out one of the rifles. His gaze was riveted on the door. For a moment he reminded her of Eric, ever vigilant and ready to kill. She shivered at the thought.

He kept the rifle down but his finger on the trigger. "When Eric first came to me about the government guy watching him, I thought he was being paranoid," he said. "He was always thinking people were out to get him. But this time he was right. Now here I am, paranoid, too."

She stood next to him in the darkened kitchen. "You have good reason to be."

They heard beeping, and the door slid open. Petra's eyes locked onto Lucas. He set the gun down, and he and Amy walked out of the kitchen. Petra ran into his arms, and he held her, stroking her hair. She closed her eyes, obviously relishing the sensation of being with him again. Amy felt odd, knowing how Petra felt about him. She sensed Eric looking at her from the kitchen, though he started unloading the two paper bags he'd carried in, including two boxes of Pop-Tarts—one chocolate, one strawberry—and a bag of chocolate-covered raisins. She mouthed the word *Thanks*. He shrugged.

Finally Lucas stepped back and looked at everyone. "We need to talk." He nodded toward the dining table.

Petra looked at Amy as if she knew what he was going to tell them. But Amy had no idea. Whatever it was, she thought, it would be serious. She grabbed her bag of raisins.

Lucas waited until they had all taken a seat, though he remained standing. Just as she tossed a raisin in the air, he said, "We've got to go back to the hospital." He glanced at Amy. "The asylum."

The raisin bounced to the floor. "No," she said, a sick feeling in the pit of her stomach.

The blood had drained from Petra's face. "No *way*."

Eric narrowed his eyes. "Why?"

Lucas walked over to the board above the desk and took down the photograph of the children by the pool. He pointed to the boy. "Rand."

Amy said, "I saw his profile on Cyrus's computer."

"They brought him in while I was there. In one of my visions I saw him strapped to a table like I was. They're using his grandmother, threatening her safety if he doesn't cooperate."

Eric asked, "What do they want him to do?"

Amy asked, "What did they want you to do?"

"It's political stuff. Spying." Somehow she knew he wasn't telling them everything; he'd turned away while answering. He continued. "They're giving him something that's making him nuts in a different way than what they gave me. He's stressing big-time."

Petra said, "That's what the woman meant when she said her boss still had another prisoner."

Lucas nodded. "He's one of us." He slapped the photo down in the middle of the table. "We can't abandon him."

Eric banged his palm on his forehead. "Oh, no, don't tell me you have abandonment issues, too!"

Lucas's eyebrows furrowed. "Huh?"

Eric pointed at Amy with his thumb. "She drove me crazy about not leaving you there. Then she had to get the car Cyrus left just because he'd left it for her. Now she wants to get some stupid parrot. This girl has abandonment issues. We can't risk our asses getting things because we can't stand to abandon them."

Lucas looked at her with such soft emotion she felt it in the pit of her stomach. He turned back to Eric. "She lost her mother and her father before she was six years old. Maybe she does have abandonment issues. I can't blame her for that. Do I have them? Who knows? But I will tell you, I'm not leaving Rand there. I know what the Devil is capable of."

"The Devil?" Petra asked.

"That's what I called the guy in charge."

Petra said, "I think his name is Darkwell."

Eric pinched the bridge of his nose. "How do we even know Rand will trust us? He doesn't know who we are."

"Because we're a better bet than the people who have him now."

"And it's not only Darkwell we have to worry about," Petra said. "The enemy Offspring can remote view, though apparently only to me. We have some kind of connection, like you and Amy, only a bad one. Figures. That's how they found me at the asylum. They call him their 'star Offspring.' Darkwell told him he probably has other skills—like yours, Eric. He's eager to work on them, and . . . practice on us."

Eric's eyes hardened. "Then we'll get him while we're there."

Petra said, "Eric, what happened to laying low for a while? That was a really, really good plan."

He ground a fist into the palm of his other hand. "I need to kick some ass. These people have to go."

"So you're in," Lucas said. He took in Petra and Amy. "Not you two."

Petra looked relieved, but Amy shot to her feet. "No way. We are a team. We've proven that we're stronger when we work together."

Lucas said, "Amy, I saw you fall."

"So I fell. Big deal."

His voice got low. "It was more than a fall. You were shot."

She sank back into her seat. "You didn't tell me that part."

"I was waiting for the right time."

"Then we change it," she said. "You saw your death, but you didn't die."

Eric smiled in that know-it-all way. "See, told you she was a pain in the ass."

Lucas gave her a wry smile. "I see that."

"We are a team," Amy said again. "Stronger together. I'm not going to play the little woman back here all worried while the menfolk are off to war. I'm in." She looked at Petra. "Are you?"

She swallowed hard. "Okay. The good news is, they don't think we'll be back."

Lucas leaned forward. "Eric, our mission tomorrow is to get Rand. I know you want to take the enemy by storm, and believe me, I want to annihilate them as much as you do. But we need to focus on one thing at a time. Rand is at the rear of the east wing, where I was. It's an easy in and out. To get the others, we have to go farther in. It's too dangerous. We need to find more of us. Amy's right. We're a team, and if we're a bigger team, we've got a better chance.

"After Rand," he continued, "what we need is information. Why are our psychic abilities so strong? Did our parents die because of the original program? What are we up against? We need to take one of them, and Robbins is our best bet. I could tell he was uncomfortable with what the Devil was doing to me."

Amy said, "We know what he looks like." She glanced at Eric. "We saw him when we remote-viewed you."

"Good," Lucas replied. "If we see him in the east wing, we take him. But we don't hurt him." He leveled his gaze at Eric.

Amy said, "Cyrus told me that the two men in charge of the program were extremely dangerous. It sounds like Robbins is the Devil's right-hand man."

"Maybe he was only pretending to be your ally," Eric said. "So you'd cooperate."

Lucas shrugged. "Maybe. I'm not saying we'll be

his buddy. But we don't take him out. We give him the chance to tell us what he knows. If he doesn't, we return him—alive."

Eric's eyes narrowed. "Since when are you the boss? I was the one who took charge and got you out of that place. Now that you're out, you want to take over."

"I'm not trying to be the boss, Eric, but you have a tendency to go off half-cocked. We can't afford to do that. We're not playing a game over at Radical Paintball."

Eric pushed away from the table and went into the kitchen. He grabbed a beer from the fridge and took several swigs before returning.

Petra turned to Lucas. "I heard the woman talking to someone named Peterson."

Lucas nodded. "He was a combination strongarm and nurse."

"He was supposed to give you a shot the night you were rescued. Darkwell implied that it would . . . kill you."

Lucas looked at the inside crook of his elbow where a faint red mark remained. "They gave me three injections of something called the Booster. It was supposed to boost my abilities."

Amy said, "That's what Cyrus called the nutritional cocktail the people in the original program got."

Petra said, "He didn't give you that last shot. The woman called him right after you got busted out. He asked her to cover for him and tell Darkwell you'd gotten it. He was worried."

"Thank God." Lucas's face looked haunted. "Each one made it worse."

"Made what worse?" Petra asked.

"I get this storm of images now that kicks me in the ass."

Petra's face creased in worry. "Lucas, if you go in . . . if they get you again, they'll give you that shot. And you'll die."

His expression remained passive. "Then I won't get caught." Lucas turned to Amy. "Did Cyrus tell you what was in it?"

"He didn't know. He said a scientist created it, and the ingredients were top secret."

"This is what our mothers were involved in." Lucas looked at Amy, Eric, and Petra. "And your dad, Amy. The Devil—Darkwell—mentioned my mom, said she was talented, a dreamweaver, but wouldn't say much more. That's how I can get into other people's dreams."

"Other people's dreams?" Eric asked. "Not just Amy's?"

"I was able to get into Rand's dreams, too. Last night I told him we were coming."

Eric said, "I went to my . . . my father's house. Before the bastard turned me into the police."

"Turned you in?" Lucas said. "Dad?"

"Yeah. Because I'm wanted for arson. Anyway, I found a letter from the president of the Society for Psychic Phenomena, sending condolences for our mother's death. He was suspicious of the program she was involved in."

"What did your father say?" Amy asked.

Eric and Petra exchanged a meaningful look and he subtly shook his head. "He didn't say jack. We figure the trust funds we have are blood money, paid by the government to shut him up. Or at least stuff his curiosity. He didn't deny it."

"I got some money, too," Amy said. "Cyrus told me it was an insurance policy, one that didn't exclude suicide as a payoff." She cleared her throat. "There's something else Cyrus told me. Something I didn't mention." She looked down at her hands on the table for a moment before meeting Lucas's gaze. "You and Eric are Ultra Offsprings."

"Say again?" Lucas said.

"You were born of affairs between two of the subjects in the program. I told you about the sexual side effects. Well, some of the subjects got involved with each other, and their offspring are even more enhanced, more powerful."

Just as she suspected, Eric's face lit with pride. "Cool."

"There's something else, before you get too cocky. It also makes you more susceptible to the other side effect . . . mental instability. Cyrus said one of the subjects went on a rampage and killed three people."

A shadow passed over Lucas's face. "You mean we could go crazy."

Eric leaned across the table, aiming a hard look at Amy. "Why didn't you tell us this after you talked to Cyrus?"

"Remember why you didn't tell Petra that her extraordinary hearing was probably bioenergetic? Ditto. I didn't want you to get full of yourself."

Lucas said, "Wait a minute. Eric, if you're born of an affair between two program members—"

"My father isn't my father," he finished.

Petra said, "Yeah, we know that."

A breaking news announcement caught their attention. With Eric wanted by the police, they left the television on and kept one ear open for any more broadcasts.

A woman was saying, " . . . a follow-up on the mysterious death of Major General Napoleon Darkwell, a highly respected and celebrated war hero who was found dead in his bed early Saturday morning. A preliminary autopsy indicates heart failure, and an investigation is under way. We will bring you updates as we learn them . . . "

Amy said, "Darkwell! Is that the man who's in charge?"

Lucas stared at the television. "No, but I'll bet it's his brother," he said in a low voice.

Eric went to the desk and returned with a piece of paper. "This is the sketch we made of the facility's layout. We'll make a plan."

Petra said, "There's still a hole in the fence where Amy drove through. I overheard that it's supposed to get fixed tomorrow morning by the Calistoga Fence Company. Their truck is in the shop but will be repaired by then."

Lucas pulled his dark gaze from the television. "First thing tomorrow we call the fencing company and tell them to never mind, we got it fixed."

"Robbins was the one who called, so pretend you're him," Petra said.

Eric's face lit with the momentum of a good idea. "And we steal the truck from the repair shop and show up to fix the fence."

Petra said, "They change guards at nine in the morning, so we'll have to be out of there before then.

Otherwise there will be twice as many armed men during the overlap."

Eric held up a finger and then disappeared into the gun storage room. A few minutes later he leaped out, his arms extended. "Boo!"

They jumped at the sight of him in a gas mask that made him look like a sci-fi movie bug creature. He lifted the mask and held up a silver canister that was about six inches high and four inches around. "We have several of these and this canister of tear gas."

Lucas raised an eyebrow. "I understand the gas masks, but why would the people who built the shelter have tear gas? That's an offensive weapon, and everything down here should be defensive."

Eric shrugged. "Who knows? Maybe one of them was paranoid like I am." He slammed the canister on the table. "We go in with this and set it off in the hallway where Rand is. Anyone who comes down the hall will choke before he gets off a shot." He looked at them for their reaction. "Well?"

Amy almost wanted to laugh at his childlike enthusiasm. "It might just work." She liked the idea of the bad guys incapacitated while their guys were in the building, the most vulnerable place for them.

After more strategy, Eric said, "I think we've got it covered."

Amy saw Lucas's pale face and the smudges beneath his eyes. "Are you sure you want to do this tomorrow? You just got out of there, and you haven't really recovered from that."

"The fence gives us the perfect opportunity, but it's a limited one. It'll be an easy rescue, in and out, minimal violence, and you and Petra stay in the car ready to rock and roll."

Once more, it was the only way he'd let them participate.

Petra covered her face and groaned. "Here we go again."

CHAPTER 26

Amy woke sometime later sensing that Lucas was no longer in bed. It was only two in the morning, too early to start their mission. With visions of him collapsing under the storm of images, she put on his shirt and tiptoed out into the hallway. Lucas's and Eric's voices floated to her from the living room. She knew eavesdropping was wrong, but maybe Lucas was telling Eric what had happened to him. When they'd gone to bed, he vehemently opposed the light being off and insisted the radio be on. He was haunted by his sensory deprivation but wouldn't talk about it. How could she help if she didn't know what was going on in his head?

Lucas said, "I heard you killed Gladstone."

Eric said, "I hope Darkwell didn't punish *you* for it."

"I didn't know anything about it. Eric, you burned the guy."

"Yeah, well, turns out he was going to kill me, just like you sketched. Amy got onto his computer's hard drive. He kept a journal on the three of us. He didn't like any of us, especially me."

"With your charm, I can't imagine."

"Ha ha."

After several moments of silence, Lucas said, "What Cyrus told Amy about us being Ultras. The mental thing—"

"It has nothing to do with that," Eric said.

Amy pressed against the wall, her eyes closed.

"What about our stepmother? The house burning down?"

"I'm not going there." She heard Eric stand and stiffened, ready to slink back to her room.

"Sit down," Lucas said. "It's time to stop running away from this discussion. We didn't talk for years because you were too afraid to answer my questions."

"Because whenever you ask, you look at me like I'm a murderer."

After a moment of tense silence, Lucas asked, "Are you?"

"I was a teenager, for Pete's sake."

"So? You'd set a bunch of fires before you ever hit your teens. I know you did, Eric. I've seen your face when you watch flames. Darkwell said you did it psychically, which explains the lack of evidence."

After a moment Eric said, "I'm surprised Amy didn't tell you. It wigged her out big-time."

"You did it in front of her?"

"She was about to get either caught or shot. It wasn't like I was doing it for fun."

No, but he had enjoyed it. She'd never forget the look on his face when he watched that man burn. She hadn't told Lucas, though, because she wasn't sure he was ready for that yet.

Lucas said, "You hated our stepmother."

"So did you."

"I didn't burn her to death." His voice was rigid, accusing.

Eric let out a huff of breath. "Yes, I did it, but not on purpose. Petra heard Ingrid talking about us, wheedling Dad—our so-called father—to send you into foster care and to send me and Petra off to some boarding school. She was a gold digger, taking advantage of a weak, lonely man, threatening to leave him. And he was caving. So I sat in school that day hating her, stewing, imagining the worst things happening to her, and . . . hell, you have to believe me. I didn't know I was setting a fire. Normally I focus my attention on a specific place and I work hard at sending thoughts of fire to that spot. I didn't do that with the house. I just sent hate. If I'd wanted to kill her, I wouldn't have done it at the house. Hell, we lost about everything." He paused. "I'm not a murderer, Lucas."

Lucas hesitated. "Thanks for finally telling me the truth."

"I'm not a murderer," he repeated. "I only kill when I have to."

After a moment, Lucas said, "I know."

"Don't tell Petra. I know she wonders, but I don't want her to know for sure."

"All right."

Eric said, "There are things you don't tell us either. Like connecting to Amy's dreams."

"That's personal. It has nothing to do with murder."

She heard someone push away from the table and walk toward the hall. She ducked into the bedroom, ready to jump into bed if it was Lucas. A few minutes later she caught the scent of paint. She got out of bed again and hovered at the doorway.

From a different direction Lucas said, "How did you find out about your father?"

"He told me, just before he called the police on me."

"I'm sorry, man." She heard the sincerity in his voice.

"It's no big deal," Eric said, but Amy could hear pain in his denial. "Do you ever wonder who your father is?"

"Not really." A pause. "Sometimes."

"I want to find out who my father is. What could he do? Maybe I inherited the remote viewing from him. Maybe I've got other abilities. I want to find out everything I can about BLUE EYES. Darkwell said you'd inherited your dreamweaver ability from your mother. My mom could probably set fires the way I can, which is why she burned to death. But why burn herself?"

"Cyrus said they got crazy. Maybe my mom's car accident wasn't an accident after all."

"No, man, go with the accident. It's easier to live with."

"I know. Amy's had a hard time with her father's suicide. Your mom's death was probably an accident, too."

Eric's voice revealed emotion when he said, "I hope so." After a pause, he said, "Petra knows where the files may be kept at the asylum. Getting to them is going to be tricky, though."

"Do you want to risk your life to find the truth?"

"Yes."

"Even with your ability, you're not invincible. We need to focus on rescuing Rand. Offspring come first, the truth, second. Don't get crazy." After a minute of silence, Lucas said, "I saw Amy getting shot, and dammit, I can't tell whether it's going to happen today or not. Eric, you have to promise you'll watch out for her. Keep her and Petra safe."

"You make it sound like you won't be around."

"I'm just asking in case . . . something happens to me. What they put in me, I don't know what it's going to do." After a pause, "And promise me something else: if I go . . . crazy, put me out of my misery. I don't want to hurt anyone."

"You're thinking of that guy in the first program who went nuts and killed people. But that's not going to happen to you."

"Promise me, Eric."

"All right, all right."

She felt dread wash over her. No, that couldn't happen.

"I'm going to sleep for another hour or so, if I can," Eric said.

She closed the door and heard Eric return to his room. She knelt down at the cabinet and pulled out the sketch Lucas had drawn of himself dead. There wasn't a lot of detail. He was lying down . . . on the ground, on a table? She wanted to believe this was from his captivity and that they'd circumvented fate.

Please don't let it be anything to do with this mission. She knew he wouldn't be dissuaded. Stubborn recognized stubborn, after all. She put away the sketch and walked out. Lucas sat in front of an easel, wearing nothing but jeans so ratty she caught glimpses of his skin through several holes. For a moment she saw intensity in his eyes as he painted, but then he saw her and stopped.

"What are you doing up?" he asked with a soft smile.

"Couldn't sleep. Like you, I'm guessing." She came up behind him and slid her arms over his shoulders. The waves in his hair were soft, not as tight now that it was freshly washed. He had just started a new canvas with abstract ribbons of cobalt blue. "Whatcha painting?"

"Anything. Nothing. I just needed to smell the paint, feel the brush gliding against the canvas."

She leaned forward and pressed her cheek against his. "Don't let me stop you. Can I watch?"

"Better yet . . . " He took her hand and led her around to sit in front of him. Then he put a brush in her hand. "We can make it a collaborative effort."

She turned to him, feeling his smile all the way down to her stomach. She dipped the brush into the deep red paint and mirrored his ribbons. With her back against his chest, every movement made them rub against each other. She wished she could strip out of her shirt so she could feel his skin against hers. She painted random dots, changing colors every so often. It was nice to just be silently with him.

"Not bad," he said behind her, tickling her ear with his voice.

"Really? I've never done this before." She turned to him. "You're just saying that."

"Not at all. See how you've got the balance of color there, and design here. It's good."

She smiled, feeling like a little kid who just got a supreme compliment from her parent. Feeling pumped up, she put squiggles on the canvas with a flourish of her brush.

He laughed. "Uh-oh, now I've given you a big head!"

"That's never going to be a problem." Before he could inquire further about that, as she suspected he would, she looked at the painting above the easel. It was of her lying on the ground, looking up at the sky. "You paint me so beautifully."

"It's what I see."

She balanced her brush on the palette and settled against him. "When did you first start seeing me?"

"Soon after you moved away, I think. Just brief flashes, sort of like I get now, but not painful. When I became a teenager they got stronger. Then I thought, oh sure, adolescent boy daydreaming about a girl. At least I was trying to convince myself. But these dreams were more than daydreams. I'd suddenly be somewhere else, seeing this girl who was my age. The fleeting glimpses became longer, more intense, and I began to feel what she was feeling. I knew that this was related to my other dreams, but it was as if I was getting something good, too. I seemed to tune in whenever she was experiencing some strong emotion. Good ones and bad ones. I thought she must open herself up then. I wasn't even sure she was real, to be honest. She was my secret girlfriend.

"I started to get my premonition dreams more in my late teens and early twenties. They always involved someone I had contact with. It spooked me. I thought I was bringing bad luck to them. As you can imagine, I didn't really want to get involved with anyone. It's kind of hard to explain that I might wake in the night and maniacally draw some scary picture. 'And oh, by the way, it'll happen four days in a row.'"

She liked the idea that he hadn't been with a woman in a serious sense, but it saddened her, too. She turned to give him a smile. "I suppose most women might have an issue with that."

He grazed her cheek with his hand. "You were the only woman in my heart. You brought light to my darkness."

That made her want to cry. Because she didn't want him to think she pitied him, she held back any words of sympathy. "I'm glad." How could she tell him how much that meant to her? She snuggled against him a bit more in a silent gesture.

"Then one day I was going through some of my old stuff that I'd boxed up after the fire and I found that picture." He nodded toward the one on the bulletin board. "And I knew she was real. I knew her name was Amy, and I remembered having a bond with her even then."

She turned around again. "Why didn't you ever try to find me?"

"I didn't want you in my life."

He was trying to hurt her, push her away. That was her first thought. But this was Lucas who would lay down his life for her. She recalled something he'd said in one of their dreams: *There are things you don't know about me . . . dark . . . you safe . . .*

She came to her feet and faced him, her hands on his shoulders. "You think you've got some dark place inside you because you see people's deaths."

"It's more than that."

"What?" She waited, seeing the darkness shadowing his eyes. When she knew he wasn't going to answer, she said, "You *saved* my life. At the marina," she clarified.

"I should have destroyed those sketches."

She touched his cheek. "I'm glad you didn't. You probably wouldn't have told me."

"Why relive it?"

"I *want* to relive it. I want to hear what happened from your side."

The terror of that dream still lived in his eyes. "I don't know if I do." He must have seen her need to know because he took a deep breath and said, "I freaked when I realized the woman I'd already sketched being attacked was you. I thought I was keeping you safe by staying away from you. Then I saw my Amy getting raped." He managed a smile. "You were my Amy, even if I didn't know who you were."

She settled onto his lap, facing him. "I *am* your Amy." Something about those words caught in her throat. She belonged to him. Belonged. All these years she'd felt she didn't deserve someone to love.

His eyes darkened, becoming more intense.

"What?" she asked.

"It's just that . . . well, you've always been mine in a distant way. But no one has ever really belonged to me."

She smiled. "I know exactly what you mean. Go on; you saw me getting . . . well, you know."

He blew out a breath. "I knew I had to do something, especially since that was the third sketch. But there still wasn't enough detail to see where it was. I was frantic. I told myself to wake up right after doing the fourth sketch, when I might still be connected to the event. I did, and I reached deep inside me, feeling I could know more if I dared. I didn't want this gift or curse, but now I welcomed it. I stared at the sketch so hard, it was like that scene in Xanadu, where the guy looks at the painting of the muses and then skates right into it.

"I saw what I probably experienced while in the trance. I was in the guy's head, watching women walking by. He was building up to, planning, his first taking. He would wait until a woman walked by alone, grab her, and then drag her onto his boat. I knew you would be that woman.

"I had thirteen hours to find that marina. I was a man crazy, going from place to place trying to find the one that matched what I'd seen. I got there right after he grabbed you. He didn't see me until I was right on him."

She traced the scar on his abdomen. "You could have gotten killed."

He shrugged as though it was no big deal. "I didn't think about that. I just wanted you safe."

"My own guardian angel." Gratitude and love swelled inside her as she hugged him. "You could have come forward. The cops wanted to know who my hero was. So did I."

He shook his head. "How could I explain why I was there? And I didn't want you in my mess of a life. Then I saw your name on Gladstone's computer." He looked past her, recrimination in his eyes. "I pulled you into an even bigger mess."

She took his hands in hers and forced him to look at her. "I was already in the mess. You tried to save me. You're my hero."

Surprisingly, those words made the shadow in his eyes even darker. "No, I'm not. Don't say that."

"You're my hero," she whispered, leaning close to kiss him. She wanted to chase all those shadows from him.

The groan she heard did not come from Lucas. She turned to find Eric standing at the entrance to the hallway, looking away. "You have a bedroom, you know. And it's time to get rolling."

Petra was right behind him, not looking too happy herself.

Amy blinked at the sight of Eric. His hair was now a dark brown and combed straight down.

He ran his hand over it. "Time for a change."

Petra gave him a friendly shove. "See, you need change, too."

"For a disguise," he said.

Amy kissed Lucas, a much more chaste kiss than she preferred, and climbed off him. "I'll throw some breakfast together."

Eric grimaced. "Not Pop-Tarts and yogurt, I hope."

"No, we need something heartier than that."

Lucas got up, a bit, ah, stiffly, making Amy grin. "I'll load the gear. We'll call the fencing company at seven, cancel the work order."

Eric said, "I remote-viewed the local garages and found the truck. We've got to move out in the next twenty minutes if we want to snag it before they open."

Amy took a deep breath as she gathered eggs, bacon, and toast. Petra joined her, looking as worried as Amy felt. What concerned her most was that Eric might break with their plan and go looking for the files. Which might put him in danger. Which would send Lucas into danger going after him. She couldn't lose him again. No way in hell would she lose him again.

CHAPTER 27

Amy and Petra waited in the Camry while Eric and Lucas scaled the garage fence in the predawn light.

The world outside the tomb seemed different—colors more vivid, the air fuller, the sunlight painfully bright. Amy inhaled deeply. "Do I even want to know where Eric learned to hotwire cars?"

"When he realized he was being watched by Gladstone, he went into survival mode. He got two untraceable guns, the cell phones, and went off the grid." She kept her gaze on the men as she spoke. "He learned hotwiring from a friend. Eric was the boy who played with toy soldiers, then those video games about war, and then it was paintball. This is natural for him." Her forehead creased. "It's what worries me the most about him."

Eric worked in the cab of the truck while Lucas opened the gate.

"And he has the most powerful weapon I've ever known," Amy added. "Even scarier, he likes using it. When he burned that guy at Quiet Waters Park, he enjoyed it. I don't know if it was the power or the actual killing, but he had a smile on his face while he watched the man burn to death."

"He's always been . . . on the edge. He jumped off roofs, climbed up on those bulletin boards you see by the side of the road . . . and set fires."

Eric started the truck and pulled up to the gate.

"What was Lucas like as a kid?" Amy asked.

"He was quiet, seemed to live inside himself more than in the world." Petra smiled. "But he jumped off the roof right along with Eric. No peer pressure necessary."

Eric drove through the open gate. Lucas closed it and hopped into the truck. They paused by the car and Petra transferred the gas masks and canister to the truck bed. Amy followed as they left the lot. Lucas was wearing a baseball cap and sunglasses. The same gel that Petra had used on her hair made his waves straight. He was going to play the silent partner, keeping in the background while Eric talked to the guard in case they recognized him.

Amy and Petra hung back while the truck drove down the road to the asylum twenty minutes later. Lucas would ring the phone once when they had the guards at gunpoint. Petra would get into the truck and be ready when they emerged with Rand.

That was the plan.

"I have a bad feeling," Petra said, cracking her knuckles.

Amy didn't want to voice her agreement and add to it. "You know, you'll get arthritis doing that."

"That's just a myth. And it's better than chewing my fingernails." She spread her fingers, showing red-painted nails. "Hey, where's your pep talk?"

"It's going to be fine," Amy said without much conviction.

"You're thinking of that sketch Lucas drew, aren't you? Or that he saw you get shot."

"I'm trying not to think of either, thank you."

Petra settled back in her seat. "It'll be fine. Lucas said it was an easy rescue. We have tear gas. And the element of surprise. You won't get shot because you're not leaving this car. It'll be fine."

Amy wasn't going to point out that the quiver in Petra's voice undermined her sentiment. She wrapped her fingers around the steering wheel and waited for the call.

"We're so going to get caught," Petra said, her eyes wide. "And we'll be guinea pigs for the enemy Offspring. He'll practice—I don't know—setting us on fire or something."

Amy put her hand on Petra's shoulder. "It'll be fine. Really."

Petra opened the phone for the umpteenth time. "Oh, no."

"What?"

She held up the phone with its blank screen. "The battery's dead."

"But we made sure to plug it in so it would charge all night. It worked this morning."

Petra slapped her hand over her mouth. "We plugged it into one of the hot outlets, I bet. The switch has to be on, and it wasn't. The phone must have still had a little power left. I didn't check the bars because I assumed it had charged."

Amy stared at the long road going in. "Now what?"

* * *

Lucas got out of the truck and went to the bed to ostensibly pull out fencing poles while Eric made small talk with the guard.

"What is this place, anyway?" he asked, nodding toward the building, an agreeably curious expression on his face.

"How long is this going to take?" the guard asked, ignoring his question.

"What, maybe an hour?" he asked Lucas.

"About," Lucas mumbled, laying out the poles, which were obviously not tall enough for the job. Fortunately he was on the back side of the truck and mostly out of view. He pulled out the roll of fencing, grabbing the shotgun, masks, and canister as he did.

"Well, we'll get to it," Eric said, and headed around the back to help Lucas.

They set the roll several feet from the truck so it wouldn't impede their escape. A flash of movement directed Lucas's eye to the road leading in. His heart nearly stopped when he saw the Camry backing up. What the hell were they doing?

When the guard began to follow his gaze, Lucas started coughing and choking. Eric slapped him on the back while Lucas made sure the guard's attention had been snagged enough for the car to get out of sight.

Just in time, too. The other guard came around the back of the east wing. That would save time if he were in the vicinity. Once they had the gun on the near guard, they were to have him call the other guard and then walk the two of them into the side exit where Eric had gone in for Lucas. Then they'd set off the tear gas and lay them out, along with anyone who happened to be in the area. They'd brought an extra mask for Rand.

The guard remained close. Eric pulled the roll as he scooted backward, ending up next to the guard, and then pressed the gun into his waist. To the second guard, he said, "You, come over here."

The man weighed his options until he saw Lucas with the shotgun aimed at him. He walked over.

"Nice and slow, hand over your guns," Eric said. "At this angle if I pull the trigger, I'll get both of you with one bullet."

Both men complied. Eric stuffed their guns into his waistband as Lucas walked over with the gas masks and canister.

Eric nodded toward the side door, and, with a nudge, the two men headed over. "Open that door."

Eric and Lucas kept their movements casual and the guns hidden in case anyone was looking out the windows. Lucas pressed the Send button on his phone and rang Petra's phone to set her into action. The guard unlocked the door, and Lucas edged it open while peering inside. "It's clear."

The smell of old linoleum hit his nose, bringing back those horrible days of captivity. He pushed the thought away and walked in, the other three following him. He passed the showers and an empty room, to a locked door. Through the window he saw Rand, pacing back and forth; at least he wasn't strapped down.

Lucas turned to the guard. "Give me the key to this room."

"We don't have any interior keys. We're only assigned to the perimeter."

He was probably telling the truth. "Set off the tear gas. I'll shoot the lock." The possibility that they might need to do that was why they'd brought the shotgun. Less chance of a ricochet.

Eric pulled out the canister. It slipped from his fingers and fell to the floor. One of the guards kicked it down the hallway. The other turned and pulled the fire alarm lever. Bells clanged, shattering the silence. A second later a guard appeared at the far end of the hallway, weapon drawn. Eric shot, dropping him, then turned and shot the guard who had pulled the lever. Lucas had the other guard held at gunpoint. His heart was hammering. It was supposed to be in and out with minimal violence. Dammit. The injured guard writhed on the floor, blood gushing from his shoulder.

"Eric—" Lucas looked up to see him tearing down the hallway toward the middle section of the building. "Son of a bitch." He turned back to the guard who was still standing. "Move." He indicated the empty room next to Rand's, pushing him in and locking the door. The other guard had stopped moving. This wasn't good.

Gerard Darkwell was in the session room with his star Offspring when the alarm pealed. Trouble. He opened the door and spotted Olivia paused near the reception desk. "Lock yourself in the resident's hall," he ordered. "Keep the girl in there, too. Go!"

Olivia jerked into action, running toward the wide doors and punching in the security code to lock them down. The hospital had been set up for riots. He heard a gunshot. Another. They were under attack again!

He turned to the muscular young man who had

jumped from the recliner, body tensed for action. "What can I do, sir? I'm trained in multiple weapons. I want these bastards."

Gerard recognized the sadistic hunger he'd seen in the mirror many times. He nodded toward the chair. "The weapon I'm most interested in is your mind. Find Petra, but don't get too close. We don't want her to sense you."

A minute later the man said, "I see Petra with another woman. They're in a car, and . . . they're out front, on the road leading in."

Petra was about to walk to the end of the road and see if Lucas and Eric had gone into the building when an alarm went off. "Something's gone wrong."

Amy pulled up to the edge of the road. She could just barely peer through the trees at the corner and see the truck. "I don't see them. They went in."

"Should I go to the truck?"

"No, let's wait. When we see them coming out, I'll tear over and you can jump in. This doesn't feel right."

"See, I knew it didn't. They should be out by now. The next shift is going to be here in fifteen minutes."

Amy's heartbeat spiked crazily. *Come on, come on.*

They didn't come.

Petra screamed at someone outside the driver's window. Amy began to turn but the barrel of a gun against her temple stopped her movement.

"Out of the car, ladies," a man said.

Amy saw his bandaged wrist. Oh, damn. Was he the one Eric shot? By the fierce snarl on his face, Amy guessed it was. She slowly got out.

He pointed the gun toward Petra, obviously adept at using either hand. "You, come out this way, too." He opened the door and trained the gun on her as she climbed out.

"Walk toward the building. And *please*, give me a reason to shoot you."

He wouldn't need much. Petra slid her hand into Amy's as they walked together.

CHAPTER 28

Lucas shouted, "Back away from the door! I'm going to shoot out the lock." He aimed the shotgun and pulled the trigger, angling himself away from the metal door to avoid a ricochet. The shot dented the lock. Two more rounds and it exploded, throwing the door open a few inches.

He pushed it farther open and found a bruised Rand eyeing him with suspicion. "Who the hell are you?"

"I'm Lucas. I—"

Lightning crackled along the crevices in his brain. *No, not now!* Images flashed: Amy with a gun to her back! Amy falling. Shot. Blood.

Was it happening now or was he seeing the future? The images kept repeating in sequence. Fear was as strong as the pain. He couldn't get his thoughts together, couldn't get his body to move. He fell to the floor.

The guard opened his eyes. Red hot pain radiated from his shoulder. He didn't know what was happening to the once-escaped prisoner. He was on the floor, clutching his head and groaning. The door to the other prisoner's room was open. He had to do something. The shotgun was only a few feet away. With a grunt he used the floor to pull himself over to it and secured the shotgun. Pain made stars fly, but he pushed past that and grabbed the guns in the prisoner's waistband, too. He pointed his gun at the other prisoner, who was poised to flee.

"Don't move."

The alarm stopped, though the sound still throbbed in Eric's ears. He aimed the gun at the locked office door. He only needed two minutes to grab the laptop on the desk and get out.

"Drop it!"

He swung his gun around to aim at the voice— and stopped when he came face-to-face with Amy and Petra held at gunpoint by the man he'd shot the day before. By the hatred in his cold, blue eyes, the man remembered him well. His mind scrambled for options.

"Drop the gun *now* or the girls get it," the man growled. "And what you have in your other hand."

Eric set down the gun as his fingers blindly groped for the ring that would release the tear gas.

"Drop the canister," the man barked.

Eric had been about to pull the pin when he realized he didn't have his mask anymore. He'd be incapacitated, too. He dropped the canister. He had only one backup weapon, but it was a hell of a backup. "Burn, you son of a bitch," he muttered.

A tingling sensation crawled up Eric's spine. Petra had described something like it when she was being re-mote-viewed. He tried to shake it off and train his gaze on the man. It persisted.

You're going to die, Aruda.

What the hell? He heard the voice in his head, but it wasn't his thoughts.

It's over. Give it up. Give up and die!

He felt a strange pressure inside his head. *Someone was in his head. Hell, someone was in his head!* He couldn't focus his energy on anything but getting him out.

The shadow of fear had left the man's eyes. He lifted his gun.

Rand raised his arms as the guard pointed the gun at him. He nodded toward the guy on the floor. "Hey, man, are you trying to make me crazy in here? Alarms, gunshots, fire, and now some whacked dude barges in and then goes into a seizure."

The guard grimaced in pain as he got to his feet. "This guy's psychotic. That's all I know."

He heard someone banging on a door down the hall. The guard looked confused. Get help and leave Rand there? Take Rand with him but leave the crazy guy on the floor?

"Don't leave me here with this guy," Rand said, injecting panic into his voice. "I'll do whatever you want."

The guard's eyes were hazy with pain as he tried to focus. He blinked, weaved on his feet. "Help me get him in this room."

Rand reached down to pull up Lucas—and drove his elbow into the guard's face. Lucas rolled to the side and grabbed the gun that the guard dropped with a gasp of pain. Rand could see that whatever had happened to Lucas, he'd recovered.

"Help me get him in this room," Lucas said.

For a second Rand stared at him. "I know you. Wait a minute. I *dreamed* you!"

"My friends and I came to bust you out of here, but things went to hell fast."

Rand grabbed the guard's legs and the two of them carried him into the room, set him down, then Lucas locked the door and tossed the guard's gun to Rand. There wasn't time for Rand to ask questions, like why this stranger was rescuing him. Or why he'd dreamed about him. "What now?" he asked.

"We get the others." Lucas ran down the hallway.

Rand followed. "How many are there of you?"

"Eric's in the building. We've got two women outside in the car ready to get us out of here."

Another guard was lying on the floor, groaning in pain. Who the hell were these people? No matter, he'd rather be on their side. He already knew what the other side was like. Now that he had a gun, he'd take out the head bastard with a shot to the forehead . . . right after he nailed him in the balls.

They took a left and came to a security gate. Lucas ran back to the guard lying on the floor and took the keys off his belt. After trying four of them, he unlocked the gate and paused to listen.

Rand heard a man say, "Drop the gun *now* or the girls get it."

Girls?

He saw Lucas blanch. Hell, they were probably the women in the getaway car.

He and Lucas went through the security gate. The hallway split both ways and continued around the corner to the center of the building. The voice had come from the left. They pressed against the wall and inched their way in that direction.

Rand shot ahead ten seconds in his mind. It wasn't enough. They were still here. He had a bad feeling, though. This wasn't going to end pretty.

Lucas peered around the corner. Frustration and fear permeated his whispers. "He's got Petra and Amy. They were supposed to stay safe in the car. Why didn't they? Why isn't Eric using his firepower?"

Rand projected ahead again. This time he saw a man sneaking up behind them with a gun: Peterson, the guy who'd given him the meal with drugs in it. Rand turned in time to catch him come around the corner. He raised his gun and shot at him, heard a gasp of pain as Peterson's gun slid across the floor. Shit. He'd shot someone.

Another shot split the air. Both he and Lucas peered around the corner again. The shorter girl with the brown hair took advantage of the distraction his shot created and grabbed at the guard's gun. The tall blonde joined in, wrestling the big guy for control. The guy with the Mr. Universe body—Eric, he presumed—was twitching his head as if he were surrounded by invisible bees.

Rand projected again. *Oh, shit.* "The brunette's going to get shot in ten seconds! From the right."

"Amy. *No.*" Not disbelief, but agony.

Lucas flew down the hallway toward the women. Three seconds left. He launched himself toward Amy. Two seconds left. Flew through the air, turning his body to the right, gun at the ready. He knocked Amy to the side, his body jerking when he pulled the trigger. Bizarrely, blood splattered from *his* chest. He fell to the floor. Lucas's run sent Eric into action toward them.

Rand ran to the other hallway in time to see one of the doors open. He shot at the door and it slammed shut. Lucas had hit his target; a man was sprawled on the floor. Rand returned to the front hallway and sprinted toward the open area. Eric was slamming the guy who'd had the women into the floor. "Get out of my head! Get out of my head!"

Amy and the blonde were screaming, Amy with her hands over Lucas's chest, his blood streaming through her fingers.

The front entrance was within easy reach. Rand's instincts said to haul ass. *Take care of yourself, dude. No one else will.*

But these people had. Lucas had. So he said to Eric, who was still beating the man even though he was unconscious, "Let's get your friend out of here."

Eric came out of his rage. "Petra, get the car."

She ran out the door, her face pale.

He and Eric grabbed up Lucas. Amy's face was wet with tears as she pointed toward the rear entrance. "More of them are coming!"

Rand shot at the rear entrance and then sent another bullet toward the door he'd seen open before. Glass shattered, falling like rain on the yellowed linoleum.

Rand and Eric carried Lucas to the door, and Amy ran ahead to open it for them. He saw a sedan screech to a stop. "You've got to be shittin' me. No way are we all fitting in that."

The glass on the front door shattered.

"Okay, maybe we will."

Amy grabbed the gun from his hand, now that he was carrying Lucas, and sent a wild shot back into the building. Petra jumped out of the car and opened the doors, whispering over and over, "Not again, not again." They slid Lucas onto the backseat. Eric jumped into the driver's seat, Amy sat in the back with Lucas's head on her lap, and as for him . . . well, hell, he didn't have time to debate. He jumped into the passenger seat, and Petra climbed in the back.

Eric tore out of the lot. One car sped out from behind the building after them. Another car raced down the road toward them. The driver turned it to block them. Eric drove onto the shoulder and around it. The dude had a fierce look on his face; veins stuck out at his temples and neck, mouth in a snarl, right hand cut and bloody.

Rand said, "Amy, give me my gun back."

God, she was wrecked, whispering Lucas's name over and over. She handed him the gun without taking her eyes off Lucas. Rand leaned to the side of the headrest and squeezed out two shots through the open window. The tire shredded, and the car swerved violently and spun out.

No time to pat myself on the back. Here comes another one.

But before he could get off another shot, their rear window shattered, crazing into pieces. Amy and Petra screamed and ducked. Rand shot again. He'd used a gun but had never shot at a human being before today. The pursuing car's windshield crazed. The driver stuck out his head. Rand shot again, hitting the metal just inches from him. The guy slammed on the brakes.

Rand said, "We got a lead. Lose 'em, dude."

Eric took a two-lane road that seemed to go nowhere, but his resolute expression showed that he knew where he was going. He turned again ten minutes later, cutting through an old neighborhood before getting onto a major highway. Rand kept his gaze trained behind them. Only when they'd gone for a while without anyone dogging them did he drop his gaze to the backseat.

Amy had taken off her shirt and was pressing the fabric against Lucas's chest. He'd lost a lot of blood already. Rand had a feeling taking him to the hospital wasn't an option. "Oh, man, he doesn't look good."

Amy lifted her reddened, streaked face. "He's going to die because of you! He had to go back and get *you*!"

He lifted his hands. "Hey, I never asked him to. I don't even know him." Except in his dreams, but that sounded hokey so he wasn't going to say it. "I also got him out of there." Hell, he did feel bad. Being accused by a pretty, half-naked woman in distress wasn't helping.

She was looking at Lucas again, and Rand wasn't even sure she'd heard him. Man, love and grief poured out of her. It hurt just to look at her. Petra was nearly as torn, squeezed into an awkward position in the tight backseat, not taking her eyes off Lucas.

He sat back in the seat. Eric was staring ahead, his jaw still tight. "So," Rand said to him. "You want to tell me who you people are?"

"What the hell just happened here?" Gerard thundered. His two subjects stared at the carnage. He ran to the residence's door and opened it with the code. Olivia stood there, her face pale.

"They're all gone," Robbins said, coming down the hallway.

"Even Brandenburg?" Gerard asked. This couldn't have happened. It was a bad dream. A nightmare.

"Apparently he's what they were after. Our guys are on them."

Olivia screamed when she saw the two men on the floor, but she gathered her wits and crouched beside Carl to check his pulse. His head was a bloody mess. Next she ran to the other guard. "They're alive. Has anyone called an ambulance?"

Robbins waited for an order. Gerard said, "Call Pope. Tell him we'll need medical assistance as well as a clean-up." That was his only option, but he didn't like using it. He turned to the others. "We need to check on the other officers."

The uninjured scrambled to help the injured. His protégé took in the two injured guards with anger and shock on his face. "We have to shut these traitors down."

Gerard found a small bit of pleasure in the young man's fierce attitude. "Good job on derailing Aruda. You kept him from torching anyone."

Gerard's phone rang. "We lost them, sir. They shot out our tire. They shot out Kaiser's windshield, and he lost them, too."

"Get back here as soon as you can. We've got men down. Any injuries on your end?"

"No, sir. We're good."

This was a battle, and the enemy had gotten the upper hand. It burned through him, the way losing always did. *You're nothing, Gerard. Always was, always will be.* He shook away his father's voice. This wasn't about proving himself to his father, the craggy son of a bitch. So much more was at stake here. He had a mess to clean up, literally and figuratively. He'd lost his prisoners. It was shameful.

Robbins returned, still looking pale. "Pope is on his way. He wasn't happy."

"I'll bet. And that's nothing compared to how I feel."

Robbins walked over to Carl and crouched down beside him. "Help's on the way. Hold on, buddy." Carl wasn't responding. "What happened to him?"

"Aruda went nuts on him."

"The guy's a psycho."

Gerard had to smile at that. It wouldn't be long before his star Offspring could do more than fill Aruda's head with words.

Olivia returned. "Peterson's shot in the hip. He's conscious. Another man is down, bullet to the upper chest, lost a lot of blood but his pulse is steady. I can hear two men banging on locked doors in the east wing. We need to get them out." Robbins handed her his keys. She looked at both men. "Is help coming?"

Robbins said, "We've called Pope."

"Who's Pope?"

"Oh, I thought you knew."

She looked at Gerard, who said, "He cleans up messes to preserve the classified status of top secret projects."

Her voice grew shrill. "Is he sending medical help?"

"Yes."

She ran to the medical supply closet.

Robbins knelt over Hanson, the man Lucas had shot. He was also unconscious, bleeding from a bullet in the shoulder. He tore off his shirt to stanch the flow, then looked up at Gerard. "For God's sake, why are you smiling?"

"We lost a small battle here, but we will win the war."

CHAPTER 29

Amy thought her heart was imploding. Lucas's breathing was becoming shallower. Now that Eric wasn't driving like a madman, she could check his pulse. Hardly there. *This can't be happening. I can't go through this again.*

"We have to get help."

Eric said, "We can't take him to a hospital. They're kinda funny about bullet wounds, wanting to call the police and stuff. Do you know anyone with medical training who would be willing to treat him and not tell anyone?"

Amy shook her head. She looked at Rand, feeling bad for screaming at him but unable to apologize just yet. It wasn't his fault, not really. Lucas had insisted on going back for him. Now she understood why Eric was so angry when Lucas had risked his life to warn her.

Rand said, "Wish I did." He meant it, too, as he looked at Lucas. "Why did you risk your lives to rescue someone you didn't even know? Not that I'm complaining, mind you."

Eric said, "We do know each other. Years ago our

parents were involved in a classified project together. We"—he nodded to indicate those in the backseat— "spent our days together. Your mom took care of us." He glanced in the rearview mirror. "You have a psychic skill, or maybe you see it as an extraordinary ability." He looked at Rand expectantly.

Rand's face was a mess, covered in cuts and yellowed bruises. He had some kind of a spike through his eyebrow, which was torn and bleeding. Traces of a blond goatee showed through the stubble on his face. "I can see ten seconds in the future." He nodded ahead. "That yellow car is going to cut over in front of the red car. The driver is going to stick his hand out the window . . . no finger."

They watched as just that happened.

"The a-hole back at the hospital was trying to get me to use it to see even further ahead."

Eric asked, "Did he do that to your face?"

"No, the guys at the casino did most of this." He gave them a sheepish smile that looked a bit gruesome with the green bruises. "My, ah, skill comes in handy at the roulette table. Casinos don't like guys who win too much." He narrowed his eyes. "How'd you know I had an ability?"

Amy looked at Lucas again, tuning out as Eric filled Rand in. She felt so damn helpless. Were they just supposed to let Lucas die? She wanted to scream, to cry, but she held onto her grief. There was something she could do, something small. She unclasped Lucas's necklace and put it on him. He needed all the help he could get.

Petra looked just as agonized. She'd spent the wild part of the drive crammed into an awkward position with her hands gripping the seats to keep her balance. Now she slid to the side and folded herself into yet another awkward position next to Lucas's chest. "I need to touch him," she said, and Amy wasn't sure she was talking to anyone in particular. Her intense blue eyes focused on Lucas as she held her hands over his chest.

Amy was still pressing down on the wound. "Your hands are hot. I can feel the heat coming off them."

"That's what happens when I rub people's shoulders."

Her miraculous massage. How miraculous? Amy doused her hope. No massage was going to heal a bullet wound.

Amy moved her hands away, settling them on Lucas's head, accidentally smearing it with blood. Petra placed her hands on his chest, closed her eyes and tilted her head back. Her forehead creased. Tears followed the tracks already going down her cheeks. She moved her mouth, whispering so softly Amy couldn't hear her words. Several minutes later she could make out, "Lucas, come back, come back . . . Lucas, your heart is strong, your body is healing. I love you, Lucas."

Amy closed her eyes, too, and silently chanted the same words. She poured her love down her arms and hands and into him. That love was a double-edged sword, though, cutting deep into her. She had believed in loving and losing, and now she was losing. But at least she had loved.

From what seemed like a distance she heard Rand ask, "What are they doing back there?"

Eric said, "Beats me."

Amy didn't know either. Their voices faded again, and in her mind she heard one of her favorite songs by Fuel: "Hemorrhage (In my Hands)." She had fixed many a hard drive with that song pounding through her earphones. Now the words about love bleeding in his hands, asking someone not to fall away and leave him to himself, resonated through her.

She cracked open her eyes. Petra was hunched over, as though in physical pain, even gasping as if experiencing pain. One of her hands was splayed over her chest. She was breathing heavily and her face was contorted.

"Petra?"

She shook her head.

Baffled, Amy shifted her attention between the two. Petra let out a breath and became completely still. Her expression relaxed, looking almost peaceful. Just seeing her that way instilled an odd peace in Amy. She looked down at Lucas. He, too, now had a peaceful expression on his face . . . or was he gone? The thought strangled her.

He wasn't breathing anymore. A gasp of grief escaped her mouth. He was gone. She was alone, because even with Eric and Petra, without Lucas she was so alone.

Lucas's eyes fluttered open and looked right at her. She blinked, sure she was imagining it. He took a deep breath and . . . smiled. A faint smile, but a smile! Petra opened her eyes, too, and the surprised look on her face morphed to joy.

"Lucas," Amy said, cradling his face.

"Why are you upside down?" he asked, his voice weak.

She laughed. "You're in the car, on my lap."

He looked at Petra, her hands on his chest. "What happened?"

"You were shot," Petra said. She lifted her shaky hands, which were covered in blood.

He tried to sit up.

Amy said, "Maybe you shouldn't—"

Too late. He lifted her wadded-up shirt and looked. His shirt and chest were covered in dried blood. He ran his hands over a red welt.

A welt?

Eric jerked the car into a parking lot, threw it into Park, and twisted around in his seat. "Am I seeing things? Maybe I *am* crazy."

Petra put her fingers over the welt. Her face was suffused with red, her eyes shiny with unshed tears.

"I don't understand," Lucas said, looking around at the stunned faces staring at his chest. "Where was I shot?"

"Here," Petra said.

"But—"

"It's healed," Amy said in an awed whisper.

He blinked, rubbing his hands over his face. "I remember . . . " He looked at Rand. "You said Amy was going to be shot. I ran, pushed her out of the way . . . "

"And got shot," Eric said.

"How long have I been out?"

Eric looked at his watch. "Forty minutes."

Amy put her arms around his shoulders. "That's why we're all looking at you with incredulous expressions, Lucas. A few minutes ago you were dying. Petra put her hands on you, and now . . . you're healed."

Petra couldn't stop smiling. "I can heal. I can heal!" She rubbed her hand over the same place on her chest where Lucas had been shot.

"Your miraculous massages," Amy said. "You said

people claimed you healed them. And your hands, they were burning hot when you put them on Lucas."

"I felt a need to touch him. I couldn't explain it; it just came over me."

"What happened?" Amy asked. "You doubled over."

"I felt his pain. Like I took it on." She looked beneath her shirt. "It still hurts but there's no mark. I actually expected to see one."

Lucas took Petra's hands in his. "I feel like I'm in a dream. It's amazing. You're amazing."

"No shit," Eric said to him. "I can't believe it, and I'm looking at you."

Amy reached out and gripped one of Petra's hands. "It's like your ability to hear from a distance. You thought it was just a really good physical ability. Those massages you gave to people actually healed them."

Petra glowed. "I have abilities! And I saved my best friend." She hugged Lucas. "And I'm so tired. It's like my energy is draining right out of me."

Lucas pulled her against him. She closed her eyes and within seconds her face was slack. Amy curled up against him, too, awash in relief.

Lucas twisted around a little and touched Amy's bare shoulder. Then he lifted the shirt, but it was covered in blood. Rand pulled his shirt off and handed it to her. "It's a little less bloody than yours."

Eric pushed it back at him and removed his shirt. "Mine's cleaner."

"Thanks." Amy laughed at all the chivalry and pulled it on.

Eric put the car into gear. "Let's get back to the shelter."

Rand was still facing the backseat, looking at Lucas. "Eric told me a little about this Offspring stuff. About how we all knew each other. This all blows my mind. And then what she did." He nodded toward Petra, who was out. "But what totally rocks me is that you risked your life to get me out of there. Eric said it was your idea. That you insisted. Man, you saved my life." He reached his hand out, and Lucas shook it. "I understand why you'd throw yourself in a bullet's path to save these two. Even Eric. But why me?"

"You're one of us."

Rand nodded, letting those simple words sink in. "Now what?"

Eric said, "We get hold of one of those bastards and find out why we're the way we are and what happened to our parents."

Amy added, "And what they injected into Lucas. Did they give you shots?"

"They slipped me some mind-altering shit, LSD or something. The nurse dude said it would open my mind, expand my abilities. All it did was wake me out—freak me out, " he explained at their puzzled expressions. He scrubbed his fingers through hair that was dark at the roots and bright blond at the tips. "So we all have abilities. She can hear and heal. What about the rest of you?"

Lucas said, "I get premonitions."

"And you get into people's dreams." He pointed at Lucas. "That was almost as weird as the acid, seeing you." He turned to Amy.

"I talk to dead people. But I don't see them. I *do* see people's glows. 'Auras,' some call them, but the colors are a little different than the aura charts I've seen."

Rand's was the same muddled mix of colors as the rest of the Offspring.

Rand turned to Eric. "And what about you?"

His mouth twitched. "I set people on fire."

Rand's eyes widened. "Seriously?"

Pride seeped into Eric's voice. "Yeah."

"Was that what you were trying to do when you were twitching in the hallway?"

Lucas added, "Yeah, what *was* that about?"

Eric's slight smiled fled. "The enemy Offspring got into my head. He was saying stuff, telling me I was going to die. I was too busy trying to get the bastard out of my head to start a fire."

That gave Amy a shiver. "That's a hell of a lot worse than someone just watching us."

"Tell me about it."

Lucas said, "You've got to stop that intrusion or function despite it. You can't let it sideline you like that."

"I know, I know. I wasn't expecting it. And it wasn't just voices. I could *feel* him in my brain, this weird, tingly pressure. They've got the government on their side and they've got at least two people like us. This guy who got into my head, he's probably an Ultra, too."

Amy tightened her hold on Lucas. "They might be powerful, but so are we. And we'll get stronger with more of us. We have two names from Cyrus's computer. We'll contact them."

Lucas rubbed the welt on his chest. "We've got to be careful, though. We don't know who the enemy Offspring are. Or how many work for Darkwell."

Eric said, "Talk to Cyrus, Amy. See if he can give

you more names. We're going to need as many of us as we can get." His fingers tightened on the wheel. "So we get them before they get us."

Gerard studied the old case files for BLUE EYES. He wasn't psychic—he wished he was—but he had a feeling there was something buried there. The attack on the facility and rescue of the prisoners was only a setback. The injured men were being treated, cover stories had been created, and now that the facility was cleaned up, he would forge on to victory.

At the knock on his door, he looked up to see Pope walk in. He stood to shake his hand.

Pope was imposing, six-foot-five, a slick, shaved head, and well-defined features. He was striking, not the kind of man to blend in.

"Thanks," Gerard said. "You saved my ass, but more importantly, you saved the program."

Pope settled into the chair, which was way too small for his tall frame. "Is this related to BLUE EYES?"

"The offspring of those subjects."

"No mysterious substances being injected into them, I trust." Pope had been there for that clean up, too. Oddly, he didn't look as though he'd aged a day since then.

"The Offspring already have enhanced powers, inherited from their parents. We're onto amazing things here, Pope."

"Tell me."

"Are you sure you want to know? Usually you prefer to stay in the dark."

Pope's smile was colored by a childlike curiosity, an odd thing on a man like him. "I'm intrigued."

Gerard hoped he didn't want to get involved as he filled Pope in on the current program, leaving out the fact that he'd managed to get hold of the essence of the Booster. "Next time I'll be ready for them. I hope I won't need you again." He waited for Pope to leave; he was never one to sit around and chat.

Pope didn't leave. He sat in silence for a few minutes, giving away nothing of whatever he was thinking about. Finally he said, "You have files on the Offspring."

"Yes," Gerard replied, drawing out the word.

"I'd like to see them."

Gerard hesitated. "May I ask why?"

"I didn't ask you why you needed my services."

Gerard hated the powerless feeling that heated his skin. He logged into the database and turned his laptop toward Pope.

He spent a long time reading the Offspring files. "Lucas Vanderwyck. Was he your first prisoner?"

"Yes."

"Tell me what he was like when he was here."

Gerard became more and more uncomfortable, but he told Pope how Lucas had killed two terrorists and become more agitated as his captivity dragged on.

Pope kept reading. Gerard walked behind him once, ostensibly to pull something out of the file cabinet, and saw that he was reading Eric Aruda's file. He was particularly interested in the Rogues.

Finally, Pope turned the laptop around to face Gerard. "I want copies."

When it became apparent that he meant now, not at some time in the future, Gerard printed out each record. As they came off the printer, Pope picked them up and thumbed through them.

Olivia opened his door after a quick knock and started to say something when she saw Pope. She eyed him with wary curiosity. Gerard didn't bother to do introductions. "Come back later."

Getting a glimpse of one of the records, she was obviously surprised that he would share his information. She didn't know Pope.

Neither did Gerard, for that matter. No one knew who he was or his origins. He went by the last name Pope, but that probably wasn't his real name. Gerard knew he had connections way up in the government, but like Steele, couldn't be tied to anyone. He had power and money. Thankfully, Pope was on his side.

Once the last file was printed, Pope put it in a folder with the rest. "Keep me informed. Maybe I can be of further help."

The prospect of that both excited and worried Gerard, but he said, "I will."

He watched Pope walk to his black Aston Martin. As soon as the sleek vehicle pulled out of the parking lot, he called Steele. Robbins knocked at the same time and entered. Since the siege, he'd had a scared rabbit look on his face. Gerard nodded for him to close the door as Steele came on the line.

"It's me. Any luck finding Zoe Stoker?"

"I'm on her trail now."

"You're having a hard time with these women, Steele. You're not soft on them, are you?"

"I don't like women," he said in a tone that showed he was serious. "Conniving, sneaky bitches. These Offspring women are even sneakier. But I'll get her."

"When you return, I have another assignment for you. For a change, we know what their next step will probably be. You can redeem yourself." He hung up.

Robbins's face paled even more. "Zoe Stoker? But why?"

"Diamond made a call to her just before he went traitor on us. We don't know what he told her, but it's likely she's not going to be an asset now. We can't take the chance in any case."

"Sir, I can't be part of this anymore."

"Once we take out the Rogues, we can proceed without risk. No need to be afraid."

"It's not that. It's . . . I can't stand taking people and forcing them to do things." His expression hardened. "The killing. I know about Leon. My God, you had Lucas kill your own brother."

"I had to protect DARK MATTER. I'm not letting anyone close me down, not this time. I'm too close to saving our country. We are the ghosts, invisible soldiers waging an invisible war on our enemies."

"How many deaths will you justify for your cause? Will you kill me because you think I might be a threat? What about any Offspring who don't measure up? They're not useful, but they know too much. Will they go, too?"

Fury raced through his veins, but he was a master of cold control. "If I have to."

"I want out of the program. I never wanted to be here in the first place."

Gerard leaned back in his chair and steepled his fingers. "There's only one way out."

Robbins's face paled, and he turned and left without a backward glance.

The man was merely shook up, Gerard thought. He'd come around.

He had better things to do than worry about his subordinate. He pulled out the BLUE EYES files. Something kept nagging him, and frankly, he needed the diversion.

Hours later he found what his sixth sense told him was there. "Son of a bitch. How did I miss this?" He inhaled deeply. Smiled. "Merry Christmas and Happy Birthday to me. I just found buried treasure."

EPILOGUE

Amy snuggled up against Lucas in bed that night, her finger tracing the red welt on his chest. "I don't think I can take much more of you almost dying."

He pushed her hair back over one ear. "Maybe we should stop this right now. It's not going to get any less dangerous. For me or for you."

She looked at those blue-gray eyes, so serious and protective. "Do you really think we can stop?"

That got a Mona Lisa smile out of him. "Only if you get away from us, from here. You said Cyrus gave you a contact for a new identity."

"I already have a new identity. I thought I was loner Amy, content in her safe little world, opening her heart only to a dream lover. I am *not* Amy who runs away from love and danger. Especially not love. All my life I felt different from other kids. Now I belong."

Lucas said, "Yeah, with a bunch of misfits."

"Just like me. Most importantly, Lucas, I belong with you. So stop trying to protect me from danger, from heartbreak . . . from you. From the time I discovered you were real—no, before that, when you broke into my apartment and they took you away—I sensed a connection between us. It would have been much easier to have believed, as Cyrus told me, that you were a psychotic serial killer. I couldn't let you go, though. Not then, not now."

He was still smiling, though it was bittersweet. He rubbed the cross pendant he'd insisted she wear again. "I just don't want to hurt you. I don't know what's going to happen with these episodes I get."

"We'll handle it, love," she said, using an endearment he'd used in their dreams. It hurt that he wouldn't use it now. He took her hand and kissed her palm, something else he'd done in their dreams. She closed her eyes, savoring the gesture. "I love the way you touch me, the way you kiss me . . . everything."

"I love you."

She opened her eyes. "Did you say—"

"I love you," he said, looking so very serious now. "I love your freckles and your wild hair and your smile—definitely your smile—and even your tears when you couldn't bear to lose me, and I thought, 'Damn, this woman really loves me. How did I get so lucky?'"

Emotion washed over her, putting a different kind of tears in her eyes. She kissed him soft and sweet. "I'm too tired to do much more than that." She grinned. "Hey, how about you come to my dreams?"

She loved his smile, too.

"I'm never too tired in my dreams," he said.

"Bring the pyramids with you." She propped herself up on one elbow. "How would you feel about an addition to our little family?"

His eyes widened. "You can't be pregnant!"

"I mean my cockatoo."

"If it makes you happy, I'll put up with just about anything."

She snuggled into his body and for the first time in over a week slipped into a contented sleep. Lucas was here, he was alive and well, and he'd said he loved her.

Before she could sink into dream bliss, though, she passed through the hypnagogic state and heard voices whispering, talking, the mix muddling the individual words.

Cyrus? Are you there?

Amy. You're all right?

I'm wonderful. I've got Lucas with me.

I'm glad. It's not over, though. You know that.

I do. We're trying to find as many Offspring as we can. Do you know how many of us there are?

At least a dozen. Probably more.

Can you give me names?

Bill Hammond, but he's dead. Zoe Stoker. Those were my other Offspring. I didn't pay attention to the others.

She started hearing other voices intruding. One man's voice stood out. *You will all be annihilated. I see your destruction.*

Amy shook away the voice. *Cyrus, who was that?*

Gladstone. The man Eric Aruda killed. He hated Offspring.

We know. We saw his journal. Can he really see our destruction?

I hope not. I can't see into the future, but I get premonitions. Right now I don't get anything.

Cyrus, before you go, there's something I have to say. I'm sorry I thought you were the enemy.

Don't be sorry. I deceived you. I was responsible for your father's death. I'll never forgive myself for that.

I forgive you.

She fell into sleep then, and waited for the desert sands to stretch out before her . . .

ACKNOWLEDGMENTS

Writing is not a lonely profession. Along the way lots of people helped to make this book come alive, brainstormed ideas, answered questions, and gave encouragement. My sincerest thanks to all of these fabulous people:

Janet Evanovich, for your butt-kicking advice. They don't call you a phenomenon for nothing!

Pat Hommel, my Annapolis Realtor who showed me your hometown through your words and hospitality.

Dave and Susi Martinson, for the use of Snowball, aka Orn'ry.

Michael Joy (aka KillJoy), for answering computer questions.

Antonio "Tony" Sanchez, MSM, CLET, Captain, Biscayne Park Police Department, for giving me feedback on all these crazy scenarios I throw your way.

My critique bud, Marty Ambrose, for just being you!

I also send out appreciation to the folks on the business end of things who have helped bring this book to the reality that sits in your hand now, including Joe Veltre, Tessa Woodward, everyone at HarperCollins, Sue Grimshaw, and all you wonderful readers and booksellers!

The following is a sneak peek at

OUT OF THE DARKNESS,

the next pulse-pounding romantic thriller
from Jaime Rush

Coming Soon from Avon Books

"This would go a lot easier if you'd stop screaming in pain," Zoe told the muscular man lying beneath her. "And you're scaring the people waiting in line."

"Nobody told me this was going to hurt so much," he said in a strained voice. Sweat beaded on his face and bare chest.

She arched one of her dark red eyebrows. "What did you think a tattoo needle was going to feel like?"

"Just finish already."

She could have pointed out the young lady who actually looked bored while getting her tattoo, no shred of pain on her expression. Zoe looked at the line of people waiting to get their tattoos at Creative Ink, and her three artists, RJ, Rachael, and Michael, all busily doing one of three tattoo designs. She could hardly enjoy the fact that her charity event for SafeHouse was a success. She struggled to maintain control, a mega feat considering how many freaking things had gone wrong. She absolutely could not let frustration bubble to the surface. Especially with the news cameras rolling. When she lost her temper, bad things happened.

She'd arrived an hour early and was psyched to find about a hundred people already waiting. She was totally not psyched to also see the cop demanding to see the owner—her. She hadn't set up proper crowd control. Heck, she hadn't expected a crowd. She made arrangements to get the velvet ropes that nightclubs used for their overflow lines. Relief. She enjoyed that for about five minutes until the power died for half an hour.

RJ's car had broken down, making him late. Rachael had a cold and barely dragged herself in. She wore one of those respiratory masks and complained about how ridiculous she looked, especially with the news cameras coming in and out.

"You look like a world-class surgeon, Rach," Zoe called out. "Work it, babe."

Rachael's eyes crinkled in a smile as she lifted one of her blue-glove-clad hands and gave her the finger. The newspaper photographer snapped the picture. If that made it into the paper, she was going to—calmly—kick Rachael's pretty little ass.

At least she had music. The Russian tunes she dug poured through the shop. Next up was some local rock band RJ liked.

They were behind schedule, amping up people's impatience. Ugly black clouds built outside, threatening to dump rain on the people waiting in the line that snaked around the block.

And now this six-foot-two bodybuilder was whimpering in pain even before her needle touched him.

"Key West," Zoe said between clenched teeth. "St. Bart's. St. Martin. Nassau." She looked at the poster of Aruba. The tack at the right corner trembled.

Breathe.

"Jamaica," she said.

"What are you doing?" the guy asked.

"I recite island names for stress relief," she said, lowering the needle to his chest. "It's my dream to go to a tropical island someday."

He screamed like a little girl, and she almost dropped her machine. She saw the flash of the photographer's camera capturing the moment. He came in closer and took several more pictures.

"Tortugas, Montego Bay . . ."

The guy in the chair pasted on a tough-guy smile. What a stooge.

Zoe took advantage of the situation and leaned forward to finish the tattoo. The guy jerked when the tip touched his skin. "Look," he said, "I'll give you the money for the shelter's playground, but no more."

She placed her hand on his chest. "You are *not* walking around with half a tattoo telling people that Zoe Stoker did that to you. Buck up, 'cause I'm finishing it."

With a sigh, he slumped into the chair again. She grinned when he said, "Nassau . . . Paradise Island . . ."

The phone rang off the hook. She couldn't afford a shop manager; she was still making payments to the guy who sold her the shop. For today she'd hired a friend of Rachael's to man the phones and collect money. Breanna walked over, her body language giving off vibes of not wanting to disturb her.

"I've got a call from a Cyrus Diamond. He says it's life-and-death important."

Cyrus? Life and death?

He was the CIA guy who was helping her to dig into her father's past. Twenty-one years ago Jack Stoker, respected army and family man, walked into the office where he worked and shot three people and wounded four more before taking his life. Her mother remembered none of the details, choosing to push the ugliness into the far past. Or even worse, acting like he never existed at all. Zoe had tried to pretend that for a while. God, her father had killed people. Then one day her mother said something that struck fear and curiosity in her, and since then she had to know more.

Her inquiries had been blocked or ignored until Cyrus Diamond contacted her. He, too, had questions about a friend who worked with her father. So far he'd found out very little. So what could be life and death? Zoe pulled off her gloves to take the phone, confused and curious.

"Relax," she told the guy. "I'll only be a minute."

She walked to the back corner, where posters showcased a selection of stock designs. The one filled with old horror movie monsters was all hers.

"Cyrus, what's up?" she answered.

"I'm sorry to lay this on you. You may be in danger because of our inquiries. I'm afraid we got the attention of someone who doesn't want us to find out the truth. I'll explain more as soon as I can."

His breathless warning seemed so bizarre, she could hardly compute it. "Cyrus—"

"I've got to go. I'll call you later. Stay somewhere else tonight. They know where you live. Beware of strangers, even the police. They're not involved, but if a more powerful agency claims jurisdiction, they have to turn you over. I know how it works. You'll be taken somewhere for questioning and no one will hear from you again. I've got to go. I'll talk to you soon. Be careful, Zoe. Be really careful."

For a moment she couldn't breathe. His fear was as solid as the phone she was holding. Now it was her fear, too.

One of the posters fell off the wall.

No, *not now. Control, Zoe, control. St. Thomas. Kitts. Fiji, Fiji, Fiji.*

She looked up at the line of people that snaked out the door and the cluster of lookie-loos crowded at the window peeking in. Beware of strangers? She was freaking surrounded by people she didn't know!

At Avon Books, we know your passion for romance—once you finish one of our novels, you find yourself wanting more.

May we tempt you with . . .

- **Excerpts** from our upcoming releases.

- Entertaining **extras**, including authors' personal photo albums and book lists.

- Behind-the-scenes **scoop** on your favorite characters and series.

- **Sweepstakes** for the chance to win free books, romantic getaways, and other fun prizes.

- Writing **tips** from our authors and editors.

- **Blog** with our authors and find out why they love to write romance.

- **Exclusive content** that's not contained within the pages of our novels.

Join us at
www.avonbooks.com

AVON

An Imprint of HarperCollins*Publishers*
www.avonromance.com